Journey
Of
The Mask

Journey
Of
The Mask

Nancy Hill Pettengill

Nancy Hill Pettengill

Writers Club Press
New York San Jose Lincoln Shanghai

Journey Of The Mask

Writers Club Press
an imprint of iUniverse, Inc.

For information address:
iUniverse, Inc.
5220 S. 16th St., Suite 200
Lincoln, NE 68512
www.iuniverse.com

ISBN: 0-595-12484-4

Printed in the United States of America

I had found a tiny flicker of hope buried in the wreckage of my life, and I would not surrender it without a fight...I would never go underground again.

—Erik

Preface

———— ✶ ————

The story of the unhappy man who lived under and terrorized the Paris Opera House has fascinated me for years. Like Christine, I am hopelessly drawn to Erik and his tragic quest for love. The character spoke to my heart like no other ever has, and one day I felt compelled, as if prompted by Erik himself, to attempt a continuation of Gaston Leroux's original novel. I wrote one paragraph that eventually became the basis for a story that I had never imagined I could write.

Erik is a dangerous, unpredictable and volatile man with a nefarious past and questionable ethics. Even so, all he ever wanted was to be loved. As an incurable romantic, I wanted to give him the chance to experience what he'd always been denied. I want the reader to suffer the pain of this man's journey and thrill to the delirious joy of his rewards. Erik must endure much before he can finally accept his ultimate destiny.

Through fascinating research, countless sleepless nights, endless questions, numerous rewrites and many doubts, writing this book has been a true labor of love for me. It ultimately became my own personal journey—one that has provided me with a profound sense of accomplishment.

I will always be fascinated by the character of the "Phantom Of The Opera", or "Erik", as I know him best. I hope I have successfully presented him in a new context.

I

———————— ✶ ————————

"Erik is dead."

The tiny notice appeared exactly as I had instructed, but I felt a strange twinge when I read it. I folded the newspaper back against itself and paced my parlor while peering intently at the words. Reading one's own obituary would doubtless be an odd experience for anyone, but it was not my own response that concerned me. I worried that she would not see it, and if she did see it, would she keep her promise?

*   *   *

I was known as "The Phantom of the Opera". I could not have come up with a name more suited to my purposes had I tried. Of course, the theater people had no idea who or what I was when they hung that name on me. I had become the talk of the theater, and consequently had to be identified in some way or another. I found myself rather pleased to be awarded a title of such distinction.

One might wonder why I should be given a title in the first place. It is a habit of human nature to assign mysterious names to anything that defies description or explanation. Something that lives hidden in the cellars of an opera house, makes its presence known only through spectral means and causes constant havoc in the name of a ghost would definitely fall into the category of the unexplainable. Indeed, I went out of my way to remain as mysterious as possible. It might be difficult to understand why I would choose to follow odd and lonely pursuits of that nature. One would require only a brief glance at me to discover the answer to that all-important question.

I was born with the ghastliest of birth defects in the most visible place possible on the human body—my face. The deformity is so horrendous that it is almost impossible to look upon it. I myself could not bear to look in a mirror until recently. I have been forced to wear a mask every day of my life and few individuals ever troubled to look beyond it to learn what was inside me. From the moment I was born, everyone around me reacted to me with horror. Consequently, I grew to be a rather morose, selfish, and unpredictable fellow. I developed habits and a lifestyle that consistently landed me on the far side of the normal limits of human decency and acceptable behavior. Eventually I found that human interaction of any kind had become almost unendurable. I had been criticized and mocked for too long. I finally retreated from the human race completely, as does a beaten dog when it is constantly subjected to nothing but abuse. I fled to the only place I felt safe. I went underground.

Up to that point I had spent my whole life wandering, unconsciously searching for the one thing I knew I would probably never find; someone with whom to share my life. That search ended when the last of my stone doors, far beneath the glittering jewel of Paris society, closed behind me. After almost forty years of running all over the globe, I finally had to let go of the absurd notion that someone, somewhere, someday would care for me.

This brings me to the young singer named Christine Daae. That "story" has been told several times by others, and I have no desire to either contradict or validate those attempts. The details of my relationship with Christine are known only to her and to me, but it was based initially on what she heard but could not see. Therefore, she truly believed that I was her mythical Angel of Music. As difficult as those months were on her, I was less than prepared for the toll the experience would take on me.

From my current perspective, I can look back with greater clarity on that time during which my heart and other equally under-utilized parts of my anatomy ran ahead of my common sense. I could not accurately interpret her emotions or my own, and admittedly I did not often perceive the situation rationally. My mind eventually could not entertain any thoughts beyond my schemes to keep her close to me. I realized then that I had never fully purged the need for human contact from my soul and could no longer bear my self-imposed isolation from the rest of the world. I was human. With new eyes I looked back with horror and revulsion on the years during which I had lived beneath the stone in my seclusion. How could I have lived like that without going completely mad? I had convinced myself that my music would be enough to sustain me. Music has comforted me during the worst times of my life, but after Christine it could no longer completely fill the void in my soul.

Tiny sparks ignited inside me as my withered emotions began to fight their way back. My mind, always so direct and focused, was suddenly incapable of settling down and my thoughts flew about me like demented birds. I had embarked upon a mission that I did not understand until late one evening when I was relaxing in my chair and my unruly thoughts suddenly came to rest. It was as if the entire stone building had crashed down upon my head. I *wanted* that girl. I wanted her for reasons that I was not prepared to handle.

Emotions and desires that I had pushed away many years ago came hurtling down upon me, cracking my carefully constructed shield of self-protection, laying my soul wide open and destroying my peace of mind and my complacency. Christ, the girl was just a child, and I was an old man who should be incapable of such thoughts and feelings. I was old enough to be her father for God's sake! I told myself harshly that I should be ashamed to be thinking the lustful thoughts of a young man. I had pushed away and buried those impulses long ago. Why should they return at this point in my life? They were completely foreign and very frightening to me.

From the moment I realized that my attraction to Christine was more than that of a helpful teacher, I began my downward spiral. I became hopelessly entangled in a web of desire, deceit and confusion that I dragged her into with me. It was neither what I wanted nor what I expected when I began the game, which had at first seemed so innocuous and innocent. I wanted only to teach her to sing and to express music the way it should be expressed; with feeling, passion and enlightenment. Music deserves nothing less. The way I thought about her went completely beyond the wretched reality of my circumstances. I became a lascivious idiot—a shameless voyeur—watching an unsuspecting woman from behind a glass. I had always prided myself on my self-taught sense of culture and refinement, and when I stopped to think about it I found my own actions quite abhorrent. Alas, I could not stop. I should not be so hard on myself, for the sight of her was constantly battering my rigidly constructed self-restraint.

There seems to be a widely held perception that when someone suffers a deformity, they must not be "normal" in other ways. In my case, that could not be further from the truth. Aside from my face, I am completely normal and, indeed, possess a strong sexuality. I had experienced the normal physical confusion of youth, but due to my forced solitude I was never familiarized with the social aspects of that development. As I grew older, I successfully learned to push that part of myself aside and soon became so adept at it that it became an unconscious action. But for my one glaring exception, I am the same as any other man. Even while living underground, my body remained firm and strong. Climbing up and down hundreds of steps several times a day along with swinging around ladders and catwalks kept me in acceptable physical condition. Enhanced by my imposing height and graceful agility, my physique matched that of a man of half my years. When I had earlier been a part of the world above there were women who obviously found me attractive in some way, but the mask halted their curiosity. A masked man can hold a mysterious attraction, but it was also clear that there might be something beneath the mask they would not care to see. As a result, I cultivated an aloof and briskly cold manner to help me keep others at a safe distance. It is my personal tragedy that I should be possessed of such a potent sexuality only to be afflicted with a physical deformity so glaringly obvious that it has taken precedence over everything else that I have ever had to offer.

I attributed my feelings for Christine to the normal male reaction to a beautiful girl and nothing more, but I was deluding myself as I continued to scheme, manipulate and maneuver for contact with the unsuspecting and vulnerable Miss Daae. While it irked me that the boy was always hanging about her, I concluded that as long as his involvement with her remained outside the theater he would not interfere with my plans. Conversations between them in her room were actually rather hilarious and entertaining at first, but it soon became clear that there was some hidden agenda in his attentions that reached beyond the childhood friendship they had apparently shared.

The boy to whom I refer is the Vicomte Raoul de Chagny. I shall refer to him as Raoul. (Do not assume any affection in my use of his given name, as there is none. I use it only for the purpose of simplification.) From my position at the periphery of Christine's life, it was clear to me that Raoul was very taken with her. I did not understand the hurt that I felt.

Desiring to go beyond our present arrangement of audile contact through her mirror, I finally invited Christine to my home. Disaster struck during her first visit there.

She likely believed that her "angel" brought her to some other world as I sang to her during our journey down the stairs and across the underground lake to my rooms. It wasn't until much later that her dreamlike trance was broken. My song had lulled her to sleep. I was reading and believed that she still slept…until she crept up behind me. The pressure of her hand and the mask leaving my face were one instantaneous movement that I could not react quickly enough to prevent. On instinct, I whirled around to face her in horror!

"You wanted to see THIS?" I cried, pointing to my naked face as my shocked surprise quickly turned to anger. She screamed and fled to cower in the far corner of the room; a reaction that I had seen far too many times in my life. "Then, LOOK at it! LOOK at me!" I shrieked, and moved towards her.

My uncontrolled rage jeopardized her safety, for when sufficiently angered I cannot be held accountable for my actions. (Indeed, I am a prime example of one who suffers from what are known as "blind rages"; occasional fits of anger so intense that one loses sight of reality.) When she tore the mask from my face I felt exposed and threatened. I had underestimated her and fooled myself. I don't know why I thought she might be accepting of my need to wear the mask. No one else was. I had not considered her curiosity about what lay beneath it. She could not have anticipated the consequences of her action.

She was speechless with fear as I reached out for her throat, but instead found my shaking fingers tangled in her hair. Abruptly I was overcome by something strange that halted me in mid-attack. I felt sick with rage and humiliation, but as I looked into her terrified eyes, suddenly I could think of nothing but hiding from that wild stare. I wrenched my hands back with a guttural cry, cruelly pulling her hair in the process. Sobbing with humiliation, I covered my ugliness with my hands and stumbled away from her toward the other room as the blood drained from my face and the sweat broke out on my body. I slammed the door shut behind me and fell heavily into a chair just as my knees began to buckle beneath me. I felt drained and weak. My heart pounded in my chest and all my breath seemed to have left me. I held my head in my hands until my sobs died away. As the minutes passed and I felt no better, however, I suspected that perhaps my physical reaction might not be solely due to the girl's impetuous curiosity. Regardless, it had been the look in her eyes that had stopped me from hurting her. I never had the slightest intention of harming her in any way, but the survival habits of a lifetime are not easily overcome.

I tried to pull myself together. Presently I remembered that Christine was still in the other room and she did not know how to get out. I dreaded facing her again but I could not just leave her there. I placed another mask over my face and opened the door.

She had sunk to the floor, in the corner where I had left her, with her hands covering her face. I walked silently into the room. Sensing my proximity, she whimpered and cowered down further. I went to sit down in a chair across from her and closed my eyes, as I still felt inexplicably weak. We were an odd pair, the two of us, as we sat there quietly, each of us apparently uncomfortable with the idea of making the first move. It would not be me, however, if I could help it. I remembered the stark terror in her eyes. I did not want her to be frightened of me. Eventually a slight rustling of her skirts penetrated my consciousness. I opened my eyes to see her silently watching me from the floor. I hoped my passivity would help lessen her fear, so I did nothing. Her tiny voice finally broke the silence when she haltingly apologized for what she had done. Whether she said it only to pacify my anger or she honestly meant it I have no idea, but it broke the stalemate between us. I told her calmly that I had merely reacted by instinct, and that I did not wish to harm her. I then added that she was welcome in my house for her lessons from now on…if she decided to continue. Showing a bit more confidence in her tone, she admitted that she was indeed desirous of continuing the lessons. I would not push my luck any further, so I returned her to her dressing room.

If nothing else, I had been revealed as human after all and thus ended her illusions of angels and ghosts. Her agreement to take her lessons in my home gave me some small hope that possibly she was not as frightened of my surroundings and me as I had feared.

Later, it occurred to me to be somewhat perplexed by my earlier bout of weak breathlessness. I had never suffered from any form of ill health until the last six months or so, during which I had experienced a few odd sensations that I attributed to tension. Christ knows I'd had my share of that long before I saw Christine. Recently, episodes similar to the one earlier that evening had begun occurring more often than I would like, leading me to think that I really must try to get myself under control. Beyond the shock of finding my face exposed to the girl and the strain I was putting myself under, I could think of no other reason for my unsteadiness of that evening. I eventually shrugged it off and turned my thoughts to the writing of Christine's next lesson.

2

———— ★ ————

The hours that Christine and I spent together after that first night brought me great relief in my loneliness. In all the years of my life I can remember only a handful of occasions when I'd held a meaningful conversation with another person. One drawback to my superior intellect that consistently frustrated me was that few could hold their own in a conversation with me. Not that there were many who tried. Only one man stands out in that respect; a man who knew me in another country and another life. He also knew more about me personally than I would have liked; a fact that caused me periodic unease since, by coincidence, he had landed in Paris shortly after I began my haunting of the Opera. He had immediately recognized my style of entertainment from the newspaper accounts and hastened to place himself where I might casually "run into" him. He was a former daroga, or Persian head of police, and his past history and mine are heavily intertwined in ways upon which I will not elaborate. He became a somewhat unwelcome part of my life during the Opera years. Owing to my previous activities in his country, once he discovered me in Paris he readily assigned himself the duty of keeping me in line. I considered him a minor nuisance, but I am compelled to admit that he had been the only person in my life with whom I had felt any connection. Still, his incessant prowling about several of my underground tunnels while searching for the entrance to my home (which he never found) and his constant reminders of past events got on my nerves until I reminded myself of the knowledge he possessed of several best-forgotten years from my past. I counted on his continued silence so I allowed him to shadow me occasionally and told him what he wanted to hear. I was quite successful at avoiding him, and was usually able to put him out of my mind altogether.

Christine spoke to my soul. Her lilting voice gave me many hours of pleasure and her increasingly frequent laughter brought me a feeling of giddiness that temporarily let me forget my sad existence. However, I did not know how to handle my growing affection for her. To be fair to myself, something was also developing in the way she looked at me. I felt her eyes following me more frequently as time went on and it unnerved me.

Raoul made increasing demands on her time and affections. He proclaimed his love for her to the world and I found it more difficult to endure the time that she spent with him. I thought having a piece of her life would satisfy my craving for someone in my life. I was mistaken. I kept returning to the fact that Raoul was young, rich and handsome while I was an old and ugly recluse with a nefarious past. The practical side of my mind did not blame her for wanting a life with him but the emotional side, the side which had been denied for so long, screamed at me to end her relationship with the boy.

My growing obsession with the girl drove me to begin plotting to drive her lover from her life, leaving only myself for her to lean on. It never occurred to me that there could always be someone else who might come along to take her away from me. I could not or would not see the reality of the situation. As time went on, Christine began to show the strain of being caught between our two worlds as she realized that two men were vying for her attentions, albeit for different reasons...or so she thought. Her lies about the time she spent with Raoul and her desire to hide her feelings for him should have warned me that what I was doing in my preoccupation was slowly wearing her down. I adored her fragility but as time progressed I failed to see how pronounced it had become. I argued with myself every night before I slept that what I was doing was for her own good and that she would finally come to believe that her place was with me, creating beautiful haunting music and filling my empty hours. Had I been in full possession of my faculties I would have realized that things could not go on, as they were, for much longer. One look at her brought back all the rejection and denial I had ever felt in my life and concentrated it in the desire that raged through my body.

My frustrations sent me back into nasty habits that I thought had disappeared forever. I was soon to curtail my successful haunting career in favor of my increasing preoccupation but, for a time, my once-innocent, ghostly games for amusement and profit rapidly escalated into senseless acts of retaliation against anyone or anything that even slightly annoyed me. Of course, it was Raoul toward whom most of my malice was directed. Even so, I found myself powerless to fight the hurtling progress of their budding relationship.

Raoul and I were participating in a remote tug-of-war with the unfortunate Christine caught in the middle. Emotionally torn and twisted between us, she gradually became withdrawn and easily upset. She began to look frighteningly pale, with sunken eyes that now appeared as dark shadows against a paper white background. Christ, she was beginning to resemble me!

I overheard the two of them one evening talking of an elopement. My stunned disbelief quickly turned to jealous rage and I felt more truly alone than at any other time in my life. To have thought that after all those years a monster like myself could actually find someone was too much to have wished for. All the fantasies I had been concocting in my feverish mind were just that—fantasies. My foolish belief that she truly cared for me melted away as fragile seedlings of newly discovered human emotions withered and died within me. Thoughts of rejoining the human race disappeared. The intensity of my despair drove deep, but I could not give up.

*   *   *

The next night Christine called for a carriage. It was very late, being after the evening performance, and the night air was damp and cold. She carried an air of secretiveness about her. What was she up to? I rarely left my haven under the Opera but I gave it no thought that night as I followed her out into the darkness. Her manner suggested something other than the usual rendezvous with Raoul but I didn't believe they were ready to run away together. My own hack left within minutes of her departure.

My body no longer handled cold very well. One might think acclimation to the cold was a prerequisite of living in the cellars of a stone building, but central heating of my own design kept my rooms at an acceptable temperature. While I had effectively buried myself alive when I moved into the Opera, I did not think it necessary to live as if in a tomb. My rooms were very comfortable, as a matter of record, and quite opulent. My personal comforts have always been high on my list of priorities.

When I thought I could take no more of that interminably long and bumpy ride through the cold her carriage pulled to a stop up ahead and she stepped down some ways beyond a small country inn. I had my brougham stop directly in front of the inn so I could exit it without her noticing me. As her carriage moved away, she looked around and began walking down a lane. Through darkness lit by a wide sliver of moon I made out her shape heading toward a small cottage set back from the road in a tiny clearing. Just after I sent my own ride on its way, I was almost run down by a third vehicle approaching at a high rate of speed. It barreled past me and continued on beyond the point where Christine had been walking along the road, and disappeared around a wooded corner. I thought for a moment that it might be her damn fool Raoul, but I must have been mistaken.

She had gone inside when I arrived at the old cottage, which sat alone in a state of run-down disrepair. I cautiously pushed on the door. It swung in easily but groaned loudly. She whirled around and her hands flew to her mouth. I could barely see her, and I can't guess who she thought I was at first. She recognized me somehow because she suddenly relaxed.

"What... What are you doing here?"

I was "caught"; a position in which I rarely allowed myself to be found, and I had no ready answer. I was already showing the signs of an increased carelessness that I could ill afford.

"I noticed you going out. It is late and I was concerned for you," I finally mumbled as I turned to close the door behind me. I pushed back my hood and faced her.

"I will come and go as I please," she stated nervously.

Christine had never seen me anywhere outside of the cellars of the Opera building. Seeing me separate from that world for the first time must have been rather startling for her. She fumbled around for a minute on the lone table and then there was a tiny flicker of light from a small lantern. We stared at each other across the barren room. She pushed her cloak hood back from her head and looked visibly uncomfortable under the intensity of my gaze. She nervously reached up to push a stray curl from her forehead. I felt my anger at her earlier betrayal returning though it was now once again tempered by my undeniable concern for her safety.

"I might also ask what you are doing. It is dangerous for you to travel this distance at night," I said sternly, recovering myself a bit as I moved slowly away from the door and into the shadows.

She replied, "This is where my father and I lived before he…I needed to get away, to think. You give me no chance to think about anything!"

I was about to confront her on the issue of her planned flight when suddenly the door burst open, rattling on its old hinges and banging back against the wall with a crash. Raoul stood in the doorway framed by the blackness of the night, his startled expression eerily revealed in the weak flickers from the tiny lamp. He saw Christine immediately and moved toward her. He was brought up short when he unexpectedly caught sight of me standing in the shadowed far corner of the small room. So it *had* been Raoul in the carriage that almost ran me down.

Uncertainty showed in his eyes as he finally understood that I was not just a product of Christine's imagination. Until that moment, Raoul had never actually seen me and sincerely doubted that I existed at all. Christine's descriptions of me carried a definite air of the preternatural. He'd been witness to my handiwork at the Opera, but no one had ever seen any more of me than I wanted them to see. Most of them still considered me a ghost, and Raoul complacently continued to think that I lived only in the imaginations of Christine and the other theater folk. Now, he looked like he had seen a ghost.

I had to force myself not to laugh out loud at the ridiculous expression on his face. He knew who I was immediately, but it was taking him some time to assimilate the fact that I was a real person and therefore a very real threat to his intended happiness with Christine. It then occurred to me that he might have suspected that Christine and I had traveled there together.

I stood in shadow. I doubted he could see much of me except perhaps a bit of my white shirt under my cloak. I decided to use that and his confusion to my advantage. The boy was only just coming to terms with the fact that I was real so, obviously, he did not yet know with what or whom he was dealing. As I watched him silently from the corner my thoughts of laughter died unheard and my anger at their plot was on the rise again. He could not take his eyes off me and we stared at each other while his expression changed from uncertainty to an anger of his own. I took the first initiative and coldly addressed him in a low and menacing voice.

"You, sir, will do well to leave these premises immediately."

Raoul's reaction to that statement was not what I naively hoped it would be. Hearing my voice startled him but he recovered himself quickly. He drew himself up to his full height (which, I might add, was considerably less than my own) but did not move from the doorway. His face turned toward Christine but his eyes remained on me.

"Christine, who is this?" he demanded contemptuously. "Can this be your wonderful and benevolent 'Angel'? Your heaven-sent 'Angel of Music'?" His eyes narrowed. "Angel indeed!" he added with heavy sarcasm. He did not wait for an answer, and then spoke directly to me.

"Who are you to be giving me orders concerning this woman? You will cease your torment of my beloved and crawl back beneath the rock under which you have been living! How dare you spirit her away with you!"

In his somewhat feeble attempt to sound authoritative, his choice of words struck me as rather amusing given where I actually did live. My amusement quickly turned to icy contempt.

"You believe that she left Paris with me. How does that feel, believing that your intended has left town with another man in the middle of the night?" I sneered.

He was gaining confidence and stared at me with undisguised scorn. "With another man? I hardly think so. I don't know *what* you are, but you are certainly not a man. Not a gentleman, anyway. A gentleman would never conduct himself as you have done." He inserted a note of mockery into his sarcastic tone while he openly looked me up and down as if measuring me. "If not a man, then, what kind of creature are you? You hide your face...perhaps you are a coward."

Those words stung. I have been many things, but never a coward. It would take more than simple intimidation to back him down, but I could not help but admire his show of courage. There we all were, in a dark cottage in the middle of nowhere. In the corner of a very small room, facing him in the dark, was something that he had consistently passed off as part of a silly ghost story and refused to take seriously. Yet, this supposed figment of someone's imagination was standing right in front of him and had spoken to him. He could no longer deny my existence or the knowledge that I was responsible for the horrors that had befallen the theater in recent months. He must have known that I was extremely dangerous, unpredictable and an experienced killer. (On all points he would have been quite correct.) There was no mistaking the menace in my voice or that I meant what I said. I could already feel the tingling rush through my body of the anticipation that always preceded a deadly contest, and my fingers began to twitch impatiently. I was surprised to realize that the exhilaration of battle was a feeling I had missed during my years of solitude. It made me feel alive again. And now this foolish young aristocrat, familiar only with petty arguments and gentlemanly duels among those of his social class, dared to confront me even while lacking any real knowledge of me as an opponent.

Neither of us moved. Our eyes met again and locked together in a standoff. Christine was standing almost directly between us, but just far enough to the side that Raoul and I each had an unobstructed view of the other. She was backed against the table and her eyes were wide. As we continued to stare each other down, a feeling of entrapment began to engulf me when I suddenly became aware that he was standing in front of the only exit. Since my earliest memories, I have suffered severely from claustrophobia. I had to get out of there, but I could not let my increasing anxiety show and compromise what I perceived as my tenuous position of power.

"I would advise you not to insult me if you are unsure of what I am," I returned icily. "It would not do for me to have to dispatch you right here in front of the girl."

"You would threaten me?" he exclaimed incredulously. "Just what do you have in mind?"

"My boy, you do not have the slightest idea of with whom you are dealing or of what I am capable." My hands clenched and unclenched beneath my cloak, both with fervent desire to be gone and the itch to be wrapped around his snobbish neck. "I warn you that I will not hesitate to do whatever I feel is necessary."

I took an aggressive step toward him and it had the desired effect. His bravado slipped ever so slightly, and I had to make my move while I had the upper hand. My desire to be out of that oppressively small building was overwhelming. Christine remained speechlessly backed against the table. The situation was not worth getting her even more upset. I could finish this at another time and under better circumstances. I was not feeling my best and needed to gather myself for a more appropriate time.

I spoke in a deceptively smooth voice that was a lot less controlled than it sounded. "I will allow you to take Miss Daae home this night, since she is obviously upset. Get her home where she belongs. This business is not finished between us. Now, get out of my way, boy, before you get hurt."

With that I boldly walked right toward him. He was forced to step aside or be bowled over by my hasty exit. As I swept past him I paused ever so slightly to look directly into his face, noting the unmistakable look of fear in his eyes. I ducked through the door into the welcoming darkness and melted into the night.

My first face-to-face encounter with the "enemy", as I now thought of him, had served me well considering that it had been unexpected and unplanned. Our meeting had made him aware that I was not one to be underestimated. It also planted seeds of doubt and insecurity in his mind as to my intentions regarding Christine. Even so, I considered myself at a dangerous disadvantage that night and would never allow myself to be caught unaware again.

I had stupidly sent my conveyance on its way without considering future consequences. I was forced to walk a long distance along the rutted roadside before getting lucky enough to have an old farmer stop to ask if I required assistance. Fortunately the night was still dark and my rescuer could not see me clearly. He generously offered me a ride in the back of his hay wagon, which I gratefully accepted. The hay, which smelled like it had been recently removed from under some horse, was warmer than the night air. I had been uncomfortably cold in the chill of the night earlier in my enclosed brougham, but it had been far better than walking for miles on that damnable country road or snuggling into freshly soiled hay. I spent much of the trip angrily cursing myself for my earlier stupidity and then I probably dozed off, because I failed to notice when we finally approached the outskirts of the city. I suddenly roused myself to note that the cart had stopped and the old man was patiently waiting for me to get out of it. I stiffly climbed out and insisted on paying him for his trouble. I am sure he wondered, as he slapped his traces and pulled slowly away, what a finely dressed Parisian gentleman was doing walking in the middle of nowhere at three o'clock in the morning.

At home I turned my heating system on to full force. After retiring with several heavy blankets and a large bottle of wine I eventually felt warm enough to sleep. I would not subject myself to such foolishness again, but would instead begin planning a strategy to win Christine. No battle in the history of the world has ever been won without an effective strategy in place. Mine would guarantee my victory.

3

---★---

I awoke the next morning with a clearer sense of purpose than I'd had in many months. My encounter of the night before allowed me to make an assessment of the pompous young fool who believed that he and Christine would marry. Undoubtedly our unexpected meeting had shaken him.

I had one advantage in that I knew my enemy. A headstrong young man who fancies himself in love can make a formidable opponent. At the same time, he was inexperienced and naive when it came to matching wits with the likes of me. And that was the source of his disadvantage in this situation. He did not have the faintest notion of me as an opponent. He knew only what Christine told him. I had told her some of my past history but, when she repeated it to him, the story sounded fantastical and largely unbelievable. I'd witnessed those conversations more than a few times and he'd dismissed her descriptions with a wave of his hand. One must always assess one's enemy before a strike, and the poor boy had no way to know what he was facing. Well, he would know soon enough, for the deck was stacked and I held all the cards. The lines had been drawn and Christine was the prize to be won.

*   *   *

I did not go to Christine's mirror for many days after our nocturnal excursion. Since I had unexpectedly lost the opportunity to confront her on her planned flight with Raoul, I nurtured the anger I still felt at what I perceived as her betrayal. The sight of her face would have set me off my course. I had been distracted enough that night and I did not need anything else cluttering up my mind. Since she had never been privy to how any of my tunnel mechanisms worked or even where the levers were located, Christine was unable to go looking for me. I was, nevertheless, able to keep tabs on her through other means. Her apparent worry over my absence was touching but I could not allow myself to go to her just yet. During this hiatus she obviously spent her free time with Raoul. That irritated me, but what they were plotting no longer mattered. I did not yet know how, but the boy must be taken out of the picture.

A week passed during which I observed Christine's increasing frustration over my lack of contact with her. The timing of my absence was also fortuitous for me since I experienced a few days of feeling a bit under the weather. Whether it could be attributed to my night out in the cold or to my unexplained bouts of weakness I could not guess, but fortunately it did not last long. When I finally went to the mirror and spoke to her, along with the relief in her eyes at the sound of my voice there was something that I could not identify. I found myself pushing aside my frustration and anger towards Christine herself, choosing instead to transfer those feelings to Raoul. I attributed my tolerance and my change of heart to her being carried away by his constant assault on her senses and with his continuous declarations of love and devotion. I could no longer sustain my anger at her for being caught up in his ardor. The boy was positively nauseating to watch, but for some reason I couldn't fathom, she was responding to his advances.

She came through the mirror with me willingly, her eyes never leaving my face. She was very quiet until we arrived on the other side of the dark lake and I was handing her out of my small boat. When she softly said "thank you" I noticed that she kept looking at me oddly. Her timid but searching glances were unnerving me by the time we reached my parlor. I sat her down on the couch and went to light a few lamps and get her a glass of wine. She had said nothing but I felt her eyes on me when I turned my back to pour our drinks. Finally I could take no more of her inquisitive silence and whirled around, sloshing some of the red wine on my trousers. I took no notice of it.

"Why, girl, do you keep staring at me like that?" I asked impatiently. She flinched in surprise at my sudden outburst.

"I was not staring at you. At...at least I didn't mean to. I mean, I..." She stumbled over her words in confusion. "Where have you been? Why have you been gone so long?" She paused to look at the floor and her voice dropped to a whisper. "I...missed you."

"Where I go and what I do with my time is of no concern to you. Especially now, since you've been planning to leave me!" I retorted angrily. I had not intended for my thoughts to come out like that. Further confusion spread over her face, so I continued. "There has to be more behind the way you are looking at me than what you..."

"How did you know about that?" she interrupted me with a low voice as she kept her eyes fixed on my expensive Persian carpet.

"It doesn't matter how I know," I replied as I handed her the goblet and sat down in a chair opposite her. I crossed my legs nonchalantly and swirled my wine around in the glass as I stared into it. "You should have guessed by now that I know everything I choose to know, and there can be no secrets from me." Against my will I felt my eyes rise to her face. My bitterness returned and my voice hardened again in anger. "You were planning to leave without having the decency to tell me to my face!"

I raised my glass to my lips and took a deep swallow. I was dangerously close to shattering the fragile crystal as my hand tightened around it. She continued to sit silent and motionless on the couch, staring at the floor as the mantel clock ticked the seconds by. My impatience grew until I thought I would go mad waiting for her to speak or move. I was about to say something when she finally raised her eyes to mine. They flashed with an expression I had not seen before as she suddenly leapt to her feet and came to stand in front of my chair.

"How dare you eavesdrop on my private conversations!" she fumed. "I don't know how or where you heard what you think you did, but it is none of your business what I do just as you say it is none of mine what you do! I have not signed a contract with you, and I certainly have never given you any control over what I do with my time!"

I'd not had much practice in reading her thoughts at that time and, honestly, I was too taken aback by her outburst to pay attention. Despite my own rising anger I had to admit that I liked this new, unfamiliar side to her personality. I sat there dumfounded for several seconds until I realized that I was about to break the glass that I still clutched tightly. Without taking my eyes from her I firmly set it down on the table next to my chair. She was standing about three feet from me, breathing heavily, with her fists clenched at her sides. Her eyes flashed, her jaw was set and her lips were pressed into a tight line. My, my, I thought, what a little spitfire she is when angered. I slowly rose from my chair and took a step toward her. As I stood well over a foot taller than Christine, she had to look up to continue staring me in the face. Her gaze never wavered. The little minx was defying me and I knew there would be no gentle words between us that evening.

I would play along with her little game of control. Locking her eyes with mine, I moved very slowly to the side and then around behind her. Her eyes followed me until I passed beyond her field of vision. She did not turn her head. Proceeding to walk around her in a tight circle, I was close enough to touch her, but did not. I moved very slowly and I thought I noticed her tremble slightly. A faint smile crossed my lips under the mask as I paused directly behind her to relish her increasingly obvious discomfort. I leaned forward just far enough that she could feel my breath caressing her hair. She stood only an inch away from my chest and the heat from her body warmed me. *If I could just put my arms around her…*

I observed the effect my movements were having on her with malicious satisfaction, but I was in serious danger of losing my advantage in our game by letting her nearness get the better of me. She was experiencing much more than anger and it confirmed my assessment of the odd looks she'd been giving me. I leaned away from her and, taking care to move slowly and silently, I resumed my circle around her, continuing around until I faced her again. Her eyes were closed. I backed away from her and she visibly relaxed as she let her breath out slowly.

She did not move nor open her eyes immediately. I watched her expression. I was still close enough to touch her, but the moment had passed and I was once again in total control. I turned away to pick up my glass and drain it before I left the room. I left her alone for a few minutes, then I took her back to her dressing room. Neither of us spoke a word. She was as silent on the return above ground as she had been on her journey down. The evening's events had proven to be very enlightening.

           *   *   *

My next observance of the most annoying Raoul took place without him even knowing it. I saw him striding purposefully toward the opera manager's office. Arriving there by tunnel well ahead of Raoul, I secretly settled myself where I could listen to the conversations in the office. When he reached the door he rudely burst in without knocking, giving poor Vaurien, the manager, cause to clutch at his chest in astonishment.

"When are you going to do something about this 'thing' that inhabits your Opera House?" Raoul demanded loudly. "Why can't you protect Christine Daae? He keeps getting to her and taking her away and you sit there like an idiot and let it happen!"

Did he still not know what I was? I chuckled softly in my hiding place. Why, he was as stupid as Vaurien.

"But Sir, I have done all I can. I have brought in the police and other authorities, but there seems to be nothing anyone can do!" the man stammered.

Raoul banged the desk with his fist. "Well, you should be able to find out where he lives at least! This place is big but there are only so many rooms in it and he obviously lives in one of them. I'm telling you that he needs to be hunted down and arrested! He should be hung for what he has done! He is a danger to *anyone* who gets in his way, but most of all to Christine. He will not leave her alone! I fear for her safety and I can't be with her at all times to protect her!"

He was ranting and becoming apoplectic. His usual aristocratic demeanor had apparently been left at home for he was screeching like a fishwife. Poor Vaurien was tripping all over himself trying to placate him. Raoul was, after all, one of the opera's wealthier patrons and it just would not do to upset or anger him. Nevertheless, Vaurien's hands were tied and he knew it.

"I will try again if it would please you. I will hire more investigators and police to track him down. Remember that I want to be rid of him too. What do you think this kind of publicity does to my business?" Now, true to form, he was thinking about himself and his cash flow.

"Your business be damned!" Raoul shouted. "This is Miss Daae's life we're talking about here! You must do something immediately to stop him!"

With that he stalked out of the office, leaving the door wide open and the speechless manager unmoving in his chair. I heard nothing further from the room but as I was about to vacate my hiding spot I heard a whispered, "What do I do now?"

Damned if I know, I thought wickedly.

                    *   *   *

Renewed efforts to protect Christine brought a dozen workmen into the Opera where they paid particular attention to her dressing room. Stupid fools, they thought they could prevent me from getting to her. It was amusing to watch them from behind the mirror. They filled up cracks, laid new flooring and inspected the ceiling. Did they really think I entered through a crack in the wall? Ghosts could certainly make good use of holes and cracks, but how did they think I got Christine through them? Really, it was all I could do to contain my laughter. I don't know what, if anything, she had told them upon their questioning her; we never spoke of it. It was one of few conversations that I did not overhear. I trigged the catches on the mirror release just in case, but I needn't have worried, for the men inspected everything around it carefully but did not disturb the massive glass.

Similar inspections went on throughout the building. At the same time, the authorities were also poking around. They dared to venture down into the cellars and it was gratifying to observe their hesitancy in looking too deeply into the darkness. Apparently my fame had spread further than I thought, and I congratulated myself on a job of haunting well done. I was not concerned with all this searching because it was not possible for anyone to find the route to my home. It was, however, annoying me to the point that I wished for them to leave me in peace. I could not go anywhere without taking the utmost care, as most of the passageways were occupied with at least one or two sets of prying eyes and ears at all times. My home was a safe haven but I was forced to curtail my playing of music. Those sounds tended to carry through the stonework farther than I would have liked. I had by then given up my pursuit of mischief at the Opera, so none of the searchers heard or saw any evidence of my presence. With the exception of Raoul's ranting at him, Vaurien might have believed I was no longer in residence. After several weeks of futile effort, the hordes of interlopers were finally gone and I could once again conduct business as usual.

That business was devising a way to separate Christine from Raoul. I vacillated, which was most unlike me. My first inclination was to remove him permanently, but as I had grown older my more hard-core tendencies seemed to have softened a bit. I wanted him out of our lives but I did not have the heart to kill the boy outright. I mentally continued to threaten him with the worst possible consequences, but my few thin threads of conscience told me that such drastic measures would also hurt Christine immeasurably. I would figure out another way to deal with the problem.

Raoul was very disappointed with the most recent efforts of the manager to dispose of me. I saw him several times in the days after the search had been terminated and he was showing signs of undeniable stress. He tried to get Christine to agree to leave with him but she steadfastly refused and he could not understand why. I saw that as a victory because she was now quite obviously torn between us. Raoul did not see the situation that way. He attributed her reluctance to leave to her fear of the unknown outside of the life she had made for herself in Paris. Since Christine was of lower class than he, it would be necessary for them to leave Paris to be together. His aristocratic family would never accept her as a suitable wife for him and the severance of his inheritance did not bode well for the couple.

I observed Raoul meeting with Christine in her dressing room and other locations around the building as he repeatedly asked her to leave with him. One day I watched them silently from the mirror tunnel as he impatiently paced around her room. She was seated at her dressing table after a rehearsal.

"Christine, please understand. We have to get you away from here. It's not safe for you to stay," he pleaded.

"Raoul, I'm not leaving! At least not right now," she said firmly.

He stopped pacing to face her. "But why? You are in danger as long as that monster knows where you are."

She looked at him through her reflection in the table mirror. "That 'monster', as you call him, will not hurt me. He cares about my career and me and would never do anything to harm me. Besides, he is very much a gentleman," she said with a note of finality. She picked up her hairbrush and began drawing it through her long dark hair. I heard the static snapping as the brush fell through her curly tresses and I longed to run my hands through them instead.

"Oh, Christine, you can't really mean that. Look at what he's done! He's a cold-blooded murderer and probably does not have any conscience whatsoever. Why, the stories I've heard about him are horrifying!" he exclaimed, his eyes wide.

Christine spoke calmly as she brushed. "The stories you've heard are largely untrue. He has never done many of the things people accuse him of. I know, because he has told me all about it. He admits there have been things that he now regrets. He is trying to change, but he can't because of the way people have treated him. People like you." The hairbrush stopped in mid stroke as she threw him an accusatory look. "It's not his fault that he must wear a mask and hide himself."

"But, darling, how can you be so sure of him? You have heard him threaten me! Don't you remember that night at the cottage when he told me he would kill me if I didn't get out of his way? How did he put it...that he would 'dispatch' me...you heard him say it. Are those the words of a man who is trying to change?" He fell to his knees beside her. "I tell you this man, or *whatever* he is, is dangerous! Are you telling me you're not afraid of him?"

Christine sat without speaking for several seconds. The next thing she said hit me hard. She turned around on her bench and faced Raoul.

"He is only a man who has endured a lifetime of painful rejection. But yes, he does still frighten me at times," she said in a low voice. In a whisper that I could barely hear she added, "Sometimes he terrifies me."

I didn't know if she spoke in that manner because she thought I might be listening or from the fear I heard in her voice.

"I know in my heart that he would never intentionally hurt me," she continued, "but he can be so unpredictable and...and so frightening. He is very powerful, but he's also intelligent and caring and I feel so different when I am with him. He is a wonderful teacher. He can be very tender, and his voice...I can't explain what his voice does to me...it draws me..." She looked off into space, as if in a dream.

I slumped soundlessly against the tunnel wall. "...*he terrifies me.*" I had not expected to hear that she was still afraid of me. I thought she was beyond that, especially after her recent display of temper. It hurt me to know that our relationship had not progressed as far as I thought it had. I did not wish to frighten her. I needed her to trust me completely and without hesitation. I must be extra gentle with her. From inside the room, I heard Raoul moving about again. I gathered myself and turned back to the glass.

"Christine, I hope you're not saying that you have feelings for this creature!" Raoul cried incredulously with his hands in the air. "How can you when we intend to be married? Oh, my dearest, what has happened to you?"

Christine's hands flew to her temples, and her eyes closed as if to shut out his voice. "I don't know, Raoul, I just don't know!" she cried in confusion. "I love you, Raoul, I really do, but...please, *please* stop badgering me about this! I do intend to be your wife, but I cannot leave right now. Please do not ask me to explain." She turned away from him and rested her elbows on the table with her head in her hands. "I'm developing a headache. Would you please leave me alone for a while?"

He stood behind her with a look of complete helplessness on his handsome face. He knew he could not press her any further that day. She was no longer listening. He backed away from her and stood there for a moment of indecision, then he turned on his heel and went to the door. He looked back and it appeared he would say something else, but he only shook his head slowly before he left, closing the door gently behind him.

This "creature" stood absolutely still. I did not want Christine to know that I had witnessed that exchange between her and Raoul. To be perfectly honest, I didn't have anything to say to her then, and I doubt she wanted to see me at that particular moment. I could not tear myself away, however, so I continued to watch her silently. She sat unmoving for some time before she finally lifted her eyes back to the small mirror. Her eyes were wet with tears and they spilled over onto her cheeks as she stared at her reflection. She must have given no thought whatsoever to the possibility that I might be near when she began to talk to herself.

"What am I to do?" she whispered, addressing her reflection in the mirror. "I wish you were here, Father, to tell me what to do. I am so confused. I know Raoul loves me, but Erik is... You always knew how to help me..." She began to cry softly and I silently crept away.

Halfway down the stairs I felt lightheaded. I leaned against the damp, cold wall for support. My heart pounded and I felt nauseated so I hastened home. I held the lantern so low that it kept bumping against my legs. If I had been any more careless I could easily have set myself ablaze. Considering the way I felt at that moment the prospect didn't seem like such a disaster. I could barely stand while I fumbled with the door releases and got into the house, almost collapsing on the carpeting. I felt weak and sweat was beginning to soak my mask as it trickled down my face. I staggered to the nearest chair and sat down. I struggled out of my coat and then leaned forward to put my head down. What in hell *was* this? I could not understand what was the matter with me.

I finally felt strong enough to walk clumsily into the bedroom. I had just enough time to pull off my sodden mask and loosen my collar before I felt faint again and had to lie down on my bed. For years I had actually slept in a coffin, but after getting to know Christine I had judged that behavior a little too morbid even for me. A good thing, for at that moment I was grateful for the oversized mattress onto which I now sank. Ironically, if Christine could have seen me then, I daresay she might have amended her opinion of her frightening and powerful teacher. I lay there bathed in sweat until my heart settled down into its regular rhythm. I soon fell asleep with the vision of Christine's tear streaked face swimming before my eyes.

*   *   *

I opened my eyes to the clock on the table. Nine o'clock. I knew it was not the same day. My clothes were soaked with sweat, as was the bedding under me. How I missed waking to greet the sun outside the window! One does not see many sunrises when one lives five levels below the ground. Even my childhood's bare attic room had possessed a small window through which the sun shone each morning. Such a simple pleasure it was, and one that most people took for granted. I figured I had been asleep for some 18 hours. I needed something to drink but was reluctant to get off the bed to get it. One of the drawbacks to living alone was that there was never anyone there to assist with such matters. One normally could call in a friend or neighbor to help, but I did not have that option. I would have to help myself. I would also have to do something about my vile condition. I passed a hand over my face and rubbed my eyes. The cold sweat that covered me caused me to shiver with a quick chill. I wiped the sweat from my face and neck with the blanket and slowly sat up, my head spinning. Damn, I was a mess. In marked contrast to the deplorable personal habits of the majority of the population, I had always been obsessively meticulous with my toilet and could not stand my condition for another minute.

I slowly lowered my body into the steaming water of a welcoming bath. Deeper than most, my brass tub was from Persia, and was considerably larger than the average man would need. It had been custom molded to fit the contours of my body. I had come to love the steam baths while living in the Far East, and it had taken much work to get this gem of a tub down into my home. At times like this it was well worth the effort. I stretched my legs out and then slid completely under the water that was as hot as I could stand. The warmth closing in over my head felt luxurious and I held my breath for a minute while I let the water warm me. Surfacing again, I used a rough sponge to soap every inch of myself, scrubbing hard to get the blood flowing. Finally warm and feeling tingly all over, I lay soaking in the water until it began to cool. I leaned against the angled back and allowed my limbs to go completely loose, savoring the sensation of weightlessness and the complete freedom from clothing and mask. Slowly I felt the tensions of past weeks leave my body as I let my thoughts drift to nothing. This was not an easy feat considering the strain I was under, but extensive training in mind control allowed me to empty my mind whenever needed. It was a skill that had served me well over the years, and probably saved my sanity more than once. I must have slept a bit more, for suddenly I realized that the water was no longer hot. I reluctantly stepped out onto a thick carpet to dry myself.

After having a few morsels to eat, I sat resting in my chair with a glass of wine. I did not feel as strong as I should; on the contrary, I felt extremely weak. The bath had drained my tension away, but it had also exacerbated the weakness I had felt since coming down from the theater. At least I no longer felt so ill. The extreme weakness and accompanying nausea bewildered me but, judging from past experience, I would soon feel well enough to resume my normal activity. Once again I put off worrying about what was causing them. Thoughts began to crowd my mind again, and I remembered what I had overheard between Christine and Raoul. I told myself to forget about that and go on as if I knew nothing of their recent argument. At the same time, I knew I had to be very careful with Christine, and not do anything to frighten her any further.

4

---- ★ ----

During the recent search of the Opera that had been conducted in response to Raoul's demands, I had told Christine that I needed time to work on new manuscripts and gave her several lessons to practice on her own. In that way I reduced the frequency with which I traveled around the building, thus making it easier to avoid detection. I now considered it safe to play music once again as it had been over a week since the workmen and the prying police had left. Christine was in fine voice. She was very appreciative of my praise, but after what had happened the previous time we had been together, I feared nothing would ever be the same between us again. I longed for those simpler times early on in our relationship when we talked for hours on end of everything and nothing. The comfortable and affectionate rapport we had enjoyed previously had vanished. The tension was undeniable, and the source of it was equally obvious. Christine did not raise her voice or her temper to me again, and for my part I had forgotten my anger at her earlier plans to leave. I knew that she did not want to leave me, but she apparently had no intention of bidding Raoul good-bye either. Christine was truly caught in the middle and probably did not realize the position in which her inexperienced heart had placed her. I desperately wanted to tip the scales in my favor, but too much pressure would drive her straight into Raoul's safely boring arms. I was gentle and solicitous but there was no escaping the change in our relationship.

The recent developments in our relationship terrified me. I wanted her to be mine but I had never fully considered what the consequences of that would be. I had never known a woman's loving touch in my entire life and now it seemed that I was as close as I might ever be to realizing that experience. Our previously tentative and gentle contact while reading or talking, the brief touch of a hand or a gentleman's arm held out in passive assistance were no longer enough for me. I was sure that Christine was also feeling the pull of awakening desire...even while knowing what lay behind my mask. I labored to keep my desires hidden. The rein I had on myself was growing looser as I observed her seeing me in a different light. I did not know how I would handle it if anything were to happen between us. I had been denied for too long. I did not know what to expect when and if I let myself go. Intense passion had been boiling inside of me since my first recognition of my attraction for her and I was frightened by its power. If my relentless and forceful attack on the intellectual passions of my life were any indication, I had good reason to be concerned. On the other hand, if things did not work out between us, I did not want to appear as an old fool. But oh, how I wanted her! It was taking every last ounce of my will to keep myself under control. Ever since the night of her outburst in my parlor, we had been swept along by something neither of us fully understood.

Raoul had no concept of the situation between Christine and myself. She continued her relationship with him without interruption. Those times when I knew she was with him now drove me mad with jealousy. I don't think she ever realized the extent to which she was playing one of us against the other. I had heard her declare her feelings to Raoul but she had not expressed any sort of commitment to me, although I was desperate to hear one from her. It annoyed me because I firmly believed, albeit prematurely, that she was beginning to have at least some of those same feelings for me.

I eventually could wait no longer. I resolved to speak frankly with Christine...to tell her how I felt when I was near her and how much I needed her. I feared I would frighten her with words of my deepest desires so I would keep those to myself for the time being. I planned her next visit very carefully and invited her to dinner. Everything must be perfect—the candlelight, the music, the food and the wine. I spent hours fussing over my dress clothes for that evening, and checking and rechecking the condition of my rooms. I was obsessive with my preparations because this night would be special.

After much thought I had come to the difficult decision that the only way to ensure the separation of Christine and Raoul was to remove her, not him, from the situation. As long as we stayed in Paris, Raoul would be vying for her affections. I think she did love him in some fashion, but I needed her more than he did. He was young and rich, and there would always be another girl waiting around the corner for him. As for me, this was my last chance at any kind of happiness. Christine would be my saving grace and only she could lift me out of the living hell of my loneliness.

I researched my plan with a renewed vigor and energy. I'd waited almost fifty years for this woman to enter my life. I had tasted true companionship for the first time and I would not live without it again. One might accuse me of being selfish with my plans to take her away from all she'd ever known and from her now successful career with the Opera Populaire. Although it was difficult for me to contemplate leaving the protective world that I had painstakingly created for myself, my need for Christine had become more important. I was willing to give up everything to have her. Yes, it was a very selfish action on my part, and I am ashamed now to admit that I placed her needs secondary to my own. All I knew at the time was how much I needed her.

I smoothed my suit once more and took the time to brush a few specks of lint from my coat. I strode over to the only mirror I owned for a final check. The satin inserts on my black waistcoat, trousers and coat lapels gleamed in the lamplight along with the tiny threads of gold woven into delicate patterns on the lower portion of the waistcoat where my gold watch chain hung at just the right angle. The white of my shirtfront was set off in drastic contrast by the dark of my suit. As I adjusted the angle of my tie, ornate, gold cufflinks peeked out from my coat sleeves. My boots shone. I reached up to smooth my hair and adjust the mask. Finally satisfied with my mirrored image, I gave my waistcoat a final tug and set my hat at its most rakish angle. I withdrew the intricately carved gold watch from its pocket and flipped open the lid. The time had come. I picked up my cloak with a flourish and draped it around my shoulders, throwing back the edges to reveal its white satin lining. Then, after taking a quick look around me, I took a deep breath and went upstairs.

Halfway up the five flights I felt the churning in my stomach of a schoolboy on his first outing with a young lady. Imagine the absurdity of a man of my years having never taken a woman out! Well, I could not afford to think about that sad state of affairs. It was bad enough that my palms were sweating and I was feeling overly warm under my heavy cloak. I could do this...I had to. I had seen how other men treated their women and I knew that, given a chance, my own innate sense of the romantic would see me through.

She was waiting for me, looking absolutely stunning in an off-the-shoulder lavender gown embellished with black lace and beading.

Her hair was piled high on her head and held by black beaded combs. I rolled the glass back silently on its pivots. She turned to look at me over one bare shoulder and I was struck speechless by her breathtaking loveliness. I stepped over the mirror's frame into the room and went to the armoire for her wrap. Never taking my eyes from her, I placed it over her shoulders. I sensed that she also felt something new in the air between us. My fingers lingered on the soft fabric at her shoulders as she fastened the cloak around her neck. I stepped through the opening into the tunnel and extended my hand back through the frame to her. With a nervous smile she placed her tiny hand in mine. Picking up her skirts in her other hand, she followed me through the mirror's opening.

There was no way to descend to the fifth cellar other than to walk, as always, down all those flights of stairs. I would have preferred to hand her into a golden lift to lower us gently into the earth. The stairs were dank, dark and very slippery. While I lit the way with my lantern in one hand, Christine firmly tucked her hand beneath my other arm. She had never done that before. Every few minutes I stole a glance at her as she walked along with me. I could barely see her face in the dim lamplight and her concentration was fixed on where she was stepping. We approached the fourth cellar and the dampness made the stale air very chilly. She had continued to lose weight and looked extremely fragile. Recently I had heard comments from attendees of the opera to the effect that they could not understand how such a huge voice could come from such a frail girl. Her eyes appeared very big in her thin face in the dim light and my concern suddenly overwhelmed me. I forced my mind back to the moment at hand. We must have appeared as if we were a couple out walking along the Seine or strolling on a Sunday afternoon through the Tuileries Gardens. For us though, there would be no other couples to greet along the way.

We arrived at the lowest level and the first of my doors. I had constructed my defenses so as to confuse and frustrate anyone who might look for where I lived. Each subsequent door was designed differently and it was necessary to know exactly what to do to gain entry to each of them. I felt above the door in the darkness for the hidden lever that would roll the first door, constructed of stone, open. The chill was beginning to get to Christine. The season was late winter and the lower levels of the stone building retained much of the cold. The door opened with a low grinding sound. It weighed many thousands of pounds. It pleased me to watch it roll back as I had put much thought into the system of weights and counterbalances that would move it so smoothly. Christine, as usual, was oblivious to what I had done to move it.

The next passageway was not as damp. I had built stops into the floor to prevent any running water from reaching that far. It was also level so it was easier for Christine to walk. She still had her arm tucked under mine. The human contact, though small, felt good. We reached the second door, which was made of heavy oak. I had blended it into the stone background just in case anyone managed to stumble onto it. After we passed through this door the air became a little warmer. I had taken care to make sure that my heating system was functioning properly and the heat radiated into this last passageway. Christine looked up at me gratefully, glad to finally feel the heat. It was the first time she had looked at me since we left her dressing room. My final door stood before us. Imported from Spain, this door was also oak, but intricately carved. I took a deep breath as I reached overhead to move the tiny lever that would release the lock. At the faint click of the latch I pushed the door open and held it as she walked in.

Warm candlelight greeted us as we entered, and I congratulated myself on the inviting atmosphere I had created for this night. At the same time, it occurred to me that the abundance of flickering candles, the earthy smell of incense and the atmosphere in general was one of pure seduction. I hoped she would not notice. I quickly shed my cloak and hat before I turned to her and eased her cloak from her shoulders. At least she couldn't see the flush I felt creeping into my face. I tried to ignore the softness of her skin when my fingers lightly brushed her neck. I asked her to sit down and went to get her some wine.

"I've been looking forward to this evening," I said, handing her the wine and sitting down in a chair across from the one she had taken.

Looking around, she said, "You have worked hard to make things very nice for me."

"I always want things to be perfect for you, my dear," I said softly. I feared I was wearing my feelings on my sleeve, and my heart was beating faster than normal. I raised my glass. "To you, Christine, and your success at the Opera."

"Why, thank you very much," she said with a shy smile. "I could not have gone so far and accomplished so much without your help."

"The pleasure has been all mine, I assure you, but all I did was bring out what you had all along, Christine."

Following a bit of small talk I rose from my chair.

"Shall we share a bit of music before we dine?"

"I would like that."

She took my outstretched hand. We went into the music room where I sat at the enormous pipe organ, throwing the tails of my coat behind the ornately carved bench with a flourish. This was the situation in which we were both at our best, and I always felt a thrill at the liquid sounds of her beautiful voice accompanying my playing. Her lips formed the complex Latin and Italian phrases without hesitation and I watched her face as I played. For the moment Christine appeared unaware of her surroundings, lost in the music as she was. She had become a true professional. After a few arias from known operas we began on some of my own compositions. Her voice filled the room and were it not for the depth of our location underground I felt that all Paris would have heard her and that those in the streets would cease their bustling to listen.

Reluctantly I called a halt to the music since she had already sung a full opera that night. She was radiant as I took her hand and led her back to the other room where we enjoyed a sumptuous feast of salmon croquettes and duck breast served with pears. We finished with flavored custards served in tiny porcelain pots. We spoke politely but very little as we ate. I could not take my eyes from her and she kept hers lowered for most of the meal. I know she wondered where all the meticulously prepared food had come from, but I would not reveal my little secrets.

After dinner I took her arm and was jolted by an intensely sexual response deep within me. I don't know if Christine also felt it; if she did, she did not show it. My other hand came up to take hers as I slid the first hand around to the small of her back to guide her. I walked closely beside her and felt the muscles in her back move as she walked. My hand crept further around to rest at her waist. With my one arm almost fully around her it was all I could do to refrain from taking her completely in my arms.

We neared the couch and I hesitated to remove my hand from her waist. I was standing behind her, in the same position we had been on that night when we had first felt the heat of our closeness. She did not move away. Hardly daring to breathe, I slowly moved both my hands lightly up the length of her back. My hands slid in a soft caress up over the smooth satin of her gown and came to rest upon the silky skin of her exposed shoulders. Her skin was so soft, like the finest velvet. I pulled her shoulders back gently against my chest. My head was reeling and strange things were happening inside me. I could barely catch my breath, and

Christine was breathing deeply and swaying slightly on her feet. I moved my hands slowly and lightly down along her arms to finally intertwine my fingers with hers. Then, following the lead of a slight pressure from her arms, our joined hands came together in front of her.

I held a woman in my arms for the very first time.

Bowing my head to her hair I breathed in her scent and was lost to the world. The heat intensified where our bodies touched. I was on fire. My knees threatened to give way beneath me. I could not get close enough to her. Only after her barely perceptible gasp did I realize that I had tightened my arms around her. The sound broke the spell and I reluctantly released her. My hands dropped slowly away as I stepped back away from her, immediately feeling the coolness of the empty space between us.

Leaving her standing in the middle of the room, I turned to wind up the large rosewood music box that I kept on a table. As the soft tinkling sounds of a simple but haunting melody began to fill the room I turned to her and took her hands in mine. When I moved a little closer she backed away slightly. She was more nervous than I was, if that were possible, and she was trembling. I desperately wanted to hold her again but she was showing signs of reluctance. I could not push her too quickly. Her hands were still resting in mine. I released one and raised my hand to her face to lightly touch one soft cheek. She raised her eyes and I saw the same confusion there as I had seen on earlier occasions.

"Christine."

"Erik, I...I..."

"I frighten you? I do not want you to be frightened of me. I would never do anything to harm you. You must know that by now."

"I know you would never intend to hurt me, but sometimes you are so different...so far away. Sometimes I feel that I don't know you at all, that you are two different people."

I sighed. "I admit that my temper gets the better of me at times. I am used to having my own way. It has become second nature."

I led her to the couch. She sat down and I sat down next to her, still holding her hand. I took up her other hand again and tried to keep my voice from shaking. "Christine, you have brought into my life the first happiness that I have ever known. You touched my heart and my soul. You accepted me when all others shunned me."

My heart was pounding and my nerve was quickly diminishing. I knew that this was the time to ask her my most important question.

"Christine," I continued, "I can never return to my lonely life without you. You mean the world to me. You are my life. There is a passion trapped inside each of us for the other that smolders just below the surface. You have feelings for me. I can see it in your eyes." I paused, searching her face for some sign. "You say you love the Vicomte." I could not prevent the urgency that was creeping into my voice. "He is a boy, Christine, and I am a man...a man whose need for you is greater than anything you or I have ever known. What we could experience together would make what you feel for him seem insignificant and pale in comparison. Christine, I can show you things that you've never even dreamed of; a world full of beauty, discovery, sensuality and passion. Please let me be a part of your life. Let us leave this life of darkness, secrets and uncertainty and begin anew, together. I need you. Please leave Paris with me."

She sat unmoving, her eyes wide, as I slowly raised her hands to my lips, barely brushing them with the lightest of kisses. I did not know what her reaction would be to the gesture; I had never been so forward with her before. It was awkward enough because of the mask, which basically covered my entire face down to the top of my upper lip and dipping down slightly further over each cheek. I almost expected her to run in horror at the sight of her hands rising to my lips but she did not pull away. After what seemed an eternity, she gently pulled them back to her lap.

"Erik, how can I...I can't..." she stammered

"Please, give us a chance. That's all I ask..."

"All you ask?" she interrupted as if she had just awakened. "You want me to leave Raoul and everything I've ever known to go away with you? Yes, I have feelings for you. I cannot lie to you about that. But I barely know you...where would we go, what would we do? What would I ever tell Raoul?"

"You wouldn't have to tell him anything," I said excitedly. "I can complete my preparations and we'll be gone." I reached for her hands again, but she once again gently but firmly pulled them away.

"Complete your preparations? It seems that you have presumed to know my mind," she said, tossing her head in mounting anger. "I am becoming very weary of men who believe they must make my decisions for me. I can make my decisions for myself. You ask me to go with you. What am I supposed to do, just walk away and leave the man whom I am to marry? You must be insane to think that I would do that without a word!"

At the word "insane" my own anger pushed to the surface. "As I recall, my dear, that is precisely what you planned to do to me not too long ago," I countered bitterly.

I left her sitting on the couch and stiffly crossed the room to get myself a drink, pointedly passing up the wine for something stronger. My mood and my patience were rapidly deteriorating. After taking several deep swallows that drained half the glass, I turned back to her.

"You've been playing a dangerous game for far too long, Christine," I stated flatly. "If it becomes necessary for me to take action to end it, then I shall. I have been overly patient with you and your 'secret' love affair with the Vicomte. I have stated my position and my feelings to you and I do not take either of them lightly. You say no to me, yet you cannot stay away from me, can you? Can you!"

She did not answer me. I stared at her. Her eyes dropped to the floor with increasing discomfort and her hands were clenched.

"This evening is over," I stated abruptly and tossed back the remainder of my drink. Turning on my heel, I went to get her wrap.

*   *   *

Damn! I don't know how I had expected her to respond to my outrageous request. She had not refused outright, but she made it very clear that she did not intend to leave the boy. In fact, what she had said about her engagement indicated that she would go through with her plans to marry, regardless of what I wanted. *Oh Christine, why must you make things so difficult?* I was going to have to take action. I could not go on without her. I had grown too fond of her, and there was no denying the intense physical desire that now threatened to tear me apart every time I so much as thought of her. My desire must be satisfied in some tangible way, and soon.

One might ask why I had remained celibate for all these years. I could have gone into the dark streets of the poorer sections of the city and tried to buy favors, but the prospect of being entertained by certain inhabitants of the street world made me feel physically ill. There were women out there who were desperate enough to lie with anyone for the right price, but the thought of watching them literally swallow their disgust at the prospect of touching me was more than I could bear. When I was a young man struggling with the same urges, I could never bring myself to take a chance on the humiliation of it. I satisfied myself in whatever ways I could until I learned not to think of such things. Unfortunately, "such things" were once again on my mind. I was losing patience. Patience was a virtue that I had never possessed in large quantity but, for now, I must bide my time and make my plans carefully—plans that were almost ended forever by an unexpected and explosive encounter with none other than the Vicomte de Chagny.

5

---------- ★ ----------

I was still smarting over what I perceived as Christine's total rejection so I stayed away from her for several days. The fact that she was still struggling with her choice between the boy and me was, once again, no longer of any importance to me. Fed by our mutual attraction for the same woman, the animosity between Raoul and me had been steadily increasing. The boy was naive, inexperienced and somewhat foolish but he was proving to be a tenacious opponent.

Meanwhile, he continued to harass Vaurien over his reluctance to investigate me further. That greedy fool did not want to rock any boats as long as his star singer continued to perform as expected. I had brought about an amazing transformation of a shy chorus girl and tentative dancer into a confident young woman with a truly phenomenal voice and an impressive stage presence. His attitude angered Raoul, who threatened to withdraw his patronage, but apparently Christine's performances were becoming so popular that people were being turned away at the door nightly. They no longer needed his money. Vaurien and the building's owners were overwhelmed with their recent success and they were not about to tamper with it. They did not want to upset whatever had created their fine new talent, be it man or ghost.

Leaving me alone also held another advantage for them. I had ceased all the mischief and foolishness with which I had formerly occupied myself at the Opera. My abandonment of malicious games had kept the previously frequent stories of odd sightings and other strange happenings at the Opera out of the newspapers. Superstitious people who had previously been reluctant to set foot in the place now flocked to the theater, complacent in their belief that the "Opera Ghost" was no longer a threat.

As for me, my patience had been pushed about as far as it would go. I had taken all I could of Christine's vacillation between us. Separate but interwoven circumstances had brought Raoul and me to the very edge of a precipice over which we both dangled with the unfortunate object of our desire balanced precariously between us. All of this increasingly virulent animosity came to a head one night in a violent confrontation that should have resulted in the death of one of us. To this day I cannot comprehend how both of us came out of it alive.

It was very late one night after a performance and I thought the theater was empty. As was my habit, I was prowling around the backstage areas examining sets, lighting and various other aspects of stage production. I was on a catwalk high above the stage when a movement below me caught my attention. There were only a few lamps lit and I strained my eyes to see who it might be. I was barely twenty feet from the floor, and as the figure below me moved into a pool of light, I recognized Raoul. What in hell was he doing here at this time of night? Up to no good probably, I thought as I silently watched him from the narrow grating upon which I stood. He moved to the one spot from where I could actually see him best, directly below me and to my left. He began to fish in his pocket for something so I squatted down and carefully leaned over the thin railing to get a better look.

Raoul's hand emerged from his pocket holding a knife. The short blade glinted in the lamplight. My intake of breath was inaudible as I observed him walk quickly back among the ropes and pulley mechanisms used for flying scenery. Looking frequently over his shoulder in a very secretive manner, he began to saw methodically at the ropes with the little knife.

Sabotage! I had not thought him capable of such an act, and watched him with disbelief. I soon noticed that the ropes he chose to weaken were those which controlled the lightest screens and backdrops. I understood then that he intended harm to no one but me. His little game would be just enough to disrupt a performance or two and I knew exactly who would be blamed for the "accidents".

So, my boy, I thought. You think you've got it all figured out, don't you? I stood up slowly. The disgust I felt at his clandestine trickery threatened to consume me. How dare he think that he could hang this petty and juvenile prank on me! I was capable of more, oh so much more! Others who had been foolish enough to cross me had been made *very* aware of what I could do. Raoul was a bigger fool than I thought if he believed anyone would attribute this silliness to me. With utter contempt my eyes narrowed to slits as I looked down at him busily working on a rope. I felt a cold sensation around my heart as my loathing and jealousy blended together and hardened into hatred.

"May I assist you with that?" I shouted from above, my voice ringing in the empty and cavernous theater. "No doubt you intend to give me full credit for it anyway, is that not so?"

Raoul dropped the knife with a clatter and looked around wildly. I decided to have a little fun with him. I threw my voice to the back of the theater.

"You did not answer my question!" I sneered.

He faced the thousands of seats out in the darkness, his eyes darting back and forth frantically. The darkness was such a wonderful friend, always there when I needed her.

"Where are you? Show yourself!" he shouted.

Really, he needn't have shouted so loudly for he was standing directly beneath me. I laughed; an ugly sound full of mockery, and threw my voice again; this time to the boxes of the grand tier at stage right.

"How do you know I'm even here?" I questioned with childlike innocence. "Perhaps I really am the specter you've always thought I was!"

I pulled from my pocket a small incendiary device of the type normally used in carnivals for light displays. Activating it with one hand, I threw it high and out in front of him towards the massive chandelier that hung from the high ceiling. It exploded with a loud "pop" and there was a bright flash that briefly illuminated the chandelier and sent sparks raining down upon the plush seating.

"I am here!" I shouted again with venom dripping from my voice, this time originating the sound from upstage. "Am I Angel or Devil? For you I prefer the latter!"

Raoul spun around to face the rear of the stage. I had him truly frightened now but my satisfaction was short-lived. His hand emerged from under his coat clutching a small pistol. At that moment the catwalk upon which I stood creaked softly, alerting Raoul to my presence directly above him. His head and arm jerked upward simultaneously. I saw his enraged and frightened face blur in an explosion of brightness as the gun went off in front of it. Temporarily blinded by the flash, it took me a few precious seconds to get myself moving before he could take aim for another shot. I carried no gun. I had never needed one. The only weapon I possessed was a thin but carefully knotted length of catgut. In my hands the lasso was an accurate and deadly tool of death but I needed to be at very close range to use it effectively. In this circumstance I might as well have been unarmed.

Raoul centered me in his sights again as I ran nimbly along the narrow platform while digging in my pocket for a second incendiary display. I watched him follow me with the barrel of the gun. He fired again. The bullet ricocheted off the iron walk with a clang and disappeared. The sound was deafening. I knew the catwalks well, but I was not fast enough. As I pulled the tiny device from my pocket and threw it, he squeezed off his third shot. The gun and my sparks exploded at the same time causing Raoul to duck under the storm of brightly burning pellets raining down around him. His bullet found its mark. With a sickening thud it tore into the back of my upper right arm just below my shoulder. The pain made me stumble on the walk. Righting myself, I saw Raoul awkwardly climbing the ladder at the end of the walk with the gun in his hand. I was at a distinct disadvantage unless he accidentally shot himself on his way up that ladder. I guessed that he did not realize I'd been shot.

Luckily I am left-handed, because my right arm was not much good to me. I hoped my shirt and coat would soak up the blood that I felt warming the upper part of my arm. I would not run from him. I could have. I knew so many ways to exit the area it would have made his head spin. I could have disappeared right before his eyes if I'd wanted to. But he had called me a coward once before and I would not prove him right this night. I stood and waited for him, forcing him to make the next move. He reached the top of the ladder and advanced slowly toward me with his gun aimed at a point between my eyes. There was a wicked smile growing on his face. Now mind you, I have looked down the barrel of many a gun in my time, but never one being held by a jealous and enraged fool whose argument with me concerned a woman. Frankly, considering my past history with those of the fairer sex, this was not a situation in which I had ever expected to find myself. It was not the sight of the blank and deadly end of the gun barrel pointed at me that concerned me so much as the crazed look in the eyes of the man whose finger was on the trigger.

With the semidarkness again in my favor I slowly and imperceptibly slid my left hand into my coat and closed my fingers on the reassuring coils of my lasso. I stood my ground as he came closer. I had to wait until the proper moment to use it effectively. I felt the warm stickiness of blood reach the palm of my dangling right hand. It began to drip from my fingertips, through the catwalk, and onto the floor below.

"So, *Angel*," he said sarcastically as he slowly walked toward me. "You're not so ghostly now are you?"

The gun was cocked; his finger caressed the trigger. He raised his arm until it was straight out in front of him, placing the gun barrel barely an arm's length from my face. I swear I could hear each individual drop of my blood fall into the growing pool of it that was collecting on the floor below us. I prayed that the sound be only in my imagination. It sounded to me like the ticking of a clock—my time was running out along with my blood. If Raoul guessed that I was wounded he would surely shoot me dead and end this whole mess. I prayed for the accuracy of his aim, for I would rather die than allow him, or anyone, to take me alive.

Raoul smiled at me again with a nasty curl of his lip. "Now you are not answering *my* question," he sneered. "Has the 'cat' got your tongue?" he asked with a tap of his toe on the catwalk. When I did not answer he chuckled egotistically at his own feeble attempt at humor.

"I warn you..." I began in a low but aggressive voice.

"Warn me of what, pray tell?" he asked incredulously while moving the ornate pistol in tiny threatening circles. "You are hardly in a position to threaten me. I fear that you are about to meet your maker, whomever that was." The smile disappeared. Coldly he added, "You will not escape this time."

As his last words left his lips he finally noticed the blood dripping steadily from my fingers.

"Well, well, it seems you are human after all..." he said as he stupidly glanced down at the large, dark stain on the floor below.

The instant or two during which he removed his eyes from mine was all the time that I needed. My hand whipped out from under my coat clutching the lasso. In a heartbeat and before Raoul knew what hit him I had the noose around his neck and brought the end up high. Stepping quickly around behind him in the narrow space I tightened the noose around his throat. The gun clattered to the walkway and fell over the edge. Since I was taller than he was I could lift enough of his weight off his feet with one hand to leaving him choking and gasping for air. From my position behind the struggling man I leaned forward toward his right ear.

"I meant to warn you, Chagny, that I am not one to be trifled with," I growled from low in my throat. "Believe me when I say that I have successfully handled myself with infinitely more accomplished assassins than the likes of you." I took him up a bit higher, leaving him slightly limp from lack of air. "I would kill you right here and now if it weren't for the fact that Christine cares about you," I hissed between clenched teeth. "And don't flatter yourself by thinking you'd be my first nobleman either, you arrogant little twit," I added nastily. His body began to sag heavily. "Do you doubt me?" I asked, and applied a bit more pressure. He tried to respond, but neither air nor sound emerged. His eyes were wild and he feebly clawed at the tightening line around his throat.

"You will leave me alone," I continued into his ear in a deceivingly conversational tone, "and not interfere with me or my plans. You will cease your pursuit of Christine. You will stop whining to the management. As of this moment, you are giving up the fight. Goodbye."

I steadily took the noose up tighter and tighter around his neck until he sank to the floor unconscious. My extensive previous experience warned me when to stop. For Christine's sake and my own peace of mind I bent over his prostrate form and felt his neck for a pulse. I removed the noose and noted with satisfaction that the mark left by it was slight. It was specially designed for the purpose to which I had put it, and there would be no evidence remaining on the neck in a couple of hours. Satisfied that he would recover, I grabbed him by his coat and dragged him a few feet so that he lay between two main supports. I didn't want him falling off the catwalk but I lacked the strength to carry him down the ladder.

Feeling a bit faint, I slowly descended the ladder and walked across the dimly lit stage. Blood seemed to be everywhere. My coat was heavy with it. The wound must be more serious than I thought, and our struggle had not helped. The thought was reinforced as if on cue by a new awareness of the painfully throbbing ache in my arm.

I was shocked at how much blood there was once I got downstairs and began taking off my clothes. I used the mirror to inspect the wound and was dismayed to find the bullet deeply lodged against the bone just below the shoulder joint. By painfully raising the arm high above my head I could reach the entry point with my left hand. I was going to have to get that thing out of there by myself. I have never been squeamish over such things, but the prospect of probing around inside my own arm for an unseen chunk of lead did not appeal to me. I had no choice.

Quickly I gathered my materials. I cleaned myself up as best I could even as blood continued to flow freely from the wound. Then I opened a vial of morphine. Taking up almost twice a normal dosage into the syringe, I plunged it into the vein of my right arm and sat back to wait.

When I felt sufficiently numb I began my unsavory work. By holding the top of the tub room door with my right hand and leaning against the wall, I was able to keep my arm high enough to work on it. I desperately wanted to sit down but there was no other way to keep my arm elevated while keeping sight of the wound in the mirror. After placing a knotted rag between my teeth, I began probing for the bullet with the blade of a small, sterilized dagger. The delicate, razor-sharp weapon with the jewel-encrusted handle had seen many purposes but I doubt that surgery was one of them. Even in my numbed condition the pain was almost more than I could handle, but I could not take any more morphine and still keep my head on straight. I finally felt and heard the tip of the blade scrape against the bullet. Gritting my teeth against the rag, I worked the delicate blade in deeper and deeper until it slipped behind the smashed bullet. The blinding pain forced a low moan from me. My knees grew weak and I fought to stand long enough to finish the job. I finally brought the bullet out far enough to work it loose. With dizzy relief I heard it drop to the floor before my body joined it on the cold Spanish tiles. I quickly cleaned and dressed the gaping hole in my arm, removed the rest of my clothing and staggered into the bedroom where, finally and gratefully, I fell into a deep sleep.

Throbbing pain woke me very early the next morning. I injected another hefty dose of morphine to control the pain. Heavy reliance on the drug would be necessary for several days. Soon the pain eased enough for me to get dressed, but not before taking a warm bath. I forced myself not to worry about the trail of water I slopped onto my luxurious carpeting during numerous trips from stove to tub. Damn, I thought breathlessly as I poured the last bucket into the tub, in all these years why hadn't I figured out some system for delivering hot water?

After my bath, I had something to eat and set about cleaning up the mess. I picked up my blood-soaked clothes, bedding and cleaning rags with distaste and decided that there was nothing to be done about them as I regretfully bundled them up for disposal.

*   *   *

The previous night's confrontation had revealed an appalling amount of hostility between the boy and me. I knew then that I had no alternative. If there was to be any chance whatsoever of my keeping Christine, I must take her away. It was too late for me to retreat to my cellars and forget the whole thing. I had cornered myself. Even in the unlikely event that I decided to give Christine up, Raoul would now do whatever it took to have me hunted down even if it meant taking the building apart block by block with his own hands. I knew full well the fate that awaited me at the hands of the authorities. My public execution would be swift and sure, but the treatment I would endure prior to it would make the gallows seem a welcome sight. Even if I managed to elude them all, I had not the heart to begin again elsewhere if it meant doing it alone. I had hoped that Christine would leave with me by her own choice but circumstances now called for me to fall back on my carefully conceived plans. I had so much as told Raoul outright that I would not hesitate to carry out those plans.

After extensive research I had formulated my plans around one location that seemed to fit my rather unique needs. I pored over volume after volume describing many places and of course I had the experience of my own travels throughout the continent and beyond. We would be sailing for America. To be specific, New Orleans, Louisiana.

Many people called the place the "Paris of America" because of the numbers of French who had settled there. The city was a central point for the cream of society and sported a vigorous enthusiasm for the opera. New Orleans also had a history of strange traditions and practices of peculiar and deliciously macabre beliefs that made for a unique blend of the bizarre that I found immensely appealing. This was a place where people actually *chose* to wear masks during massive street celebrations. I could find no better or more appropriate hiding place than a city steeped in superstition and mystery offset by a healthy gaiety and the air of romance.

My plans for our departure could be carried out at any time and at a moment's notice. My solicitor had booked undated passage for two on one of the newer luxury steam passenger vessels out of Le Havre. The route would necessitate a journey up the Seine, which connects Paris with Rouen and eventually with Le Havre. I briefly considered traveling north by rail but travel by boat was more suited to my sensibilities. I was accustomed to luxury and comfort. I had parted with enough cash over the years to keep myself at a consistently high level of comfort. Extensive investments, real estate holdings and other less upstanding endeavors prior to and during my years at the Opera had resulted in my amassing a considerable fortune that was as yet untapped. The liquidation of my many assets would provide Christine and me a more than comfortable lifestyle for the rest of our lives.

Several trunks of the latest and most impressive of ladies' fashions had been purchased and everything Christine could possibly need was duly arranged for and at the ready. My one trunk held a few of my custom-made dress suits, shirts, shoes and other necessities. All my clothing was black. With the exception of my white shirts I'd worn nothing but black for many years and I honestly could not remember wearing anything else.

A few waistcoats and several intriguing items I had picked up in foreign countries had some color in them but even they were predominantly black. I noticed this continuity for perhaps the first time during packing and it struck me that the lack of color was rather funereal. I consulted my mirror. Christ, I even looked like a mortician! I would have to amend my sense of fashion for Christine's sake. In addition, we were going to a warmer climate. The concessions I must make for this scheme of mine were mounting up.

My manuscripts and what little else I had of true importance went into my trunk along with a few extra hand-made masks. For years I'd had them custom fitted and made by an aged craftsman just outside the city. They were made of superbly supple kid leather. These too, had always been black. Recently I'd had some made in natural, which was not too far removed from human skin tone. I always had several extras on hand for fear of being caught without one. When I paid my man the last time for his beautiful work and loyalty he gifted me with a mold and a list of materials. The gesture touched me and I was very grateful; it would make my job of finding a new craftsman that much easier. The last purchase I made was that of a small, plain gold ring, which I slipped onto the little finger of my left hand. There it would stay, without explanation, until and unless Christine accepted it from me without reservation.

The thought of leaving my home saddened me greatly. The comfortable rooms hidden far beneath the stage had been the only place in my life in which I felt I truly belonged. The pain of leaving was softened somewhat by the belief that I was leaving for a better and brighter life, full of the hope of a more normal existence. Renewed optimism had accompanied each of the innumerable times I relocated since the night I last walked out of my parents' home, and each time my dreams were shattered; my hopes drowned in hatred and fear. All I ever wanted was to live like everyone else.

Everything was ready. All that remained was to get Christine on board ship. After the events of our most recent evening together there was no possibility that she would have dinner with me again so soon. Nor would she leave with me willingly. I must therefore take her without warning; right from under Raoul's aristocratic nose, thus adding kidnapping to my list of crimes.

I had sent the trunks on ahead to storage in Le Havre. My solicitor had informed those in charge of passenger services that the gentleman for whom he booked passage was taking his ill wife back home to her family at the first sign that she was stable enough for travel. No one would question my boarding during this or any other night with an unconscious woman in my arms. I would make my move when the time was right.

*   *   *

Later that night I was lurking behind the mirror when Christine and Raoul entered her dressing room laughing and holding hands. Waves of jealousy hit me. He started to leave, then returned to her side, smiling wickedly.

"By the way, love, that 'thing' that's been stalking you won't likely bother you again," he said smugly. "He's probably realized by now that his efforts are in vain. Perhaps he's gone back into whatever hole he came out of."

Before she could answer he pulled her carelessly into his embrace and tilted her face up to his. The sight of his lips fastening on hers made my stomach lurch. The gorge rose in my throat as I watched him draw that kiss out, holding her tightly and tangling a hand in her hair. Christine's slim neck bent backward as he pressed down harder upon her soft lips. It was as if he knew I was watching. When her arms slowly encircled his neck I began to sweat with jealousy at the sight.

They stood barely two feet from the glass of the mirror. The sound of my ragged breathing echoed back to me in the dark tunnel. I wanted to go through the glass and kill him on the spot. I knew just how to do it—quickly and efficiently. The arrogant highbrow wouldn't know what hit him. However, that would not do much to further my case with Christine, now would it? Well, this pompous and complacent fool will soon find out that he is no match for me, I thought. He should remember this moment because it's the last one he'll ever spend with her.

Less than an hour later, Christine disappeared from the stage...smack in the middle of the second act.

She had just finished a brilliant aria. The lights inexplicably failed for a few seconds. When they returned to full strength, the actors blinked in confusion, then gallantly tried to pick up where they left off. They were unable to do so. Their star had disappeared.

Unseen by the audience and the other actors, I had swiftly emerged from the trap door by Christine's feet at mid stage, grabbed her and dropped back down through it. One whiff of the cloth I held to her nose and mouth put her out and, ignoring the painful throbbing of my right arm, I carried her quickly downstairs. I planned to keep her under sedation until we were away from Paris, but I waited too long and the drug wore off before I could reinforce it. Everything then happened at once.

Pandemonium had broken out in the theater far above our heads. I was wasting time, listening to the commotion above with a twisted sense of accomplishment, when I heard the tinkle of a tiny bell that would announce the arrival of someone in my torture chamber. (I had built the chamber years earlier simply to keep myself occupied. I never thought it would be used.) There must be a mistake. Who in hell could possibly be in there? My confusion turned quickly to outrage when I looked through a one-way mirror into the chamber to see the damned Vicomte accompanied by none other than my dear daroga!

I knew what would happen to the men in that chamber when it began heating itself to ungodly temperatures, but I was desperate to get Christine away from there. Imagine my shock when I turned around to find her groggily sitting up on the couch! Christ, could anything else go wrong? Then she heard the shouts of the two men and realized that something terrible was happening to her lover in the next room. They, in turn, could hear what was transpiring on my side of the wall. As Christine began to cry and beg for their release, my mental state, under heavy duress and tenuous at best by that point, suddenly began to fall apart. I believe I must have been somewhere between one of my blind rages and a mental collapse. They all must have thought me quite mad, for my subsequent ranting and raving made little sense. I loudly declared that two tiny knobs on my mantel would decide all our fates and that Christine would make the choice. It was simple, really. The turning of one would ignite an old wartime supply of gunpowder stored in hundreds of barrels hidden under our feet and blow the Opera and a large chunk of Paris into the next century. The other would activate a rush of water from the lake that would soak and destroy the powder. Christine stared at me in growing horror as she listened to the muffled shouts of the men in the chamber. Her own mind began to shut down and she dropped to her knees in despair, then began to dash her head against the floor.

The sight of her pain, the interruption of my meticulous plans and the threat of my own devices suddenly overpowered me. I pulled her to her feet and screamed at her to choose a knob even as my heart thudded with dread while I watched her make her decision. She chose blindly but wisely. Would I have stopped her had she reached for the other knob? I was far enough off my head that I honestly cannot answer that question now, but it was with an unexpected sense of relief that I heard water begin to fill the subfloor below us. The floor of the heated chamber then opened up and dropped the men into the swirling waters below. When I observed the naked agony on Christine's battered face as she listened to their screams, something let go inside me and I finally conceded defeat.

I had quite a job reviving them. Christine sat, silently and in shock, while I worked feverishly to purge the water from their lungs. Once both men had unconsciously resumed breathing on their own, I spoke with Christine quietly and rationally for a few minutes during which I apologized and extracted a promise from her. I then retreated to give the girl and the awakening young man a moment alone while I pulled myself together enough to do what I had to do.

My dream was gone, but Christine could still realize hers. I surprised them both by asking the boy to take care of Christine and blessing their union. Then I led a listless Christine and her bewildered Raoul to the world above. Once they stood safely at the street gate, I quietly bade them farewell and turned away before anyone could say another word. Back in my rooms, I hefted my Persian friend upon my shoulders and bore him quickly through the dark streets to his flat, where I left him propped by the door.

It was over.

*   *   *

I lay in the silent darkness of my rooms for days afterward, taking no food and only an occasional sip of wine, alternately sweating and shivering with cold. Not even the constant throbbing of my shoulder wound could rouse me. I made no conscious decision to die; my mind simply ceased to look ahead. The future meant nothing to me. As for my daroga, he would likely turn his back on me for good this time. For years he had stuck by me, alternately chastising and forgiving me for my sins, but I had gone too far. He was the closest thing I'd ever known to a friend, but I was in no state to suffer from his loss. Nor would he likely suffer mine. I expected the authorities to come crashing through my door at any time led by the new knowledge of the Vicomte. They never came. I didn't have the strength to wonder why.

The pain of hunger finally ceased its grinding in my gut, leaving a feeling of shrunken pressure that weighed me down where I lay in a cold sweat. My mouth was dry but as I lifted my head toward where I had last set the wine bottle, my head began to spin with a nauseating sense of motion. I lay back with a sigh and closed my eyes. I fell into a very deep sleep and dreamed of Christine. She had shown me the only compassion and understanding that I had ever known. She was all that I ever wanted. She was gone. I don't know how long I lay there teetering on the very edge of life, but suddenly I opened my eyes and knew, with a firm conviction, that I would try again. I had sent Christine away to be happy, but I now realized that my intentions, though honorable, were in vain. I could not allow myself to die in the darkness, nor could I let her go. My mind resumed its recognition of a future, and that future was stronger than the pull of impending death. I awoke with a plan already so well developed and so potentially effective that it was as if someone else had scripted it for me while I lay in a state of suspension—someone who knew my ultimate destiny better than I did myself. Yes, I would disappear as planned—swiftly, completely, permanently—and I would not be alone.

Summoning what little strength I had, I struggled to my feet. My head ached, I shook with weakness and my clothing was damp and odorous. The stubble of new beard itched when I put on the mask. For the task at hand, I would set aside my disgust and force myself to remain as I was. I could hardly bemoan my debilitated condition, as my sickly appearance and obvious discomfort were an unexpected asset for this first and very important step. Once my daroga caught a look at me he would be unlikely to doubt the news that I planned to tell him. The heavy feeling in my stomach intensified when I got up. I couldn't get enough breath. Short stabs of vaguely familiar pain skittered through my chest. I hunched myself over the pain and, looking and feeling like the walking dead, donned hat and cloak and made my way unsteadily up to the darkened streets of Paris.

Huddled on the doorstep of the daroga's seedy flat, I could barely stand long enough to ring the bell. His man reluctantly ushered me in and I sank thankfully into a chair before I collapsed on the worn carpeting. My breath was short, my chest and stomach hurt and my hands shook. My visit was brief and to the point. Between gasps, I informed my old friend that I was not long for this world. I told him what had happened while he lay unconscious in my apartments, and swore that I had sent Christine and the Vicomte on their way alive. My mere mention of the girl caused tears to run down my hidden cheeks and my voice to shake, which added to the effect that I was trying to achieve. The words caught in my throat, and several times I motioned for him to stay seated as he rose to assist me. Indeed, he did look very concerned. With my stomach grinding anew and my arms clutched around myself, I told him, as quickly as possible, that he must agree to do one last thing for me in this lifetime, for I would soon be dead and there was no one else to help me. Upon receipt from me of several personal items once belonging to Christine, he was to place a short notice in a certain newspaper. The notice would be her signal to return to Paris to fulfill the promise that she had made when I let her go—the promise to bury me. I left him then, with tears of a different sort running down my cheeks.

       *   *   *

"Erik is dead."

Christine obviously expected me to meet my maker at some point, but when the notice appeared in the paper only weeks after she had left me it probably came as a bit of a shock. As I stood reading the notice in my parlor that night, I realized that the twinge I felt was of guilt. I don't think I'd ever actually felt guilt over anything before that night. I've spent most of my life living one lie or another, but this was a colossal manipulation of her loyalty and a promise she had made in good faith. It was a blatant, hurtful lie that would irrevocably change her life forever. Abhorrent as my method was, I knew it was the only way I could get her to return to me.

I knew when Christine arrived back in town. I won't bother to explain how; suffice it to say that I always knew exactly what was going on when necessary. I felt a curious mixture of pride and relief that she at least cared enough to keep her promise. Perhaps she trusted me more in death than in life. Regardless of motive, she and Raoul had returned. I spotted the two of them just hours before her rendezvous with destiny and I was appalled at her appearance. She was thin and serious and exhibited none of her former youthful gaiety. She looked haggard and much older than her years. Had I done that to her? I knew nothing of where she had been since she had left or anything about the circumstances of what I assumed was her marriage to Raoul, but it was obvious that something was wrong in her life.

I had no way of knowing when she would come for me, so I waited, hidden in the shadows of the cellars by the lake. The dampness was so pervasive that it possessed a smell. Occasionally I heard water dripping from the walls into puddles and into the lake itself. The one lantern that hung on the far side of the cavern cast a dim and eerie glow that provided just enough light to find one's way through the dark.

The light crunching of distant footsteps alerted me to the approach of another figure. My heart pounded in my chest. Although I was once again fit and healthy, I suddenly felt weak with anticipation. I waited silently for whomever it was to approach the dark form lying on the floor next to the old well. The corpse was clothed in black, fitted with one of my masks and wound in a cloak. The figure slowly moved closer and, as the feeble beam of light caught the shine of tear tracks on her cheeks, I recognized Christine's face. I stood a scant 5 feet from her when she noticed the dark shape on the floor. I held my breath as she raised her hand to her mouth in a now familiar gesture of shock. She began to cry softly. Several interminable minutes passed before she summoned the composure to kneel beside the body.

"Oh, Erik," she sobbed, "I'm so sorry. So very sorry…things had…to end like this." She wiped the tears from her face and sniffed loudly. "I didn't want it to be like this." She then reached out toward the body.

"Christine."

The girl shot to her feet with a cry and looked wildly around her. I stepped up behind her and laid my hand lightly on her shoulder. She jumped at my touch and whirled around to look directly up into my masked face. Her eyes widened and she opened her mouth to scream but no sound came from her. Instead, she went down in a dead faint. I caught her in my arms and laid her gently on the floor. Quickly I lit another lantern and brought it close while I pulled a small vial of laudanum from my pocket. Her eyelids flickered so I reached into my pocket to pull out a cloth soaked in an anesthetic. I laid it gently over her nose and mouth until her body went slack. I cupped my hands around her face and my eyes fell upon her lips. I took a long look at her beautiful face as framed by my own hands, then moved one hand under her head to cushion it while I drew the fingertips of my other hand lightly down her cheek. Wasting precious time, my hand shook as my fingers moved on to lightly trace those soft red lips which I longed to meet with my own. I knelt there beside her and held her head in my hands as she slept unknowingly before me. She was so beautiful...so soft. I leaned down toward that luscious pair of red lips and my breathing became more labored with every inch I closed of the small space between us. I was almost close enough to feel the caress of her breath. *Oh, Christine.* I stared at her mouth, and my tongue flicked out to lick my own lips with desire. My tongue touched the inside edge of the mask and my mouth went dry. Damn! Damn, damn, *damn*!

I shook it off angrily. There was no time for that now. I lifted her head slightly and poured the contents of the vial into her mouth, working her throat to get it down. I was very careful with the dosage; enough to ensure that she was out for a long time. The laudanum would kick in before she recovered from the inhalant. I was safe for many hours. I pulled the corpse around behind the well, into the shadows, where it would likely not be discovered for years...if ever. Returning to Christine's side, I softly muttered an apology for what I was doing to her, then lifted her limp body and returned to my haven for the last time. I placed Christine on my couch and wrapped her in a cloak and blanket. The trunks were long gone and waiting for us in Le Havre. My rooms were immaculate. My magnificent organ would never again be heard and my imported tapestries, furnishings, and carpets would rot away to dust. I felt their loss acutely but it could not be helped. I had carefully concealed my home, but I could not see a return in my future. I assured myself that no one would ever find it, at least as long as the Opera stood. Tears of regret and uncertainty clouded my vision and I impatiently blinked them back. Saying a silent goodbye to yet another phase of my life, I put on my hat and cloak and returned to Christine's sleeping form. I gathered her into my arms and went to meet my waiting carriage.

6

———————— ★ ————————

The night watchman on the docks nodded sleepily to me and motioned toward a narrow gangway. I paid the hack driver and walked up the slightly sloping gangway with Christine nestled in my arms. She had settled into me as a child would in the arms of her father. I thought it comforting until I remembered that she knew nothing of what she did.

I found my way to my cabin and opened the door. In the cloud-filtered moonlight I could barely make out the bunk as I laid Christine gently upon it. I turned away and fumbled with the lamp. I opened her blanket and removed her shoes. I reached out to loosen the collar of her dress but thought better of it. The gesture did not feel right to me. I carefully covered her and, after making sure she was still deeply under the effects of the laudanum, left the cabin and locked the door behind me.

I spent the first lonely night of our journey pacing the deserted decks. In the early morning hours I noticed signs of her returning to consciousness and induced her to swallow another draught laced with laudanum. I kept her in a state of suspension during which we slowly traveled the distance to Le Havre. We were able to board the much larger and more opulent ocean going steamer directly and without incident, again under cover of darkness and using the same ruse of illness that I had previously. I spoke to a steward who arranged for someone to unpack Christine's things to the wardrobe and prepare her for bed. I could finally relax a bit. I found a spot in the corner of an alcove in the darkened saloon where I could catch a few hours' sleep.

Throughout that night I periodically returned to the room to check on Christine's condition. She continued to sleep heavily as the pale dawn of our third day away from Paris shone dimly through the large square window. Its frosted glass gave the impression that the day was very foggy, but as I strolled the decks alone in the early morning light the sun rose to what would become a beautiful blue sky. What a gorgeous sight it was! I had lived for too many years in almost total darkness. Standing there, with the morning sun on my face and the cool sea breeze washing over me, I felt that I could accomplish anything. I felt renewed, the way I had when I first left home so many years ago; fresh and ready to begin a new life with new dreams...before life had crushed me like an insect under its feet.

Abruptly my thoughts came crashing back to Christine. I had deceived her in the worst way imaginable. My confidence wavered as I wondered if she could ever forgive me. I took several deep breaths of the vibrantly fresh air and slowly wandered back to the stateroom. I dreaded her first moment of clear understanding of what had happened to her. I could not keep her drugged forever. She had to know. When I opened the door she was still lying in the brass bed, barely awake and staring at the ceiling with unfocused eyes. I moved to the side of the bed and leaned over her.

"Christine," I whispered. Her drifting gaze slowly shifted to my face. Confusion was rampant in her eyes.

"Erik?" she said weakly.

"Don't try to talk yet." I told her. "Just rest."

I wanted to delay the moment when she would come fully awake. She would realize what I had done and probably hate me for it. She looked around groggily.

"Where am I?" she asked. She put one thin hand to her brow. "What happened?"

"You are with me and you are safe," I began. "Why don't you try to go back to sleep?" I suggested, trying to postpone the inevitable.

She looked at me again and disbelief flooded her eyes.

"Erik! But you're...you're," she stuttered. "I came to bury you...I saw you lying there..."

I reached for her hand but it was too late. Christine suddenly sat up in the bed and stared wildly at me.

"Erik, you're dead!" she cried. "How...?"

The expression on her face suddenly changed from one of confusion to one of understanding. She knew what I had done. Her eyes narrowed with suspicion, then she broke down.

"I cried over you," she whimpered incredulously, her eyes spilling tears, "I kept my promise, I went to you and I *cried* for you! You were there, all right, but you weren't lying dead on the floor, you were *watching* me. You saw my grief and you *used* it! You used it! How could you? How could you do such a thing to me?" She buried her face in her hands and I could barely make out those last words.

At that point the ship heeled broadly to the port side. Christine looked up again in wide-eyed fear and flung the bedcovers from her legs. She staggered from the bed and rushed to the window, almost knocking me to the floor in the process. She wiped her hand across the glass in an attempt to wipe away the frosty coating. The ship suddenly listed to starboard, throwing her against the mahogany washstand in the corner. She winced as her hip struck the edge of the mounted washbowl. Turning back to me in sheer panic, her hands flew to her mouth as the realization struck her that she was aboard a ship.

"Erik, what else have you done?" she demanded in an accusatory tone. "Where is Raoul?"

"Christine," I began gently. "There is no one else with us. We are on our way to a new and wonderful..."

"Life?" she screamed, cutting me off. She stared at me with a mixed expression of horror and hysteria.

Then she looked down at herself, noticing for the first time that she wore only a nightgown. She halfheartedly arranged her arms in front of her body to cover herself. She threw me a sideways glance of embarrassment.

"Don't trouble yourself over that," I reassured her, as if it would make the situation better, "I found female staff to care for you."

Without looking at me again she whispered, "How long has it been?"

"Three days," I said quietly and dropped my own eyes to the floor, cowed by her expression.

She turned back to the sightless window. "Then Raoul doesn't even know what happened to me?" she asked the window with disbelief.

"I'm afraid not," I admitted. This was not going well at all. "No one knows where you are. Christine, it was the only way..."

"How dare you make my decisions for me!" she shouted, whirling around to face me. "Who gave you the right to take me away? I said that I would not leave with you!"

"Christine, I... Please understand..."

She did not give me a chance to explain or even to finish my sentence. I had not thought her strong enough to display this kind of emotion. I'd seen her angry, but I never anticipated anything like what came next.

"How dare you, how dare you!" she screamed at me, over and over. I thought my ears would shatter from the shrill sound of her voice.

I tried to calm her by putting my hands on her shoulders, but it only made matters worse. It was not the time to touch her and I was surprised by the vehemence of her reaction. She violently threw up her arms, throwing my hands off her shoulders. I was too horrified by what was happening to react when she came at me in a rage.

Christine beat upon my chest with her tiny fists, her eyes tightly closed in anger, fear and frustration. She continued to rain blows upon me while I stood there and took them, silently letting her play herself out. Her arms soon grew weak and slow with the exertion and tears slid down her cheeks from her tightly closed eyes. Abruptly, she was still, and her hands rested on my chest. She met my gaze briefly with her eyes swimming with tears of pitiful helplessness. Then, as I looked down at her, her eyes rolled up into her head and she passed out. Her weight seemed like that of a bird as I laid her gently on the bed. I stood looking down at her with my heart in the pit of my stomach. What had I done?

*   *   *

Christine slept all through that night. I had no choice but to remain at her side. She could not be alone when she awoke. Her present exhaustion was most likely brought on by the combination of her body coming off the drug and her fear.

I had no firsthand knowledge of narcotic withdrawal. Although I had experimented heavily with many different narcotics some years ago, I had never allowed myself to become dependent upon them. Experimentation, I sincerely believed, was the best source of knowledge. I had kept morphine on hand for years for various reasons. Aside from my bullet wound, which remained painful, I'll admit that it had helped me handle some other recent physical discomforts brought on by my unfulfilled desire for the woman who slept in the bed before me. For whatever reasons, I had kept a supply of the drug on hand for years. One never knows.

I sat in the chair alongside the bed and watched Christine in her heavy slumber. My thoughts drifted back to my own health. I must remain well enough to be a proper protector for Christine. I'd had no episodes for months and felt younger than I had in years. I must be up to the task that I had set for myself because there could be no turning back now. I knew full well that the morning would bring with it a second confrontation. I rearranged my long form in the small chair to get more comfortable. It would be a long night.

*   *   *

Dim light forced my eyes open. I groggily reached up to rub them and found that my mask had ended up in my lap. I glanced quickly at the bed and was relieved to see that Christine had not stirred. From my slouched position I moved to sit up and every muscle in my body screamed with pain. I was not used to sleeping in chairs. I would have to find better accommodations until Christine and I could come to an understanding. I got up and silently moved about the room to get the circulation going in my stiff legs, and adjusted the ventilators to get a little fresh air into the tiny room. I must have been asleep for hours. Since most of the passengers and crew alike would still be abed at this hour, I thought of going out after some tea. Movement from the bed halted my progress toward the door.

Christine's eyes were on the ceiling and her hand was moving to wipe the sleep from them. I anxiously went to the edge of the bed but said nothing. She turned her head toward me.

"What...?" she began. "Oh," she muttered. Slowly she sat up, her luxurious curls cascading around her shoulders. I longed to reach for them, to slowly entangle my fingers in their softness. Seeing her fresh from sleep brought back my aching desire for her. Her hair looked so soft, and her mouth... I pushed the thought away. It would take her a long while to forgive me, if she ever did.

"Good morning, Christine. What may I have brought for you?" I asked eagerly as I reached for the electric bell. "What do you need?"

She looked directly at me with clear eyes for the first time since we left Paris. My heart sank. The look that I dreaded was there. Her eyes were completely cold.

"What do I need?" she repeated flatly, "Nothing from you. Except perhaps leaving so I may put on some proper clothing."

"But..." I stammered, needing to do something for her.

"Erik, please!" she hissed, anger now joining the coldness in her eyes. "Just leave," she finished stonily, turning her face away from me.

Without a word I left the room, exiting without a backward glance into the light rain and fog of an already less-than-perfect day. It was no longer necessary for me to watch her for there was nowhere for her to go. She could not escape me, but that look in her eyes haunted me as it showed clearly that escape was precisely what she wanted.

The ship was waking up. People moved along the decks toward a hot breakfast. Summer had not yet begun and the sea air was cold and damp. My most pressing dilemma was finding a place to pass the time where I would not be seen. Finding myself in public for the first time in so many years was decidedly unnerving, to say the least. I had lived in public for much of my life, but my years of

solitude had dimmed the memory of the pain associated with living among men. In the excitement of making all my plans I had
not thought much about the exposure that leaving my home in the
cellars would inevitably bring me. It was not only unnerving, I
concluded, it was positively frightening. The saloon where I found
isolation a couple of nights ago would be teeming with passengers
at their morning meal so I decided I might try the smoking room.
I had gotten a few hours of sleep in that abominable stateroom
chair so I was not in need of rest. I was not hungry, so I thought I
would stop in at the library first where I might find something of
interest to read. Choosing a thick volume on ancient civilizations,
I continued to the smoking room and was relieved to find it quite
empty. There was one other advantage to this room; women were
not allowed to enter it.

Two days passed with almost no contact between Christine and
myself. I remained on the very outskirts of life aboard ship, avoiding people when I could and enduring the inevitable stares and
whispers when I could not. I continued to check on Christine periodically, but she would have none of me. The coldness in her eyes
pierced my heart and robbed me of my confidence and my hopeful
visions of the future. What future, I thought grimly as I prepared
to spend my second night in a dark corner of the saloon. Hell, I
was better off back in my lonely house under the opera dreaming
about what I could never have. Anything was better than being
with this woman, whom I desired above all else, only to have her
totally reject me. Christine herself had ordered the few meals that
she had eaten in her stateroom. I finally recognized the look in her
blue eyes for what it was. She hated me.

The next morning came quickly. I'd slept for most of the night
in spite of my thoughts and surroundings. I'm too old for this, I
thought, as I unfolded myself once again from the stiff dining
chair. It took me quite a few steps to get the cricks out of my legs.

Soon afterward I found myself again in the smoking room. After what seemed like endless hours, I was lost in my book when it occurred to me to check the time. It was already late morning. I sighed and turned in the richly upholstered maroon leather chair to look out the window. The fog was heavy and the waves looked as cold and forbidding as Christine's eyes. Raindrops trickled down the windowpane. I noticed a lone woman standing at the outside deck rail. I couldn't be sure, but it looked like Christine. I did not have my cloak and hat, so I was forced to go out on deck without protection from both the elements and curious eyes. I left the warm impression I had made in the comfortable chair with resignation and left the book in it.

When I opened the door to the outer deck the wind caught me. Christ, it was cold! Fortunately my mask was of such a good fit that I did not worry myself about losing it. That would have been a disaster in itself. I turned up my collar and folded my arms around myself. Against the force of the wind I walked briskly but carefully along the wet, deserted deck toward the woman at the rail. Not many would venture out in this weather and the woman was, indeed, Christine. One of the cloaks I had bought for her was wrapped tightly around her but the hood was down and her hair was wet. She looked pale, lost and bedraggled. She did not acknowledge me. The light rain was just enough to be annoying. I stood next to her for a few moments until the wind began to seep through my coat and down my neck.

"Please, child, come in from the cold. You'll catch your death out here," I coaxed from between teeth that were beginning to chatter. At no perceptible response from her, I tried again. "If not to the stateroom, then please come into the saloon and have something hot to drink. I fear that my old bones do not take well to this cold wind."

"Well, then," she replied briskly, still staring out over the waves. "You should have considered your old bones before you decided on carrying out this bit of foolishness." She turned her head to look at me. I forced myself not to turn away from the cold hostility in her once warm eyes. The weather gave them an extra cast of gray. "I have already had something to eat, thank you very much, and I am on my way to the Captain's quarters."

She turned on her heel toward the stern. I could not allow her to talk to the Captain. With several strides I was alongside her and firmly took her by the arm.

"Don't you touch me!" she hissed while trying to pull her arm away from me. "Don't you dare touch me. I will do as I please."

"Christine, you really don't want..." I began.

"Let go!" she shouted, sounding like a very spoiled child.

The frustration of repeatedly receiving her cold shoulder caught up with me. My patience suddenly snapped and I contracted my thin fingers around her arm. I pulled her toward me so that my face hovered only inches above hers.

"Christine, you will do well to listen to me right now," I ordered in a low voice. "You will not find any sympathy in the Captain's Quarters nor anywhere else on this ship. I suggest that you accompany me to the saloon for a civil meal. If you don't think you can be naturally civil to me, then you'd better lean on your considerable acting talents, my dear, for you have no choice." I tightened my grip on her arm until I saw pain reflected in her eyes.

"What do you mean?" she asked fearfully as she tried unsuccessfully to pry my fingers from her arm. Her eyes widened. "What have you told them?"

"Why, I only told them the truth, my darling," I continued in a conversational tone that dripped with sarcasm. "The Captain of this ship and his entire crew know that my *wife* suffers from illnesses that can cause certain forms of…how shall I put it…dementia." My eyes narrowed as I leaned forward even closer into her face. "No one will believe anything you say," I spat.

With a small cry she tore loose from my grasp, turned and ran. Cursing under my breath, I began to walk after her. Well ahead of me, she reached the furthermost end of the stern rail and I thought she may have lost her mind when, with disbelieving eyes, I saw her appear to lean out over it. She could not possibly be in such despair that she would throw herself into the cold waves! I couldn't bear for anything to happen to her! I broke into a run. My boots rang on the wet planking. Through the fog I could barely see her outline at the rail. I reached her with my breath rasping in my throat and my heart pounding. She was leaning much too far out. I grabbed her and spun her around to face me. Without thinking, I wrapped my arms around her in a massive embrace and buried my masked face in her hair.

"Oh, Christine, Christine…" I murmured into her hair, which smelled of the sea and the fresh air. Her body stiffened. I lifted my head and released her. I looked into her eyes, which now showed both confusion and shock. I stepped back nervously from her, as surprised at my own reaction as she was. "Don't ever frighten me like that again," I said in a quaking voice.

"I don't…" she said, but stopped when she realized what I meant. "Oh, no! I wouldn't do that!" She was aghast. "I could never do that!"

Tears shone in her eyes. I think she was frightened that I would believe she could consider such a thing. She took a further step back from me. Her head shaking in disbelief, she turned to look out over the water again, her hands resting on the rail. She was silent a long time before she spoke.

"Erik, I am weary and I am angry. You hurt me. I cannot trust you. I don't know if I can ever forgive you for what you did. It seems that you must always have your way no matter who else is hurt in the process."

I stood there like an idiot with my emotions a tangled mess. My own frustration was forgotten.

"Since it appears I have no choice in the matter, I will be civil to you for the remainder of this voyage." she continued coldly. She spoke to me as if I were an errant child and would not look at me. "I shall even be good company if that will please you. I shall play your good wife for now, but in public only. In return, when we reach our destination, you will immediately send me home to Raoul. After that I shall not expect to see you again." She paused. "I suppose I should ask where we are going?"

"America. I will do anything you ask." I said quietly. I meant it. "Please accompany me to the saloon so we can get you out of this wet," I added with a note of resignation. She placed her hand, in a thoroughly businesslike manner, under my offered arm. "One more thing, Erik," she said with cool detachment. "I hope you have seen to accommodations for yourself."

I was relieved. I was loath to spend another night sleeping in a dining chair. There must be one extra cabin on this ship that I could purchase. Although I would lose her soon enough, a truce of sorts had been reached between us. If nothing else, I had what was left of our voyage to collect a lifetime of memories.

True to her word, Christine publicly became my dutiful but distant wife. We planned our meals around the beginning or end of the serving hours to avoid the bulk of the diners. What a topic of conversation we must have made; a nervous man in a mask accompanied by a young wife who was reportedly mad. There were the expected stares and whispers for a few days but I found myself adjusting slowly to my unaccustomed exposure. I am sure this was partly due to my preoccupation with Christine. I did not even notice when interest in our activities diminished and finally stopped altogether. I found, to my surprise, that I was beginning to enjoy the comforting sounds of everyday life that surrounded me; the clink of glasses, the murmur of many voices blended together and a child's laughter. All of these sounds had been shut out of my life by five floors of stonework for far too long. In my self-pitying solitude, I had not realized how much I missed being a part of life.

Christine and I settled into something of a routine. I arranged accommodations for myself in the second class section and found it comfortable, albeit lonely. But then I was used to being alone, wasn't I? I always rose very early. After taking the sea air in a lonely dawn walk around the decks, I presented myself at Christine's door to take her to breakfast. With her arm through mine, we entered the saloon and chose a table in one of the alcoves along the side. I held the back of her revolving dining chair and she thanked me politely as I swung her around to face her meal. Quite handy for the ladies, these chairs were, for they were afforded the opportunity to arrange their skirts before moving them under the table.

Christine spent the remainder of her mornings in the library. I could usually be found in the deserted smoking room. After the noon meal we spent time together. These hours were difficult for me. A friendly but distant girl who treated me as politely as she would a companionable stranger had replaced the warm Christine whom I had known in Paris. We spoke of many things as we strolled along the decks or sat on deck and listened to the sounds of the piano coming from the music room, but our conversation lacked the warmth and affection that we previously shared. I suppose I should be thankful that she was speaking to me at all. There were no more displays of anger from either of us. We kept any thoughts of the future to ourselves. Her thoughts and mine were undoubtedly worlds apart and we did not speak of anything beyond the moment.

Evenings were spent separately until I asked her to accompany me to the music room for some entertainment. My request left my lips without forethought. I had not actively sought public situations for many years. She looked at me with surprise when I asked her about going and, to my delight, she agreed. Regardless of what she thought of me, she was also bored and tired of our inactivity. That night I appeared at her door as any gentleman would call for a lady. I wore my best suit and adopted my most charming attitude, such as it was. She called for me to enter. When I stepped into the stateroom I was overwhelmed with the vision of loveliness that I beheld. I smiled at her. "Miss Daae, you look lovely tonight," I said, bowing slightly. "Surely you are the most beautiful woman on this vessel." The stateroom suddenly seemed very small to me. Christine was standing much too close for my comfort.

"Thank you, Erik, you flatter me," she replied with a tiny hint of a smile playing about her lips. "We will be docking eventually and I didn't want all these lovely gowns to go to waste. I must admit," she continued while taking one last look in the mirror and adjusting a few strands of hair, "that you went to a considerable amount of trouble and expense to make sure I had everything I would need on this voyage. Your judgment has seriously been in error, but I do appreciate your efforts toward my comfort."

"I only want to make you happy," I replied. I am sure that I wore a schoolboy's admiration all over me. "And tonight you are making me happy."

"Well," she said as she took my arm, "Since I am here I might as well try to enjoy myself. There won't be many more evenings left."

With that painful reminder of events to come hanging in the air between us, we walked down the deck. As we neared the music room, I couldn't help myself and stopped a few feet from the door. Damn, the room was crowded with people. The large room was brilliantly lit and the effect was as if the overhead glass dome were filled with sunlight. People stood around in small groups chatting. Others danced to music from the grand piano in the corner and many relaxed at tables with drinks and conversation. The atmosphere was one of crowded gaiety. My mouth went dry at the thought of entering that world. Christine's progress was halted abruptly when I stopped dead in my tracks.

The blood drained from my face and I felt disoriented. Without a word Christine pulled me by the arm over to a row of deck chairs along the darkened outside wall and pushed me down into a chair. I dropped my head into my trembling hands and swallowed several times trying to wet my dry throat.

"Christine I'm sorry, I can't...can't go in there," I whispered. I was sweating even though the night air was cold.

"Wait here, Erik," she said with authority, and left my side.

Before I could wonder where she had gone she was back and pressing a glass of brandy into my shaking hand. I took several sips and felt a little better. I straightened up in my chair and looked at her helplessly.

"I apologize," I began again, "but it seems that my invitation may have been ill-considered. I fear you shall have to go in alone."

"We are both going in there," she said firmly as she sat down beside me.

"No," I said with resignation, "I don't know what I was thinking. It's been too long. I can't do it. They will all run from me."

"No one is going to run from you," she said. "And you *can* do it, Erik." Looking at me intently she added softly, "You can do it because I am right here beside you."

I searched her face in the beam of light that shone on it from one of the nearby windows. In her eyes I found the strength I needed to take this most difficult step. True, her eyes did not hold what they once did for me, but I saw compassion there and a total empathy for my position. Christine, like no one else ever had, understood and accepted me with all of my faults. It was true that I had acted with poor judgment in stealing her away. I had hurt her and used her, and it was true that at the end of this journey I would lose her forever. Right now, none of that mattered. We shared something very special; an understanding and acceptance of each other's fears and weaknesses. At the moment, mine was the greater weakness and the lovely woman beside me was offering to help me overcome it.

We sat there in the darkness for a few minutes without speaking while I sipped the brandy. My right hand was resting on the arm of my chair and presently I felt the warm weight of Christine's smaller hand upon mine. It was the first time I remember her voluntarily touching me. I accepted it for the sympathetic gesture that it was, for I knew she offered it only as strength. But perhaps it also meant that she didn't hate me as much as I feared and that we might possibly part as friends when the time came. That was the most I could hope for. I drained the brandy and set the glass down. The smooth and warming liquid coursed down my dry throat and I felt renewed strength flow through my body.

"Thank you, Christine...I don't..." I faltered.

"No," she said, motioning for me to say no more. "Everything will be all right."

And it was.

*   *   *

A bit of our old rapport returned after that night. We set aside our differences in favor of making the best of the situation. I was relieved to hear Christine's laughter again. Walking into that crowded room was one of the most difficult things I have ever done. But never before had I been able to rely upon the strength and support of another person to help me face life's unpredictable situations. Christine's smiling greetings to those we passed and the slight pressure of her arm under mine gave me new courage. Inevitably, there were hushed whispers and covert glances and some did actually leave the room, but very quickly the majority turned back to what they had been doing prior to our entrance. Christine and I made it a nightly habit to go hear the music after that. The mutual appreciation that we shared for music once again brought us together and served to lighten our moods even further. How we had both missed our music! Christine especially enjoyed our evenings among the dancing and laughter.

One night I observed her foot tapping away in time with the music. I watched her for a while. She was totally taken away by the music. On impulse and without giving myself time to change my mind I bowed in front of her and extended my hand along with an offer to dance. The surprised delight I saw in her face tugged at my heart.

"Oh, Erik, are you sure you want to do that?" She looked past me at the people who crowded the floor.

"I will try if you will allow me," I replied. "I have not danced before, but it does not look too difficult," I added with not a little uncertainty.

"Then I shall help you learn," she said as she rose to the challenge and took my hand.

I led her to the very edge of the dancing area where the shadows met the light. The thought of trying this strange new thing in the midst of strangers frightened me. We stood awkwardly staring at each other for a moment. I, of course, did not have the slightest notion of what to do first. Fortunately one of us knew how to proceed. Christine reached down and took my left hand in her right and brought her left hand up against the back of my upper right arm. I flinched quite unintentionally as her hand contacted firmly against the still-tender area.

"Oh!" She stepped back in surprise. "What is wrong?"

"It is nothing," I managed to say quite normally as the pain subsided. "An old injury that continues to annoy me. Nothing to concern yourself with." I drew her back toward me.

"If you say so," she replied doubtfully.

She moved back into my arms and replaced her left hand; this time lightly on my shoulder. I moved my right hand to her waist and we began to move to the music.

I cannot express with mere words the ecstasy I felt that night, dancing on board a luxury ship upon the Atlantic under a full moon with a woman in my arms. These were things of which I had hardly dared to dream, and I feared that I should wake up at any moment to find that it was indeed only a glorious dream. I caught on to the simple waltz rather quickly and, since no one paid us any undue attention, I enjoyed myself immensely. I was hesitant to hold Christine in that manner, but, as time went on, I found myself holding her a little closer than when we had begun. She didn't seem to mind so I slowly drew her in until we were as close as common decency allowed on the dance floor. Only inches stood between us, and I could not help but allow my eyes to drop every so often to that space—how I wanted to close it! When I looked down my gaze unavoidably fell right into the front of Christine's décolletage and I stumbled a few times. Hopefully Christine assumed it was from watching my own feet and my inexperience in the dance. Her chest rose and fell with each breath and I had to force my attention back down to my feet. Christ, if she had guessed my thoughts on those nights, she herself would have run from me screaming. And I would not have blamed her. Her eyes were usually fixed at a point high beyond my shoulder, but, every so often, I would catch her looking up at me. She would not meet my eyes while I held her and turned away swiftly to avoid them. I wanted the music to go on forever so that we could dance forever. Alas, it came to an end all too soon.

*　　　*　　　*

I was surprised to find Christine missing when I went to her room for breakfast early the next morning. I found her sitting in one of the wooden deck chairs looking out over the blue Atlantic. I sank down with relief into the chair next to hers. She turned her face toward me. Tears were running down her cheeks and it appeared that she had been crying for some time.

"Why, Christine, what's wrong?" I asked. "I thought we had a very nice evening last night. Did I do something to upset you?"

"No. I mean yes...well, no, not last night," she stammered between the occasional sob. Finally she blurted it out. "I can't stop thinking about Raoul."

Her crying began anew and she covered her face with her hands and turned away from me. It broke my heart to see her so unhappy, but I didn't know what I could do to make it better. I had done this to her, and I didn't see how she could accept any apologies for the way she was feeling. I listened to her cry for a few moments and decided I would try anyway to do something to help her...anything. I fished out a clean handkerchief and handed it to her. She turned back to me to accept it. Wiping her eyes, she looked off to the east.

"He doesn't even know what happened to me, Erik," she said, trying to get her voice under control. "I told him I must return to the Opera...for you...but I would not allow him to come to the cellars with me. He surely sent the authorities after me...and they will think that is you lying down there. There will be no trace at all of me. He must be wild with worry." She looked back to me hopefully. "He doesn't know I'm with you. We can fix this, Erik. If you'll just take me back I can make up a story...I can convince them not to..."

"After the things I've done?" I asked incredulously. I looked out over the water and sighed. "My dear Christine, I am a wanted man. Returning to Paris would mean the end of the road for me. I would be lucky to get so much as a trial."

"But I could tell him..."

"Let it alone, girl. Just let it alone."

"But he'll listen to me, I know he will. He always does what I want him to, and you saved his life."

"That doesn't matter. Trust me."

"Erik, you're being difficult," she said petulantly.

I turned back to her. "Christine, there are things you don't know. Regardless of what happened the last night I saw him and whatever you might tell them, nothing will satisfy him but the sight of me swinging at the end of a rope."

"But Raoul wouldn't do that," she said firmly. "He isn't like that. He's compassionate and kind and...he wouldn't do that, especially if I asked him not to." She paused and looked at me intently. "Erik, what don't I know?"

I stared at the water. The waves sent a bit of spray our way once in a while where we sat along the rail. The air was brisk. I must tell her the truth about the state of affairs that existed between the boy and me. I motioned to her that we should move to a more protected area of the deck. We settled into a new set of chairs out of the wind.

"Aside from the Vicomte's and my first tense meeting in your father's country cottage, there have been several incidents that you know nothing about," I began. "We have tangled more than once over you and the last time things got ugly between us. Believe me when I say that if I had not left Paris when I did, one of us would not be alive today."

"But why, Erik? You must tell me what happened!"

After all I had done to her, I owed her a bit of honesty.

I sighed again and leaned back in my chair while crossing my long legs on a foot bench.

"All right, Christine. For quite some time Raoul was repeatedly and adamantly demanding that Vaurien resume his search for me. His demands were the reason for the army of men who recently descended upon the theater wielding their hammers and lanterns. It was a massive effort to protect you from me, and to forcibly remove me from the premises. It was also a huge waste of their time and money for I am never that careless. Do you know they filled the cracks in the walls of your room? I daresay they thought I must leak in through them like smoke to spirit you away. I really found it quite amusing."

I stole a glance at her. She did not appear to find it amusing, and was waiting for me to go on. "Well, anyway, I knew everything that went on within those walls. The search yielded nothing and the fool refused to put any more effort into the matter. Raoul was livid. He tried to force cooperation with threats to no avail, so he resorted to more drastic measures. On the night in question," I continued, "I caught him in the act of setting up an 'accident' on the stage for which I would be blamed. His intention, obviously, was to force the issue by proving that I was up to my old tricks. And yes, my dear, you are hearing the only admission that will ever pass my lips that I am indeed the infamous 'Opera Ghost'. Your Raoul wanted me hunted down and hanged, to be rid of me once and for all." I watched her face as she listened but was unable to read her expression. "We had words and the encounter soon escalated into violence. I had to prevent the chance of any future altercations between us because I know how much you care about your young man."

"But you still haven't told me what happened," she persisted.

"Raoul tried to kill me that night. He fired repeatedly even though I had no gun, and I was lucky that he did not kill me. But he did hit me, and I left enough blood at the scene that he very reasonably could have assumed that I had crawled off to die...at least until the night I took you off the stage."

Christine's sharp intake of breath was muffled as her hands covered her mouth. Her eyes were wide with disbelief and... yes...concern.

"Blood? Where..." Then she remembered. "Your arm! It's not an old injury is it? That's where Raoul shot you."

I nodded, keeping my eyes on the deck planking. She was seeing Raoul in a slightly different light that I had no wish to contradict.

"So that was what he meant when he said that you would not be bothering me any longer," she said thoughtfully and half to herself. To me she said, "But why did you feel you had to leave?"

"Because I didn't want to kill him." I stated bluntly. "You must remember that I am very experienced in such matters. He was lucky that night but he would not be again. I have no doubt that another confrontation would have resulted in my killing him. I rather loathed the idea of letting him kill *me* just to avoid hurting *him*, and I knew how much my killing him would hurt you, Christine."

Of course I didn't add that my killing the boy would have turned her against me forever. "I had to leave. I tried to do the right thing...to send you away to spend your life with him...but after you were gone I realized that I could not leave...or live...without you. You would never have agreed to return to me so I handled things in my own—rather drastic—way. As you have said yourself, that is the only way I know."

Silence fell between us. Each of us was lost in thoughts of the past. The next time she turned to me, tears were trickling down my face under the mask. I turned quickly away from her, embarrassed by my sudden and unbidden show of emotion. Now where in hell had this come from? I could neither control it nor stop it. I buried my face in my hands when I began to cry.

"I'm sorry Christine, so sorry…" I sobbed. "I didn't know any other way. I need you so much…you are the only one I've…I'm sorry that I've…I…Oh…God help…me…" I could no longer choke out the words.

I felt her arm creep tentatively around my shoulders, carefully avoiding the right side. I was racked with sobs as a lifetime of grief and despair washed over me. I had somehow destroyed everything and everyone that I had ever touched, and the weight of the guilt I carried with me was heavy. I felt Christine's hand upon my arm, which she held tightly until my sobbing subsided. No one was about so I turned further away from her and removed the mask. My outburst was brief but very humiliating. I was attempting to wipe my tearstained face with my sleeve when Christine handed back my handkerchief. I quickly dried my foolish tears and replaced the uncomfortably damp leather on my face. I was completely drained of emotion except for the gratitude I felt towards this woman whose strength once again promised to lift me from my despair. I straightened my jacket and told her that she should go inside where it was warm. After making me promise that I would be all right, she left me sitting alone with my miserable thoughts. I felt as completely adrift as the ship under me.

7

———————— ★ ————————

We were both unaware of how accurate Christine was about the situation back in Paris. I learned much later that Raoul had indeed panicked when Christine did not return from her mercy mission. He pressured the authorities into mounting a massive search during which he loudly and publicly broadcast my evilness even though I hadn't been seen or heard from in weeks and he had, by his own admission, returned Christine to the city so she could "bury" me. (I would question the thoroughness of their "massive search", because they apparently never found the body lying in the shadows behind the well.) The search was suspended after a fortnight due to the lack of evidence.

As in the past, Vaurien and the authorities were reluctant to take Raoul's claims regarding my involvement too seriously. Raoul was the only one of them to have actually seen me up close and he was in such a state that they began to doubt his sanity, going so far as to question him about his own whereabouts during the past several weeks. There was no evidence to link Christine's disappearance with the earlier vanishing act of a questionable presence that seemed to exist only in the minds of a certain few. The case was officially closed, effectively ending forever any threat of official action against me as long as I stayed away from Paris. The news also meant that my beautiful home would never be discovered. Somehow that comforted me, for the image I carried with me of it being destroyed during a search had distressed me greatly.

The theater went back to its business, but Christine's departure meant the end of an unusually successful period in the Opera's history. As for Raoul de Chagny, he stubbornly continued to search Paris and the surrounding countryside on his own. He thought there was something very fishy about Christine disappearing while on a mission connected in any way with me. Due to my reclusive nature he apparently failed to recognize the possibility that, if she were with me, Christine might be out of France altogether. He traveled endlessly within our large homeland, searching in vain for a woman who had, in fact, traveled a thousand miles away upon the ocean. I covered my tracks well, using carefully chosen people who would have sold their souls to the devil for the amount of money I paid them.

*   *   *

I remained on deck for a long time after Christine retired. I shivered as the wind came up in cooler blasts from the north. The waves grew with the hint of an oncoming storm. I finally went to my cabin, weaving my way down the deck with an uneven gait as the ship rolled slowly from side to side.

The wind and waves increased throughout the day. Christine and I quietly followed our usual routine. Much had passed between us and we spent the better part of that day in our own reflective thoughts wrapped in a silence that can only exist between two people who know each other well in some way; a comforting companionship born of something shared.

By the time dinner was served, the storm had escalated to severe proportions. The entire saloon reflected a reserved and cautious atmosphere since most of the diners wanted only to finish their meals quickly and return to the relative safety of their accommodations. Christine and I were no different. We silently finished our beef tenderloin and I walked her back to her room without delay. It became hazardous to walk on the decks as darkness fell and I was anxious to get her safely to her room. After returning her wish of a good night and seeing her door safely closed behind her, I continued on to my own small but comfortable cabin.

The crash of my washbowl hitting the floor woke me with a start. I fumbled for my pocket watch, which was foolish because I could not see it in the darkness. I guessed that it must be well after midnight. The ship was pitching wildly and I heard the sounds of frightened passengers as they experienced similar disruption of their sleep. I got out of bed and tried to light my lamp but the ship rolled an appalling distance to the port side and I was thrown against the bed. I reached for my clothes and dressed as quickly as possible, wondering how Christine was faring in her room on the other side of the ship. Donning my heaviest cloak, I crept to the door to open it cautiously.

The waves rose like mountains alongside the ship. The lights in the public rooms were all on and their feeble beams revealed rivers of seawater running down the decks. Rain and spray mingled together to drench everything not soaked by the sloshing seawater. Deck chairs had been thrown in a tangled pile against the railing at the stern and other items were scattered around on the deck. A massive wave appeared at the very rail along which I walked. I watched in trepidation as it rose higher than the very topmost structure of the ship. The wind howled and I heard screams from the saloon as the ship mounted that immense wave and then dropped with a lurch into the trough it had created. Christ! I quickened my pace along the wet deck.

I banged on Christine's door with my fist and shouted her name over the roar of the wind. She pulled it open almost immediately and threw herself into my arms with a cry. I didn't even notice the way she threw herself at me because my only thoughts were of her safety. She wore only her nightgown and was shivering. I sat her down on the edge of the bed and went to her wardrobe to fetch her cloak. She needed to calm down before I could give her the privacy to get dressed. I paused to turn the ventilators up to as high a temperature as they would go, but they were woefully inadequate in this weather. When I brought the cloak back to the bed she clutched my arm in panic and pulled me down beside her. I could barely see her in the dark.

"Erik, are we going to die?" she questioned in a shaking voice. "Is the ship going down?"

Waves threw the ship from one side to the other and we heard distant crashes and thuds. At each sound she clutched my arm tighter.

"No, my dear, the ship is not going down."

Having never been in this position myself I honestly did not know what affect a storm of this magnitude could have on the ship but it would not do to upset her further. "It's just a bad storm, and it will all be over in the morning."

A sudden roll of the ship threw both of us to the floor. I could not light a lamp and Christine was getting hysterical. Everything that could fall had already done so. The safest place in the room was the floor. We were already sitting on it so I reached up to the bed and pulled the blankets from it. I then took Christine's arm and drew her to me, covering her with the blankets. She leaned back against me and I tucked the blankets in tight around us.

"Relax, Christine," I said soothingly. "I will not let anything happen to you. Try to rest a bit. I assure you that the storm will be over soon. Are you warm enough?" I asked.

"I am better, thank you," she replied, leaning her head back against my shoulder much as she used to when I told her stories months ago. I hesitantly put my arms around her outside the blankets and she seemed to welcome the safe enclosure. After a few minutes of listening to the wind howl outside the door and the occasional crashing of deck furniture she spoke in the darkness.

"Erik, about what you told me before; did Raoul really try to kill you?"

"Yes," I said quietly, "it is the truth."

"And you have not tried to kill him?" she queried, not letting the subject drop. I envisioned a mental picture of Christine holding a scale with Raoul balanced at one end and me at the other. She was weighing us against each other in her mind. Christ, we were miles away from that damned boy and still I had to compete with him!

"Christine," I said wearily, "I have had many chances and he has given me enough reason to do just that. Killing that boy was not something I wanted to do." I paused thoughtfully. "You have changed me in ways that you can never understand."

We fell silent as we listened to the storm wreak its havoc upon the ship. I began to tell her a concocted story about my past experiences on ships. It was total fabrication but it served to calm her like a child's bedtime story. After only a few minutes I realized I was talking to myself; she had fallen asleep. I would give her a few minutes of peace to allow the storm to pass a bit before disturbing her to have her get dressed. If anything happened to her out here on this wild ocean, I thought, I had better die alongside her because I could never live with the guilt.

*   *   *

I opened my eyes to the gray of early morning slowly filling the tiny room. Christine slept peacefully in my arms. I looked down at her sleeping face with its long dark lashes and smooth pink skin surrounded by the most luxurious hair I have ever seen. I was struck by something profound from deep within me. My heart began to beat faster and odd sensations flooded through me. This was not the physical lust I had felt for some months, but something else entirely. I watched her sleeping face quietly and with a growing sense of peace. Suddenly all of the strange feelings and confusion that I felt whenever she was near made perfect sense to me. Everything that I had questioned was brought into crystal clear focus and I finally knew what it all meant. I loved Christine with all my heart. I was in love with her!

Revelation coursed through me when I realized just what this precious child meant to me. For the first time in my life, the warmth of love for another person enveloped me, threatening to suffocate me in its deep, soft folds. I thought I had lost the capacity to love many years ago. Tears stung my eyes and I held her tenderly, almost without breathing, for fear that her waking would break the spell under which I had fallen. Inevitably though, the light that shone through the large window made her stir.

Christine's eyes fluttered open and then closed again against the light. She stretched languidly as if she were alone in her own bed. Her sensuously slow writhing against me awakened my desire. She was not aware of where she was. She began another long stretch, this time raising her arms above her head. During the course of the night both of us had slipped down from our original position sitting against the wall. The bulk of her body now rested between my splayed legs and her head was almost in my lap. I could not move until she did. Her rising arms came up toward my face and, as her hand touched me, she abruptly sat up and swiveled around to face me.

"Oh!" She exclaimed with surprise. She looked around with sleepy eyes, then reached for the blanket lying on the floor next to us and wrapped it tightly around herself. Then she noticed that she was sitting between my legs and her face blushed as red as rose petals. She struggled to her feet and went to sit on the edge of the bed.

I remained where I was. I sincerely hoped she would not notice the somewhat obvious (to me, anyway) problem that her sleepy movements had caused me. I had no wish to embarrass her any further than she was already. My discomfort was further complicated by the fact that I could not immediately move to hide it. I had spent too many hours in that position under her weight, slight as it was, and my back and legs were painfully stiff. A night on the floor in the damp sea air was not what I had planned or needed. I discreetly folded my hands across my lower lap and silently regarded her on the bed.

She seemed not to notice anything unusual, probably because she didn't take her eyes from my face. We stared at each other for a few moments as I waited for both my desire to subside and for the blood to get moving in my legs. She was shyly watching me, and when I made no move to get up, she finally asked me what was wrong.

"Erik, are you hurt?" she asked in a small voice and with concern in her eyes.

"No, my dear, not hurt," I replied, "but I thank you for your concern. I have only spent too many hours sitting on this hard floor and a man of my age shouldn't do such things."

The awkward moment passed and I made the effort to get to my feet, smoothing my suit and adjusting my mask as I walked stiffly toward the door. I would go to my own cabin and freshen up before we went to breakfast. My tortured back could use a few minutes stretched out on my own bed. I also wanted a moment to bask in my new understanding. Christine's voice stopped me as I reached out to pull the door open.

"Wait..." she said softly as she stood up, flinching when her bare feet came in contact with the cold floor. "I...thank you for taking such good care of me last night...I was very frightened."

"Christine," I went to her and took her hand gently, "I would give my life for you." I bent over her hand and placed a light kiss upon it. Straightening up, I nodded slightly to her and left to prepare for breakfast.

*   *   *

The state of affairs between us was definitely improving, I thought with satisfaction, as I changed into fresh clothes and performed my toilet that morning. Since the night when we enjoyed our first dance I had been extremely cautious in not pushing Christine too quickly. For a man of notoriously short patience, I thought I was doing rather admirably. Several situations had presented themselves, including last night's storm, during which I felt her warming to me without any undue effort on my part. Each evening brought us a little closer. Those nights were among the happiest of my life. I discovered that I enjoyed the disciplined movement of dance, especially since it involved close physical contact with another person. I studied what the other men did and managed to pick up several different dances. We entered American waters and were expected to dock at Norfolk, Virginia the next day. I was running out of time.

My last day at sea was spent in the leisurely and pleasurable company of a very warm and friendly Christine. Her eyes sparkled, her cheeks were pink and she had put on a little weight. I am sure this was somewhat due to the fact that she was no longer performing and rehearsing for so many hours a week, along with the hearty meals we had been enjoying on our voyage. The sea air became warmer and it was a joy to spend many hours on deck watching the waves and the sea birds that were beginning to appear. I was accustomed to the people with whom we had been traveling so I no longer felt the need to keep to the outskirts of activity. We still did not openly socialize but neither did we avoid the other passengers. Christine, in fact, had enjoyed many a conversation with some of the other ladies while I waited patiently in the background or spent quiet hours in the smoking room or library. If anyone questioned the reason for her "husband's" mysterious appearance, they possessed the good graces not to mention it.

Our voyage came to an end under beautiful sunny skies and warm temperatures. We stood at the rail as we approached Hampton Roads Harbor and enjoyed watching the busy activity all around our vessel. We drew closer to the teeming waterfront and I tensed as my reluctance to be among people returned. I must leave the familiar cocoon of shipboard life and venture out into the world. Christine herself had grown quiet when we first came into sight of land. As we stood waiting, she looked at me and read the uncertainty in my eyes. She placed her hand firmly on top of mine on the railing. I turned my hand over to grasp hers like a life-line and we silently stood hand in hand watching the docking process. The trunks and other baggage were soon ashore and it was our turn to disembark.

We slowly made our way down one deck to the gangway. Christine was also nervous. She was entering a new country where the language and customs were completely foreign to her. We were the last passengers to leave, having waited for most of the crowd to leave the pier. We looked at each other for mutual strength before going down the sloping ramp. She hooked her arm firmly through mine and hugged my arm tightly to her. She picked up her skirts with her outside hand and we descended to the pier.

There were a number of hacks waiting at the roadside while the horses stood quietly munching in their feedbags amid the din of the waterfront. I handed Christine into the nearest one and got in myself to wait while our luggage was loaded. I was grateful for the enclosure of the carriage.

People in the street and the lobby stared at me when we entered the hotel. I tried to ignore them by remembering that Christine's arm was firmly wedged under mine. Again, I had not thought much about this part of life away from the safety of the Opera. I knew that I would not be able to hide away any longer, but those thoughts were nothing compared with actually being here surrounded by people. Well, the trip had been my choice and I would have to do it for Christine's sake. I had done it for many years before hiding myself away in the cellars, and I could do it again. This time it would be on my terms. I looked down at the beautiful woman on my arm and approached the desk to deal with the nervous desk clerk.

Although not quite as elegant as I preferred, our rooms were most adequate. I requested a connecting door between them. I would retreat to my own room for a little rest after I had done some business.

"Christine, I hope you will be comfortable here," I said. "I shall leave you alone. Please rest. In a few hours I will order us up our noon meal." I turned to leave and remembered the door. "There is a connecting door between our rooms," I continued. "You may wish to lock it on this side. I assure you that I will not come through it unless you call for me. It is your decision."

"You have always been a perfect gentleman with me, Erik," she said quietly, "and I might need something."

"As you wish, my dear," I replied. She had not mentioned her return trip to France, but her subdued manner troubled me. I returned quickly to the lobby to exchange some of my funds from

francs to dollars. I steeled myself to ignore the pointing and staring that I would inevitably encounter on such excursions. It was
easier when Christine was with me but she was very tired. Upon
pocketing my newly exchanged currency, I asked the clerk to book
two cabins on the next steamer bound for New Orleans, which
would leave in a few days. Back in my room again, I lay down for
a while but could not sleep. I dreaded the moment when Christine
would tell me that she wanted to return to France.

I had promised her that I would send her back. There was
nothing I could do but follow through on my word. She had
already given me more than I had ever dared to hope for. She had
brought me my first real happiness while we traveled upon the
ocean. My head was filled with wonderful memories that would
last me a lifetime with or without her. In that short time, I had
rejoined the world of the living. I had learned to dance and to
enjoy the sounds of life around me. I had welcomed back the
fresh air and the splendor of a sunrise. I discovered that I was still
capable of love for another person. I had thought my heart was
so damaged and blackened by my previous life that I could never
learn to love. Now the heart that had been empty for so many
years was overflowing with the richness of my love for Christine.

Nevertheless, if Christine wanted to return to Paris, I would
send her back. I would not go with her. Aside from the hangman's
noose that awaited me in Paris, that part of the world held nothing but painful memories for me and I had no desire to return. If
Christine left me, I would seek a new life in this new land. I would
continue on to New Orleans alone and lose myself forever in the
bizarre and boisterous life of that mysterious city. I loved
Christine, and with that love came the first feelings of true self-
lessness that I had ever known. I would do anything for her. If that
included letting her go, then so be it.

I said nothing of the steamer reservations to Christine when we dined later on the simple meal in her sunlit room. I knocked softly on the connecting door and waited only a moment before she called me in. She was more talkative after her rest and now seemed excited to be in a new and strange place. Her rapidly shifting moods confused me.

"Oh, Erik!" she exclaimed over her meal of tiny watercress sandwiches and tea. "These are adorable and they are so delicious! You must try one!"

I did not feel hungry and was silently picking at a plate of shellfish. I was busy asking myself why in hell I had arranged further passage for two to the South when I would not need them both. It was foolish of me to be so presumptuous. Her suddenly lighthearted attitude was unexpected and it was difficult to determine what she was thinking. I was chiding myself when her voice finally penetrated my thoughts.

"Erik," she was repeating, "Are you listening to me?"

I looked up from my plate, my fork hovering over my food. "I'm sorry, what were you saying?"

"You haven't heard a thing I've said," she pouted. "What is the matter?"

I could not take the suspense any longer. I must prepare to get on with my life without her.

"There is something we need to discuss." I put the fork down, laid my napkin on the table and pushed my almost untouched plate away. I sat back in my chair and cast around in my mind for the right words.

"Christine," I began hesitantly, "I promised you that I would submit without question to your wish to return to France at the first available opportunity."

She stopped eating her fascinating little sandwiches and stared into her plate.

"I need to know what plans I should make for you at this time." I sounded all business. I could not put it any other way and still get the words past my rapidly constricting throat.

Her silence hung over us like a curtain. I watched her stare at that plate for what seemed like forever. She rose without speaking and went to the window. She stood there for an eternity before she slowly turned around to face me. Her eyes were wet and her hands were clenched at her breast. One large tear ran dramatically down her cheek. She was thinking of Raoul. I waited for her to speak the words.

"Please," she whispered, "I fear that I am more fatigued than I thought...I need to lie down and to...to think. Yes, Erik, I need to think. Please...I need more time."

"As you wish, my dear," I said with an unintentional note of resignation in my voice. "Please call me when you are ready."

"I will."

Nodding curtly to her I got up and left, this time through the door that opened onto the main hallway. In my own room, I removed my mask and coat and went to sit at the window. The time slowly ticked by and I sat staring idly at the clouds passing outside. My mind began to drift to things I had not thought of in years, going back to my lonely childhood that could not even be called a childhood and my years of wandering the globe. Moving from place to place had shown me the world, but my experiences had proven that, for all this world had to give, I should expect nothing from it for myself. The vast knowledge I had gained meant little to me because I had no one with whom to share it.

I reflected on the iniquitous years that followed my reaching adulthood. The wickedness of my life then had not been my choice, but the memories of the things I did to stay alive now filled my heart with horror. Circumstances had taken me beyond the law and to the very edges of my sanity, blurring forever my sense of the frequently fine line between right and wrong. Nevertheless, I cannot deny the activities of my past, and I alone must take responsibility for them.

Then came my dark and lonely existence as a half-dead recluse living like a mole under the Opera House. As I looked back on all the phases of my life from that window in Norfolk, every last one of them seemed impossibly empty. My eyes felt heavy and I rested my head back against the tall chair in which I sat while scenes from my sad life continued to swirl about me in a kaleidoscope of painful memories.

Time passed. The waiting was killing me. I had already waited almost half a century for my life to begin. Would I ever be accepted for who I was or would I be doomed to live the remainder of my life under this mask of hatred and fear? I did not have the slightest idea of what I would do when Christine left me. All I knew for sure was that my future could not be any worse than my past. I had found a tiny flicker of hope buried in the wreckage of my life, and I would not surrender it without a fight. Christine had changed my outlook forever, and I would never go underground again. I stood before a locked door at the most critical of many crossroads in my life and Christine held the key.

          *   *   *

Christine and I were performing a beautiful aria together on an ornate and brilliantly lit stage. We stood close together, bathed in the footlights, holding hands and singing of everlasting love. Her eyes met mine with the unmistakable sparkle of love. The heat from the footlights and from our mutual passion threatened to consume me. The audience watched our scene with rapt attention. We reached simultaneously for the highest note and our voices soared together, perfectly matched and filling the theater, when acute pain sliced through me, taking my breath away. Christine continued to hold her note long after my own had died, totally ignoring my distress until she had finished. I looked imploringly at her. She turned to me with an odd look on her face, then casually dropped my hands. I reached out to her in a frantic plea for help...she was backing away from me...further and further away...and then her mouth opened in a soundless scream as she ran from the stage! I was alone when the weakness finally overtook me. The audience rose to its feet with a collective gasp when I sank slowly to the floor. Concern turned quickly to horror as someone shouted and pointed to the mask, which lay upon the boards in front of me. A hush fell as they stared at me, weakened and horribly exposed in the spotlight...then someone screamed...everyone was screaming! I was on my knees with one hand grasping the clothing over my chest. I reached out for the mask and pain shot through me again...

I awoke in a cold sweat clutching my chest and panting in an agony that was all too real. It had never been like this before— what was happening to me? I got out of the chair with difficulty and staggered toward the bed. I must have made some awful sound for the last thing I remembered was the sight of Christine flinging her door open and rushing toward me. I reached out to her as the room tilted and the floor came up to my face.

*   *   *

Cold and wet—what was that? My eyes fluttered open to see Christine's blurred face hovering above me. I was lying on the floor and Christine was wiping my face with a cool wet cloth while cradling my head in her lap. The pain had passed but I felt weak and nauseated. The cold wetness on my face felt so good...the cold wetness... The mask! It was still on the table where I had put it.

"No!" I choked out in a strangled voice, raising my hands to hide my face. "Please don't look at me!"

"Erik, be still!" Christine ordered firmly. She tried to catch my hands as I flung them around in panic, trying to cover myself. "It's all right...don't be frightened."

She caught my wrists and slowly pulled my hands away from my face. I knew I was in no position to argue with her from the way the ceiling was spinning above us. I looked up anxiously into her clear blue eyes.

"It will be all right," she repeated soothingly. "Let me help you."

I allowed my arms to fall with great apprehension. I felt naked and vulnerable. She wet the cloth again in the washbowl on the floor beside her and wrung it out. Taking great care, she wiped my forehead with its coolness. The poor girl probably hadn't the slightest idea of what to do for me, and I honestly didn't know myself. Fortunately, this was not the first time she had seen my face or it might have caused her to run screaming into the foreign streets. I don't know how long I had lain there unconscious, but it appeared Christine had time to study my face before I came to. It is the only explanation I could think of, because she did not appear repulsed or frightened by my ugliness. I suppose that if anyone looked at me long enough it might be possible to grow accustomed to the sight, even if I had never been able to get used to it. But then, for me it was a matter of personal pride...or the lack thereof. After wiping my face gently for several minutes she laid the cloth aside.

"What happened?" Her concern was evident.

"I don't know, nothing quite like that has ever happened to me before," I answered truthfully. "There was so much pain..."

"Are you feeling better now?" she asked.

"Yes, much." I replied weakly. "I'll be fine soon." I wished I could believe my own words.

Her smile was replaced by a look of uncertainty that I did not immediately comprehend. I saw the curiosity grow in her eyes and then I knew what she wanted.

"May I...?" she asked hesitantly

"Yes," I whispered like a frightened child.

Christine laid her hand gently alongside my cheek. I held my breath for the first brush of human touch upon my face. She lightly traced the uneven features of my ruined face, gently following the alternately rough and smooth surfaces over the distorted bone structure as if her touch might hurt me. She could not hurt me, of course. My face was not a painful injury, and it felt totally normal to me. Her fingers tenderly found the tiny bump of my nose, my unmatched eyes and finally the oddly large but soft lips of my misshapen mouth. I searched her eyes while she gently explored me.

"Oh, you poor..." she began softly, her eyes becoming moist with tears of compassion.

"I do not want your pity," I said abruptly as I pushed her hand away. Ignoring my lightheadedness, I got unsteadily to my feet. The spell had been broken. I pushed this latest and most serious affront to my health to the back of my mind and went to the table where I had left the mask earlier. I picked it up and fingered it absently.

"I want no one's pity." I kept my back to her so she could not see the hurt in my eyes. "All I've ever wanted was acceptance— never pity!" I spat the word as if it left a vile taste in my mouth.

"Erik, I didn't mean..."

I surreptitiously placed one hand on the table to steady myself. "As long as you are here," I interrupted impatiently without turning around, "I must know your plans. You have had sufficient time to decide when you want to sail. Further delay will benefit neither of us." I rushed on, aware that my nerves were on edge and I was talking too much. "I understand why you cannot stay with me, I should not expect that anyone could stand to look upon my hideousness for a minute much less…"

"I will stay." It was a whisper.

My ears must have been damaged when I hit the floor. I continued on almost without stopping, the words tumbling from my lips like water over rocks as I stared at the mask in my hand.

"…perfectly understandable, you are a normal young woman and I should not have expected anything else." *What did she say?* "I shall make your arrangements as soon as…"

"Erik."

I ceased my foolish chatter, donned the offending mask and turned around slowly. She was still sitting in the middle of the floor with the washbasin. I had not heard her correctly. As I stood staring at her in disbelief, she got to her feet and came to me.

"Erik," she began again, "I have thought all along that I would be making my life with Raoul, but I cannot ignore what I feel for you." I held my breath, wondering where she was going with this. "Remember what you said the night you asked me to go away with you? You said we would experience things together that Raoul could never give me." She looked into my eyes. "I believe you now. There is something that draws me to you. When I saw you reach out to me for help just now I realized that I really care for you. When I am with you there's an excitement inside me that I do not feel with anyone else." She paused and added, "I can't resist it any longer, Erik."

"I deceived you, drugged you and took you from your husband. Can you tell me you forgive me for what I did? I saw the cold hate in your eyes, Christine. I've seen hatred too many times to mistake it for anything else. I will never forget the agony of seeing it in your eyes and hearing it in your voice."

"Raoul is not my husband. We were never married." She went to the window and spoke to the street below. "I did hate you for what you did to me. When I woke up on that ship and realized what you had done, I hated you. Making me believe you were dead...you can't imagine what that did to me. When you cruelly told me that the captain and crew thought me to be mad, I hated you. I hated you for putting me in a position of insecurity and fear, and I hated you for thinking that I could throw myself into the sea."

"Then, why...?" I was completely confused.

She turned back to me. "It was what I saw in your eyes the night we went to the music room for the first time, and again the following morning. Uncertainty is not something you show often. I have begun to see more of the sensitive man underneath the angry, manipulative and vengeful exterior you show everyone. During the storm your concern was only for me, and it was real. You sacrificed your own comfort to protect me, and it showed how much you care for me." She sighed and looked me in the eye. "Erik, there is much more to you than what I've seen. You have changed since we left Paris, and I believe I'm finally seeing glimpses of the real man who is trapped inside you. I cannot explain this to you or to myself, but something in my heart tells me if I leave you now I will regret it for the rest of my life. I want to be with you. We will find out together if what my heart says is true."

I looked down at the lovely woman who had just made me the happiest man on earth. One look at her face convinced me that she was speaking from her heart. Tears stung my eyes. I took her hand in mine and lifted it to my mouth to brush it with a light kiss.

"Christine," I whispered, feeling as if in a dream. "I shall be honored to take you to New Orleans with me. I shall be the proudest man in the city with you on my arm and in my home. But, I must know this first. This mask has always caused me to be hated and feared everywhere that I have ever lived. You need to understand the hostility that I attract. Remember too, that I am a man of dark moods and a frightfully bad temper. It will also require a great deal of adjustment on my part to live again among men, but I am willing to work at it once more if you believe that you are strong enough to handle it. You must understand what I am saying."

"We will discover this new life together. Sometimes you do still frighten me, but I know in my heart that you would never willingly hurt me." She stopped, searching my eyes. "There is so much I don't know about you…" Her voice trailed off.

"I frighten you. I don't want that."

"It is in your eyes, there is something in your eyes sometimes that I don't know…there's a part of you that is beyond reach. That part of you frightens me."

"I could never hurt you." I moved a little closer. I looked down at her hand in mine and began to stroke her fingers absently. "What about the Vicomte?" I had to know. "I sent you away to be married because I thought you loved him. What happened?"

"Raoul wants me to marry him and I do love him, but we…it was not easy for us after we left you, for reasons that I don't want to explain right now. I have known him since we were children and I will always care for him. But I must leave you alone to be with him. My heart will not let me do that."

"I care for you very deeply, Christine," I admitted, although it didn't come close to how I really felt about her. "I would give my life for you." I removed my mask without warning and leaned down right into her face. "Can you live with this?"

She did not react at all to the sight of my hideous face. She reached up and touched my poor excuse for a cheek. "I see beyond this face to the soul of the man who lives beneath it."

I gently enfolded her in my long arms, drawing her tenderly against me. Hers crept hesitantly around my waist and she laid her head on my chest, enveloping me in a sweet sensation of warmth and caring that was totally new to me. At long last I had someone to care about. And she cared for me.

8

---★---

Christine's eyes shone with a child's wonder of seeing new places. The next few days were lost in a flurry of anticipation as we prepared for our departure. New Orleans was a city of great mystery, excitement, unusual customs and an eclectic mix of people. From what I had read, it seemed the perfect place for us to begin our life together. I could barely contain myself as I saw the excitement in Christine's eyes and heard it in her chatter. This Christine was so different from the girl I had taken away from Paris. She was a lively, happy and thoroughly charming young woman and her excitement now included me.

With the tensions of our mutual uncertainty eased, we fell quickly back into our old habit of talking for hours on end, discussing any subject that came to mind. I was shocked to hear her say that she and Raoul had never married but, since she obviously didn't want to talk about it, I did not ask. We took long walks at dusk or in the evening when there were fewer people on the streets. Walking the streets was much easier when Christine was with me. Her laughter and jovial mood transferred itself to me. I was becoming foolishly complacent in my renewed role as a member of society so it quite threw me late on the second afternoon when we were accosted in the street by a couple of gentlemen who had obviously been a little too far into their cups. My mask caught their attention and they were not willing to let the matter drop. I was concerned not for my own safety, but over the vehemence of their attitude and their total lack of courtesy toward the woman on my arm.

It was growing dark and we were close to our hotel when the two men came around the corner. I heard the sounds of other men's loud voices coming from the establishment they had exited down the street. Still unaccustomed to meeting people head on, I preferred to continue walking past them with a slight but courteous nod of my head and the brim of my hat lowered. Christine and I had done just that, when the taller of the two turned and shouted at me.

"Well, what's this we have here?" he sneered, walking back towards us.

I tightened my arm down on Christine's and continued walking. I warned her under my breath to say nothing under any circumstances. They caught up to us and came around us to block our path.

"Who're you s'pposed to be," the short one slurred, "a circus freak? Barnum's left town a week ago, fella."

"Well, they forgot this one," the first one said with a nasty grin. "Let's see what's under that mask, huh? Are you real scary or just plain ugly?"

Both men erupted into laughter.

"If you gentlemen would kindly let the lady and me pass, we will be on our way." I said evenly. I spoke many languages flawlessly and they accepted my English without comment. I believed, if they recognized us as foreigners, that the consequences might be worse for us. I did not want them to address Christine. She knew no English.

"Not before you show us what's under that mask," the taller man said, with all humor gone.

They stood in front of us, waiting for me to remove my mask. They showed no intention of backing down and it was getting late. Christine's arm began to tremble under mine, but I dared not look away from the two drunken fools in my path.

"I would advise you gentlemen to let us pass. I have no wish for any trouble here."

I was hoping they would give it up, but it was not to be. My concern for Christine's safety increased as the men slowly began to move closer.

"Well, trouble's what you're gonna get, buddy, if you don't take the mask off right now."

My voice was low. "I am warning you…"

"No one threatens me and gets away with it," snarled the tall man as he nodded to his friend, "and that mask is comin' off."

I disengaged Christine's arm from mine and had my coiled rope ready in my left hand. I pushed her out of the way and was ready for them. They made a grab for me and my rope shot out to snare the taller man about the neck while I fastened my right hand around the throat of the short one. Since my right arm was still a bit painful it was all I could do, but it was enough. My hands were enormously strong and my long fingers reached around his neck with the heel of my hand resting firmly upon the most lethally vulnerable area of his throat. I shoved both men up against the brick of the building next to us and tightened my hold until their eyes bulged and they ceased to fight.

"You are mistaken, sir," I growled, my face only inches from that of the man who now felt my thin but deceptively strong lasso around his neck. "It is I who will not be threatened." I looked into his wide eyes and noted the fear in them with satisfaction. I tightened my grip slightly for emphasis. "Get out of here while you still can," I added shortly. After one last squeeze I released them.

They fell to the ground, gasping and choking. I stood over them watching their discomfort. As soon as they could move they scurried out of my reach and ran down the street, never looking back.

I quickly returned the rope to its hiding place within the folds of my coat and turned to find Christine standing off to the side where I had pushed her. Her hands covered her mouth and her eyes were wide with fear and something else I couldn't read. When I reached out to her she retreated a step. I stopped with my hand suspended in the air between us. Her head began to slowly move from side to side, her wild eyes never leaving me. I guessed what was wrong. It was the first time she had actually seen the potentially lethal results of crossing me. She had heard stories of my violent and unpredictable nature but had never seen any evidence of it for herself. I had been very careful of that, and indeed, continued to take great care with all of my words and actions. I had to move quickly to snap her out of her renewed fear of me.

"Christine!" I said, taking her shoulders in my hands firmly before she could back away from me any further. "Christine, we must get back to the hotel...it's getting dark."

She began to tremble. She lowered her hands from her mouth but kept her arms tucked in tightly with her hands locked together up under her chin.

"Those men...what you did to them..." she whispered. "There were two of them, how did you...?" She looked up at me incredulously. "Erik, you're...it's just like everyone said! I did not believe them." She looked off in the direction of the men's escape, then back to me. "That's what I see in your eyes, isn't it? Danger. You could have killed them with your bare hands, couldn't you?

"I..."

"Erik?"

Would the truth drive her away? I decided my best choice was to admit it. "Yes, but it was only to protect you from..."

"You've done it before, haven't you?" she interrupted softly. "I mean, killed people like that. With only your hands and that...that thing."

"Only to protect myself," I answered honestly. Well, it was true as far as the lasso was concerned. I had used it only in self-defense. Even in sport it was still considered self-defense, was it not? "Now I have you to protect," I continued, "and I couldn't let those men get any closer. I am dangerous only to those who would threaten us." I waited for a reply that never came. "Christine please, let's get off this street."

She allowed me to lead her back to our hotel, but remained distantly silent. I feared that the progress we had made in our relationship might have been severely damaged by her realization that the side of me she'd heard about was real; the side I'd always tried to hide from her. Even with our newly found trust in one another, I had no intention of telling Christine that at one time I might have killed those two men, stepped over their bodies and walked away without a second thought. There would always be things about me that she was better off not knowing. I must learn to keep a tight rein on my temper. Still, I could not have let them hurt her and I would stop at nothing to protect her.

Back in our rooms, she went directly to the edge of the bed and sat down. She still held her arms pulled in tightly against her chest and wore that frightened look. This was exactly the kind of situation I had been referring to when I warned her about the consequences of staying with me. The experience would either strengthen our relationship or send her running back to France; straight into the waiting arms of her safe but dull Raoul. While she sat on the bed I paced the room. I didn't want to leave her alone in that condition but I didn't know what I could say to help her. After a few minutes she buried her head in her hands and began to cry.

I stopped my pacing to watch her with concern. Her sobbing continued so I finally went to her. Kneeling in front of her, I gently put my hands on her shoulders. I couldn't help but notice that she flinched when I touched her. I didn't know if she was crying because she could take no more of me or from a belated reaction to our street encounter. When she raised her face her eyes were full of tears.

"I didn't know it could be like that," she sobbed. "I was so frightened. I was frightened for you. You told me what people might do, but I didn't realize…"

"Hush," I said, rubbing her arms and trying to calm her. " They won't bother us again."

"But Erik, I was frightened of you too," she cried, looking down at her hands fidgeting in her lap. "I've never seen you do things like that before. They warned me…they told me that you were a mur…a mur…that you had killed, but I didn't believe them. You told me things yourself but I never dreamed…watching you was…" Her eyes met mine and her tone changed to one of warning. "There will be others like them."

"Yes, my dear, there will always be others," I admitted. "That is why I wanted you to understand what I must face every day. If you are with me, then you must face it too. Even when you are alone, you may be ridiculed because of me. You must be very sure, Christine."

"Oh, Erik, the things you've put up with!" she cried with a note of anger creeping into her voice. She wiped her face with the back of her hand, drying it as best she could. "I want to stay with you. I must be strong, because you need me." She shyly reached for my hands. "These hands have killed and that frightens me…but I know how gentle they can be." Her eyes met mine again. "You are such a contradiction, Erik." She paused with a slight wonder in her eyes. "Maybe that is part of what I find so exciting in you," she finished softly.

"Christine," I whispered, pulling her hands gently toward me.

She leaned forward from the bed and wrapped her arms around my neck, hugging me close. I returned her warm embrace and truly believed that together we could conquer our fears. Tomorrow we would sail for New Orleans and the beginning of our new life. I would try my best to leave my unsavory past and my fears of the future behind. I had started over many times before only to discover that the same frustrations and pain always seemed to follow me. This time I faced a new beginning with Christine beside me. I would finally be rewarded for all the years of humiliation and degradation that I had suffered. No one would stand in my way.

Unbeknownst to us, the path on which we idealistically set ourselves that day would be twisted and strewn with obstacles which would test us in ways neither of us could ever have anticipated.

9

———————————— ★ ————————————

"No, my dear, your rook cannot move diagonally," I repeated patiently. I was intent on teaching Christine the game of chess. It was a favorite of mine since it required a sophisticated combination of skill and strategy. At first she seemed baffled and confused by the intricately carved pieces and their individual movements on the board, but she soon began to catch on and, before we docked at the levee of New Orleans, she was able to play a simple game with a certain amount of confidence. Not many women played chess and I was proud of her dogged determination to master it even if it was only to please me. It was somewhat exasperating for me to play at such an unchallenging level, but at least she was a willing student. Her game would improve given time and encouragement. How I longed for a truly decent game of chess! It had been many years since I had the opportunity to play with someone who could even come close to my skill level.

The ship that took us to New Orleans was smaller than our transatlantic vessel and, with less to do, we spent most of our time quietly talking, reading or playing games. The other passengers caused no trouble for me and we were left to our solitude. They talked behind my back and some rudely pointed, but I had grown somewhat accustomed to people's stares to the point where I was having an easier time ignoring them. Christine would just smile at them and we would walk on. Her attitude helped me immeasurably as I learned to come to terms with my new public status. My ability to shrug off offending comments and rudeness was slowly growing and I had her to thank for it. She was extremely gracious even when people were unintentionally rude. It was amazing how strong she really was. Watching her sometimes, it seemed that she was indeed calling on her acting ability and certainly on her stage presence when she greeted people. This enabled her to approach people more easily at first. Slowly the veneer of shy vulnerability was being stripped away to reveal the inner strength that she always possessed, heretofore buried under her insecurities. The recent, drastic change that had taken place in our lives had enabled both of us to begin to shed some amount of our personal facades. Christine was quickly blossoming into a confident young woman who was willing to take chances to find her happiness. I saw a dramatic physical change too. She was putting on more weight and had gotten her color back. She was no longer the lost soul with whom I had fallen in love but a beautiful, vibrant young woman who looked at me with shining eyes and who every day made me love her even more.

We talked a lot while we sailed along just off the East Coast of America. Christine talked more about her childhood and admitted that she had been exceedingly lonely. Her father had been her only companion and apparently because of his vocation as a musician they moved about constantly. She was unable to make friends easily and, though she did have the love of her father, she had felt "different" during her childhood. She openly spoke of Raoul, which rather surprised me. It was during childhood that they had first met and apparently the young Vicomte was the only real friend she had ever made as a child. After many years apart,

Christine and Raoul had only recently met again at the Opera through sheer coincidence. After hearing the story, I could better understand what drew them together and why she had felt a strong kinship with him in such a short time.

She wanted me to tell her of my childhood but it was a difficult topic for me to discuss. Even after all these years I found it very hard to open that locked door on my life. Her gentle yet persuasive coaxing finally wore down my defenses and I told her something of my tormented childhood years, the ugly truth pouring out in a torrent of relief. I had never been able to talk to anyone of those early years when I existed as a lost child, alone and unloved, with nothing but my burgeoning hatred of mankind to keep me alive. Christine was struck silent by my bitter accounts. The sympathy I saw in her eyes and the firm squeeze of her hand around mine were very helpful.

I still wore my mask most of the time when we were alone together, but when I needed to remove it for some reason it no longer bothered me to let her see my face. She had gone past the horror of it and now I needed to do the same thing. My own inner strength had always been grounded in that mask. It hid my one and only weakness and psychologically put me in a position of strength and power. I felt helpless without it. Christine's support of me and my love for her were slowly replacing the mask as the main source of my strength. I could never stop wearing it in public, but it no longer represented what it once did to me.

                    *   *   *

We stood at the rail watching our ship slide into the harbor at New Orleans in the late afternoon sunshine of a beautiful southern day. Docking in New Orleans was a unique experience. The city was built on a level even with the river that wrapped halfway around it. During high water one could look from the deck of one's ship across the top of the levee and directly into the second story windows of the buildings on the waterfront. The earthen levees were the only barrier that stood between the city and the waters of the great Mississippi River. There were a number of rough looking warehouses at the upper end of the city which I found out later were for the storage of salt. From the look of the worn planking of the piers and the general appearance of the waterfront, I guessed that the area had seen better days.

My solicitor in Paris was to have obtained me a lease in a fashionable section of the French part of town, known locally as "The Quarter". I wanted Christine to feel as much at home as was possible in a strange country. He was to have procured a home befitting the manner in which I was accustomed to living and which would also make Christine proud without being ostentatious. While the home must without question be a fine one, I had also added the requirement of a generous amount of privacy, both in and out of doors. A small staff was to be chosen with extreme care. It was a tall enough order to fill by someone in town, let alone someone working from across the ocean for a client whom he'd never actually met. I had to trust that for what I paid him he had found what I wanted. Since I had set these plans in motion just before departing France, I did not know what had been accomplished in my behalf. The details of his arrangements should be waiting for me in the form of a cable at the St. Louis Hotel, to which we were headed as soon as we docked. We would be staying there tonight so that I could meet with the man in New Orleans whose name would be provided for me as a new solicitor. For obvious reasons, I hoped this new man had been chosen as much for his discretion as for his business acumen since, from that day forward, I would be dealing with him in person.

"Erik" was the only name I'd ever used. It had never been necessary to divulge any more information than that and I did not
wish to connect myself with anyone either living or dead. My
business dealings had always been handled under an assumed
name. I had to choose a new name for travel, the hotel register
and for all future business. There was also the question of
Christine's relationship to me. In Paris it was not proper for an
unmarried couple to travel together unescorted—living alone
together was unheard of. I had never been one to stand on tradition, but I did not know the customs of our new city, so I must be
prepared to speak to Christine about such matters soon. For the
time being, I had two rooms waiting for us at the hotel. I looked
down at my hands resting on the rail and at the tiny gold ring
gleaming on my little finger. Would I ever see it on Christine's
dainty hand?

Following a burst of bustling activity we found ourselves
deposited on the pier and we entered a carriage for our short trip
to the St. Louis Hotel. The enclosure of the carriage provided me
with a brief respite from the eyes that followed me from the ship
to our conveyance, eyes that I ignored with great effort. While it
was true that this city saw more than the usual share of strange
people, I could not help but feel self-conscious and conspicuous.
All about me I heard strange French dialects and unfamiliar, heavily accented English. I must learn quickly.

The waterfront streets were filled with dust and bits of waste
paper flying in the breeze. The gutters along the high sidewalks
were high with water. I learned later that the oddly high brick
walkways were called "banquettes" because they rose above the
water like tiny banks. I was aware of New Orleans' severe drainage
problem, but I sincerely hoped the area in which we were to live
was a little more acceptable than what I saw on the waterfront.

I was delighted with the hotel building. I could not help myself, having done extensive architectural work in the past. The lobby was resplendent with murals, arches and colonnades, and boasted a grand spiral staircase. I deposited Christine in the waiting area and went directly to the desk to get our room keys and, hopefully, my information from France. There was a young clerk sitting behind the desk with his back to me, working on some papers. I cleared my throat gently and he held up a finger next to his head to indicate that I should wait. I silently drummed my fingers on the desk while he completed his task. He swiveled around in his chair and was rising to his feet when he looked up to see me standing there. Immediately his face went white and his eyes widened. His mouth opened and closed a couple of times but no sound emerged. He stepped backwards awkwardly and without a word abandoned the desk area through a door at the back. I prayed that Christine had not witnessed that display. She was facing the other way looking out the window. My face burned with embarrassment and I was wondering what I would do next when another clerk entered through the same door. Having obviously been forewarned, he came straight up to me.

"I am terribly sorry for the rudeness of my staff, sir," the older man said to me. "I will not excuse his behavior, but he is new here and has not yet learned his manners." He looked at me with a slight embarrassment of his own. "Please accept my sincere apologies, sir, and what may I help you with today?"

It took some effort, but I forced myself to let the unfortunate incident go. I nodded my acceptance and said "Good afternoon," in English, with as friendly a voice as I could muster. "I trust you have two rooms and a cable waiting for one Erik Devereaux and companion?"

"Yes, sir, I do indeed." He conducted himself professionally but his gaze lingered upon my masked face. This was considerably after the season of the city's famous street festivals, so he was likely surprised to see someone masked at this time. He turned to fiddle among the room boxes. I glanced self-consciously over my shoulder to notice several hotel guests eyeing me suspiciously. Their glances turned quickly elsewhere, but they could not hide their curiosity. I turned back to the desk and felt their eyes burning into my back. This will not be easy, I thought to myself. The clerk finally returned with two keys and an envelope. He set them on the counter and rotated the registration book toward me.

"If you will please sign in, sir. A down payment of one night's lodging is required."

I took the inked pen and began to write my name in the book. Christine came up silently behind me to look over my arm at what I was writing. I remembered that she had never known what my name was. I hesitated for only a second before adding "Devereaux" in my backward left-handed scrawl. (I had been repeatedly punished as a child for my left-handedness. Severe beatings and frequent comparisons to the devil had only strengthened my stubborn resolve to remain that way. As a result, I never learned to form my letters in the flowing hand that was expected of me and my writing remains clumsy to this day.) I finished with "and companion" and laid down the pen. I looked over to meet Christine's eyes and saw, in her tiny smile, her triumph at finding out another informational tidbit about me. I would not disappoint her by telling her that Devereaux is not my real name. I would later obtain the proper documents to verify my identity as Monsieur Erik Devereaux of Rouen, France. She put her arm through mine and stood beside me while the arrangements were completed.

"Here are your keys, Mr. Devereaux," the clerk continued after checking my name in the book. "I hope you will find everything in order. Your rooms are connected as requested." He cast a sideways glance at Christine, probably wondering what we were to each other. "If you need anything you will find a bell button on the wall by the door, and we have telephone service from each room to the front desk. Enjoy your stay."

"Thank you." Pocketing the two keys, I picked up my envelope and tore it open. As promised, the cable listed a name and address. Mr. Jean Vaillancourt lived in the Rue St. Anne. I was pleased to note that his offices should be relatively close to where we would live since the Quarter was not a large area. Christine and I were silent as we waited for the elevator to take us to the third floor. Our baggage had gone up ahead of us. I unlocked her door and pushed it open. I remained in the hallway.

"Why don't you go in and rest for a while, Christine," I said. "I will go meet with Mr. Vaillancourt. I would like to get us situated in our new home as soon as possible." I took her hand and kissed it. "Our long journey is almost over, my dear, but the adventure has just begun." On impulse, I leaned over to place a light kiss on her cheek. As my mask made contact with her face I longed to remove the leather to feel her warm and silky skin against my own. She smiled somewhat shyly at me. Then, to my astonishment, she stood on her toes to return the gesture with a tentative brush of her lips upon the mask. Her closeness washed over me like a wave and I didn't want to leave. Soon we would be settled in our own home and this phase of transition would be over. We would be living together, alone... *Don't think of that now!*

"I must go," I said in a husky voice, resisting the urge to take her in my arms. "I will return as soon as possible, and will expect you to have gotten some rest."

I turned and walked down the hall, leaving her at the door. I decided to use the stairs. Once in the stairwell my breath left me in one long gush and I leaned against the wall until I could recover it. Christ, I couldn't take much more of this torture. Being so close to the girl day after day was becoming more and more difficult. I quickly took my mask off and wiped my sweating face, hoping that if anyone came by they wouldn't notice that I was having a hard time gaining control of myself. Christine was beginning to take some initiative by occasionally making her own shy and tentative advances toward me, making my predicament even more difficult. To be perfectly honest and somewhat rudely frank, it was becoming almost impossible for me to keep my hands off her. I knew, though, that if I lost control and did something I would regret I would lose all the ground that I had gained in winning her trust and confidence. Damn it, I loved the woman! I would not hurt her like that. Fortunately no one else had need of the stairway at that moment and by the time I reached the lobby I could walk through it with my composure intact.

I hailed a carriage to take me to Vaillancourt's offices in Rue St. Anne. I managed to get into one right at the curb before the driver got a good look at me. I was already sitting in it by the time he noticed that he had a passenger. Without looking at me he listened to the address I gave him and we were off. Just getting away from Christine and out into the fresh air made me feel much better. My ride served to acquaint me with some of that part of the city, and as we rolled through the neat blocks of the French section I liked what I saw. The houses for the most part were old and quaint but many of them were also quite elegant. The architecture was not what I was used to, but the buildings did possess a certain charm all their own. There was an eclectic mix of architectural themes including French, Georgian and Spanish influences which blended together to form a charming collection of homes. The area was also much cleaner than the waterfront.

My carriage pulled up in front of a well kept home that looked like plaster with a design of stonework drawn into it. It was painted a bright white topped by black shutters, and the doorway with its fanlight above looked very welcoming amidst its side gardens of lush green vegetation and multi-colored blooms of azaleas, camellias and magnolia. The gallery overhead was trimmed in lacy ironwork, also painted white. It looked quite inviting for relaxing on a hot afternoon. I was out of the carriage and calling over my shoulder for the driver to wait for me before he'd even brought his horse to a full stop. I stepped up to the door just above street level and lifted the knocker, letting it fall softly. It seemed a shame to disturb such a peaceful setting.

A large woman of color wearing a bright colored wrapping on her head and a huge white apron around her ample middle opened the door. Mr. Vaillancourt must not stand too stiffly on formality, I thought. The poor woman's eyes widened in her round black face and her mouth dropped open as she stared at me with undisguised alarm. It took a minute for her to gather herself enough for me to state my business. She had already begun inching away from me.

"Good afternoon," I said. "I believe Mr. Vaillancourt might be expecting me. My name is Erik Devereaux."

She swallowed heavily and finally found her tongue. "Yassah, this way, suh," she said as she turned back into the dark recesses of the house. It was cool and pleasant inside. She pointed at a room to the left of the hallway across from an ornate staircase. "Wait heah, suh," she said and scurried off with obvious relief.

While I waited I reflected on her reaction to me. I had forgotten these colored people here had beliefs that I did not yet understand. I had read something of voodoo and the black arts, but I had much to learn. The whole idea of possession, conjuring, fetishes and other such oddities fascinated me. I intended to pursue it thoroughly at some point after we settled into some sort of routine home life. This poor woman probably thought I was something out of her worst nightmare.

I had just arranged myself in a comfortable chair in the parlor and picked up a copy of a newspaper called the *Times-Democrat* from the adjacent table when a balding, portly man wearing a pince-nez came down the creaking carpeted stairs. He came at me with a jolly smile covering his red face and held out a beefy hand to me. I quickly stood up and stared in surprise at his outstretched hand. Suddenly I realized I was being inexcusably rude and I accepted his hand rather hesitantly. I prayed that he was not offended.

"Mr. Devereaux, pleased to make your acquaintance!" he said with an enthusiastic smile. "I see you look a little perplexed, is it perhaps at my greeting? Your man in Paris told me that you had a rather, er...unique...problem, so I was quite prepared for you, really, quite prepared." He then winked at me, which really surprised me, and in spite of myself I found I already liked this jovial man. This was unusual in itself, for I never entered into friendship easily with anyone. As I explained earlier, there had been only one person in my life whom I could call a friend, and I would never see him again. I was understandably suspicious. He motioned to the sideboard. "Would you like a bit of brandy after your long trip? I trust you found your accommodations acceptable and in order?"

This man liked to talk, that was certain. I was wondering when I might get a word in when he suddenly stopped talking and stood waiting for my answer. Startled by the abrupt silence, I managed to say yes, thank you, for the brandy.

"The hotel and rooms are fine," I continued as he indicated that I should sit down. "My companion is waiting for me there. I wanted to meet with you as soon as possible so I may get the details on the house you have leased for me. After weeks of travel I am, as you can imagine, very anxious to be settled."

"Yes, yes of course," he said with continued enthusiasm. "I do understand, yes, do understand. I have the information you seek right here." He went across the room to a massive roll top desk and removed a packet of papers tied with a red cord. He handed it to me and sat down. "Here is everything you need. The address of your residence is number 1104 in the Rue Royal. The Quarter is small, that is only several blocks from here. Also enclosed are your lease contract, which you will need to sign, of course, a house key and a bank draft for some American dollars. We have arranged for the funds that you identified to be sent to the Bank of Louisiana, located at Royal and Conti Streets. The draft will enable you to draw against those funds immediately as you see fit. They can also assist you with the exchange of any francs you carry into dollars. Also in that package you will find your identification papers, which will verify that you are who you say you are, Mr. Devereaux. I assure you that everything is in fine order, yes, fine order. Will there be anything else at this time, sir?" He almost leapt to his feet, rubbing his hands together in anticipation, apparently, of the possibility of receiving another request for his services.

"No, I believe you have taken care of me quite nicely for now, thank you," I said. "I am feeling a little tired from my trip and wish to return to my hotel for the evening." I had been scanning the papers as he spoke about them, and everything appeared in order, just as he said. I retied the packet of papers. "Everything seems to be in order, and I thank you for your services, Mr. Vaillancourt. I will be in touch soon for any future business arrangements that I may require."

I got to my feet and started for the door, but turned back. "Mr. Vaillancourt," I began hesitantly. "I also wish to thank you for the respect and courtesy you have shown me today. With or without warning of my unusual situation, I am not accustomed to people being so accepting of me. You will pardon me if I seem a little bewildered; I am more accustomed to hostility than courtesy. I believe I have chosen the right city in which to begin my life again. It will be my pleasure to do future business with you."

He smiled and stuck out his hand again, which I accepted this time without hesitation. "We're a friendly city, we are, full of all different types of people and customs. One more person who's a little different won't matter here, no, won't matter here! Good day, sir," he said with the same enthusiasm as when he had greeted me. He laughed with delight, his watch chain bouncing around on his considerable midsection.

I came back out onto the street chuckling to myself. What a funny little man, I thought. I made a mental note to send my solicitor in Paris a fat bonus for finding me this man. So far my introduction to the people of New Orleans held great promise for the future.

My carriage was waiting for me as instructed and I got in quickly, hollering out the address of 1104 Rue Royal. I would have the driver stop there briefly so that I could see it for myself before I brought Christine there in the morning. I wanted her to be with me when I entered our home for the first time. I had enough confidence in Vaillancourt to know that the house, inside and out, would be perfect.

We turned into the Rue Royal and I began looking for 1104. I never had a real house before. I'd lived in a tiny cottage with my parents, and I had my elegant dwelling under the Opera which was extremely comfortable and all of my own creation. I'd lived many places in between, none of which I had ever called home. This was different. This was a real house in a real street among real people. This was normal. My heart leapt when I finally saw it.

The exterior of the house was brick, the only one like it on the street. The style was a combination of Georgian and something unique to this city…Creole…influences. The recessed front door was flanked by sidelights and topped with a huge fanlight. The design was repeated for a matching door on the second floor. Black shutters framed the windows, which showed white lacy draperies hiding the darkened rooms. Along one side of the house stood a tall brick wall with a solid oak gate, which led to what appeared to be a large side garden completely hidden from the street. A beautiful gallery stood out at the second story level surrounded by an intricately woven design of ironwork to form the railings. Four large chimneys, two on a side, rose proudly to the sky to top the structure. I looked with longing at the key in my hand, and reluctantly asked the driver to return to the St. Louis. Jumping down quickly from the carriage step, I reached up to hand the driver my fare. He took one look at me and almost dropped his money. I thanked him and crossed the sidewalk to the hotel, leaving the poor soul staring after me with his mouth hanging open. I very likely could have walked away without paying him at all, but that would not have been a very nice way to begin life in my new city.

Into the hotel elevator with me stepped an older couple who could not have stood more than five feet tall, either of them. Both gray-haired and the same overall shape, they had the look of a pair of matched bookends. They entered without looking up, and the bored and oblivious operator had pulled the door shut before their glances rose to my face. I must have stood close to eighteen inches taller than they, and when they finally caught sight of the mask atop my imposing height both faces immediately went white. Well, I had certainly seen that expression before. I moved over as far as was possible in the small space behind the operator and nodded my head to them. Nothing I did would have mattered; I could read the suspicion in their eyes. They said nothing to me, but if the elevator door had not already closed I had no doubt they would have put as much distance between us as possible. They stood waiting like statues, unmoving and stiff. When we arrived at their floor they exited hastily without looking back. I sadly watched them go. I must learn to accept these things as a part of my life.

Christine was ready and waiting for me when I returned. It wasn't until our meal arrived that I realized my own hunger. It was odd, but since I left France I had gained a new appetite. Food had never meant much to me except as a source of nourish-ment...a necessary ritual. I had never taken pleasure in different foods and experimentation with them held no interest for me. Now, however, I found myself looking forward to mealtimes. Several times recently I had been somewhat embarrassed over the amount of food I had consumed. I originally attributed this phe-nomenon to the sea air. Now I thought it had more to do with my improved outlook on life along with the sight of Christine happily wading through her own hearty meals across the table from me.

For the first time in my life I was gaining weight. My coats did not fit as well as before and the waistbands of my trousers were uncomfortable. Thank God my masks still fit, since it would be some time before a new leather worker could make more. Ill-fitting masks were a painful problem from my childhood that I prayed I would never experience again. I hoped the weight gain would not go much farther. I had always been painfully thin and, though I probably looked less like a walking corpse now than before, I had no desire to become as round as my friend Vaillancourt was. I also hoped my improved overall health might prevent any repeats of my mysterious—and recently frightening—attacks.

Later that night, Christine and I decided to take a stroll through the darkened streets of our new city. Since leaving Norfolk, a tentative initiative toward the physical had developed between us. It was an unspoken decision on both our parts. Though it was proving very difficult, I attempted to match the level of my own need for contact to Christine's. She needn't know how tightly wound I really was. The direction of our relationship had not yet been established, yet it seemed a natural progression that we become closer after having been practically living together for weeks. We walked hand in hand under the lamplight until an unusual chill in the night air forced a shiver from Christine. I instinctively put my arm around her, enveloping her in the folds of my cloak. I would have to see about getting some more appropriate clothing for the climate but tonight the cloak was a welcome addition. She snuggled into my side as we walked, and presently I felt her arm creep around behind me. I resisted the urge to take her past our new house. We were both tired. We rounded the last corner on our way back to the hotel. The street lamps had not yet found us. I pulled Christine with me back against the wall of the nearest building, further into the darkness.

"Erik, what's wrong?" she asked quietly. "It's very dark here."

"I know. The darkness is my friend." I put my finger to her lips as she opened them to speak again.

"You have made me so very happy." I stroked her hair away from her face with a finger. "We are beginning a new life together, a life that I never expected to know, and I owe it all to you, Christine. I am forever in your debt."

"A life which we still would not know had you not taken me from Paris, Erik. What you did was terrible, but...I am happy to be with you right now." She looked up at me in the darkness.

Hiding my surprise at her admission, I leaned down and took her gently in my arms. She sighed, whether from relief or warmth or happiness I could not tell. My heart began to pound and I felt warm all over. As Christine's small body melted into mine I straightened up, lifting her off the ground and hugging her more tightly to me. Her arms went around my neck and I rested my face against her soft hair. The embrace felt so different from others we'd shared. We embraced with mutual affection for the first time, and it felt wonderful to hold the length of her body against mine. I suddenly felt very brave in the familiar darkness. I slipped the mask off and reveled in the feeling of the night air on my uncovered face.

She looked up, then gently returned her head to my shoulder, with her face toward me. Slowly, I lowered my head to brush her cheek with my lips. I slid my lips gently across the smoothness, then tentatively touched my cheek to hers. The softness of her skin against mine was indescribable. I waited, expecting Christine to pull away at the sensation of my ugliness against her face. On the contrary, her arms seemed to tighten slightly around my neck. The beating of my heart threatened to burst right out of my chest and I finally accepted her unspoken invitation. I pushed her hair aside and buried my naked face in her neck, thirstily drinking in her smell and her warmth and the feeling of her soft skin against my own uneven features. *Christine.*

"Erik," she said breathlessly in my ear.

My arms tightened around her. I moved her body against me and a low moan escaped my throat.

"Oh, Christine, I...Oh..." I breathed urgently into the warm soft skin of her neck. I was losing control.

"Erik...please," she said again, but even as I heard her voice say my name I could not respond. I was getting lost...so lost...

The clattering of a lone carriage approaching brought me abruptly to my senses. The mask found its way to my face automatically.

I tried to disentangle us before the carriage came around the corner. "We must get back to the hotel," I muttered, only half meaning it.

I set her feet firmly back on the ground. I felt disheveled and out of sorts, and oddly empty. She stepped back from me without a word and shivered. I reached out and pulled her back under the protection of my cloak, then set off at a good pace for the hotel, making her jog to keep up with my long strides. We said nothing as we hurried down the street and into the warm lobby. Upstairs I unlocked the door to her room and stepped aside for her to enter.

She moved past me but grabbed my hand as she did, pulling me into the room after her.

"Erik," she began tentatively as she crossed the room to look out into the dark night, "I don't know what's happening to me. I've...I've never felt this way before or thought about the things I've...been thinking about. Not even with Raoul." She turned back to me, her face flushed with embarrassment. "I don't know what I'm doing." She sat down on the edge of the bed and looked down at her hands clenched in her lap. "I want to stay with you, but..." She paused and added in whisper, "I shouldn't be thinking about these things."

Apparently some of the discussion I had planned for tomorrow would not wait. I felt drained and weary, but I went over to sit in the chair opposite her. I crossed my long legs and looked at the woman on the bed, who one minute could be so in control of herself and in the next become once more a frightened little girl.

"Christine, tell me what I can do to help you," I said gently.

"I'm so confused...about you and me," she admitted, not looking at me. "First you were my angel, and I didn't think you were real. Then you were like my father, teaching me about many things and taking care of me. Now, I...I don't know...I think of you...differently." She took a breath and rushed on. "Tonight in the street I didn't want to stop, and that frightened me. I am not sure what it was that I didn't want to stop doing. But part of me did want to stop...oh, I'm not making any sense!" She looked up at me shyly and with confusion written all over her face. "I never thought you would mean those things to me, I mean you are much...and I didn't think you..."

"Older?" I snorted with amusement at her discomfort. "You think I am too *old* to want you in that way? My dear girl, the upper forties are not an age when people are usually considered to have one foot in the grave. I am perfectly capable of anything your little dreams could conjure up, I assure you."

My frankness embarrassed her further.

"Oh no, I didn't mean that," she said, flushing to a deep red color. "I meant what would people think; you are old enough to be my..."

I was tiring of this roundabout conversation. "Look, Christine, I don't give a damn what people think. All that should matter to us is how we feel about each other. The difference in our ages is of no consequence to me. You mean the world to me, Christine. If you stay, you must accept our relationship for what it is and where it is heading." (That was big talk from me, who was as nervous about things as she was.)

I leaned forward to rest my elbows on my knees and softened my voice. "Christine, I am sorry about what happened in the street tonight. I should not have frightened you like that. Sometimes when you are near I forget myself. I apologize. I shall be more solicitous of your position in the future." I stood up and started for the door. I could take no more of this tonight.

"Erik," she said, stopping me at the door, "I really do care for you."

"Christine," I said wearily over my shoulder, "it is late. Please let's get some sleep. We have a house to move into in the morning. It will be a very busy day."

"All right, Erik," she said petulantly. "I am rather tired."

I walked back to her and placed a chaste kiss on her forehead. "Good night, Christine."

"Good night, Erik," she replied with a tired smile.

I retreated to my own room to mull over what had just happened between us. I had come very close to losing my tightly held control and it could not happen again. The girl was wrestling with feelings for me that she didn't understand. I must let things happen naturally.

My impatience must not be allowed to get the better of my judgment. I didn't know how long I could continue like this, not knowing how things would go. I loved her. I knew that she had strong feelings for me, but until I heard from her lips the words I longed to hear, I would continue to doubt my position. I prepared for bed and went to sleep with those questions burning in my mind.

10

---★---

I had not chosen the house, but I was as proud as I could be when I saw her face. I watched her as we approached it and was delighted to see that she seemed very pleased. I only wanted to make her happy.

The inside was as pleasing as the outside. The entryway was dim and cool and more spacious than it looked from the street. It was in the elegant yet simple style of the area. It was an older house, probably built around 1830, but newer than many of the Quarter's homes. Its furnishings reflected that period but showed no obvious signs of wear. The house had a lovely curving stairway with a brass newel post, polished to perfection. Upstairs it had tester beds of rosewood and mahogany, which featured carved finials that could be raised to support the mosquito netting that hung behind the headboards. Delicately carved furniture filled every room. The double parlor was spaciously light and airy and the dining room was resplendent with its red and gold draperies and matching upholstery. An arched doorway led out the back into an expansive courtyard filled with exotic plantings surrounding a working fountain and delicate wrought iron furniture. A winding staircase in the back corner led to a private gallery and ended in a set of French doors that opened into the master suite on the second floor. Leaning against the back of the house was a massive iron cistern that would collect rainwater for use in the home. Wells were unheard of here. Yet another archway at the rear of the courtyard led to the servants' quarters and the stables, along with the entrance to the side garden that I had noticed from the street. The house and grounds were compact but we certainly had enough space indoors and out and still have our privacy. A smile of satisfaction touched my lips. I must thank Vaillancourt properly for finding me this house.

I found a note from Vaillancourt on a small table by the newel post instructing me that I would find my servants in their quarters located in the garconniere off the walled garden. As I understood from my papers, they were a middle-aged couple. Robert and Deliah would handle our stable, cooking, housework and gardening. It seemed that here in New Orleans great pride and care were taken with one's gardens and they should not be left to the inexperienced. There would be no argument from me on that; I could not count any knowledge of gardening among my varied accomplishments. These people came with high recommendations for both their service and their discretion. Leaving Christine to admire and explore her new home, I set off through the garden to knock on the couple's door.

If I was expecting a reception like that which I had received from Vaillancourt I was disappointed the second that Robert opened the door and saw me standing on his doorstep. His eyes almost popped right out of his head when he saw the mask and my funereal attire. He was about to close the door on me when I put my foot forward into the doorway, blocking its path.

"Robert? I am Mr. Devereaux. I trust that Mr. Vaillancourt told you of my arrival and my lease of this property?"

Robert's jet-black face reappeared around the edge of the door. His eyes were still wide but he had gained control of his voice.

"Yassah, Mista' Devereaux, suh. I jus' didn't expect…"

I removed my foot from his doorway. "I am sorry that I frightened you. I assumed that you would have been told about my 'accident' and that, for the comfort of others, I feel I must cover my disfigurement."

If he knew the truth about my being born with this face I could never have convinced him that I was not the devil or some other equally evil character. These people were too superstitious to convince otherwise. I decided right then that it would be better for me to tell anyone who had the courage to ask about the mask that it was to cover the result of an accident. For the time being, I would also allow our servants to believe that we were married.

"If you and your wife...is it Deliah?...would come up to the house a bit later I will have some simple instructions for you. You must excuse my wife and I, we have not had any previous experience with servants and will have to become accustomed to having you around. We will not require much, but I do request that you honor our wish to be left alone as much as possible. Perform your duties as required and you will be rewarded with a generous salary and an enviable amount of time off, to do with as you wish. I would also require your utmost secrecy in all matters pertaining to our private business or situation. Do I make myself understood?"

Robert had now opened the door fully and was listening to me openly. "Yassah, I understand, suh. Thank you, suh."

"Well then. You and your wife may take your time in coming to the house. We have no immediate needs so anytime will be fine. And please, Robert, give your poor wife some warning about me. I should hate to have her faint at my feet. Please assure her that I am quite harmless."

I re-entered the house to hear Christine squealing in delight at what she was seeing in the bedrooms. I walked up the main stairs to the second floor just as she came flying out of a bedroom to fling her arms around my neck. Her momentum sent me back against the landing rail, on which we teetered a bit before I could regain my balance and wrap my arms around her.

"Easy my dear!" I exclaimed. "You'll send us both over the edge. I take it you like the bedrooms." She nodded eagerly.

"You shall have your pick of any room you want," I said. I didn't know how long our servants would continue to believe us married. The temptation to go out into the streets with the news that one's new employers lived together in sin would be a juicy tidbit. It would certainly be a good test of their discretionary credentials. Well, it could not be helped.

The master suite consisted of two large bedrooms connected by a smaller room that served as a dressing room and bathing area. The gallery that ran full length outside the French doors of both rooms afforded a commanding view of the beautiful courtyard. Christine's eyes shone with delight when she saw it and she immediately chose one of those rooms. I took the adjoining one after repeating my promise to Christine that I would not enter her room unless she needed me. I was very comfortable, at least as much as I could be while knowing that she slept in the next room.

I lost no time in purchasing a beautiful grand piano, and while it was not the same as the organ I had left behind in Paris, it would do for my composing. I could unpack my manuscripts and resume my work. I also wanted to get Christine singing again but since she had not mentioned it I would give her more time. It didn't matter how good her voice was if her heart wasn't in it.

Deliah always had a wonderful breakfast ready for us in the morning, then she would do her chores around the house and disappear. I was disappointed that she seemed to be very fearful of me even after Robert explained the fabricated reason for my mask. The good woman tried valiantly to hide her uneasiness but I could sense it whenever I was in the room with her. It hurt me more than I realized to hear her singing and talking to Christine in the kitchen, only to have her fall silent when I entered the room except to mutter about something that needed doing elsewhere. I didn't know what I could do to change her mind so I tried to keep out of her way. Robert was rarely in the house at all, having most of his work located in the gardens, courtyard and stables. They were perfectly willing to give us all the privacy we wanted in return for a few extra hours off.

I set about getting a horse and light carriage, and Christine spent a good part of her time having Robert drive her around to the best and most exclusive shops to be fitted for new dresses, shoes, coats and other sundry women's items. She had the small but complete collection that I brought with us from Paris, but if shopping made her happy I was not about to stand in her way. She had grown up relatively poor and having money to spend was a new experience for her. I was wealthy enough for her to have whatever she wanted, but I never told her just how well off I was. I had seen what vast wealth could do to some women of society, turning them into carping hens who looked down their upturned noses at those with lesser fortunes. Christine would want for nothing, but neither would I give her any idea of the extent of my wealth.

Robert took quite a liking to "Miz Devereaux" and I had no cause to worry about her when she was out with him. I knew he would take care of her. I met with him privately not long after our first introduction and warned him, in very clear terms, that if anything happened to her while she was in his care, he would answer to me. I need not go into details, but I made it clear as crystal to him that I was not to be crossed and that I had a history of getting exactly what I wanted.

There followed several months of quiet happiness during which Christine and I got to know each other better. I was very careful to watch my deep-seated tendencies to be critical, impatient or sarcastic, to name a few of my less desirable qualities. I also kept a firm lock on my temper, although no one so far had given me any reason to worry about it. I had worked hard to create the façade of respectability that I had so far presented to her and others, and I would not allow a moment of carelessness to ruin everything. Supporting this illusion took concerted effort. I felt as if I was acting a part. Eventually I would become more at home in my new persona, but it would not be easy. My love for Christine, however, were totally genuine along with my desire to make her as happy as possible. If that meant my changing for her, I would make those changes happen. I can guarantee that she would not have cared at all for the Erik of years past.

The reclusive instincts born of many years of habit were difficult for me to shake off, and I remained reluctant to go out and about the city. As the months passed, however, I became restless and bored with my lack of activity. My new home, with its curtained windows and walled gardens, was a solid comfort to me in this strange country. I had so far been lucky in dealing with the few people I had met. I was hesitant to take the initiative and put myself in a position of vulnerability. I stayed at home during those first months, enjoying a new form of solitude and writing music.

My purchase of the piano brought music back into my life. I never realized how much I missed it until I laid my fingers on those silken keys and coaxed the first soft sounds from them. Soon I was playing for hours on end and the house was filled with music. In the evenings Christine would sit on the bench beside me listening to me play. Eventually I added my voice, encouraged by the fact that it did not seem to have suffered too much from lack of practice. It felt good to sing again, and my expansive range grew limber once more as I let it out, not caring about who heard me. For so many years my beautiful tenor voice had been muffled or silenced, first by rejection then by tons of stone and earth, to be enjoyed by no one but myself. Never again would I bury it like that. To my great disappointment, Christine showed no interest in singing.

I hadn't pressed Christine for physical contact beyond what she initiated. We held hands frequently and warm embraces were common. She seemed to have cooled since that last night at the hotel but I rationally supposed it could be from the excitement of all the new things she was doing and seeing. She did not turn away from me however; far from it. I took that as encouragement. We grew closer on other levels including the most important one. A physical relationship was what I lacked and needed, but without a stimulating mental relationship to sustain me as well, I would be lost. We were as close as any husband and wife would get, excluding the physical aspects of a marriage. I wanted her to be my wife, but I would not mention it until it was right for both of us. I relied on the very ends of my patience to get me through the days and the nights were increasingly difficult for me. My thoughts drove me mad, and many nights I was awake long into the hours of the morning, unable to slow my thoughts and calm my mind and body.

Following the daily lessons in English that I had been giving Christine since we arrived, we went driving around the city in the late afternoons. We began with the French Quarter and then expanded our drives to reach as far out as Lake Pontchartrain to the north and the American Garden District to the southwest.

"Erik," Christine began as we drove home from an afternoon excursion, "When is your birthday?"

The question startled me. It had come from nowhere. "I don't know," I muttered evasively while my eyes remained fixed on the road ahead. "My birthday was never honored."

"Never honored? Do you mean your parents never even told you when you were born? How positively awful!"

"To be truthful, my dear, I have never really missed it. One tends not to miss what one has never had." I finally glanced sideways at her. "Why do you ask?"

"I just wondered, that's all. You don't even know how old you are?"

"I am reasonably sure of the year." At her expectant look I sighed and relented. "1834."

I looked back to the road. She slid over closer to me on the seat and rested her hand sympathetically on my leg.

*   *   *

I had battled solitude and increasing boredom long enough. Staying home for months while Christine explored the city wore on me. I didn't understand how I could have spent so many years by myself, but my life had been so different when I went underground. I had something to live for in New Orleans, but now I felt that life was going on about its business without me. It was time for me to get out and discover what made the city so unusual. There were many things out there for me to learn, but the subject that intrigued me the most was the practice of the black arts. For reasons that should be obvious, I kept my interests in that direction a secret from Christine.

Christine's reluctance to sing bothered me. Music was the original basis for our whole relationship and she seemed to have turned her back on it completely. That perplexed me and the frustration I felt with the halt of progress in our physical relationship was not helping. Against my will and despite my efforts to keep things on an even keel, these strains began to show in my shortening temper and a rising degree of irritability. I began to snap at her and became overly critical of little things she did which should not have annoyed me. One day I shouted at her and then stalked upstairs angrily when all she had done was to enter the parlor while I was wrestling with a particularly stubborn piece of music. Soon I was criticizing her habits, her clothes and her interests. The hurt that showed in her eyes before she turned away did nothing to change my mood. My already sharp sarcasm honed itself to a more hurtful level. I felt like a caged animal. I did not mean to take my frustration out on Christine, but one afternoon when she returned from town, I let it get the best of me.

She had been gone longer than usual. I was not worried because she was with Robert, but I felt left out and isolated. My cursed face still prevented me from living life like a normal man, and nothing I could do would ever change that. I had made great progress in reacquainting myself with life above the ground, but my efforts alone could only take me so far. Christine was my ticket to the world beyond the walls of our home. I needed her like I'd never needed her before.

I was working at the piano in my shirtsleeves. When I checked my watch and noted the time, my frustrations came to a head and my temper flared hot for the first time since I left Paris. With a sudden and inexplicable anger that I could not control, I leapt up and swept the top of the piano clean, sending ink, pens, coffee and manuscripts flying all over the room. I stalked over to the mantel and swept its contents to the brick hearth with a growl that was lost amid the sounds of breaking glass and the crashing of books and candlesticks. The many shelves of the bookcase along the wall succumbed to the same fate. I whirled around in a rage, seeking something else to throw. I had picked up a heavy wing chair and was heading for the large back window when Christine appeared in the doorway. Behind her bobbed the terrified faces of Robert and Deliah.

"Erik!" Christine's sharp command penetrated the haze of my anger. "Put that down!"

I blinked at her standing in the doorway and stopped with the chair balanced over my shoulder. She sent the servants away and came toward me while I slowly lowered the chair and set it on the floor. I looked dazedly about me. The mess in our beautiful parlor was incredible; had I done that? I looked back at her face and read the disappointment in her eyes. I was ashamed of what I had done but it was what I saw in Christine's eyes that caused me to react in the worst way possible.

"Don't you speak to me like that!" I spat, covering the space between us in two long strides and taking her roughly by the shoulders. "No one talks to Erik like that!" I was quickly losing my temper again and did not realize I was painfully squeezing her shoulders with my long fingers. Christine just stood there silently, which only served to incense me further. I needed to lash out at something and she was the closest target.

"Where have you been?" I shouted, giving her a little shake. Her silence was maddening…why didn't she say something? My hand shifted with lightning speed to her fragile neck and I wrapped my inhumanly strong fingers around it. I pushed her back against the wall with a thud. "All these little errands of yours into town…do you think I am stupid?" I sneered in an ugly tone. "You think I don't know that you are up to something besides endless shopping for your pretty little dresses?" Her gaze never wavered but the pulse of her neck quickened under my fingers. "What have you been doing behind my back?" I screamed as my fingers begin to contract, working their way into the soft flesh of her neck. "Tell me! Tell…"

"Erik."

I stopped shouting and stared at her as if I had never seen her before. One hand was wrapped tightly around her neck and the other was holding her against the wall.

"Erik."

The sound came from far away. I shook my head as her patiently gentle voice found its way through my rage and into my muddled brain. I shut my eyes tightly and shook my head again, trying to rid myself of whatever possessed me. When I met her eyes again calmness finally descended over me and I saw that I was hurting her. I released her and was appalled to see the imprint of my hand on her neck. I brought my hands up in front of my face and stared at them as if they belonged to someone else. Christine had stood her ground, and now she reached up to take both my hands in hers. At her gentle touch I crumbled and sank to my knees at her feet. My head went down and my eyes closed. I felt drained and empty...and lost.

Shame boiled up from within me and I began to shake with silent sobbing. She knelt in front of me and put her arms around me. Like a drowning man grabbing a life ring, I flung my arms around her and cried into her shoulder. Her hand stroked the back of my head. I don't know how long we remained on the floor amidst the shambles I had made of the room. My shameful display abated after several embarrassing minutes.

"Was it something I did?" she asked, nodding her head toward the mess on the floor.

I got up and walked over to the hearth, kicking at the broken glass. I pushed a hand up under the mask to wipe the tears from my face, then leaned forward to brace both hands on the bare mantel and hung my head between them. My thin white shirt was soaked in sweat and sticking uncomfortably to me.

"No, it is not your fault. I just used you as an excuse." I addressed the fireplace in a cowed voice, poking at the still intact petticoat mirror with my foot. "I'm glad you came in when you did, or I fear we would not have a house still standing."

"What's wrong, Erik?" She came to stand behind me.

"A lot of things, none of which are your fault. Things that cannot be changed," I answered with a sigh. "I guess it's mostly because I've missed you," I finished in little more than a whisper.

"Missed me?" she questioned. "But I'm right here."

"Yes, my dear, you are right here," I replied with resignation. I turned around to face her while unconsciously twisting the tiny gold ring around and around on my little finger. "Christine, on the night we stayed at the St. Louis something happened between us. I know it frightened you, but it was the beginning of something. Since then there has been nothing. I feel that we have put one foot forward into tomorrow but left the other firmly planted in yesterday. I can't seem to reach you the way I used to. We were doing so well, and it all just...stopped. I don't know how to fix it."

"I don't know what to..." she stammered.

"I thought you cared about me, that we were getting closer."

"Well, I do care..."

"Then what is holding you back?" I asked. "Is it this?" I removed the mask. "You must be completely honest with me now."

She looked directly into my eyes. "I told you before that your face no longer frightens me. It is a part of you Erik, a part that you can never deny and never change." Her hand slowly rose to my face and she stroked my cheek, trailing her finger down to run it lightly across my uneven lips. I caught her hand and pressed my lips into her palm. "Maybe I've been denying my own feelings," she mused softly as she lifted her other hand to frame my face. "I do care about you Erik...very much. I don't ever want to leave you."

"Christine, I would die if you left me...you mean so much..." It was difficult to read the expression in her eyes, but at that moment I could swear that it was hope I saw in them. My breath caught in my throat. We had arrived at the crossroads and there was no turning back. The course of our lives would finally be decided. In all my hideous, barefaced glory, I took both of her hands in mine and knelt before her in the middle of the chaos. I looked up at her lovely face, which wasn't that far away considering my height.

"Christine, my life began the day you walked into it. It will end the day we are parted. I was alone and you rescued me. I want to share my entire life with you, not just pieces of it. I need you, Christine, and I love you more than life itself and with all my heart." I took a deep breath. "I love you, Christine Daae, and I would be very honored if you would become my wife. Will you marry me?"

"Oh, Erik," she said softly with tears filling her eyes. "Yes, I will marry you. Because I love you too."

I stood up and leaned down toward her face as she slowly lifted it to meet me. Her exquisite lips at last met my ugly ones. Shock waves shot through me at the actual sensation of the touch I had dreamed of for most of my life. I drew back quickly in surprise and my eyes went wide with wonder. The serenity in her face brought me back. Hesitantly I moved toward her again until our lips gently met a second time. Again I felt an indescribable thrill when her lips briefly touched mine. She began to smile. Her warm smile gave me confidence and when our lips met a third time I did not back away. I was transported instead to the most beautiful place I had ever known. Our arms crept around each other and our lips moved together in total and final acceptance of the fact that we were meant for each other.

I had finally celebrated my birthday.

II

———————— ✶ ————————

The engagement ring was the most exquisite in all of New Orleans. I picked it out myself, braving the exposure to enter the city's most prestigious jewelry establishment. The shop owner tried in vain to hide his trembling hands as he showed me tray after tray of sparkling gems. I waved my hand haughtily at each of them, for I knew he had much better to offer than what he was showing me. I knew gemstones, and these were quite inferior. Finally I leaned over the counter toward him and asked him quietly and politely to please fetch his finest selections, or I would take my money elsewhere. Apparently he wanted a sale more than he wanted me to leave, for he finally produced the tray that I was waiting for. After making my choice I paid him in cash without dickering over the price, which I'm sure made him feel much more at ease. I had wasted enough time already and Christine was worth any price. The ring, an exquisite marquis ruby flanked by two matching diamonds, was both impressive and dainty. I passed over the larger stones in favor of a more understated elegance. I abhorred a flashy show of wealth.

My other errand that morning was to the small shop of a local craftsman. He handed me the most beautifully crafted mask I had ever seen. The fit was beyond perfect, and as I turned back to him wearing the new one I noticed that the materials he had used were also different. Unlike the flat tan of my kidskin masks, this one matched my pale skin tone almost perfectly. It fitted the contours of my face while hiding most of the deformity, and even had a built-up section to give the impression of a normal sized nose. The overall effect was impressive, and from a distance the mask would be barely noticeable. Flexible and lightweight, I felt like I was wearing nothing at all. If I'd had masks like this earlier, my life might have been made a bit easier in some respects. After making sure that he had already begun work on extra masks, I paid and commended him for his superior work and turned away again to put my old one back on. The handsome new one went into its box to be hidden away until my wedding day.

Jean Vaillancourt and his wife, who had quickly become close friends, agreed to help with my plans. Though nothing had been said, I suspected that they knew from the start that we were not married. The wedding was planned for a week hence, on Wednesday, 27 September 1882. The brief ceremony would take place at the St. Louis Cathedral in Jackson Square. Jean and his wife would be the only witnesses. In order to give Christine the most traditional wedding possible under the unusual circumstances, Jean agreed to deliver Christine to the church and to give her away. He would take her to his house that morning so that she could prepare herself in the gown that she had purchased with the help of Mrs. Vaillancourt. I don't know what I would have done without this couple's generous help from the day we arrived in New Orleans. Louise Vaillancourt had received me with the same open manner as her husband, reinforcing my belief that there were other good people out there who would accept me as well.

Christine's acceptance of my proposal gave me a much-needed shot of courage. If she would be my wife, then I must become a proper husband to her. Whether I liked it or not, that meant taking her out in public. I planned an engagement dinner for the following night at the elegant Antoine's in St. Louis Street. All during that day the ring lay in the pocket of my coat safe and secure. I could not wait to slide the perfect blood-red gem onto her finger. It was the symbol of my love and a declaration to the world that she was mine.

Dinner was an incomparable affair from start to finish. I hired an elegant enclosed carriage to take us to Antoine's, and excitedly admitted to Christine that it was a celebration of our engagement. The establishment had a pervasively romantic atmosphere and the table was just what I ordered, set off to one side with candles and flowers, and very private. We walked between the grand pillars and lanterns of the front entrance and were escorted to our table without delay. The interior was rather dark, so we were seated without undue disturbance of the other diners. Having seated Christine I went to my own chair, sweeping back the tails of my new camel colored coat with a flourish. Even the momentarily wide eyes and the occasional stammering of our waiters failed to diminish my good humor that night. Along with a magnificent wine, we dined on pommes soufflés; a unique potato dish, and pompano en papillote; tender fish covered with a sauce of shrimp and wine and baked in a sealed parchment envelope. Christine was stunning in her off-the-shoulder gown of a deep emerald satin. I could not take my eyes from her. For some reason the hollows formed around her collarbone as she moved fascinated me, as did the single dark hollow further down. I watched the sparkle in her eyes, the rise and fall of her pale skin above the dress, and the way her hair caught the candlelight. She could never know the impatience with which I waited for the moment that our intentions would become official. I fear the fabulous meal was wasted on me, for my attention could not be divided that night. Christine filled every one of my senses to capacity.

Our appetites satisfied, we were relaxing over drinks and enjoying the atmosphere when my hand went to my pocket to feel the tiny gift that waited there. We were almost alone in a secluded section of the restaurant. I moved my chair around the table closer to hers as she looked at me expectantly.

"Christine," I began, then paused for a sip of wine to ease the dryness in my mouth. "Your acceptance of my proposal has made me the happiest man on earth. Please accept this ring as an expression of my intentions and of my love."

I drew the ring out of my pocket and reached for her left hand. As I slid it slowly onto her finger, she gasped and her right hand flew to her mouth. "Oh, Erik," she whispered tearfully, "it's beautiful."

"As are you, my love," I replied softly. I leaned toward her and placed a light kiss upon her lips. I began to back away but her hand reached behind my head to hold me there. Our lips met again and lingered, tasting our mutual love and our hope for the future; a future such as I had never even dared to dream of. I ached to remove the mask and kiss her the way she should be kissed.

Christine sat within the curve of my arm in the carriage, admiring her ring in the light from each passing street lamp. She shifted herself closer to me and told me again that she loved me. I could wait no longer for a proper kiss. The mask came off and my arms went around her. My lips met hers firmly with a deep and searching urgency to which she responded with an eagerness of her own. Neither of us was aware that we had reached 1104 Royal until the driver knocked impatiently on the roof with the butt of his whip. Now suffering from an intensely uncomfortable case of physical need, I impatiently pulled my fiancée through our front door and closed it hastily behind us before I dropped the mask carelessly on the floor and reached hungrily for her. We kissed again while my hands roamed her back and shoulders and hers moved under my coat to stroke muscles taught with desire. I paused to gaze, breathlessly, into her eyes. My fingers lightly traced the lines of her neck and followed her necklace down to the top edge of her gown. They lingered there at the edge and I imagined what lay beneath the satin. My impatient lips replaced my fingers, exploring those hollows that earlier had so enthralled me. My lips met the soft swells at the edge of the satin, traveling over them to sink into the valley in between. Her deep breaths rose and fell against my face as she drew me closer. I raised my head to watch my hand slide across her skin and down over the edge of the gown to mold itself around the curve of her breast. My breath caught in my throat when I felt the firmness there. I looked at her face and I could tell by the look in her eyes that she wanted it as much as I did. Christ, how could I possibly wait another minute?

I swept her off her feet and carried her up the stairs to her room, never taking my eyes from hers. In the hall I set her back on her feet and leaned over her to once more devour her mouth with mine. I knew I had to stop. I didn't want to but I must wait until she was my wife. I gathered all the self-control that I possessed and with great effort I pulled away from her.

"I love you so much," I choked in a strangled whisper.

"And I love you," she replied and reached for me again. The sight of her reddened lips flashed a quick picture in my mind of the night I had taken her away, when I had stared at them in the dim lamplight of the cellars as she lay, unsuspecting, upon the floor. Just as quickly the image departed, leaving room in my mind for only the present. I met those moist, red lips again briefly before I reluctantly backed away.

"No, Christine, we must not...I can't...we must wait until we are wed. I want to do everything exactly right with you. I want everything to be perfect."

"It is perfect." She kissed her finger and touched it to my lips. "Good night, dear Erik."

"Wait," I said, still trying to slow myself down. "Why didn't you run from me yesterday? You know how unpredictable I can be when I'm that angry."

She smiled. "Because I know deep in my heart that you could not hurt me."

"My dear, I was in the process of choking the life out of you."

"My darling, I've known from the first night I saw you that you could never hurt me. As I recall, the circumstances were similar." At that memory, I looked down at my feet. She reached up to lift my face and she looked me hard in the eye. "Erik, you are not a bad man. Past experiences taught you what you needed to survive. Now you must learn that violence is no longer necessary in your life. You have an innate goodness and a heart that has been buried for too long. I have seen that heart, and the man you really are inside. The man I love with all my heart. Good night."

With that she went into her room and softly closed her door. I stepped back and leaned against the wall. Christ, I thought, I don't deserve this woman. I don't deserve to love anyone the way I love Christine! The next six nights would be the longest of my life.

                    *   *   *

Our wedding was to be a late afternoon ceremony and Christine was busy with her preparations. There was plenty of time that day for me to relax and reflect on the turns my life had taken. I had come so far from the lonely and horrifyingly violent young man that I had been at Christine's age. I had lived in a world of hate and scorn and became hardened against most emotions. At that time I was sure I would never live to reach thirty years of age. I believed that I would surely be struck down long before then, either for revenge or as repayment for one of any number of crimes. I lived hard and expected a similar demise. I was as inhuman as one could get and still have the breath of life in them. I cared for no one and no one cared for me. I lived any way I could and did what I had to do for survival. For some reason I never gave up. I don't know what kept me going all those years. I certainly had nothing to look forward to.

Why was I here? It was a question to which I had sought the answer throughout my life. I had been born lacking the most basic human need—an acceptable appearance. There were many ugly people in the world, but others didn't run from them in terror at first sight. No one else looked like me. It's a wonder I didn't die at birth. Even now, as I looked forward to my imminent marriage to the woman of my dreams, I still did not know the answer to that question. I had made Christine a star at the Opera Populaire, but it was possible that she might have eventually attained that without my help. Without my interference she would have been married to Raoul by now, probably very happily. I had ruined the lives of my parents and many others along the rocky road of the life I had led, bringing me finally to this chair in which I now sat looking out my window at my lovely manicured gardens. Always, I asked myself why? I had so many beautiful things about me— my voice, my talents, my intelligence and my heart. But what did any of them matter if no one would even give me a chance? Beauty was so ethereal. Anything could be beautiful to someone. No one had seen the beauty in me until Christine. I did not deserve Christine's love. She was far too good for me. I could not help but think, as she waited for me at the church today, that the best thing I could do for her would be to just go away, where she would never find me.

No. I knew I could not do that. I had thought back in Virginia that if she chose to return to France I could go on without her.

Perhaps I could have done it then, because at that time it had been a very strong possibility. But that was no longer possible. We had been too close for too long. If I lost her now I didn't know what would happen to me, but she would take my will to live with her. I had nothing without Christine.

Robert, knocking on the back door to tell me my carriage was ready, interrupted my gloomy and counterproductive thoughts. He and Deliah had taken the news of our wedding with surprise, but they were so loyal to us by then that our little deception hadn't mattered to them. Well, you've really done a nice job on yourself, I thought as I got up and put on my coat. These are wonderful thoughts to be having on your wedding day. I looked down at the tiny gold ring that I had placed on my little finger so many months ago; hoping against all odds that this day would come. It was finally here. I would marry my beloved Christine, and I would hope for the best. I knew I could make her happy if I could let go of the past. I climbed into the carriage wearing my new mask and a new suit and carrying my best intentions. My love for Christine was wrapped around me like a warm cloak. I only wish that letting go of my past had been that easy.

*   *   *

I stood at the altar of the massive, empty cathedral watching Christine walk slowly toward me upon the arm of our good friend. Their footsteps echoed around the vast room, bouncing off the marble surfaces and repeating themselves over and over again. Sunlight streamed through the stained glass windows and threw a kaleidoscope of light and color throughout the sanctuary. I cared nothing about where we were married, but since I knew that Christine would want a church wedding, here I stood. My eyes drifted from the exquisitely lovely young woman wearing white to the rows of empty seats under the sparkling chandeliers and the balconies on either side. How I wished they could be filled to overflowing with the bright colors, lively sounds and joyful weeping of the hundreds of people who should always witness the joining of two people who are in love. My reverie ended as Christine came closer and suddenly she was all I could see. Everything else ceased to exist as my eyes and my mind became filled with the sight of her and my heart threatened to burst with an overpowering love that warmed me like the bright sunshine outside the windows. Her eyes met mine through the thin veil that covered her face and she smiled shyly. She carried fresh flowers, probably provided by dear Louise. Louise stood opposite me to serve as Christine's matron, and her gaze was also fixed on the approaching couple.

Jean and Christine came to stand before me. I moved over to take my place at her side. My knees were so weak I feared they could not possibly support me. I could not take my eyes off Christine. She showed a flicker of surprise when she first saw my new mask, and I could tell that it pleased her as much as it did me. Somehow I managed to repeat the words the priest gave me. We exchanged rings, and when I slid the gold ring from my finger and placed it on hers I thought of the day I had bought it in Paris and of the months I had worn it. Through the haze in my mind I heard the priest tell me I could kiss her. I lifted the veil from Christine's face with shaking hands and laid it down in a white cloud behind her. Her wedding gown was exquisite. Heavily encrusted with pearls and lace overlaying a satin background, it contrasted starkly with her dark hair, which she had left to cascade down her back. I had never beheld anything so lovely in my life. Her face was radiant and I leaned down to briefly kiss her lips; our first kiss as man and wife. I straightened up, wondering what to do next. I had never been to a wedding before. I looked to Jean for help.

"What are you waiting for, man, she's your wife! Kiss her again!" He exclaimed with his usual burst of enthusiasm.

I smiled nervously and turned back to Christine, who was smiling and looking expectantly up at me. Without a moment's more hesitation I pulled her into my arms and kissed her as best I could while wearing the mask. It satisfied our friends, though we both knew how much better it could be in private.

We were not going home as Christine expected, but to the St. Louis Hotel where I had booked their best suite. No separate rooms for us this time. We would go there first to change and then I was taking Christine to dinner and the Opera. They were performing *Faust* tonight, which I knew to be one of her favorites. We had sung it together many times. I was hoping our attendance would renew her interest in her singing. I didn't care if she ever performed in public again, but I did long to hear her beautiful singing voice. We arrived in the lobby of the hotel to find the same older clerk at the desk as on our first day in New Orleans. He looked up and smiled when he noticed our dress, and congratulated us on our marriage. He handed me a key and extracted my promise to contact him directly if we needed anything.

My wife—I loved the sound of that—bashfully took her clothes into the dressing room to change, but not before I stopped her for our first real kiss in private. Without the mask separating us and with our vows binding us, the kiss held all the expected anticipation of what lay ahead. I forced myself to let her go before we got carried away. Anything more between us must wait until we returned from the Opera later that night. Now that she was truly mine, a little of the edge had been taken off my overwhelming rush to possess her. Before today there had always been a question in my mind as to my ability to hold onto her. That was no longer an issue. I could afford to wait until this evening, when I would make this a night Christine would always remember. It didn't bother me that she was too shy to undress in front of me. That would come soon enough. I chuckled as I recalled the reddening of her face when I mentioned changing her clothes. I stripped off my wedding suit and put on a new set of trousers, socks and shoes. I was standing at the washbasin carefully and laboriously shaving what little facial hair I had when I sensed a presence behind me. I turned to find Christine silently staring at me. She was resplendent in a satin and lace gown of deep sapphire. Her hair was piled atop her head in a mass of soft, dark curls with several loose tendrils hanging down around her face. I was naked to the waist, and it occurred to me that she had never seen me without at least a dress shirt covering me.

"I'm sorry," she said nervously as her face began to match the color of her lip rouge. "I didn't mean to...I'll just go back in..."

"No, my love, it's all right," I said quietly. I set down my straightedge and turned to face her. "I am your husband now." I sensed her uneasiness over things to come. She stood in front of me and her eyes slid from my face down over my upper body. I could swear that at first she wore a look of surprise in her wide eyes, as if she were not seeing what she had expected. I wondered if she thought there was anything else unusual about me; possibly something that might rival my face. I had never thought of that before. Had Christine at any time considered that my elegant and expensive dress suits might be hiding further deformities? I didn't know, but as she looked at me the expression in her eyes gradually changed from surprise to admiration. I stood patiently while her virgin eyes examined me. I could almost feel the heat upon my skin from her increasingly appreciative gaze. I spread my hands slightly in a gesture of welcome, and at my slight nod of encouragement, she reached up hesitantly to touch my wet face. Ever so slowly, she slid her hands down my face and over my shoulders and chest to linger on the tight muscles of my abdomen where they met the partially unbuttoned waistband of my trousers. I suppressed a shiver of desire as her hands ran over me. No one had ever touched me like that. In fact, I had always been overly sensitive to anyone touching me in any way at all. Eventually it had become almost a matter of life or death for anyone who so much as laid a hand on me. Christine's hands traveled back up my body to caress my chest and shoulders, then slowly slid down along my arms to my hands. Her eyes remained wide as she looked at me—the first half-naked man she had ever seen up close.

"All this time I never guessed..." she said softly. "You are so beautiful."

My gaze locked into hers as we stood silently holding hands. Christine wanted me. I could read it in her eyes as clear as newsprint. She wanted me as much as I wanted her. Christ, how I wanted her! Against my will, my eyes dropped down from her face to focus upon the flesh above her daringly low cut gown. I hoped she would not recognize the undisguised lust that must have been glowing in my eyes. I tried to control a trembling that was taking root deep down inside me and slowly working its way to the surface, where I feared she would see it. I resisted an overpowering urge to grab her and take her right then and there. A vision of two unused seats at the opera helped me to reach for a towel instead, winding my hands into it to hide the white knuckles that would betray my battle of mind over body. I certainly had no objection to us missing the opera in favor of a more intimate performance, but I was determined not to deviate from my carefully laid plans for the evening. I summoned every last ounce of my self-control to break the overwhelming sexual tension between us. I dried my face and leaned down to kiss her quickly and lightly.

"There is much more where this came from," I said suggestively. I winked wickedly at her and she blushed. "But there is no time for that now. We must leave for dinner."

*   *   *

The fact that I was willing to attend an event like the Opera was a testament to how far I had come from living like a rat in the cellars. It was far more crowded than the music room of the ship and I was very nervous about it. Christine must have sensed it as we rode over in the darkened carriage, because she held my hand in her lap and kept patting it reassuringly. The improvement of the new mask over the old one made me feel a bit braver about the whole idea but my knees were weak. We walked in the door and were immediately surrounded in the lobby by the people of New Orleans.

The French Opera House in New Orleans, with its red carpeting, towering mirrors and gleaming crystal chandeliers, was the center for the cream of New Orleans society. It had been built from the profits of the New Orleans Lottery. I had no use for the silliness of the regular gatherings for the feverishly anticipated announcement of the winning numbers but I certainly appreciated this magnificent monument to the huge cash flow involved. Much like the Opera Populaire in Paris, it was *the* place to be seen. And seen I was. Almost everyone who saw me that night did some amount of staring, but when they noticed the radiant Christine on my arm many of them seemed to lose interest in me. Those who did not simply moved away from us. Her beauty was overwhelming, and even the curious looks of many of the other women present were drawn quickly away from me by my beautiful wife. I noted with relief that no one appeared ready to run screaming from the room. A good thing I had gotten over my phobia about mirrors, for the massive panels of reflective glass were everywhere. The jewelry that flashed on the necks, ears and fingers of the ladies coupled with the chandeliers in the lobby were multiplied many times over in the huge mirrors, making the entire lobby incredibly bright. Soon we were able to take our private box seats and I could relax. I had attended many an opera, but, admittedly, had never enjoyed any of them from a legitimately purchased seat.

Christine enjoyed the performance immensely, as did I. I actually caught her singing softly along once or twice. Little did the audience in the house that night guess that within their midst sat one of the Paris Opera's most successful divas (accompanied, I might add, by its most successful Opera Ghost.). All humor aside, I thought of the tragic waste of Christine's beautiful voice never being heard in public again. I glanced over to observe the rapture on her face. I squeezed her hand and forced my attention back to the action on the stage.

Faust had one of the most sublime of scores; it was certainly Gounod's best work. This particular opera would always be dear to me, for its success and popularity were responsible for the building of the Paris Opera House. Sitting on the front edge of her seat, Christine's face showed her joy as she enjoyed the soaring strains of the Soldier's Chorus. More than once I had reflected on the parallel between this wonderful story and my own life. Like Faust, I had thought of death often during my loneliest times. Faust desired youth and was willing to sell his soul to the devil to attain it. I had desired love, and I had been the devil incarnate in my search for it. I alone had triumphed, for Faust lost everything in the end while I won my beautiful wife. It pleased me to see that she remembered and seemed to still enjoy the music. Her face was a study in contentment as the final trio was performed. I sincerely hoped this night was what she needed to get us back on the musical track we had enjoyed so much in Paris.

All too soon it was over. As our carriage drew up to the hotel's entrance, its magnificent dome was outlined against the night sky. The hotel was designed in a Classical Revival style, and I had made a mental note to study the dome when we first arrived in the city. It had been built using a method not seen for over 1400 years. It employed the use of an earthen shell constructed like a honeycomb, thus making it much lighter in weight. New Orleans, having been built on a swamp, needed architects who understood the city's unique needs. The St. Louis Hotel's dome was a fine example of adapting a design to the surrounding area. While I was distracted by the local architecture, Christine was silent for the entire ride.

I had thought about this night for a very long time. Ever since I was old enough to know of such things I had been thinking about the time when it would happen to me. As I grew older and it appeared that it would never happen, there remained a small hope that I could find a way to experience, in some fashion, what happened between a man and a woman. I never tried to pay for it; I said earlier that I could not have accepted having my money refused. I suppose I could have found someone who would take my money if I tried hard enough, but the thought of lying with a dirty stranger in a filthy roach filled room down on the waterfront did not appeal to me. My standards were too high for that. So I had waited patiently for almost fifty years, if you count from the day I was born. And I do count from that day, because I received no love whatsoever even as an infant. Love in some form is a necessary human condition. Without it we wither and die a slow, lingering death, as I had been doing over a period of many years.

I had been to the ends of the earth and back in my lifetime, but never found what I was looking for. It had found me. I now shared my love with a beautiful woman and I was about to experience the physical joys of that love. We had inevitably grown more physically intense in our anticipation of being together and it was enough to give me an idea of what lay ahead. Of course, it was the same for Christine. She had not waited as long as I had, but we would discover it together. We came to it from two different worlds, but the result would be the same for each of us. My only advantage was that I had been witness many times to the love-making of others. That may sound rather crude, but I had seen places where those living in the civilized world would not believe the customs. I believed I knew how to make our first experience enjoyable for us both. Yes, I was nervous. I just didn't want Christine to know it.

Christine still hadn't said much when I opened the door to our suite and followed her inside. She casually dropped her wrap and reticule on the chair by the window and stood looking down at the street below. It was very late and the last of the opera crowds were disappearing into their homes and hotels. I closed the door gently and walked up behind her, putting my arms around her waist and kissing the back of her head. She played with the two new rings on her finger. When she felt me behind her she rested her head back against me and sighed.

"Did you enjoy the opera, Mrs. Devereaux?" I asked, using the name for the first time. My lips traveled down behind her ear to her exposed shoulder as my hand crept down her leg and back up again.

"Yes, Mr. Devereaux, very much," she replied. She turned around in my arms to face me. "Erik, I…"

"I know," I said as I took her face in my hands and kissed her softly. "Why don't you get ready for bed?" At her somewhat stricken look, I tried to comfort her. "Really, Christine, it will be all right. We are married now, and the moment is here for us to be together. Don't worry, I'll take care of you."

She gathered her things and left the room. I prepared myself as quickly as possible; I wanted to be ready when she came out. I turned the lamps out but for one small one and removed everything but my trousers and mask. I didn't want to shock her too much all at once, and the sight of a completely naked man standing there may have given her apoplexy. I decided to give her the option on the mask, just in case. I turned down the bed and, after performing my own toilet, went to the darkened window to wait for her. The stars were brilliant and moonlight filled the room as if the heavens were trying to show us the way.

I never heard her come into the room; I felt her presence behind me. I turned and my sharp intake of breath revealed how beautiful she was. She wore a white silk gown trimmed in lace. Surely intended for a wedding night, it was full and flowing and closed in the front with tiny ties of white satin ribbon.

"Christine, you are the most beautiful woman in the world," I said, taking her hand and kissing it.

"And you are the most handsome man," she whispered and reached up behind my head to untie and remove the mask from my face. I ached with love and leaned down to her.

She responded shyly at first, barely caressing my lips with hers. Our lips met and came away countless times as we tentatively tasted each other, taking and giving a little more of ourselves with each tiny kiss. I felt her warm, sweet breath on my ugly face as my lips discovered hers with gentle determination. I savored their soft moistness, then allowed my lips to travel over her eyes, to nibble an ear and then slide back once again to her mouth, where I lightly traced the shape of her lips with the tip of my tongue. A deep sigh escaped her and suddenly she was kissing me back with a passion I had only glimpsed before. I pulled her against me and her arms encircled my neck to draw us even closer together. Deeper and deeper our kisses became until soon they were no longer enough. My heart was racing when I raised my head to look into her darkened eyes. I picked her up and carried her to the bed, laying her down gently on the fresh linen. I lay down beside her and we continued kissing while our hands discovered each other and our passion built higher and higher. I was drowning in my passion for her. I never imagined that being with a woman could feel like this. Darkness enveloped us when a cloud moved across the moon and I felt exhilarated and free in the familiar, cloaking blackness. My hands sought every part of her and I could not get close enough to her. Then I began to realize that something was wrong.

As my passion rose higher and I felt myself getting lost in the sense of her, something else that should have been happening to me...wasn't. I slowed down, figuring that I was pushing myself too far too fast. I kissed Christine's face, her hair, her neck and on down to the first ribbon on her gown. I slowly untied it, spreading the silk just a bit. I followed the opening with my lips. She was breathing heavily and her hands were at the back of my head, drawing me down to her. I drew my hand slowly down the front of her thin gown, intimately feeling everything that lay beneath it. She moaned softly and her eyes closed. Nothing I did helped me. I was mortified. My lips returned to hers as I desperately sought to force myself into the correct response. My passion was quickly dissipating. I didn't know what I was going to tell her. My own body was committing the ultimate betrayal against me, and there was nothing I could do about it. I drew away from her. Christine opened her eyes and knew something was wrong.

"Erik, what is it?" she asked tentatively.

"Nothing," I muttered, wildly trying to think of a way out of the situation. All I could think of was my own shame and humiliation. Then I panicked, and did something that illustrated my complete lack of experience in dealing with other people and my deeply ingrained tendency to think only of myself. Still wearing my trousers, I jumped up from the bed and quickly gathered my other clothing.

"Erik?"

I could not answer her. I blindly went for the door and wrenched it open, only to remember the damned mask. After a panic-stricken moment of not remembering where it was, I snatched it up and left the room, slamming the door behind me.

I hoped no one would come by and see me hurriedly dressing myself in the hallway. I saw no one and made my way quickly to the street below. I shook with humiliation when I stepped out into the darkness. I walked aimlessly down the street, wondering what to do with myself, until I heard the sounds from a nearby saloon. Well, it was better than wandering the streets, and a good shot or two might calm me.

After openly staring at me, the barkeeper finally served me what I ordered. I rudely asked him what in hell he was staring at. He loudly planted a bottle of whiskey and a glass on the bar in front of me and walked away, muttering under his breath. No doubt he wanted to throw me out on my ear but he had no valid excuse to do so. Now in a thoroughly foul mood, I thanked him sarcastically and took them up, leaving several crumpled bills in their place. I didn't bother to count them. I went to a table in the far corner, well away from the few drunks who populated the place. Only after I had quickly finished off two full glasses of whiskey with a shaking hand did I calm down enough to think about what had gone wrong.

What in hell had happened to me? This was my wedding night, for Christ's sake! Granted, I had never done it before, but the signs were there that I was perfectly capable of performing given the chance. My virility was unquestionable! I thought of what Christine must be thinking back at the hotel, and dropped my masked face into my hands, shaking my head. *I'll take care of you.* That's what I told her. I had been so damned sure of myself. I was an egotistical jackass and a self-centered fool.

I had just finished my third glass and was feeling more relaxed when I noticed someone standing silently at my table. I did not look up.

"Go ahead, stare if you want."

There was no reply. I continued examining the bottom of my empty glass and demanded, "Tell me what in hell you want or leave me alone."

"You a little out of your element here are you?" a voice said.

"Meaning?" I asked, still not looking up. I reached for the bottle instead.

"Meaning I'd have guessed you'd be over near Marie's instead of in this part of town."

Without an invitation, the man sat down with a grunt across the table from me while I poured myself another glassful. The neck of the bottle clinked against the glass and I realized my hand was still shaking slightly. The last thing I wanted was to talk, but I finally raised my eyes to look at him. He was a nondescript, heavyset man with a cigar and a rough manner.

"Marie?"

"Marie Laveau. You never heard of her? Jesus, you look like one of her people." Noting my lack of understanding he continued. "Marie's the Queen of the Voodoos. She's the one to see if you've got a problem you want taken care of, if you know what I mean." He had lowered his voice to a conspiratorial whisper.

Voodoo? Perhaps this was my opportunity to find out about the strange practices that fascinated me so much.

"Where do I find her?"

The man eyed me warily and flicked the ashes from his cigar onto the middle of my table. He'd been sucking on it so long that the end of it looked like a piece of meat and there was a trail of brown spittle down his once-white shirtfront. After taking another juicy drag from it, he rudely blew a column of smoke past my right ear.

"And what's it to you?" he asked.

I have little patience for those who would dangle a tidbit of information before me only to refuse to elaborate. I began to tell him to leave when he reconsidered.

"Okay, okay. Prob'ly won't do no harm. You look like you might need her services yourself." He lowered his voice and leaned across the table toward me. "And we can always use one more, if you know what I mean." He sat back. A nasty grin approached the corners of his mouth, which quickly disappeared at the look in my eyes. "She's got a cottage over on St. Anne, between North Rampart and Burgundy," he said, getting up from the table. "Tell her Francois sent you." He walked away without another word.

Now what in hell was that all about? I subconsciously filed the information away in the vast library of my mind for future reference.

I stayed with my whiskey for a long time, swallowing another glassful of it before I even noticed how little was left in the bottle. Christ, I hadn't drunk that much in years. I felt sleepy and decided I'd better get back to Christine. I owed her an explanation, if I could find one. The little wife, I told myself, who by this time should have been good and properly laid by her strong and handsome husband. But no, I sit in a goddamned saloon all alone and drinking like a fish on my wedding night. The mysterious, powerful and talented Erik, I thought bitterly. You can make women swoon and men obey with your voice alone, but you can't even bed your own wife. A poor excuse for a husband, if you ask me. "Well, who asked you?" I said aloud into my empty glass.

I had been a fool to think that I could make this thing work between Christine and me, and an even bigger fool to think I could live a normal life like any other man. I should have stayed in my safe, dark cellar and been content with the goddamned rats for company. I could hand myself enough rejection to last a lifetime. I didn't need to be out here in this nasty world to get that. Experience had taught me again and again that being alone was all I should ever expect from life. What in hell was I trying to prove, and to whom? I had brought Christine nothing but grief so far. It was inexplicable to me why the woman had stayed with me this long. She must now loathe me as much as I loathed myself.

I poured one more full glass, drawing the process out as I watched the whiskey trickle out of the neck of the bottle into the clear glass. The liquid became darker with the rising level. When it reached the top I looked at the bottle and at the inch or so of whiskey that was left in it. I picked up the glass and sipped it slowly, swirling it around with my tongue and savoring the flavor and the feel of it going down my throat.

Hell, I'd made a good botch of this night—made a complete mess of things. I was drunk as a skunk and now must go back and face my beautiful young wife with shame in my eyes and liquor on my breath. A fine state of affairs, and not part of my meticulous plan.

I eyed the last of the whiskey. I had finally had enough. Though my capacity for alcohol was high, I had consumed most of the bottle and I was going to pay dearly for it. I could not remember when I had last been this inebriated. Right. I really should stop putting on so many airs. Who was I kidding but myself? Inebriated? I was goddamned drunk. In my former line of work, if you could call it that, one's instincts and awareness were paramount to one's self-preservation, which allowed little room for any interference with one's faculties. In more recent years my imported wines and brandies had smoothed the rougher edges of my life, but I had lost my taste for any heavy drinking years ago. Drinking was for cowards and fools. I had been away from that other life for too long and I was getting careless.

I slowly got to my feet and walked out and down the street. I found my way unsteadily to the hotel and up to our room. I struggled to get my fingers around the damned key in my pocket. After several moments of clumsy fumbling around the tiny keyhole, I opened the door to find Christine asleep in the bed, almost as I had left her. I also noticed in the moonlight that her face still showed the streaks of her tears. I was relieved that I would not have to face her again that night. My failure had shaken me to the core. I wished there was somewhere to hide, but I no longer had anywhere else to go. Thoughts of my lonely refuge under the opera pricked my heart. An image of it waiting safe and dark and silent for someone who would never return filled my mind. I forced the thought away. That trusting young girl in the bed before me was my wife now, and she was my responsibility. All my scheming and planning got me what I wanted, and now I was damn well going to have to fix it. I took off my coat, trousers and shoes and crawled meekly into the side of the bed, staying on the edge and taking care not to disturb her. My first night sharing a bed with Christine and she didn't even know it. Yes, you've really done it now, I angrily told myself. You've been married less than one day and you've already let her down.

I had let her down terribly, and I dreaded what the morning would bring.

*   *   *

I awoke with the inevitable headache. I reached toward Christine and felt nothing. I turned my head and blinked painfully in the bright light, only to find that she wasn't there. I hauled myself up on one elbow and saw her sitting, fully dressed, in the chair across the room. Thank God she hadn't walked out on me, although I thought she had the perfect right to do just that.

"Christine," I mumbled groggily, rubbing my eyes. "What... time is it?"

"Half past nine," she said flatly.

I fell back on the pillow and swore under my breath.

"I want to go home," she stated, and stalked to the dressing room for her things. Fighting the sick feeling in my stomach and my pounding head, I quickly crawled out of the bed and got my trousers on. I was a complete disgrace, having slept in my shirt. I tucked it in anyway, hoping it would be all right. I didn't feel well either. Christ, I'd forgotten how bad a hangover could be. I met her coming out of the dressing room struggling with her small trunk.

"Let me help you with that," I said, wrestling it from her and setting it on the floor. "I need to talk to you."

"You should have done that last night," she said curtly, staring in disgust at my disheveled clothing and wrinkling her nose. "You have been drinking."

"Yes, Christine," I said wearily, wincing as the throbbing in my head threatened to split it in two. "Regrettably, I have been drinking, and I fear I have presented you with a decidedly unsavory introduction to married life." I spread my arms carelessly, swaying a bit on my feet. "Behold your new husband, who is at this moment presenting a slightly different picture than what you're used to, heh?" At the stony look on her face I dropped my arms and became serious. "Sit down...please. I will explain myself but you must excuse me for just a moment."

She stared at me with disgust written all over her face. After what appeared to be a moment's indecision, she sat herself rigidly in the chair and waited. I went to the corner and lowered my whole face into a basin of cold water. Straightening up, I reached for a towel and a drink of water and caught sight of myself in the mirror. Christ Almighty! If I were she, I'd walk out the door right now rather than face me. I leaned on the washstand and took a deep breath before I turned back to her.

Her veneer of cold indifference was cracking and she fidgeted with the handkerchief in her lap. The hurt in her eyes plunged a knife through my heart.

I eased myself down onto the edge of the bed facing her and closed my eyes momentarily while the pounding in my head subsided. There was no way around it. This situation of my own making presented me with one of the most important decisions I would ever make. I was accustomed to using manipulation and intimidation to get what I wanted, and either obscuring the truth or lying outright when it benefited me to do so. But if I lied to Christine now she would know it, and I might as well go directly to the lobby this minute and book her passage back to France. If I wanted her to stay I would have to be honest with her, no matter how much it wounded my pride and my masculinity. She had a right to know why her husband of eight hours had abruptly abandoned her bed amidst the throes of passion on the most special night of a woman's life. Christ, thinking about it like that made me feel even worse about what I had done. *Just tell her the truth.*

"I went to a saloon and got disgustingly drunk." I took another breath. She sat stiffly watching me and the silence stretched between us. I plunged in again before I lost my nerve. "Everything was going so well yesterday. We had our beautiful wedding and suddenly I had a beautiful wife on my arm. We had a lovely dinner and went to the opera. Everything was perfect until...until..." She was waiting. *Just say it and apologize before she walks out on you!*

I got up and nervously paced the room. I didn't know how to explain it, so I swallowed my pride with an audible gulp and just spit it out.

"Until I tried to make love to that beautiful wife." She looked at me in alarm and I rushed on. "I couldn't...it just didn't...I don't understand it, Christine, I don't know what went wrong." I was talking too fast, the words were gushing out and I couldn't stop them. "I wanted it to be so perfect for you and all along it was me I should have been worrying about. It must have been too long, much too long that I've waited for this. I never thought I would have that kind of problem, and I wanted you so much...I've always been so sure of myself and of my ability to...to..." I ran out of steam and looked at her helplessly. Trying to be honest with someone for once in my life was proving to be quite difficult.

"To what, Erik," she asked gently, "to be my husband?"

I sat back down weakly, holding my head in my hands. "Christine, I shouldn't have run out on you like that. I'm sorry. I didn't know what to do, I was so embarrassed," I admitted in a whisper, not looking at her. Lord, this woman was wise beyond her years. I continued to talk to the floor. "Christ, Christine, all the months I have been holding myself back, fighting my desire for you." I looked up at her to note the surprise on her face. "Yes, my love, months. I have needed you from the first moment I saw you. I didn't want to frighten or hurt you. But Christine, no matter how hard the waiting was for me, I could never force myself on you. It's been hard, Christine, so very hard to wait and to hide my feelings all this time. That's why I don't understand what happened when I finally had the chance to show you how I feel about you." I looked at the floor again. I could not meet her eyes. "Maybe I can't when it comes right down to it. Perhaps it's just been too long and that part of me is gone. Maybe I'm just too old." Resignation flooded into my voice. "I'm too old for you, Christine. You were right. You are a healthy young woman with needs that I obviously can't fill. I don't blame you if you decide you have to leave now. We can get the marriage annulled...you can go back to Paris and..."

She had been listening quietly to my shameful agony without moving. My heart was dead and heavy in my chest at the thought of ending the marriage before it even began. I could not forgive myself for what I had done to her. Not only had I not been a proper husband to her, to make matters even worse I had left our bed with rude haste and without a word of explanation. My foolish damnable pride would now be responsible for the end of my dream.

She rose from her chair and came to sit next to me on the bed. "I'm not going anywhere, Erik," she said softly. "You are more of a man than anyone I have ever known...the strongest man I have ever known. How else could you have survived what you did for all the years that it took for me to find you?" She paused and all that could be heard was the ticking of the clock. "But why didn't you just tell me? When you left our bed I thought I was doing something wrong and that you'd had enough of me. That I didn't know how to..." She appeared close to tears.

"Oh, no, my love," I said emphatically, lifting my head to look toward the window. I was close to tears myself. "You could never disappoint me like that. No one ever taught me how to love, Christine. I don't know what I'm doing." I finally met her eyes and saw with relief that the love was still there. "You keep saving me from myself, Christine, and I don't know how to thank you except to tell you again and again that I love you more than life itself. Please don't ever leave me."

"I won't leave you, Erik. I love you," she said, putting her arm around my shoulders. "Maybe when we're home again things will be better. Please take me home, Erik."

I turned within the curve of her arm and pulled her to me, burying my face in her shoulder. Tears of relief threatened to overwhelm

me but I choked them back. I asked for her indulgence while I went
to clean up a bit and then I took her home.

12

───────────── ★ ─────────────

I considered it important to treat our return home as something special, as if we had never been there before. If I wanted to split hairs, I could say that we hadn't, at least as man and wife. Ignoring the painful throbbing in my head, I leaned down to sweep Christine into my arms and carry her through the front door. Our homecoming was, on the surface, a happy affair but I could not cast off the lingering doubts in my mind and the shame of the previous night. Our marriage had begun on a sour note and it was my fault. Christine seemed to have forgotten the incident but I could not.

After enjoying a quiet noon meal in our wonderfully private courtyard, Christine decided to nap and I retreated to the parlor to work on my music. I did not blame her for the nap on our first day home; she had probably gotten little sleep on her wedding night, but for all the wrong reasons. For the time being, I had no desire to touch her. It was the first day in many months that my intense passion failed to rise at the very sight of her. Thoughts of my failure haunted me all that day.

Deliah had worked wonders in cleaning up the parlor after the mess I made there. My musical scores had been piled carefully back on the piano and the ink cleaned out of the carpets. My pens and other instruments were arranged on the side table and all the books were back on their shelves. Unbroken mantel items were restored to their places. I decided first to go right out to the servant's quarters and thank her in person for her consideration. I wore my new mask and hoped she would not find me quite so frightening in it. To my surprise, I found that feelings such as this were no longer part of an act. I actually cared. As I walked out there I could not help but recall the terrified looks on the faces of my servants when they witnessed my violent temper only a week before. The memory made me all the more appreciative of this opportunity to express my gratitude to Deliah. She had been doing a wonderful job for us and I was very bothered by her continued fear of me.

Not seeing Robert about, I knocked on the door softly. Deliah opened it but as soon as she saw who had come to visit she shrank back into the darkness of the room. At least she didn't close the door in my face. I stood on the doorstep without moving.

"Deliah," I began. "I am grateful for your hard work in cleaning up the unfortunate results of my deplorable temper. I am sorry you were witness to that."

She remained where she was, but she was listening to me so I decided to go on. "I trust that Robert explained to you long ago about my accident and my wish to cover my face in public? I am sorry that I still frighten you so; I do not mean to do that."

She still did not say anything, but I had said enough. I cleared my throat awkwardly.

"Well, anyway, I wanted to thank you myself for the fine work you and Robert are doing for us. Good day."

I returned to the house and lost myself in my composing. I was working on several large pieces, which I may or may not put together at some point. It had taken me many years to compose the amount of music that I had stored on the shelves and here on the piano. It was a pity no one would ever hear it.

*   *   *

After a late dinner I sat in the parlor reading the *Picayune*. The warm darkness outside the open windows enveloped the house with a feeling of homey comfort and the fragrance of bougainvillea and jasmine filled the air over the smell of tropical dampness. The smell of the night air had become one of my favorite things about New Orleans. (I must say that when I opened my trunk to unpack it in our new home I was appalled at the odor that escaped from it. The dank and musty smell of the cellars hit me full in the face, and I was horrified to discover that everything I owned smelled like that. I lost no time in replacing what I could and giving the rest a good airing. It is an odor I hope never to encounter again.) The only sounds were the clock ticking and the rustling of my paper when Christine appeared beside my chair.

"Erik, I'm going to bed," she said softly. "Are you coming up?"

Was it that late? I had lost all track of the time. I was taken completely off guard when I looked up from my paper to see her dressed in the same gown she'd had on the night before. Her soft dark hair framed her face and her eyes were dark. I laid the paper and my mask aside and reached for her hand, drawing her down onto my lap. She cuddled like a child in the shelter of my arms with her head on my shoulder. Neither of us spoke. I put my arms around my wife, rested my head back against the chair and closed my eyes. We sat that way silently for a while, enjoying the closeness that now felt different; we were really and truly married. She was mine and no one would ever take her from me.

Christine lifted her face to me and I bent my head to her. I felt around on the table for the lamp and put it out. My hand sought

the front of her thin gown to feel the shape of her body beneath
it. I untied a couple of the ribbons and slid my hand inside. I had
never known softness like that, and at the same time my hand felt
as if it were on fire. Still kissing me, she began to undo the buttons
of my shirt. The chair in which we sat would not do for much
longer. I moved us to the edge of it and rose to my feet with
Christine in my arms. She laid her head on my shoulder and I
carried her up the stairs to the bedroom, setting her down just
inside the French doors where the moonlight reached us. I stood
staring at her, suddenly unable to move. My confidence had been
broken and I was frozen with the memory of it. The last thing I
wanted to do was hurt her again. Sensing my reluctance, Christine
continued to undo the buttons of my shirt. Slowly and
deliberately, she followed each opened button with tiny kisses. She
pulled the shirt from my trousers, reached up and drew it slowly
down over my arms, and dropped it on the floor. I closed my eyes
as her hesitant, inexperienced but loving hands explored me like
before. This time there was no rush to go anywhere. She reached
up to trace my uneven features with her fingers, once again
illustrating her apparently total lack of concern over the
appearance of my face.

"I don't know if I can..." I whispered.

"Don't," she interrupted as she moved her fingers across my lips.

Standing on her toes, Christine's lips gently brushed mine with
the softness of a feather. Then, as I stood there in total disbelief,
she began to spread slow, gentle kisses all over my horrible face.
Her lips were soft and moist, and if I'd harbored any lingering
doubts about her tolerance of my ugliness, they were now gone
forever. My internal fire ignited with a sudden rush of heat. She
brought her lips back to mine and whispered my name against my
mouth, making it sound sensual and erotic. I took her face in my
hands and began to kiss her again, hesitantly at first, then with

more confidence as her lips parted and let me in. It wasn't long before I found myself once more falling into that special place in my mind where everything but Christine disappeared.

"Love me, Erik," she whispered in my ear as my lips moved down over her throat.

The way she caressed those three simple words totally undid me. Thoughts of the previous evening's disaster went out of my head as if it had never happened. I fingered the tiny ribbons of her gown and slowly untied them one by one. I pushed the garment from her shoulders and watched it fall in a white cloud at her feet. Christ, she was lovely! The sight of her nakedness after all the months of my dreaming about it drove me mad with desire. I picked her up and turned to lay her down in the middle of our bed.

I slowly divested myself of the remainder of my own clothing as she lay there watching me. I hid nothing when I finally stood naked and proud in the moonlight. My former confidence returned to me in a rush as I looked at her lying on the bed. As long as I live, I will never forget the sight of my beautiful Christine lying naked and waiting for me on that night. I dropped the last item on the floor and joined her on the bed. Feeling her softness against the full length of my naked body drove my passion higher, and I began to kiss her again, deeper and deeper until we were a part of each other. Instincts as old as time itself took over, guiding and teaching me. Moving away from her mouth, my lips and hands covered every inch of her body, bringing her with me into a new world of erotic sensation and discovery. Shyly at first, she touched and explored what she had never before seen. Her touch grew more confident as her own passion mounted. She was breathing heavily and I was literally drowning in my desire, being pulled relentlessly beneath the surface of reality into the depths of a world of incomparable need. When I thought neither of us could

possibly take any more, I moved over her and, with great tenderness, slowly enclosed myself in her warmth and her love.

Later that night I lay awake with my sleeping wife curled
against me, her head on my shoulder and my arm around her. The
woman who now slept so peacefully in my arms had given me
more than she would ever know. No one can possibly imagine
what was in my heart that night as I held her sleeping body in the
warm afterglow of our first union. For the first time in my life, I
had competed with other men on the battlefield of love and I had
won. This woman had chosen to marry *me*. It was true that I had
pushed her, but in the end the final choice had been hers alone.
She had accepted me first as a human being and then she had
accepted me as a man.

When I first saw Christine I was teetering on the brink of
becoming completely emotionless and was well on my way to
becoming totally inhuman. I was doomed to live the remainder of
my life in a cold stone vacuum that promised to be even emptier
than all the years that preceded it combined. Christine pulled me
back from the edge at the very last possible moment; only just
before I began my final plunge into the darkness of a true living
hell. I had been very close to dying of loneliness and I hadn't even
known it.

Her tiny hand, adorned with its two rings, lay upon my chest
and moved slowly up and down with each breath I took. Those
rings were the symbols of my new life. I put my hand over hers
and she stirred, nestling her body even closer to mine. *Oh,
Christine. You will never know how much you mean to me.* The
tears began. Falling down the sides of my hideous face, they wet
my pillow and Christine's hair. I cried myself to sleep.

I thought a lot about what happened to me on our wedding
night. I had undoubtedly built the event up so high in my mind
that I fell apart under the pressure of my own impossibly high

standards. The false start backed me off and shook my infallible image of myself just enough so when it finally did happen my expectations of myself were far more realistic. I allowed my body to take the lead over my mind for the first time and, in doing so, relinquished all concern over my obsessive need to control every moment. Spontaneity is a difficulty concept for one who is accustomed to the studied manipulation of everything around one. I was discovering that the path of human relationship cannot be charted. It must be left to seek its own way, either good or bad. I had forcibly set us on our present course, and now I must learn to stand back and let it go.

*   *   *

The days that followed were filled with the discovery of each other at night and the city by day. We took the streetcar and our own carriage all over the city. I held Christine's hand tightly during our first few streetcar rides when I felt the hot stares of the people all around me. The new mask definitely was an improvement, and for the most part people said nothing to us. They did not wish to be so openly rude but they could not hide their fascination with a man wearing a mask. Their eyes darted from me to Christine and back again as if they could not believe that such a beautiful woman would accompany someone who wore a mask in public. Then they would make a supreme effort to cast their gaze elsewhere. I'm sure they wondered if it were my appearance or my sanity that was in question. Once in a while someone would move to another seat. Over time I began to relax a bit; there was only so much discomfort to be felt over these situations. The problem would never go away, and I had to get used to it. It was as simple as that.

Christine delighted in the gardens and the windows of the many shops, and I continued my lifelong observation of architecture.

The city was a vast mix of every kind of architectural influence, especially beyond the streets of the French Quarter. I saw evidence of American, Spanish, Greek, Georgian, French and other unidentified styles that took their roots from the American South. Homes in the newer American section of town, called the Garden District, were massive but splendid mansions; spacious and often painted snow white with wide single and double verandahs supported by massive white columns of Doric or Ionic designs. These mansions sat on expansive manicured grounds overflowing with lush greens, white crepe myrtle trees, roses, iris, bougainvillea, magnolias, azaleas and many other colorful blossoms. The whole area was like one huge garden. The combined scent from all these blooms wafted on the humid breezes and created a fragrant backdrop to compliment the quiet streets shaded by towering oaks. While many of the houses were elegantly designed and very pleasing to the eye, I could not say the same for some of the public buildings. As an example, the massively granite U.S. Customs House is absolutely devoid of any design whatsoever. For sheer insult to the architectural mind, there is the Bank of Louisiana Building. Nothing is centered, pilasters do not line up with pedestals; in short it is a ghastly enough work that the designer should have been taken out and shot. I enjoyed the elegant symmetry of the French Opera House, and having had so much input into the same in Paris I had inquired about its designer. I wished to talk to this man Gallier who was so famous in these parts. Alas, I was told that he had been lost at sea some years ago.

The little "shotgun" cottages charmed Christine. Very popular here, they were so named because their rooms lined up with one another along with the doors. It was said that if all doors were opened one could shoot a shotgun through the front door and it would exit the back without hitting anything in between.

Everywhere we found the ornate iron balconies and railings that were so much a part of this city we had come to love. We explored the city, ate in restaurants, went to operas, sailed the Mississippi and in general had a very grand time.

At the end of all our days, no matter where the evening found us—in a hotel, on a riverboat or in our own comfortable home— we had each other. I could not get enough of the sight and the feel of Christine by my side and I reached for her every chance I had. We continued to explore new ways of pleasing each other as our passion grew with each passing day. Christine lost her little girl looks and her body filled out to that of a very desirable woman. She also quickly lost her naiveté in matters of the bedroom. I discovered that she was an extremely passionate lover once her initial shyness had gone and she had begun to learn how to please a man. I loved the surprisingly passionate nature that finally emerged in her but I'll have to admit that at times she wore me out.

We had been extremely lucky that there were no other serious incidents such as the one on the streets of Norfolk. I had dealt with my share of uncomfortable situations since coming to New Orleans, but they were easily handled and fortunately Christine was not always with me when these minor incidents occurred. As a couple, we simply avoided several establishments that had shown me less than average courtesy but the fear of another true confrontation remained in the back of my mind. It was to be expected as far as I was concerned; I could not forget the treatment that I had received in the past. I knew much of the reason we had been left alone was because of Christine's presence at my side. Most people, ignorant or not, are reluctant to cause trouble when there is a woman involved. To be honest, I felt that our luck would soon run out. I lived with that knowledge hanging over my head but I said nothing to my wife. My premonitions proved accurate during the cool months of that winter of late 1882, although the incident had nothing to do with my face.

It was reasonably early on that evening just before Christmas although it was already dark. The day's drizzle had finally stopped and left a cold and damp atmosphere behind it. I was feeling restless. I had spent the entire day at the piano and my legs were feeling achy from the cramped position and inactivity. I went upstairs to tell Christine I was going for a walk.

"Must we go out in this miserable wet, Erik? I don't feel like getting cold," she pouted, snuggling deeper into the big chair where she had retreated with a book.

"I shall go alone. The cold will bother me less than the ache in my legs at this moment, my dear," I replied, going over to give her a long kiss. She touched me suggestively, trying with an innocent expression to interest me in something a little more involved.

"Not now, my love," I smiled warmly at her efforts. "I really do need that walk."

"Well, be careful," she said, going back to her book.

At the front door I donned hat and cloak and stepped out into the misty night.

I walked for a long time. How I missed the soothing darkness! It had been such a large and important part of my life for so long. I'd been away from my dark home under the Opera for little more than eight months, but it felt like a lifetime and I found it hard to think back on it. I still loved the darkness. Along with my memories of the friend the darkness had always been to me, I now had my memories of more recent nights, in which the darkness meant something totally different. It meant my time alone with Christine.

I was lost in my thoughts and wandered further afield than I intended. I found myself on the outskirts of the Quarter on North Rampart Street. I was just thinking that I'd better turn back when I passed a particularly dark building. Too late, I saw the three men who silently emerged to walk closely behind me. I hoped it was coincidence. I tensed when I heard their footsteps slow down when mine did. I began to walk faster but two massive arms grabbed me from behind, pinning my arms to my sides. The man who held me was even taller than I am, and considerably heavier. I could not use my hands to any effect. I could do nothing. My mind flashed back in memory to a similar circumstance from when I was very young but I was brought abruptly back to the present when one of them spoke.

"Quick, get it!" A gruff voice said to my left. Hands began searching my clothing on both sides. It was money they were after! I rarely carried much cash on me, preferring to have Jean handle most of my acquisitions. If it was money they wanted, let them have it. I put my head down to shield the mask from their eyes. I put up just enough struggle to make them think they had me good. I sensed a slight relaxation of the arms which held me captive while the other two were trying to count the bills they had taken from me. With a growl I heaved both of my arms up and dislodged the big man's grip on me. I ducked out of it, knocking my hat from my head and exposing the mask. I hoped the light was too dim for them to see much and was thankful for the realistic color of the leather.

I dropped one of the men to the ground with a well-placed elbow to his chin and turned to look for the others. All I wanted was to get back to Christine. My careless complacency of recent months had dulled my combative reactions and I had difficulty tracking the movements of all three men. The killer instinct in me was not as strong as it used to be. I did not have the lasso on me. In short, I was totally unprepared. It was ironic that now, when for the first time I had a reason to keep myself alive, I was no longer at the peak of my defensive prowess.

I had just delivered a hefty left into the second man's gut when I was hit over the head from behind with something heavy. The few street lamps in the distance swam before my eyes and I swayed on my feet until a second blow dropped me heavily to my knees. I tried to get my bearings. The blows to my head were severe but I was conscious enough to realize they were not through with me.

The first brutal kick knocked me over onto my side. I wrapped my arms tightly around my head to protect it from further harm. I have endured many beatings in my life but few had been worse than the one I received on that winter's night. The blows came at me from every direction, connecting solidly with every part of my body. Working together as an efficient team, the men were strong and obviously well versed in how to inflict the most agony possible in the shortest time. Pain exploded inside me as one heavy boot connected with my kidneys just as I received another directly in my gut. I tried to curl up into a ball, but that left my back horribly exposed and open to invitation. They worked me over good. I heard their heavy panting over the roaring in my ears and I could no longer hold my fetal position. I had rolled over onto my back and was losing consciousness when I heard a gruff voice above me.

"Damn, look at that fool! He don't even know Mardi Gras ain't started yet!"

For some reason they didn't touch the mask. I still don't know why. I heard their footsteps melt away into the darkness and I passed out.

*   *   *

I tried to sit up. I couldn't. Every part of me screamed with pain. I stiffly lifted one hand to check the mask and was relieved to find it still on my face. I opened my eyes and turned my head painfully to look around.

I wasn't lying on the street, as I expected, but on a simple cot in a small room lit by a few candles. I reached up to touch the side of my head and winced from the pain. There was no blood, confirming that I had been hit with something blunt. With great effort I rolled to one side and got myself up on one elbow. My dirty coat, cloak and hat were thrown over a nearby wooden chair. I groaned when I tried to move my legs. A small colored woman entered the room and pushed me back down on the cot.

"Jus' lie still," she commanded in an authoritative tone.

She turned away and left, only to return a moment later mixing something in a cup.

"How did I get here?" I asked in little more than a hoarse croak.

"Drink now," she said.

She slid one hand beneath my head and raised it enough to begin pouring the vile liquid into my mouth. I coughed and choked but most of it went down my dry throat. She did not mention my mask. I don't know what was in that drink but the warmth from it soon spread throughout my bruised and aching body. Whatever it was, it contained a good amount of whiskey.

The next thing I knew the woman was gently unbuttoning my shirt and spreading it open. I tried to protest, to say that all I wanted was to get back to my wife, but the words didn't come out. I lifted my head just enough to see that my entire chest and stomach area was beginning to show a deep bruising. I dropped my head back to the bed and resigned myself to whatever she planned to do to me. She picked up a small bowl and began massaging a generous portion of the contents into my chest. Her hands were gentle but it hurt like hell. Her fingers lingered on my ribs, feeling each one carefully.

"You's lucky. No ribs broke, tho' some is cracked. You'll live."

She repeated the process on my back after turning me onto my side. I groaned when she touched me.

"I give you somethin' for that," she murmered.

She left the room again and returned with a large cup of straight whiskey. "Drink," she said and disappeared again.

After I finished the whiskey I felt a little stronger. I sat up and swung my legs painfully over the edge of the cot to the floor. I had buttoned my shirt halfway and was reaching for my coat when she returned. She was surprised to see me up, and pointed to the cot.

"No, please," I said. "I have to get home to my wife. She will be worried about me. Please understand; I must get home."

She looked at me sideways. She reached up to gently touch the mask, stroking her fingers down the sides of it. "You is special. Yassah, a special one. Don' you forget dat."

She helped me with my coat and cloak. She called out to the other room and the largest, blackest man I had ever seen ducked through the door. She motioned toward me and the man gingerly drew my arm over his shoulders and helped me to the door. At the doorway I turned back to the woman.

"Thank you for helping me," I said with gratitude. "What is your name?"

"Marie," she answered. "Marie Laveau."

Marie La... The big man pulled me through the door as something clicked in my mind.

With the ease of handling a child he set me upon the seat of a small cart. He then climbed up himself, tilting the small rig precariously, and took up the reins. I gave him the address and within minutes we pulled up at my door. He helped me down and up to the doorway, then quickly drove off without a word. I searched my pocket for the key. Luckily it was still there, untouched by the thieves. I got the door open and limped inside to lean heavily against the wall in the entryway. Christine came running from the parlor followed closely by Robert.

"Erik! Oh my God, Erik, where have you been?" She rushed to me, throwing her arms around me in relief. I could not stifle a whimper, and she fell back in confusion.

"Are you hurt? What has happened to you!" she cried in alarm as she noticed my dirt covered clothes and disheveled appearance.

"I...I was accosted...for money," I whispered. "I...fear I was...beaten quite severely..." I tried to smile and make light of it for her sake, but I was not very convincing. "I'm sorry I worried..."

I couldn't focus on her face. I felt dizzy and began to slide down the wall to the flagstones at her feet.

Christine and Robert got me off the floor and upstairs where they laid me carefully on the bed. After sending Robert out with an order to remain close by, she closed the door behind him. She gently removed the mask and was relieved that my face wasn't any more damaged than normal. I could do little but watch her. My head was swimming and I could not see very clearly. I suspected that I suffered a major concussion from one or both blows to my head. She unbuttoned my half-open shirt and her eyes grew wide with shock. She reached out to touch me but thought better of it. She put the mask back on my face and went to the door to call Robert back. Between them they got me undressed and into bed.

Robert was horrified by my injuries. "Miz Devereaux, he hurt bad. He gonna be aw'right? Mah uncle got beat like that once, an' he..."

"Yes, Robert, and thank you. He'll be fine. You go back to Deliah and tell her everything will be all right."

Their voices sounded like echoes through the deepening fog in my mind.

"Christine," I whispered.

She returned to the bed and leaned over me, placing her hand gently on my chest.

"Erik, what is this all over you?" she asked when her hand came away coated with the greasy substance.

My mind wasn't working right. "Can't think... Christine?"

"Yes, Erik, I'm right here."

*   *   *

I was awakened by pain in the gray light of early morning to find Christine sleeping as tightly against me as possible without hurting me. A light sheet covered us both and I pushed it back to take a look at myself. They hadn't missed one inch of me. No wonder I was in so much pain. It was as severe a beating as I'd ever taken, and I was not as young as I used to be. When I remembered the size of the largest of my attackers, I knew it was a miracle that his kicks alone had not killed me. If I remained in the condition I had been in when I first left the cellars of Paris, they would have killed me for sure. The weight and health I gained had saved my life.

I must mention here that I continued to suffer sporadic bouts of weakness and lightheadedness that I hid from Christine whenever possible. I still had no explanation for them. I considered myself to be relatively healthy, especially since I'd had no further episodes like the one in Virginia. Hopefully, that would continue to be an isolated incident caused by the stress I was under at the time. Regardless, it would take days to recover from the beating and it was only a week before Christmas—our first Christmas together and the first one I would ever celebrate. I covered myself and closed my eyes again.

Christine's soft lips moved upon mine. The sun streamed in through the French doors. There was no better way to wake up and I wanted to take my wife in my arms and make good and proper love to her. I realized soon enough that it was out of the question. Ironically, my face was the only part of me that didn't hurt, so I got a good kiss before Christine got up and readied herself for the day. She came back to kneel beside the bed.

"Erik, I was so afraid last night. I didn't know what had happened to you," she said quietly. She trailed her fingers through the coarse hair on my chest. "I thought I had lost you."

"My dear, you won't get rid of me that easily," I smiled, trying to lighten the mood.

I would not tell her how close she *had* come to losing me. I ignored the pain in my arms and reached up to pull her face down to me. After another long and very satisfying kiss, I took charge.

"Christine, please help me up. I cannot stay in this bed another minute," I ordered, my authoritative tone as much for my own benefit as hers. "I have composing to do."

She asked me again what happened after I was attacked, but I put her off with an explanation of a kindly old woman who took me in and put salve on me, gave me whiskey for the pain and had me driven home. I said I was too dazed to remember much more, which wasn't too far from the truth considering the way my head felt. I did not mention that I planned to investigate that "kindly old woman" further.

After several days of painfully creeping around the house I felt mended enough to go shopping for Christine's Christmas present. I informed her that she must stay at home that afternoon and asked Robert to drive me into town. I already had a special present to give her, but I was headed for the jeweler's again. My goal was a necklace and earrings that would perfectly match her ruby and diamond engagement ring.

With the small, gaily wrapped package safely in my pocket we returned home. I hid it inside the piano where I knew she would never look. Every time I played that piano between now and Christmas Day, I would think of the jewels waiting there for her. The thought gave me great pleasure. I was sitting in the parlor later that afternoon reading my newspapers when a small sound at the door caught my attention. I looked up in surprise to find Deliah standing there.

"Deliah, please come in!" I exclaimed with a wave of my hand. "Do you need something?"

"No suh," she mumbled. "I mean, suh...I jus' want to say I's glad you aw'right, suh."

Pleasantly surprised, I got up and went over to her. "Thank you, Deliah, for coming to tell me that," I said warmly. "I am feeling much better." I wanted to say something else to her. "Please tell me if there is anything you need," I added.

"Yas suh, thank you suh. Good day, suh." She scurried off.

I returned to my papers with a smile upon my face.

13

———————— ★ ————————

On Christmas Eve I took Christine to dinner and then out driving to see the decorations and feel the Christmas spirit around us. I had given her the jewels earlier that night, saving my other gift for the morning. She squealed with delight when she opened the box, and instructed me to fasten them around her neck and to her ears at once so she could wear them to dinner. It was a relatively warm evening for winter in New Orleans and the weather was quite pleasant. It was a nice change from the damp and cold weather we'd had for the past week. We stopped in at the Vaillancourt's for a little cheer and a glass or two of wine, and Christine proudly showed Louise her gifts. At Christine's request, I then took her to midnight mass at St. Louis Cathedral.

I had not been inside the church since the day of our marriage and it brought back many pleasant memories. Christine attended Mass occasionally, but I had not chosen to accompany her. My belief in God had been severely tested over the course of my life-time. I renounced Him completely at a very early age, blaming Him for the horrors of my life. As a child, religion was the only thing my parents saw fit to teach me and it was relentlessly drummed into me. It was also made very clear to me that I was considered an abomination that could be linked only to the work of the devil. I believed early on that God had forsaken me, and for many years afterward carried the belief that He did not exist.

After Christine came into my life I began to rethink my position on the subject. I slowly came around to a tentative belief that He might truly be there, if one wanted to believe it hard enough. When Christine agreed to marry me I thought there must be a God to have brought me to that point, but I never pursued the issue further. We sat in the beautiful candlelit church listening to the sounds of a huge pipe organ. I soon felt a sense of calm—of serenity—as I held Christine's hand in mine and let the music and the voices wash over me. I could not see who was playing that wonderful instrument because the organ box was tucked out of sight behind the altar, but I envied them.

We arrived home to our own simple decorations and a candlelit bedroom celebration all our own. We stood at the French doors overlooking our private courtyard for a long time, listening to the sounds of the night, someone caroling, and our own hearts beating.

"Merry Christmas, my love," I whispered into her ear as I playfully pulled on its lobe with my lips.

"Merry Christmas to you, darling," she answered with a giggle. "I hope your first one is special."

"Very special indeed," I agreed, and grinned wickedly at her. "And I plan to make it even more memorable right now." I swept her into my arms and we collapsed in a heap of satin, jewels and linen upon the bed. It wasn't long before the jewels were the only things she wore, and we set new meaning to the word "memorable".

    *   *   *

Christmas Day was a gay but low-key affair, which suited me perfectly. Deliah prepared an amazing Creole dinner, and Jean and Louise were our happy guests. Gifts were exchanged all around, including some simple things we had for Robert and Deliah, who were embarrassingly appreciative when summoned in to receive their gifts. I even managed to wring a shy smile from Deliah when she opened her box to find a new shawl. I thought to save my gift for Christine for last, and when it appeared that everything had been opened, I brought the heavy box out of hiding. Christine looked at me in surprise, expecting nothing more than her beautiful jewels. I watched her face with anticipation as she carefully opened the top of the box. When she looked in and saw the large music box that I secretly brought from my home under the Opera with its simple, familiar design and haunting melody, it brought tears to her eyes. I helped her set it on a table and wind it up. The gentle sounds transported me in a bittersweet memory back to my home in Paris. I felt saddened when I thought of all the other beautiful things that I was forced to leave behind—the collections of a lifetime of wandering. Christine sensed my melancholy and came to sit close beside me. I received nothing from her, but I would never mention it. She had already given me my life, and I could not ask for more than that.

Jean and Louise left after our delicious Christmas dinner. We bid them goodbye after promising to see them again soon. They were truly good friends. We went into the parlor and Christine came up to me.

"Erik, you have not mentioned my gift to you," she stuck her lower lip out in mock indignation.

"My love, you have already given me more than I can ever repay." I leaned toward her but she ducked away from me.

"No. I have something for you, but we must leave to get it. Please get the carriage."

She directed me to drive to the St. Louis Cathedral, and as we walked inside I could not imagine what she was up to. She kept looking at me with strange smiles and a secretive air. She pulled me along by the hand up the length of the center aisle and onto the altar itself. The building appeared to be completely empty, but within minutes the priest appeared from somewhere in the back.

"Ah, I see that you have arrived, Mrs. Devereaux. Mr. Devereaux," he addressed me, shaking my hand. To Christine he said, "And he still does not know?"

"Know what?" I asked stupidly. I hate being the last to know anything.

"Mr. Devereaux, your wife has made arrangements for you to play our magnificent pipe organ. You may play now or anytime you wish, as long as your schedules are checked with me first. That is, if it is your wish to do so." He looked at me expectantly. "Your wife has assured me, sir, that you possess some degree of musical competence," he added, as if my hesitation might stem from lack of confidence. His innocent comment was truly an understatement if I ever heard one. Some degree of musical competence? I might have laughed out loud if I had not been so overwhelmed with the whole proceeding.

I looked from the Father to Christine and back again. I was stunned and speechless. I sat in this very church thinking of this very wish just yesterday, and now it had come true. I turned to him with humility.

"I would be honored, Father. Thank you."

He pointed out the tiny hallway and several steps that led to the organ box.

"Enjoy yourself. Play as long as you like, there is nothing scheduled here for the remainder of today."

My heart went into my mouth when I saw it. Three manuals gleamed in the lamplight and the multitude of stop knobs that surrounded the manuals in many rows suggested endless possibilities of sound. Unlike the one long keyboard of my grand piano, these three would allow me the full range of my composing capabilities.

The organ was even more than I dreamed it could be—much larger and more powerful than the one I had built in Paris. Above my head soared the ranks of pipes; many hundreds of them, maybe thousands. I ran my fingers reverently over the smooth keys and the shining mahogany. Christine stood back silently to watch me. I slid onto the massive bench and tapped my feet gently on the pedalboard beneath me. I stared around me for several minutes trying to take it all in.

I began with tiny one-handed melodies. I gradually added more keys and volume, familiarizing myself with the organ's touch and its beautiful tones. I reached out with both hands to move stop knobs in and out, instinctively knowing the precise combinations that would produce the sounds that I wanted. I laid my fingers again on the keys, and one of my own compositions sprang forth. The piece began gently and gained power and strength gradually. The notes rolled from beneath my fingers and I swayed back and forth on the bench as the miles fell away. I was once again sitting at the instrument of my own creation, writing and playing the music that had kept me alive. Yes! Yes! It had been the music all along! It was glorious, wondrous music that kept me alive until the day I was delivered by God to Christine's waiting embrace!

Music thundered out from beneath my fingertips, filling the empty church from the columns of its balconies to the very top of its steeples. Deeper and deeper I fell into music's welcoming and loving embrace until I knew nothing else. I was home again. Music had always been like a lover to me, caressing me as I loved it in turn. Now that relationship took on a whole new meaning as I combined my immense love for Christine with my lifelong love of music, melding them together into an ecstatic euphoria that went beyond words or thought. I don't know how long I played—it might have been two hours or five for all I knew. When I finally lifted my aching hands from the manuals I felt drained and exultant at the same time. The keys and I were both dampened with the sweat of my passion. I exhausted myself, but could think only of the next time I would sit on that bench. I looked at the rows of white and black keys before me and suddenly I was crying, overcome with the joy of what I had just experienced. Christine's arms came around me from behind. I swung around and buried my face in her breast, crying like a baby.

It was the most thoughtful and insightful gift anyone could have given me. I played that organ for hours on end. I worked on compositions over its manuals and played for masses and weddings. I could not be seen by anyone while I played so no explanations were needed. Father Etienne offered to pay me for my services. He was visibly shaken by what he heard the first time I played in his church late on that wonderful Christmas day, and he was quite obviously anxious to have me play in public. I refused all payment. Access to his beautiful instrument was all that I required.

14

★

I was jolted awake to find myself covered in sweat and feeling uneasy. I had dreamed of something but I could not remember what it was. I looked over at my quietly sleeping wife. I passed the incident off as indigestion and went back to sleep. Four nights later it happened again. I got out of bed and went to the window, trying to remember what had disturbed my sleep. My body was running with sweat for no apparent reason. I felt all right, so I didn't think it was one of my episodes. I'll admit right now that I had become a little too complacent about that. No, this was something different. I felt the same heavy sense of dread that accompanied the first dream. Again I had no answers and went back to bed.

It was early 1883 and the season of our first Mardi Gras celebration was just around the corner. We had left Paris almost a year ago. That year had brought so much change in my life it seemed too good to be true. From my lonely existence under the Opera, through my selfish and cruel kidnapping of Christine to the love and the life that we now shared seemed an impossible transition. I'd tried hard to put my past behind me and I'd adapted reasonably well to being a part of the world again. We socialized little but neither did we stay at home all the time. There had been uncomfortable situations and there would be more. I knew there would always be the possibility of someone overreacting to me. I had learned to live with that. I believed Christine had too.

A week or so later I had a terrible nightmare that was a swirl of images, all terrifyingly real. Ghoulish faces surrounded me with large mouths opening and closing in awful screams. Daggers dripping blood flew through the air and crowds of people pointed at me and laughed. Dueling pistols clattered repeatedly to the floor and I saw my own hands covered with blood. Finally, in the clearest image of all, I lay on the ground, unable to lift my arms. A large, dark figure lifted a huge rock high above me and then let it go. I screamed when I saw it falling directly toward my face. I was still screaming when my eyes flew open to see Christine above me, shaking me awake.

"Erik! Wake up! Erik!" She was shaking me by the shoulders. My breath came much too fast and my heart was pounding. I sat up and looked wildly around the room. She had lit the lamp and I found myself staring at the shadows on the far wall trying to remember where I was. I was dripping wet. I must have looked dazed for she grabbed my face none too gently in both hands and forced me to look at her.

"Erik! I'm here! What is it?"

My eyes finally focused on her. "I had a nightmare. It was awful," I panted, trying to catch my breath. I rubbed my eyes to erase the pictures that were still horrifyingly fresh in my mind. I knew what they were, you see. They were scenes from my own horrible past and that scared me far more than anything my mind could have conjured up. I was still shaking when she put her arms around me. I couldn't tell her what I had seen, because most of it was from events in my life that I never wanted her to know about. I did tell her, though, about the last part, about the man with the rock. We agreed that it must be a delayed reaction to the attack on North Rampart Street. I went along with this for her sake, but the other images in the dream haunted me. I thought I had successfully closed the door on that part of my life. Why was this happening now?

I slept well the next night, and for many nights thereafter. I prayed there would be no more dreams. I immersed myself in my composing and my playing at the church. I began to spend so much time in the cathedral that I forgot all about the dreams. I also got involved in a bit of private architectural design work for several of Jean's associates. Jean had noticed some of my drawings lying on a table one day, and although I lacked the requisite professional references, he managed to find me several clients. Things were coming together for me. Around that time I fell quite by accident into another way to occupy my time. I was visiting Jean one day and was telling him about my frustration with my attempts to further Christine's knowledge of the strategies of chess.

"It's not that she cannot play, Jean, but she cannot possibly hope to challenge me," I said in a complaining tone. "It takes many years of discipline to play at such a level as I require. She tries very hard and I enjoy the time spent with her, but it is not enough."

Jean thought for a minute.

"Well, Erik, I can play but I'm sure you would not be very challenged by my playing either. No, not very challenged! However, if you would like to play a real game we have someone right here in New Orleans who has been considered a world class player for many years. Even as a child I believe. In fact, he played competitively in England and France back in, I think, '58 or so. I'm surprised you never heard of him, very surprised. His name is Paul Morphy."

I could not recall the name. "I can't say that I remember, but in those days I was doing quite a bit of traveling." 58...58..., I thought, where was I in 1858? "No, I was not in France at that time." I was certainly not keeping up with world news during those years either.

"If you'd like to talk to him, he lives right on Royal Street. I'll give you the number." He rooted around in some papers and wrote something down. He handed me a slip of paper with 417 Royal written on it. "Be advised, though, that he isn't quite right. He may not want to talk to you at all if you mention chess. No, not at all."

"Why on earth not?" I queried, not understanding his statement.

"Poor Morphy has suffered from depressions and other forms of mania over the years; he has even spent time in the Louisiana Retreat. He has always been very cynical about the public aspects of being a professional chess player and has been largely unable to cope with his success. Unable, indeed. He loathes the public chess world and will always tell you that he is a lawyer first."

"He is a member of the bar?"

"Oh yes, yes he is. He opened an office some 15 or so years ago, but it was not successful. The man has had problems ever since. He may not talk to you at all, no, not at all. He lives with his mother and sister at that address, but he can often be found in the afternoons walking along Canal Street. He wears a top hat and carries a very unusual walking stick."

Christine had gone to visit some new friends with Louise so the afternoon was mine. I would try to intercept Morphy on Canal Street rather than appearing at his door and likely frightening his mother or sister to death. I walked over there and, after a quarter hour or so of scanning the street, I was inconceivably lucky to spot a man carrying the most ornately carved stick I had ever seen crossing the intersection at Canal and Bourbon who looked to be a likely prospect.

"Pardon me, Sir, I was admiring your stick. German, isn't it?"

I walked up behind him and spoke gently, remembering what I'd been told of his nature. He stopped and turned around. He visibly started when he saw the mask, but to his credit he recovered himself quickly and only retained a somewhat nervous look. It must be this city, I thought as I faced yet another person who had not turned away immediately at the sight of me. Of course, I had not yet experienced Mardi Gras.

He glanced down at the stick in his hand. "Why, yes, yes it is. From Germany, that is. I spent some time there many years ago." He had relaxed a bit but was still looking at me suspiciously.

"As did I," I offered in a friendly manner. "The Germans certainly have a way with wood. They have a carving style all their own." I admired his stick for a moment before I spoke again.

"Pardon my being so forward, but are you Paul Morphy by any chance?"

Surprise flickered across the man's face. "I am, sir. Why do you ask?" He was once again on his guard. His head began to dart this way and that as if watching for something.

"Chess, Mr. Morphy," I replied. "I would like to play some challenging chess, and I have been given your name."

"I don't play anymore," he said and began to turn away.

"Please sir," I said, stopping him. "I have no agenda other than to sit in the parlor and enjoy the experience of having my own considerable talents on the chessboard properly challenged." He did not turn away again so I continued. "For many years I have been unable to find an opponent who could match my intellect in the game. I would truly be grateful if you would do me the honor of allowing me a game or two." I finished my pitch with an attempt at humor. "I may even let you win a game," I concluded with a smile.

At that he seemed to relax. "All right," he said. "I shall play with you, but there is a condition. You must not tell anyone of our games. I do not wish it to be known that I have played again."

"Agreed, sir." I said and held out my hand.

We made arrangements to meet at his home in the Rue Royal in a few days at a time when the ladies of his house would be out. He seemed to understand my lack of enthusiasm for wanting to meet them, as he had his own problems with his public image. I have to say that when we sat at the board and I observed his first moves, I began to wonder if he still possessed the strategic abilities of his younger years. He appeared to be a few years younger than I am, but he did not look well. It took me until halfway through the first game to realize that he had been holding back; probably to give himself time to gauge my expertise. When he began to play in earnest I was faced with a true and proper challenge. He won our first game and subsequent games showed us to be quite well matched.

So began a satisfying and enjoyable relationship between Paul and me. We both had our problems and we took comfort in each other. We spent many hours facing off over that chessboard, and regardless of who was the victor on any given day, we always enjoyed a good humor and a relaxed camaraderie. We talked of many things. Eventually he did ask about the mask, and I comfortably fell back on the aging story of an accident. He appeared perfectly content with my answer and questioned me no further about it. I said nothing about what I'd heard regarding his delicate mental state. Paul became a very important part of my life as one of my very few close friends.

                    *   *   *

I came home from Paul's one day to find Christine silently sitting in the bedroom. She was staring at something, but since her back was to me I could not see what it was. I quietly walked over to her and was startled to see my knotted lasso stretched out on the bed before her. The sight of it caused an unexpected lurch in my stomach. I did not carry it as often as I used to; I had not, in fact, carried it for months. For many years I had never gone anywhere without it. Along with my uncommon strength and combative expertise, it was my only source of defense and the only weapon I had ever carried. Our life in New Orleans was so civilized that I ceased to feel the need of carrying it constantly.

Words momentarily failed me when I observed the mixture of horror and fascination on Christine's face as she stared at it. I touched her gently on the shoulder and she jumped, moving quickly to sweep it behind her. I reached around her to retrieve it and slowly coiled it back into the compact loop that had always fit so perfectly into a special pocket on the inside of the cloaks and coats I wore for many years. I thought it was well hidden away in a drawer.

"I'm sorry…I found it…" she began, faltering with uncertainty. She looked like a child caught with something naughty.

I sat down next to her on the bed. "I am not angry with you, Christine."

I looked down at the innocuous looking piece of catgut in my hands. It represented violence and death. Looking at it now I saw it for what it was—a gruesome reminder of a life I no longer led. I was staring at it, remembering, when Christine's question interrupted my thoughts.

"How does it work?" she asked in a tiny voice.

"It will work for no one but me." I got up to return it to the drawer. I don't know why I did not dispose of it. It was certainly not something commonly seen on city streets, at least in this part of the world. She halted my progress across the room when she said, "Please show me."

"You saw me use it in Norfolk," I said without turning around. The conversation was making me uncomfortable. Especially after a vision of the same lasso wrapped tightly around Raoul's neck sprang into my mind. "I see no point…"

"Please, Erik?"

She fell into her most wheedling tone, the one she used when she wanted to get her way and my goat at the same time. It didn't often fail.

My darkening mood lightened and I could not help but smile to myself at my wife's expert use of her considerable feminine wiles to get her way with me yet again. I turned back to her, stopping halfway when she stood up to meet me. Without taking my eyes from hers, I launched the lasso at the nearest bedpost. Before she noticed that I had moved at all, I stood with the noose wrapped tightly around the post and the end held high and taut in my left hand. She looked at it, then looked at me again. She had missed the movement, but I would not repeat it.

"Surprise, my dear, is more than half the trick," I said calmly as I walked over to the bed and expertly slipped the tightly drawn noose from the post with a flick of my wrist.

I coiled it and replaced it in the bottom of the drawer under some clothing, then turned to find her right behind me. She put her arms up around my neck and pressed her body against mine, backing me up against the bureau.

"My Erik. My husband, my lover and my protector," she cooed. "You are full of surprises."

The look in Christine's eyes told me that what I had just done somehow excited her. Perhaps it was the mystery of the life I had once led, and the parts of it that I would never tell her about. If she wanted to believe that parts of my life had been exotic and dangerously exciting, I would let her. It was infinitely preferable to the truth. She moved suggestively against me, then lifted one shapely leg up to rub it up and down against my inner thigh. Her blue eyes darkened and searched my own. Her lips curved into a sensual smile as her hands slid up over my chest and under my jacket to slip it off my shoulders. I leaned down into her embrace and it was a long time before we left the bedroom.

*   *   *

Christine and I were very happy. My new life and the gentler personality that was emerging in me were becoming more natural and comfortable. It was likely that I would always possess a volatile streak in that personality, but as my temperament evened out I gradually dropped most of the pretense with which I had begun our life together. The closeness we shared was beyond my wildest dreams, especially in bed. I took great pleasure in waking to find her beside me in the morning. I reached for her as soon as she woke to pull her on top of me, covering us both again with the blanket and taking my strength for the day from her loving embrace. Often we remained in bed for hours discovering new ways to find pleasure in each other.

Although I was happy with the activities that filled my days, I remained on the lookout for new challenges to feed my mind's ravenous appetite for learning. A constant through my entire life, my insatiable desire for further knowledge continued unabated. I thought to return to my studies of local architecture but I was sorely disappointed by our city in that respect. Aside from the homes there was little to study, or so I thought. I was out driving with Christine one day when we came upon the most intriguing collection of structures I had seen in years. It was located in the most unusual of places; the St. Louis Cemetery.

Actually this particular cemetery was called St. Louis No. 2 as there were three in all. Many other cemeteries like them were located nearby. In New Orleans it is customary for the dead to be buried above the ground in vaults. Because of the mix of architectural styles found within them the cemeteries are referred to as "cities of the dead". Traditional, underground burial was rendered almost impossible by the city's drainage problems. Stories were told of coffins floating in dug graves. Several men would stand on the coffin or hold it down with long poles until the water entered it through holes bored in it for that purpose. The coffin would then sink with a gurgling sound into the muck. It was not the kind of sight the bereaved mourners needed to remember their departed loved one, so the use of above ground vaults was adopted. My interest was piqued.

We returned home that day in the midst of one of our few heated arguments. Christine was appalled at my excited declaration that I would spend time studying vaults and mausoleums.

"Why would you want to spend time in such places?" she pouted as I returned to the carriage after having taken a quick perusal of the vaults nearest the road. "They are so...morbid."

"My dear Christine, I have studied far worse in my time," I said firmly, letting her think what she would of that statement. "I cannot spend my days admiring items in shop windows, taking tea with the ladies and sitting with my parasol in the courtyard."

She took that as a personal attack on her pleasures.

"Well, what would you expect me to do?" she asked with an angry shake of her head. "I do nothing different than the other ladies around town do. Besides," she whined, "you spend so much time with your music and drawings that you have no time for me anymore."

It was a senseless argument. Her last remark was unexpected and groundless and I'd had enough. I pulled the horse to a hard stop in the middle of the road. "So, I don't have any time for you, do I?" I dropped the traces and roughly pulled Christine toward me. "How about right now, my love?" I asked sarcastically. Before she could respond, my lips had covered hers in a cold, hard, impersonal kiss with no hint of romance in it. Christine pushed at my shoulders in an unsuccessful attempt to back away. In seconds I felt her responding to me against her will, and I purposely softened my lips and began to kiss her more deeply. When I was sure that she was completely lost in the kiss I let her go without warning. She sat back onto the seat with a jolt. I looked coolly at her reddened mouth and her wide eyes.

"Don't you ever tell me again that I don't have time for you," I admonished flatly. "You enjoy your pleasures and I will enjoy mine. It might be in your best interest to stay out of some of mine if they don't appeal to you."

The remainder of our drive home was accomplished in silence.

I was not proud of that little episode in the street. I suddenly felt very impatient with Christine's frivolous pursuits and her condemnation of my interests. I was also hurt by her complaint about the time that I spent with her. I spent more time with my wife than many husbands did, mostly because of my not having to work for a living. I believed the comment to be intentionally hurtful, and designed more to get back at me for finding yet another interest than having any basis in reality.

The woman-child who was my wife was a contradiction who never failed to confound me. She loved me like a woman—she frequently acted like a child. In bed it was easy for me to forget that she was only in her early twenties with no experience in the world before I literally carried her out into it. On those occasions when we argued over petty and frivolous topics such as that day outside the cemetery, she was a naïve and spoiled little girl. At those times the difference in our ages became more pronounced. Regardless of what I had or hadn't done in my past life, I was a man of the world. I had seen and done more than my wife could ever hope to dream about. Still, we loved each other and I prayed that we would get through the rougher times. This thing called a marriage was proving to require more monumental effort than anything to which I had ever set my hand.

*   *   *

We were politely cool toward one another for a few days afterward. Christine left one afternoon on another one of her endless trips into town. Robert had taken her along with Deliah, who would do some marketing. I had the house completely to myself and I sat contentedly working at the piano. I was soon scheduled for some time at the organ so I stood up to gather my papers. I felt a light tingling in my left shoulder and arm. I thought I had been playing too long so I began to move it around in circles to get the circulation going. I had picked up my things and was walking across the parlor floor when a dull ache began to spread through my chest, blossoming out until it felt as if someone were sitting on it. The ache quickly became stronger and more intense before excruciating pain suddenly exploded through me like a canon going off! My papers dropped to the floor. I grabbed for the doorjamb and ripped my collar open to get more air. My legs gave out and I fell to the floor, gasping. There was no one home but me, and the pain was intense and unbearable, going far beyond what I'd felt in Virginia. I knew immediately that I was not going to handle this one on my own. I needed help. We had a new telephone, but it was in the hallway and I was going downhill fast in the parlor. *Someone please help me!*

I can recount the events of that afternoon after piecing it together from what they told me. I passed out on the floor of my parlor only a few minutes before I was due at the church for my scheduled practice time. A quarter hour later, Father Etienne became concerned when he noted that I had not yet arrived. I had never been late before and had never missed a session. Apparently he'd run into

Christine not too long before that and knew that she planned to be out for the entire afternoon. Finally he rang up our house. When he got no answer, he grew worried enough to call on Jean.

Jean knew me better than to think that I would miss any time at all on that organ. That is, if I could help it. For some unknown reason he thought the worst and urged his horses quickly to his physician's home to drag the poor man from his table, telling him to grab his bag on the way out the door.

Jean and the doctor broke through my front door to find me crumpled on the floor between the parlor and front hall, unconscious and bathed in cold sweat. My heartbeat was weak and irregular and I had only the faintest of pulses. They rolled me onto my back and the doctor went to work on me. My heart stopped twice, but the doctor managed to get it going again by pounding me on the chest. The two men were on the floor kneeling over me after just having gotten my heart restarted the first time when a carriage pulled up in the street.

In walked Christine to find a splintered front door and the sound of men's voices in her house. She almost fainted at the scene that met her eyes. I was lying stretched out on the floor surrounded by musical scores and medical equipment. My shirt was torn wide open and my skin was ashen. I was unconscious and Jean and a stranger were leaning over me. At the exact moment that she was taking in this grisly sight, the doctor shouted that he'd lost me again. He raised his fist and brought it down hard with a sickening thud upon my chest.

Christine screamed.

"No! What are you doing to him! Don't hurt him!" Jean struggled to his feet quickly to grab her before she could reach me. Dragging her back away from the doctor and me, he tried to explain.

"Christine, he's had a heart attack, a bad one," he said gently, trying to calm her. "The doctor is doing what he can. This is the only way to help him." She helplessly stood there with Jean's arm around her, staring at me with panicked eyes as the doctor feverishly continued to work on me. He considered me dead, but he did not give up. Finally my heart began to beat rhythmically again. As they watched, color began to return to my skin and my pulse slowly stabilized.

Dr. André Sorel sat back on the floor and wearily wiped his brow.

"That was a close one," he muttered. Looking up at Christine's worried expression he asked, "Are you his wife?" She nodded. "Does your husband have a heart condition?" At her blank look he tried again. "Has this ever happened before?"

Christine nodded again. "He passed out, but it wasn't like this," she replied in a shaky voice. Jean let her go and she knelt beside me to lift my limp hand to her cheek. "Once..." She began to cry. "But it's been so long...almost a year...and he recovered so quickly..."

"Mrs. Devereaux, your husband is in very serious condition. I can't know the extent of the damage this attack has caused. I hate to frighten you, but his heart has already stopped twice and the fact that he has not regained consciousness is of great concern to me. He is stable for the time being, but I am hesitant to move him very far. Do you have somewhere close by?"

At her direction and with the added help of a frightened Robert, I was put to bed in a room on the first floor off the parlor. When Dr. Sorel told her he needed to remove my mask to monitor vital signs, she adamantly refused to allow him near me. Jean told her it was necessary and pulled her from the room. When the doctor called for her to come back in the mask had been replaced but his face was drained of color.

"Lord Almighty," he said to her. "What happened to him?" Our standard answer seemed to satisfy him. Being a doctor, I'm sure he may have guessed differently at the cause, but he didn't question her further. Our accident story was believable only to those who had never actually seen my facial deformities. After Christine promised that I would be checked frequently, he left with strict instructions that, if I did wake up, I was not to be allowed to leave that bed until he saw me again. It was his use of the word "if" that worried her most.

I opened my eyes to afternoon light. The light was too bright, so I closed them again. As my consciousness slowly returned I remembered being in the parlor, playing the piano, walking across the floor. The last thing I remembered was feeling totally and help-lessly alone. I opened my eyes again and hoarsely whispered Christine's name. Her face replaced the ceiling above me.

"Oh, Erik, you're awake!" she cried. "Thank God!" She reached over to stroke my hair.

"I had another one," I whispered, and she nodded.

"Yes, darling. It was very bad."

"I guess my face isn't the only..." I began, but was silenced by her finger across my lips.

"Don't think about that now. It's your heart, darling, and the doctor thinks this has been building up for a long time. It doesn't matter why it happened, just please get well." She tried to hide the tremor in her voice.

"Christine, there were strange things happening to me back at the Opera, but I refused to believe anything could be wrong. And then since we've been here...I didn't tell you...and in Virginia...I should have known. What if my ignorance costs us our happiness?"

"Please don't worry about it now and try to rest. It will be all right." She tried to assuage my guilt, but I remained skeptical. I would always wonder if I could have done anything to prevent the attack. The problem had been my heart all along and I'd been too stupid to see it.

I turned my head to look around. "What am I doing in here, why am I not in our bed?"

She told me what happened. She also told me that I had been out for almost twenty-four hours. I was extremely weak and my chest felt as though a horse had kicked me. I was shocked and frightened by the grave seriousness of this attack. I had shaken previous incidents off with little effort once they passed. Now I understood the true threat my condition posed to my very life, and ultimately to Christine.

I was ordered to spend a week in that infernal bed and I was not a model patient. I became irritable and short with Christine to the point of rudeness. She helped me with everything for several days, as I was told not to sit up, let alone move around much. Fortunately, she knew that my bad humor was not her fault. My favorite time of day during that week was when she brought a bowl of warm water, soap and a towel and proceeded to wash every inch of me with her gentle touch. I think she enjoyed it as much as I did, and I ached to take her in my arms and show her how sorry I was for the horrid way I had treated her on our last outing. The fact that it literally could have been our *very last* outing made me doubly regretful, and frightened for Christine's safety should anything happen to me.

It was the longest we'd been apart at night since our marriage. At the end of the week the doctor was quite surprised when he walked in to hear me telling Christine forcefully that I refused to spend another minute in that damned bed. Jean told me much later that Dr. Sorel had confessed to knowing of no medical precedent for the fact that I had survived that severe an attack at all, much less recovered completely.

*   *   *

Two weeks later, as the city prepared for its annual celebrations of Mardi Gras, I finally could be found contentedly studying and sketching the vast variety of vaults in the city's cemeteries. I found all the architecture of the world in one enormous cemetery— Metairie. I won that little battle with Christine, although she made her distaste in my pursuits loudly known to me. I shrugged it off and left with my charcoals and my paper, promising that I would not overdo it. I had been ordered to avoid strenuous activity for a while longer.

If by "strenuous activity" the good doctor included sex, then I was guilty of disobeying his orders. I returned to Christine's bed as soon as I felt strong enough to climb the stairs, and subsequently we resumed our nightly habits. That was, in my estimation, the best medicine in the world for me, although I did refrain from the more athletic pursuits such as carrying my wife up the stairs. She treated me gingerly at first until I firmly told her one night that I was tired of being fussed over and I would not break.

15

★

Mardi Gras rolled around and I was feeling myself again. Christine and I joined the celebrations, and I finagled us an invitation to the Comus Ball, the most exclusive and envied party of all. We attended the Rex Parade and thrilled to the music and the revelers in the streets. Maskers were everywhere, and I purchased special masks for both Christine and myself. During those wonderfully hectic days we wandered the streets unnoticed and blending in with everyone else. It was an exhilarating time for me as I experienced a sense of freedom that I had never before felt on a public street. Evidence of an unknown and untapped sense of flamboyance showed itself in my personality and I reveled in it. This one time during the year when I could enjoy total anonymity confirmed my belief that New Orleans was the city for me.

We watched in delight as the Boeuf Gras, or fatted bull, paraded down the street on its lead followed by decorated carriages and floats. Music was everywhere. The strains of *If Ever I Cease To Love* rose all around us. The song, with its nonsensical lyrics and catchy tune, had been the anthem of Mardi Gras since 1872 when it was sung by Lydia Thompson, who traveled from New York to present it at that year's celebrations.

At night, as if we had not had enough, we attended the great nighttime parade of the Krewe of Comus. The carnival organizations, or Krewes, labored long and hard for many months over these spectacular parades. The torch-lit parade began with its flambeaux held high by men on horseback followed by brightly lit floats, bands and thousands of masked marchers resembling witches, ogres, fairies and rainbows to name only a few. It celebrated the coming of Comus, the most dearly loved of the Mardi Gras kings. The tinkling of bells were heard from every corner of every street. There were glittery metal headdresses, ballet girls in black and white costumes, stilt-walkers and skeletons with scary faces. Christine laughed at the fat men dressed as little girls who smoked cigars. Beads were thrown to the crowds from the many floats. The smells of a cornucopia of foods assailed us from every direction. The grand celebration culminated at the French Opera House with the Comus Ball. The parade turned from Canal Street into Bourbon, where the narrower street caused much crowding among the marchers until it reached the Opera House. Around the corner on Toulouse Street stood long lines of elegant carriages on the cobblestones. Finely dressed ladies and gentlemen entered the building through a side door. This was society's entrance to the Comus Ball, and this was where Christine and I began an enchanting evening of revelry and dancing.

Inside we found a madhouse as people milled around everywhere. The short ceremony, which presented King Comus and the announcement of his queen, took place on stage and the evening was given over to the dancing. I swept Christine around the floor, for once feeling totally and gloriously inconspicuous. Why, I could even have asked one of the other beautiful ladies to dance with a reasonable possibility of acceptance, had I wanted to do such a thing. During the course of the evening I noticed many of them staring at me. It was not the same type of staring that I was accustomed to;

these were warm, lingering looks that any man would appreciate. I had eyes only for Christine. Her beauty and radiance stunned me. Once again I marveled at how lucky I had been to find this wonderful wife of mine. Only Christine had been able to see beyond what her eyes showed her to find and touch my very soul. Her beautiful gown flowed around her and the deep red of it matched her lips and the rubies that she wore.

Later, from our bedroom, we heard the partying in the streets continue throughout the night. I stood shirtless in the doorway looking out into the dim courtyard when Christine came up behind me and slid her hands up my back and down my arms. I felt her hand stop just below my shoulders as her fingers fell into the hollow where the bullet wound had not healed completely. It never would. I lost too much flesh in digging that slug out, and a deep, uneven indentation in the flesh of my arm remained. She gently caressed it.

"I never noticed this before. Is this what I think it is?"

I nodded silently, still looking out the window.

She moved around to face me, her body silhouetted in the moonlight coming from behind her, and slid her fingers up into the hair on my chest. I put my arms around her and kissed the top of her head tenderly.

"I've never understood about it," she said. "Raoul was not like that. He was gentle and kind."

"He was not gentle the night he gave me that little memento," I said. "He meant to kill me." I looked down at her, and I had to ask the question. "It has been almost a year since I took you away. Do you miss him?"

"I did for a long time, Erik. I can't lie to you about that. I used to think often of what might have made him react the way he did to you."

"He realized how serious a threat I was to his plans. I didn't even know that myself." I took a deep breath and let it out slowly, gazing out over her head into the darkness. "I don't think he could ever have understood how much you meant to me. It was life, Christine, you meant my life to me. Without you, I would have died in that hole and no one would ever have found me." I paused as another thought struck me. "Christine, why were you and Raoul never married?"

She faced the courtyard again and leaned back against me. "I suppose you've always wondered about that, haven't you?" She sighed and sadness crept into her voice. "Things weren't easy for us after what happened in the cellars that night. Both of us left there badly shaken. We already knew his family would not accept me, so Raoul said we would go to Sweden to find what is left of the Daae family. I remember him talking to me about such plans, but I am afraid he was frustrated by my lack of response. I couldn't plan and I couldn't think. I felt empty and could not recapture the excitement for marrying him that I once felt. It was Raoul's idea to wait and marry later, after we found my family, so at least one of us would have people there. He wanted me to rest for a while before traveling so we were still on the outskirts of Paris when I saw the notice about you in the newspaper. I was more affected by it than I cared to show him, but I insisted that I would not marry him until I fulfilled my promise to you. We argued about it. He did not understand why I would return after what you had done to us. I only knew that I must do as I promised. He finally agreed to take me back, but he changed after that. He looked at me in a different way."

When Christine turned around to face me again she was wiping tears from her face. She took a deep breath and continued.

"I'm not superstitious, but I've come to think fate must have played a hand somewhere in all this. Even in death, Erik, your presence was strong enough to keep Raoul and me apart. I began to suspect back in Norfolk that Raoul would never be enough for me. I thought I loved him but I've since realized that I didn't know what love was until I found it with you. I only hope that Raoul has also found someone to love."

"I'm sorry for all the pain I caused you," I said quietly.

"Don't be," she replied softly. "The time for apologies and regret is long past. You are my life, Erik, and I am where I want to be."

I had no response. I hugged her as we stood silently at the window for a few more minutes. Then we both fell into bed and immediately into an exhausted sleep.

       *   *   *

I fell into taking long walks, both on orders of Dr. Sorel and for my own amusement. Over a period of time I believed I covered most, if not all, of the French Quarter. I did not venture on foot beyond the imaginary barrier of Canal Street. I was reluctant to find myself in an undesirable circumstance so far from home. The only other area I avoided was that of Gallatin Street. I'd been told of things that could happen to people down there and of its rough reputation. People disappeared from there without a trace. Although I had frequented areas like that all my life, I valued my life with Christine far too much to place myself in that kind of jeopardy.

I felt comfortable in the streets of the Quarter, and many people there became accustomed to seeing me on my daily excursions. One might ask why I had not experienced more of the same rejection and scorn in public as I'd had at other times in my life. I had pondered it, and decided it might largely be due to my own attitude. During those years when I was most feared and avoided I had purposely cultivated and maintained a very cold and uninviting manner about me. Developed over time as a defense mechanism, hostility had emanated from me like a strong odor. I was aloof and adopted an intimidating air of mystery. Those attitudes were an intentional effort on my part to keep people at a distance. My improved outlook on life had driven all that away. A smile on my face had indeed been a rare occurrence in the past but now the expression came easily to me. The mask hid the upturned corners of my mouth, but my good humor showed itself in my eyes. Laughter had never been a part of my life before Christine entered it—only a sarcastic chuckle or a disdainful grunt had ever passed my lips. She brought my innate sense of humor to the fore and she told me how my deep rolling laughter delighted her. My whole manner had changed. In short, I was no longer unapproachable. I was not usually approached, but neither did most people literally try to avoid me. I found it very refreshing. I also thought the city itself was in part responsible for my transformation. New Orleans was home to such an odd mix of people from all parts of the world that one more slightly different person did not matter in the grand scheme of things. The people of New Orleans prided themselves on their diversity. The time I spent researching the world for a place to begin over again had paid off.

One afternoon I found myself in the neighborhood of Marie Laveau's cottage. I had not been back to that area since I was attacked and beaten there, and it was purely accidental that I was there a second time. The sun had plenty of hours left in it. My other pursuits of the past year had kept me so busy that I'd had no time to think much about my desire to delve into the rituals of the Black Arts. I stood on the street looking at what I believed to be the cottage I had left so painfully that night when the door creaked open and Marie herself stood silently on the stoop.

On closer look she appeared to be somewhere around sixty years of age, but it was hard to tell. It was obvious, though, that she had led a hard life.

"Well, well," she chuckled softly, her dark eyes smiling. "Ma special one."

No one but Christine had ever called me special, and the term brought back a dim memory of the last time I had been there. Marie had said the same thing that night. I was intrigued.

She invited me inside. I stepped into the tiny, dark cottage. Smells confronted me that I could not identify and smoke from something that had been cooked hung in the air. She closed the door behind me and immediately walked right up to me, raising her hands well above her head to my mask. She ran her fingers over every inch of it, then let them slide down to my shoulders and finally patted me confidently on the chest. I was not used to being touched like that by anyone other than my wife and it unnerved me, especially the way Marie did it. Every movement she made was as if she were making some sort of discovery and passing judgment upon what she found. She stared at me a while longer with her head cocked, then reached down to take both my hands in hers. Turning them over and over, she finally dropped them. She pointed to a wooden chair and told me to sit.

"You wear da mark o' de' debil, but you ain't." She looked at me, waiting for me to say something. When I didn't she continued. "You was born like dat, ya?" I nodded my head in silence. Christ, she must have looked under my mask that night while I was unconscious. "Naw, you ain't de debil. You's special!" Here she was using that term again. What in hell did she mean?

"I want to know…" I began, but she held up her hand, stopping me.

"You want ta know 'bout da Black Arts." She peered at me through narrowed eyes, as if weighing things in her mind. "Marie show you, but you cain't tell no one, unerstan?" She stood up and I took her hint, getting to my own feet. "T'ree nights hence,

814 No'th Rampart. Mi'night. And," she added, "you be safe in ma streets from now on."

I left St. Ann Street with a sense of dangerous excitement that I hadn't felt in a very long time. To what had she invited me? I did not fear for my safety. The woman's manner suggested that she, at least, thought there was something special about me and that it would be safe for me to return. At the time I did not know that the best thing I could have done for myself and for Christine was to never have gone into Marie's house in the first place.

*   *   ⋈

That night my nightmares returned with a vengeance. I thrashed around in the bed grappling with an unknown assailant. I clutched wildly at my chest, leaving marks upon my skin as I tried unsuccessfully to withdraw the lasso from the folds of my coat and save myself. Once again Christine tried to bring me out of it by shaking me, but this time her actions entered into my dream and I fought her. She could not hope to compete against my strength and as she became more frightened she did the only thing she could think of—she slapped me hard across the face. Believing that I was being attacked, I sat bolt upright and grabbed her, quickly and skillfully twisting her body around to pin her under me with one forearm across her throat. She cried out in terror, and I finally woke up. Seeing what I had done frightened me as much as her. I was horrified to learn that I had bruised her arms in our struggle. I held her gently and poured my apologies over her repeatedly until she finally told me to stop. I did not intentionally hurt her but that could not erase the guilt that I felt.

The nightmares did not go away. They continued to disturb our nights. I had at least one every week; sometimes more. They were always different but all were based in some way on things from my past. Soon the memory of these images began to haunt me during the day, interfering with my composing and other studies.

The stress of my nightly horrors did not prevent me from keeping my appointment on North Rampart Street. I crawled out of our bed quietly and slipped away into the night. I did not tell Christine what I was doing. If she thought the cemeteries were bad, she really would love this. I walked to North Rampart. I would not involve Robert in trying to sneak my carriage out of the stable. I also did not want my rig seen in the area to which I was headed. The night was cool but not unpleasantly so and soon I approached the address I had been given. From somewhere in the distance I heard the sound of a policeman dropping his club. It was an old custom that signaled he was on duty and everything was well in the streets. I knocked upon the door of 814.

Several colored people I saw inside stared at me. They did not show fear, but something else I couldn't figure out. They had obviously been told of my impending arrival. I was shown through another door by a small colored man and through darkened hallways lit only here and there with a single candle. The hallways were narrow and I had to duck through the doorways. Finally we came to a room that had a fire burning on the hearth and that was furnished sparsely with wooden furniture. It was obviously an old slave quarters and there were many people present. I was told to remove my coat and to sit quietly in a chair off to one side. I guessed that I was to witness a voodoo ceremony.

I folded my coat over the back of the chair indicated and sat down. I was lost in the shadows and felt oddly at home in my surroundings. The air was heavy and smoke filled and had a vile smell. The atmosphere reminded me of the opium dens of exotic places. While I waited for something to happen, I looked around the dimly lit room. A tiny glow suddenly caught my eye and I saw someone familiar standing in the dark corner. I searched my memory and placed him as the crude man from the saloon on my wedding night. The glow was from his lit cigar. What was his name…Francois. He had talked about Marie, but I wondered what he was doing there.

There was a stir in the room as several people entered escorting a white man amongst them. From the conversation I learned that this man felt he was losing his woman to a rival. He wanted the rival "taken care of". He was given a faded robe and told to go to the other room and remove every item of his own clothing. When he returned with the robe loosely tied around his middle he was seated before Marie, who had silently emerged from the shadows to sit on the floor. Between them was a tablecloth piled with food and three black candles. After much talk from Marie about "seein' 'im" the man was told that his rival would be "fixed". Marie nodded to a mulatto girl seated near her, who opened the first bottle of wine. Marie drank deeply from it and then spit it out all over herself and the white man.

Marie then produced a piece of shapeless black wax. She worked it between her hands until it looked like a crude man. Another man approached the white man who looked terrified when he saw the large knife that was headed for his arm. A tiny bit of blood was coaxed to flow before Marie took the knife and plunged it into the middle of the wax figure. Removing the knife, she then pressed the figure to the wound in the white man's arm. She then dropped to the floor and began to roll around, drooling and shrieking. The wine bottles and other spirits were passed around and everyone drank from them, myself included. I did not want to offend them. A large man and another mulatto girl approached the white man and handed him the things he would need—a small leather bag, something that looked like horse hairs, dried leaves and a handful of black chicken feathers. He was instructed to throw these items into the path of his enemy.

At the fireplace a thick gumbo was being served up in bowls. The drinking continued non-stop and I grew very relaxed. The whole thing felt like a dream. I passed the bottle along after drinking long from it and accepted the small bowl of gumbo that was handed to me. A drum began to beat and the people began chanting, louder and louder. They got up off the floor and left the shadows to dance in the firelight. Through a wine induced haze I watched them writhe and move in time to the beating of that incessant drum. I glanced over at Francois, and in the firelight I saw the same secretive smile on his face that I had seen before. He was looking right at me. I turned away and leaned back in my chair to close my eyes while the chanting grew louder and more urgent.

I felt something strange. I opened my eyes to see a delicate mulatto girl crouching on the floor in front of me, between my knees. She had run her hands lightly up my thighs to my waist and was unbuttoning my shirt. My words of protest never made it past my lips. Her warm hands slipped inside my shirt. I tried to get up but she pushed me back into the chair. It didn't take much; I had drunk enough to make me a bit too relaxed. She stood up between my legs. She was naked to the waist and her generous breasts swayed in front of my face as she began to dance. I could see the firelight right through her thin skirt. Suddenly I was grabbed under both arms and hauled to my feet by two unseen men. The girl's arms went around me and we were jostled from every side by the mad dancing and orgy style lovemaking of the others. She pulled me into the middle of the group and began to move erotically and suggestively against me. As if having a mind of their own, my arms went around her and I spread my hands below her lower back to pull her hips tightly against me. Our bodies moved sensuously together to the lulling beat of the drum and the chanting all around us. The tempo of the beating drums increased. *Just let go, let go and enjoy yourself...* said a strange, haunting voice that came from somewhere inside my head. The wine and the firelight and the feel of the girl's half-naked body pressed against me were carrying me away. Her hands moved back around to my chest and down between us. I didn't even notice that she had loosened my trousers. I was swaying in a trance-like state when I felt her hand slip quickly down inside and grab me. Abruptly I became fully aware of what was happening. Christ, what was I doing? Holding onto my clothing, I pushed the girl away firmly and stumbled back to the chair for my coat. Fighting my way through the mass of now naked bodies writhing upon the floor I found my way through the maze of hallways and out into the street. I rearranged my clothing and began walking home.

I let myself quietly into the house where I undressed downstairs and crept up to the bedroom. Oblivious to the smoky smell that clung to my clothes, I dropped them with uncharacteristic carelessness on a chair. Christine was asleep. I got into bed beside her and my thoughts drifted to the evening and to my many questions. How had Marie known that my affliction was a birth defect? Why had she invited me to a ceremony that was obviously a well-guarded secret? Why did she keep calling me a "special one"? I turned onto my side, draped my arm over my sleeping wife's hip, and drifted to sleep with those questions circling in my mind.

*   *   *

I was alone in the bed when I woke the next morning. I went downstairs to find Christine sitting in the courtyard reading a novel by a local man named Cable. His books were about the New Orleans society of which she now considered herself an upstanding member.

"Good morning, my love," I greeted her as I went over to her and leaned down to kiss her. She turned slightly away from me to take a drink from the glass on the table. I knew her too well. I waited, and finally she looked up.

"Where did you go last night, Erik?" she asked bluntly.

Damn! Stalling for time, I went around the table to take a seat. I sat down and looked innocently at her.

"I took a walk."

"At one o'clock in the morning?"

She didn't seem to know that I had been gone for almost three hours.

"I had another nightmare and I thought to walk it off," I said, smoothly lying through my teeth.

"Why didn't you let me help you, like always?" She sounded hurt.

"Because I didn't want to disturb you. Christine, you have lost enough sleep over my nighttime demons lately. I didn't want to wake you for something I could handle myself."

She seemed to accept the explanation although she looked at me oddly as I got up to go back into the house. I felt her eyes burning into my back as I walked away. It was the first time I had blatantly lied to her since we had been together, and I was not proud of it.

I lied about having a nightmare the previous night, but I wasn't far off. I probably just hadn't been in bed long enough that night to have one. The next night the dream was as terrifying as the last one and although I did not hurt Christine again I was still concerned for her. Flying, laughing faces. Whips, bloody knives and hangman's nooses. The dream ended with a young girl who looked at me and screamed in terror. I tried to tell her I would not hurt her, tried to make her understand, but she wouldn't listen. Her eyes were popping out of her head as she stared at my naked face, and she continued screaming until I woke up with a cry. I sat in the bed catching my breath while Christine got me some water and wrapped her arms around me. She rocked me back and forth, telling me it would be all right, but I knew it wouldn't be.

Months passed. I played chess, worked on my music and played at the church. I also developed a heavy schedule of nocturnal excursions. Christine seemed tired and appeared to be content with social visits and her novels. I made it a point to be home in the afternoons so that we could spend time together. I was content.

I left the house regularly at night to witness the fascinating rituals and ceremonies of the voodoos. Each visit brought me a little more understanding of its background. I could not read up on the subject, for even if anything had been available I could not have had it in the house anyway.

Although voodoo bore little resemblance to Christianity, Marie's form of the practice of voodoo had twisted the original beliefs brought here by the slaves from Africa to conform to the worship of the virgin and other religious figures. Along with idolatry she introduced a certain amount of blasphemy to make "voodooism" her own.

Voodoo commonly combines a belief in one god with belief in different spirits, who serve as intermediaries between the god and the people. It is believed that upon death, one of a person's several souls could take possession of a living person. The possessed could then offer counseling and advice. There was also a strong belief in the workings of spells and incantations. I learned of the charms and gris-gris that were used to bring about the desired effect. Gris-gris were tiny bags that contained red powder ground from brick, yellow ochre, cayenne pepper and other bits of specially chosen materials. A gris-gris found on the doorstep in the morning was cause for great anxiety, and it usually precipitated a visit to Marie for measure to counteract that particular spell. Usually the offending item had come from Marie in the first place. She ran a successful business, if you could call it that. Her self-proclaimed expertise ran from invoking evil spirits to offering protection from same. Often one night's ritual was a counteraction of a previous night's ceremony. She held these people in the palm of her hand, and she was like a god to them.

I felt there might be some basis for the religious aspects of the practice. I saw a few things that I could not explain, but I considered most of it to be just so much hokum. I've seen many alternative forms of religion in my time and their similarities are apparent to anyone who takes the time to look at them closely. Many of them require only a consummate actor and a room full of believers. A bit of magic didn't hurt either. That was where I came in.

Marie assured me that I would not be asked or manipulated again into engaging in any sort of sexual activity after I firmly stated my position on the matter. I did, however, continue to participate in the ceremonies to the extent that I left there quite intoxicated most nights. I had initially accepted the wine and other spirits to avoid offending them, but I quickly fell into expecting it and eventually enjoying it. Before long I became a knowledgeable participant in the rituals themselves. The colored community accepted me with reverence.

I began to feel a strange, addictive power. My duties grew more important with time and soon my participation, and indeed my presence alone, were almost essential for an effective spell. Costumed in a deep red robe and hood and wearing heavy, ornately carved ceremonial rings on every finger, I became an ethereal presence that lent an air of the supernatural to the proceedings. I called on past experience to push that effect to the limits with feats of magic and slight of hand. I began to see awe, worship and sometimes fear reflected in the black faces around me. Thus costumed and employing a disguised voice, I was unrecognizable to people whom I knew as prominent citizens who came to the voodoo world seeking help for their petty problems.

It never failed to amaze me that such civilized people might stoop to that form of remedy. I was skeptical of why so many of them came to Marie for help rather than the more accepted measures that society offered. Many of these people were quite wealthy and could afford any kind of help they desired. But no, they took their chances to come to the less desirable section of the Quarter to seek out Marie.

Marie astutely recognized early on that I could be of tremendous use to her. She exploited my unusual talents to her advantage in her ceremonies. Marie was an enigma. If one chanced to meet her on the street during daylight hours she looked about as harmless as they come. She was small and slight in stature and legitimately worked as a hairdresser. I believe she used the information that she constantly overheard in her line of work to help her maintain her aura of clairvoyance and mystery. I would discover later that she also employed other means of gaining useful information. It was amusing to see the looks on the faces of her voodoo "clients" when Marie told them of things that someone in her position should never have known. Numerous gentlemen whom I knew from around town came to North Rampart Street for an array of problems ranging from help with a poor business deal to a cheating wife. Imagine the awed uncertainty of an otherwise intelligent businessman when Marie spoke of the recent dinner party gone awry or the thousands of dollars lost in a poker game! These pillars of the community would have been horrified to discover the identity of the cloaked form that silently moved with a godlike presence throughout the proceedings. By that time I had become a quietly enigmatic but familiar and respected resident of the French section of the city, and many of the citizens who sought out Marie's help knew me by name. I would say nothing about anything I witnessed, but had I been in the same position years go, I would have taken malicious pleasure in exposing the whole sorry lot of them.

Even so, I took increasingly evil delight in watching all of this. My participation in the ceremonies became indispensable. I was taught the rituals and I usually performed as well. To my knowledge I am the only white man to ever have been accorded the honor of being taught the black arts by Marie Laveau. It was predominantly a practice of the colored people, although whites had been known to participate in the revelry at more "public" ceremonies. The colored people who surrounded me were driven back to the far corners of the room in fear when they observed the sparks emanating from beneath my robes or heard a disembodied voice address them.

I used my skill with ventriloquism to the greatest effect when the ceremonies took place out in the swamps or on the shores of Lake Pontchartrain. Some of them were held out there to provide for larger capacity. I had thought the carrying on and frenetic dancing were wild during the first smoky ceremony I attended on North Rampart, but that was nothing compared to what went on out at the lake. Local newspaper reporters would often attend these larger ceremonies, which were very elaborate and mostly staged for outsiders. The more sinister aspects of voodoo were carefully kept secret and the public did not see them. The curious crowds observed only what they were allowed to see, which was mostly overly embellished but meaningless incantations, lots of smoke, and some strategically placed snakes surrounded by much dancing and carrying on. When I mysteriously appeared amongst them in my blood-red hooded robes, those who were not familiar with my role in the proceedings were visibly frightened. Often emerging from explosions of equally red smoke, I glided slowly through the crowds in my robes like a dark god while they shrank back from me as if I would strike them dead with a wave of my hand. I would lift my covered head and arms to the dark sky and throw my voice to the trees. Sometimes my voice would emanate from far out on the lake, and the distance that it traveled over the still, misty water made it sound eerie and ghostly. I sang haunting songs of nonsensical syllables that meant nothing. At other times I sang in Latin, which lent a religious flavor to the evening. It did not matter what I said or did; to these people it was all magic.

I lived a double life. I had my sunlit world with my wife during the day and my dark, secret world of pagan rituals, alcohol and crowded rooms at night. The latter was very much like the world in which I had felt I belonged for so many years.

Inevitably, the dark world of my nights eventually altered my personality and my disposition. I became more moody and my temper shortened. I also lived with my lies. Christine was not a fool. She knew something was going on with me but I could not tell her what I was doing. It is impossible, in a marriage, to keep secrets like those I was keeping and not suffer the consequences. I saw the strain in her face and I knew it was not bad lighting that caused those shadows around her eyes. She approached me several times with questions that pointedly left the door open for me to unburden myself to her. She obviously thought something was bothering me that I should talk about. I waved her concerns aside. I preferred to let her think the nightmares were the cause of my gradual decline in temperament because I was largely unaware of the extent of my increasingly odd and distant behavior.

We tried to continue our outwardly happy home life but the magic was gone. Christine lost much of her exuberance in bed and the distance between us was growing. My nighttime disappearances were wearing on her but I refused to acknowledge it. Even if I did see it, I was too caught up in the powerful position I had found in my new dark world to give it up. I could not or would not see how much I was hurting her although I never intended to hurt her in any way. Christine likely got no sleep at all. Her nights alternated between dragging me out of my nightmares and lying awake wondering where I was.

For our first wedding anniversary we enjoyed a night on the town and the opera. I gave Christine a diamond and emerald bracelet that cost an obscene amount of money. Never before had I spent so much money on an item like that, and it went quite against my reluctance to flash wealth. I did not leave our bed that night, and our lovemaking showed many hints of a closeness we had not felt in months. She was very taken with the gift but I believe my choice had much more to do with my own heavy load of guilt than with what might actually please her.

I gradually filled more of my days with my composing and time spent at the church. Christine spent more time with her friends. I completed my studies of the city's cemeteries, and it pleased Christine to know that I would not be spending my time in those "morbid" places. She had no argument with the many hours that I spent down Royal Street with Paul. Since Paul always seemed to be available for play, the frequency of our games increased along with the distance between my wife and me. The hours I set aside to spend with her in the afternoons became fewer as she began to make other plans. I felt her drawing away from me but my mind was not ready to do anything about it.

The changes in our home life should have served as warnings, but they failed to interrupt my participation in the dark nighttime world of North Rampart Street. My extensive practical experience in ghostly endeavors made me fully qualified for the job. Alcohol was passed around continuously at all these events. It flowed freely, and a staggering amount of it was flowing into me.

16

———————— ✶ ————————

At Christmas I bought Christine the gift that I thought would please her the most. After our customary holiday dinner with Jean and Louise, the four of us sat in our attractively decorated parlor to exchange gifts. I was very happy with my new supply of score sheets and pens specially designed for musical composition. In addition, Jean had assisted Christine in her choice of a handsome and powerful gelding. Jet black and sleek, he was magnificent and the sight of him made me anxious to sit a fine horse again. I named him Onyx.

Christine had two packages from me. The first held a new driving cloak in a rich midnight blue. The other tiny package contained a tiny item. She looked up at me in confusion as she held the key in her fingers. Wordlessly I spread my arms expansively and looked around the room. She threw her arms around my neck. I had purchased our home.

The holiday season may have seemed a happy affair in our home, but it did little to alleviate the tension between Christine and me. If I had been using my head at all I would have realized that she was fully aware of how frequently I left the house at night. One could not repeatedly leave a marriage bed night after night without one's wife suspecting something. Why she did not ask me about it sooner I can't guess. Well, yes I can. I would have become impatient with her, and that was happening a little too often as it was. The guilt I felt at my deception of the woman that I had promised to love and cherish for life unfortunately did little to curtail my activities. My guilt grew along with the distance between us but for some reason I was powerless to stop it. I thought I was presenting the picture of a happy home life to the outside world, but apparently I was wrong.

In the early spring just after another exciting and liberating Mardi Gras celebration, Jean delivered Louise to my house in the early afternoon to accompany Christine on a visit to an ailing friend. After the women left we sat down in my parlor. I politely offered to pour us a drink but Jean waived my offer with a slightly astonished expression. I shrugged, poured one for myself anyway and sat down opposite him. He stared at me uncomfortably for a few seconds before he drew himself up and asked me, point blank, what I was doing to my wife. His usual jovial disposition was nowhere to be seen. I had never seen him so serious.

"Just what the hell is going on with you, Erik?" he queried when I still had not answered his question.

"I don't know what you're talking about, Jean," I said evasively as I took a sip of my bourbon. "There is nothing wrong, and Christine is fine."

"Damn it man! You've got eyes in your head don't you? You know as well as I do that something is very wrong between you!" He was extremely upset.

"I don't know what you want me to say." I tensed. "I have done nothing to Christine. It may be that she's lost a little weight recently, but..."

"A little weight? My God, man, she's a shadow of herself, a shadow! I think you'd better adjust that mask a bit or get yourself some spectacles." He squinted at me. "As a matter of fact you're not looking too well yourself lately, no, not well at all." His searching gaze made me uncomfortable. "I'd swear that if I could see your eyes better, I'd find they are bloodshot."

I'd noticed a slight looseness in my clothes, but my eyes? I decided to throw him a scrap to get him off my back and out of my house.

"If you must know, I have been having terrible nightmares for months now. Both Christine and I have lost many nights' sleep over them." I injected weariness into my voice and hoped he would be satisfied.

"Nightmares," He replied dubiously. "What kind of nightmares?"

"Horrifying things that I usually cannot remember upon waking." He knew nothing of my past and I had no intention of enlightening him. Indeed, if he had known of my past history he might have reconsidered his decision to continue pushing me for information. My patience was wearing thin.

"That still doesn't explain the tension I sense between you and Christine." He paused and waited. "You're not going to talk to me are you?"

I got to my feet, sending him an obvious message that I wanted him to leave.

"If my wife and I have any problems we will work them out on our own, thank you. Now, Jean, if you don't mind I am due at the church."

Jean stood up hesitantly and inched toward the door. He looked as if he might say something else, but changed his mind. He stopped again with his hand on the doorknob and looked back at me.

"While you are there, Erik, you might take a moment to say a prayer for your marriage. You are going to need it."

He turned and left without saying good-bye, leaving the door wide open. I walked over to close it gently and returned to my chair.

I didn't move until I heard his carriage disappear down the street. Damn him, I thought. *Don't let him push you*, said that strange, new voice inside my head. I went to the sideboard and poured myself another glassful of bourbon. (I had begun drinking more at home in addition to my growing consumption on North Rampart Street and out at the lake.) I had just alienated my closest friend.

Curious, I went to the mirror that hung in the hallway. I took the mask off and looked at myself. Ignoring the usual revulsion I felt whenever I looked into a mirror, I concentrated objectively on what might be different. I looked at my eyes and saw what Jean thought he saw. They had a marked red tint to them that looked quite horrific given the rest of my visage. New streaks of gray shot through my dark brown hair, making me look older than I was. The uneven flesh of my cheeks hung looser and my skin was gray. I looked down at my hands and found the same shade of gray. I returned to my chair after automatically stopping to refresh my drink yet again. I leaned my head against the high back of the chair while the warming liquid spread through me. I was not expected at the church. I told Jean that only to get rid of him. I was not only lying to Christine but to my friends as well.

What in hell was happening to my life? Suddenly everything was coming apart. The gap was widening between Christine and myself. I saw the concern in her eyes when she looked at me. (That no longer surprised me after seeing what I just did in the mirror.) I loved her more than life itself and I hated the distance between us. I held the glass up in front of my face and looked through it to the sun-drenched courtyard beyond the windows. There wasn't enough of the amber liquid in the glass to see what I wanted so I drained it and refilled it again. I could now see the courtyard with the desired amber tint. Deciding I'd had enough of that, I emptied the glass once more and set it down on the table.

My thoughts began to drift. I was walking a thin line and I knew it. But then, I was used to living on the edge, wasn't I? I'd done it since the day I was born. I saw no reason why I couldn't manage the two halves of my double life; to maintain the separation between them while not giving either of them up. I would not waste my time thinking about the possibility of life without Christine. I thought I had it all figured out, but I could no longer ignore the fact that something else, beyond what I was doing at night, was now threatening our marriage and our happiness. The more I thought about it, the more it seemed that my past was trying to intrude on my present.

Despite all my efforts to live life like a normal man, I overlooked the fact that I had never fully excised the past from my mind. It lurked just below the surface where I had forced it; festering in my subconscious. Both my nightmares and my clandestine activities reeked of my former life, and somehow they had released memories of the past to haunt me. My past now lived again inside me where it had lain dormant and silently waiting for its chance to ruin me. Its evil presence was finally making itself known and was fighting to be free. I recognized it now. The nightmares reminded me of the things I had tried to forget, dragging me back through time to the man I had been long ago. This presence was the source of the voice in my head, and it said things that I would no longer utter. It was me talking, but it was the me of twenty years before. Why was this happening now, after my life had become so full? Perhaps the guilt I lived with wasn't enough, perhaps I could never be rid of my past. I looked at the empty glass on the table. I was thirsty, and a little more wouldn't hurt. The glass was once again empty when Christine returned from her outing.

She went directly upstairs to change and returned to find me in the parlor. I was reading the paper, although I couldn't really see the words all that well.

"Did you enjoy your outing, my dear?" I inquired without thinking. I kept my face buried in the newspaper.

"As much as one can enjoy visiting a dying friend," she replied in a clipped tone. "Are you attempting to be amusing or did you forget where I was going?" She was not pleased.

I lowered the paper, but kept my eyes averted.

"I am sorry, Christine, I did forget the nature of your outing. Forgive me."

Over my newspaper she caught sight of the empty glass beside me. Her eyes then darted to the sideboard and rested on the quarter-full bottle of bourbon with its glass stopper sitting next to it. She walked around in front of me just as I moved the newspaper back up in front of me and tried again to focus on the newsprint. Suddenly she snatched the paper away and peered intently at me.

"You've been drinking again," she stated in an accusatory tone. "Why? It's the middle of the afternoon."

"I've not..." I tried to protest. I could not prevent my eyes from rising to her face.

"I'm not blind, Erik! I see the glass and I see the bottle! I can see it in your eyes! I know how much was in that bottle this morning! Why are you lying to me?"

I blinked stupidly at her. At that inopportune moment, the evil presence that lurked inside me decided to make its first appearance. There was nothing I could do to stop it. I leapt to my feet and caught her by her wrist.

"My dear wife, if I wish to have a drink in the comfort of my own home, that is precisely what I shall do. It is neither your nor anyone else's place to tell me otherwise," I said in a too-quiet manner. "I apologized to you for my insensitive remark about your friend. I would appreciate you dropping the matter."

I held onto her wrist while I looked down directly into her eyes until I could see uncertainty grow in them. I dropped her arm.

"I am going walking and I would thank you not to attempt to dissuade me."

Stalking to the front hall, I wrenched my hat off its hook and walked out, slamming the door behind me.

I was more than three blocks away before my hurried steps slowed and I began to relax. I continued on to Jackson Square where I deposited myself on a bench in front of the Cabildo. The liquor had already begun to wear off. The effects of alcohol never lasted long with me. Whatever had possessed me was also gone, leaving me weary and remorseful.

I was concerned about my failure to control the unexpected surfacing of what had, until now, lived only in my mind. I began to fear the presence inside me, and what it might do to the life that I had so carefully constructed. I now thought of the presence as a living, breathing entity that was out to destroy my life with Christine. When it was finished doing that, it would destroy me.

I sat on that bench for a long time. A young mother was taking a walk in the park with her two small children. They passed close by and I touched the brim of my hat to nod a casual greeting to her. I will not easily forget the look that immediately crossed her face. She gathered her children to her and rushed them from the park. She looked back at me as they crossed the street, then hurried them along. I slumped and stared at the ground. I wanted a drink.

What was happening to me? Throughout all the torment of my life I had never resorted to the bottle, or anything else for that matter, for solace. Indeed, I'd always felt either contempt or pity for drunkards and, as I mentioned before, I associated such weakness with cowards and fools. I was not a coward. *No? Then that makes you a fool!* laughed the evil voice. The sky darkened and the clouds finally opened to let loose a heavy rain. I remained on that bench long after I was soaked to the skin. A light breeze sprang up and, although the day was warm, I shivered. I slowly walked home.

Christine was upstairs when I walked, dripping, into the bedroom. When she turned to look at me I saw that she had been crying. She took in my wet clothes and my remorse in one glance and the concern in her eyes caused my own to fill with tears. I reached for her, saying I was sorry over and over again. Christ, how many times had I apologized to this woman in the last two years? I could never do anything right. I held her tightly and whatever had come between us temporarily let go. The wet clothes were hastily shed and we knew nothing but our love for each other. I took her with a new and driving passion born of my desperate attempt to hold on to something that was being taken away from me by some inexplicable force. I had never made such urgent love before and Christine was left gasping from my relentless onslaught on her senses.

We lay wound around each other in the gathering darkness, our passion finally played out. Just before sleep overtook us I said, "Christine, I want you to know that I will always love you with all my heart."

I did not intend for the words to sound as if I spoke of some impending doom, but the minute they were out of my mouth I realized that's exactly how they sounded. I gathered my wife more tightly to me, as if I could protect her from the awful feeling of dread that filled my heart.

17

---★---

The hot and humid summer months of 1884 descended upon us. I dearly love New Orleans, but the damnable heat might be the death of me yet. Long ago I had taken to wearing the lighter clothing called for by the climate, but there was no respite from the relentless humidity. Everyone in the city slowed down during the day in an effort to stay cool, and we were no exception.

The annual "holiday" of those who practice voodoo is St. John's Eve. I was at the lake for most of that hot June night and returned home much later than usual. I was so drunk that I can't recall getting home and could not have been too quiet coming in. I opened my eyes in the early morning light to realize with disgust that I had slept in my clothes in my parlor chair. I got cleaned up before Christine came downstairs or Deliah came in, greeting them as if I'd risen early. The pounding in my head did not help my mood that day. My alcohol intake was reaching dangerous proportions.

I was reading my newspaper a couple of days later and chanced upon an article describing the goings-on at the lake on that special night. The press always made quite a show out of attending the annual event and writing greatly elaborated accounts of it. I scanned it and was dismayed to see a vivid description of my own contributions to the evening's proceedings.

"... A tall, graceful figure clad in blood-red robes, his face completely hidden by a voluminous hood, is the most prominent presence of the event, in part due to his angelic singing voice. This figure is possessed of a voice that surely would cause the angels themselves to cry. Fire bursts forth from his fingertips as he holds the crowds of believers in thrall for hours. Appearing and disappearing at will via puffs of smoke, he has attained the status of a god among his followers. Who is this man who lives in our midst, this man who can command total obedience? Is he the devil incarnate or is he a creature of even worse capabilities? We may never know, as those who are aware of his identity would never speak of it. Certainly he appears to be at least partly inhuman. The evening's endless drinking adds to an atmosphere of pagan wildness that eventually leads to total abandonment of moral values..."

I could not let Christine see that. It would not be hard for her to put the descriptions in the article together with my odd behavior of the past year. Christ, had it really been a year? She was not home, so I took the newspaper outside and burned it. Bourbon in hand, I watched the tiny flames lick their way through the condemning newsprint until the paper finally curled into an unrecognizable black ball. I lifted my foot to crush the ashes into the flagstones. Satisfied that the evidence was gone, I walked into the house to pour myself another drink.

*   *   *

Striding briskly down St. Ann Street after having crawled from the warmth of my wife's bed for what seemed the thousandth time, I entered the intersection at Burgundy and collided heavily with another man who came around a corner just as I did. My head was down and I did not see him until it was too late. I muttered a cursory apology under my breath and continued walking toward North Rampart but I was brought up short when I heard a tentative "Erik?" behind me. I turned around slowly to find Jean walking toward me. Damn, of all people to meet, I didn't want to see him out here. With a feeling of dread I stood and waited for his suspicious questions.

"It *is* you. I thought so." He peered at me in the light from a distant street lamp. "After the last time I tried to talk to you, should I even bother to ask what you are doing out here at this time of night?"

"I could ask you the same question, Jean," I replied warily.

"I am returning home from a lengthy business meeting at the home of a client," he stated matter-of-factly. He looked off in the direction in which I had been walking. "You, my friend, are not headed home." It was not put as a question, but as a statement of fact.

"I am also on business," I said shortly. I did not like the turn the conversation was taking and was anxious to be away.

After another look toward my destination, he said quietly, "The only business in that direction, Erik, is business you should not be involved with."

Unbidden but not altogether unwanted, the presence took charge. I walked up to Jean until my face was less than a foot from his.

"My business this night, Mr. Vaillancourt, or any other night for that matter, is none of yours."

My voice came out in the low, harsh and coldly hostile tones of years past. The presence, which had already begun to surface in my behavior, had now spoken aloud. Its voice sounded foreign even to my own ears. Immediately taken aback, Jean retreated a step and I saw unease enter his formerly friendly eyes when he acknowledged the warning, reflected clearly in that voice, that he was stepping over the line.

"And by the way, Jean," I added, "if you say anything to my wife about this, I promise that you will regret it." I turned on my heel and walked away.

The presence did not leave me when I left Jean standing dumbfounded and concerned in the street. I met only one other person that night on my journey. The walk was narrow, and as the man approached me I simply took him by the lapels of his coat and bodily removed him from my path, setting him hard against a building. I had never stopped walking. I did not know who he was and I didn't care. The presence did not leave me during that night's ceremony. I joined in the rituals with unusual abandon and those around me sensed that something was different. The atmosphere of the night's proceedings was wilder than ever before and I reveled in it. Marie was not in attendance, and one of her protégés led the proceedings. A very talented young woman indeed, she was both mysterious and sensual in her manipulation of the group. I was again approached to participate in the carnal recreation but again I turned it down. Oh, I wanted it all right. The presence and I both needed it, but I would not get it there. I was loaded with alcohol and consumed by the strongest, most animalistic sexual need I had ever felt. It had nothing to do with love. What I needed that night was raw and uncontrolled, and went totally against my normal standards of how to treat a woman. Upon leaving, a paper was pressed into my hand from the darkness. I stuffed it into my pocket without looking at it. I had only one thing on my mind.

The presence and I returned home together to walk with heavy determination up the stairs. I found my unsuspecting wife standing at the French doors looking out into the night. Without a word to her and driven by the presence, liquor and unbridled lust,

I grabbed her roughly, spinning her around to face me and tangling one hand in her hair. The mask hit the far wall as my lips came down on hers forcefully, grinding our teeth together and bending her head back. I held her mouth hard to mine with one hand firmly behind her head while I savagely tore the light gown from her body with the other. I released her for only as long as it took me to swiftly throw my own clothes off. Christine was speechlessly staring at the shredded remains of her nightgown when I reached for her again. She did not push me away, but it was not long before I sensed a change in her as she realized that something other than love drove me that night. Lacking the patience for our usually extensive rituals of foreplay, I backed her toward the bed almost immediately while ravaging her soft lips. We fell across it with all my weight landing full on top of her, causing the bed to creak and groan under the impact. Christine tried to keep up with me while I devoured her, not giving her a chance to catch her breath. The presence rode on my shoulder and goaded me on while I took her rough, hard and fast. She wasn't ready for me, but all that mattered to me was satisfying my own desperate hunger as I relentlessly worked to release the enormous pressure inside me. Fueled by forces that had been building up in me for months, the intensity of my need was threatening to tear me apart when I finally exploded into her.

Immediately, the presence left me. Everything stopped when I collapsed, spent and breathless, on top of her. The only sound was that of my laborious panting. I finally lifted my head at the first tremulous sobs from the woman who lay beneath me.

Christine began to cry. I tried to kiss her tears away but she turned her face away from me. As the sobs shook her body I rolled off her and sat numbly on the edge of the bed. I was horrified by what had just happened. It was what I had feared for our wedding night; my taking her with a savage passion that I could not control.

But I had not done this to her. The presence had been responsible. I could not explain that to Christine though, because the presence was a part of me...a part that was taking control of my life.

I stayed at home the entire following day. Christine was already gone from the room when I woke up and she was not at the breakfast table. I found her sitting in the courtyard with a book. I tried to make pleasant conversation but she was distant and cool. Damn it, she was downright cold. She would not even look at me. I followed her around for a while like a lost puppy, but I could not bridge the now gaping chasm between us. We did not speak of the night before. I didn't know what I could possibly say to her to make things right. Eventually she tired of my shadowing her and asked Robert to take her into town. She was gone through the noon hour so I went to the kitchen to find myself something to eat. I would not dream of asking Deliah to fix me anything. Recently she had resumed her old habit of avoiding me. In fact, she appeared to be more afraid of me now than when we had first moved in. I sat alone at the kitchen table and stared at the meager meal on my plate. I eventually pushed it away in disgust. I poured myself a drink, but even that lost its appeal after only one glass. I wandered upstairs to our bedroom—the room that until now had held nothing but wonderful memories. I stared at the rumpled sheets and the clothing strewn around the floor. Deliah had not been in this morning. I picked up what remained of the nightgown Christine had been wearing. It was torn to shreds. Shamefully I rolled it up and tucked it under my arm. I didn't want her to ever see it again. As I straightened out my jacket there was a rustle from the inner pocket. I pulled out a crumpled piece of paper on which I did not recognize the handwriting.

Thursday in two weeks 1am 112 Gallatin

What in hell...? Then I remembered the unseen hand pressing it into mine as I was leaving the gathering last night. Gallatin Street? What would anyone want with me down there? It was an area I swore never to visit because of its dangerous reputation. I had two weeks to decide whether I would answer the cryptic invitation. I committed it to memory and destroyed it.

Christine returned home soon after that, in tears. I tried to comfort her but she would have none of me. A few minutes after she went upstairs I heard her crying. I knocked softly on the door.

"Christine?" I called softly. "Please let me in."

"No, Erik. Please go away."

Again I spoke through the door. "Christine, I know there is something wrong when you come home from an outing in tears." I heard nothing. "I'm coming in."

She was seated at the window. She had been crying for some time from the look of her and she continued to sniff when I stopped at her side.

"Why don't you tell me what happened?" I said gently. "Did someone upset you?"

She looked at me reluctantly. Her eyes were red and puffy. "Well, if you must know, several people have upset me recently...this is just the latest."

"What..." I began.

"It's you!" she interrupted me with a tremor in her voice. "People are saying things about you!" She began to cry again. "They talk behind my back, but just loud enough for me to hear the vile things they say. I don't want to listen to them anymore!"

Christ. What had she heard? "What are these people saying?" I asked softly, trying to sound appropriately bewildered.

"Among other things, they say you are involved in things in this city, and that important people have reason to fear you." She turned away from me. "I hear it more often now, people are hurtful to me. I've also been asked why I would live with a 'man like that'. Some say that you are not who you say you are. Some even say that you hide yourself because you are...evil."

I could diffuse this one easily enough. Someone had obviously begun a rumor. If she thought it was shady business dealings that people said I was involved with, I would simply deny it.

"Christine, I assure you that I am not making threats of any sort to people in high places or otherwise. I have nothing I wish to accomplish in the political or business arenas anyway. The rumors are unfounded. Someone has probably seen me walking and decided to cause trouble." She had turned back to the window. "You must not allow them to trouble you. You have my word that I am not involved with this city's leadership or its operation."

I thought that explanation would mollify her. It was not a lie; I was not involved in what she assumed from the overheard remarks. I did have some concern over the source of these rumors. As for the comment about my being "evil", I thought that was better left untouched for the time being.

"These people who see you walking...is it at night?" she queried suddenly with a sideways glance at me. "That is what you still do at night, isn't it? Walk off your nightmares? Don't tell me you don't because I know how many nights you go out."

I didn't like the sarcastic tenor of her question. She had stopped crying and her attitude and voice had cooled.

"I suppose someone might have seen me..." I began again, but stopped when she got up to face me.

"Erik, I am not going to pursue this conversation any further. I am exhausted. If you intend to continue your nightly visits to God knows where, you shall no longer do it from my bed." She spoke as if she had memorized the lines from one of her operas. "I am tired of wondering where you are and what you are doing. I am tired of turning over in bed to smell the liquor on you. I want you to answer me truthfully for once, Erik, and I will know if you are lying." She paused, taking a deep breath. "Do you leave our bed at night for another woman?"

The question took the breath from me. The room suddenly became an airless vacuum. I regarded my beautiful, cool and distant wife standing before me waiting for my answer. How could she think such a thing?

Hurt as I was by her question, I could not resist the impulse to counter it with a little of my nasty sarcasm. I adopted a stricken attitude.

"Oh, dear. Did you find lip rouge on my collar or do I reek of scent? Yes, I admit that I have actually been keeping several women on the side. Satisfying their craving for my masculine attentions has kept me quite busy lately." My voice turned bitter. "You know how irresistible I am! I must fight them off with a stick!"

Christine was not amused. She said nothing, but the hurt that I intended was reflected in her eyes. We stared each other down for a few tense moments before I dropped the act.

"No, Christine," I said evenly, "you are the only woman in my life, and will be until the day I die."

She searched my eyes. "I believe you. About the woman, anyway. But Erik, something is happening to you. You are not yourself, and you are not letting me in anymore." She touched my face gently. "Don't shut me out, Erik. I need you." With that she turned and left the room. I was left to ponder the wreckage that was my marriage, and to wonder how to get it back the way it was.

I settled into a cold, empty bed that night. I felt lonely and betrayed, but I had only myself to blame, for the only person guilty of any betrayal was me. It took me a long time to get to sleep. Later on when I was violently awakened by yet another of my relentlessly consistent nightmares to see Christine's worried face, I thought for a minute that the whole thing had been just another bad dream. I was brought back to reality with a crash when she kissed me on the forehead as if I were a child and returned to her own room.

*   *   *

I exited a local shop late one afternoon in time to overhear two men talking in the street. I caught a few words as I passed by and I paused behind them to listen.

"...and that pretty young girl, what's she doing with him?" one said. "I've heard he keeps her with him against her will; I wonder what he's got on her?"

"I don't know, but he can be creepy as hell. Frank has seen him in action, and says he's got a lot of stuff up his sleeve that you wouldn't believe. He's not one to mess with."

"He's either done something to that girl or she's totally mad. What the hell is he hiding, anyway?" the first man added. "Anyone who wears a mask all the time must have something to hide."

"I've heard they are legitimately married, but I don't know. I wonder what the real story is with them?"

I had heard enough. The subject of their conversation was apparent and I would not stand by while ignorant fools slandered my wife. The presence, of course, was with me when my iciest voice cut into their conversation.

"If you gentlemen intend to continue discussing me I would appreciate you doing it to my face."

Both men turned around slowly. They looked at each other and back to me. When one of them finally spoke up, he made the mistake of incensing me further.

"To your *face*, sir?" He replied sarcastically. "But since you asked, why don't you tell us about your wife; is she really mad? She must be to be living with…"

Furious, I grabbed him by his coat and dragged him into the adjoining alley. A red haze filled my mind as the presence eagerly encouraged my increasing predisposition for violent confrontation. His companion tried to pull me away but I threw the smaller man off me with one massive sweep of my arm. Luckily for my victim I no longer carried my lasso, but my hands were wrapped tightly around his throat when I was again grabbed from behind and dragged roughly away from him. My arms were wrenched painfully back behind me and I heard two ominous clicks as I felt cold metal encircle my wrists. The presence fled immediately at the sound. I looked around and into the faces of the two policemen who held me. Without a word I was pushed into the back of a police wagon. *Come back here!* I silently called to the presence as I sat in the wagon alone and handcuffed. *Don't leave me here alone like this!*

There is nothing I hate more than being restrained. It makes me remember things I don't want to remember. The enclosed wagon was claustrophobic and I struggled against the handcuffs, wearing my wrists raw with my futile efforts. I had to get them off! I tried to slip them but they were latched down too tightly around my wrists. The movement of the lurching wagon repeatedly threatened to throw me off the narrow wooden bench on which I sat. By the time we reached police headquarters I had been thrown to the floor twice, my knees and shoulders hurt and my wrists bled. I was still fighting with the damned things when I was unceremoniously pulled from the wagon and hustled inside.

That was one of the most humiliating experiences I've ever been put through. There have been many times in my life when humiliation and degradation were my constant companions, but I could not remember a time when it hurt me more than right here in the city in which I finally valued my place as a citizen. I sat mutely staring at the floor while they processed my assault charge. I prayed that I would not see anyone I knew—my shame was complete enough. They did not demand my mask, and I could only assume it was because I was a familiar sight to many of these same policemen during my numerous walks. They finally removed the painful cuffs, but I further embarrassed myself when I was ordered to enter a cell until someone could come for me. At the sight of the bars I panicked. No, please, don't lock me in…I'll sit quietly, I promise! Anything but locks…No! NO!

It took four men to restrain me and throw me bodily into the cell. The charges were increased to reflect my resistance. When the door clanged shut behind me I backed quickly into the far corner. I looked around wildly for a place to hide. I had to get out—I couldn't take it! I squeezed my eyes shut against a rush of memories. My ears heard the laughter, and my mind's eye saw a heavy wooden door swing shut in my face over and over again with a heavy thud. I saw myself beating my little fists raw upon it only to wear myself out and sink slowly down to the floor within the inky darkness of the space not much larger than myself. The ugly memories would not stop—they filled my ears and my mind and threatened to drive me mad!

There was no place to hide. I was shaking uncontrollably when I curled myself up as tightly as possible on the bench in the corner, brought my knees up like a child and dropped my face onto them. I could not bear the sight of the cold metal bars that surrounded me. I wrapped my arms tightly around my head to drown out the sounds and memories that haunted me. I was still sitting there, trembling, when some time later the door to my cell was opened. I did not notice it. I was lost in my own world of childhood horrors and humiliation. The presence had brought me here and deserted me just when I most needed its evil strength.

A hand touched my shoulder. I jumped and whimpered, trying in vain to crawl further underneath my own arms. I did not look up—I could not look at those bars. The hand moved tenderly across my shoulders and I heard Christine's voice in my ear.

"We're going home."

Somehow Christine got me out of there after talking to the authorities for some time in low tones. I could not hear what was said and I didn't care. By the time we walked out of the police station all charges pending against me had been dropped, leaving only a warning. It mattered little—the damage to my confidence had been done. Despite numerous illicit activities littered throughout my past, the law had never caught up with me. Years ago I would not have cared what happened to me. Why did this have to happen now, when I had tried so hard to establish a respectable reputation for Christine? I had acted rashly, and it didn't matter whether the presence was responsible or not. I paid the price.

Robert was waiting for us outside with the carriage. Stiffly and silently I allowed Christine to lead me by the hand out through the offending bars, out the door and into the sunlight. What a sight that must have been, to see Christine leading her strong and protective husband by the hand like a child! I was too caught up in my own misery to give it a thought. It was not until we were home and Robert had gone to stable the carriage and horse that she turned to me for an explanation. She was understandably angry at having to journey downtown to bail her husband out of jail. Just what was I thinking to attack someone like that?

Humiliation caused me to sound more ungrateful than I intended. "Christine, please drop the matter. There was a disagreement and I lost my temper." Thinking then of her adept handling of my release, my voice softened. "Thank you, though, for getting me out of there. The bars...I...I could not take much more of those bars...I hate bars..."

She put her hand on my arm. "I knew when I saw you sitting in that cell that something was terribly wrong. You...you've been locked up before, haven't you?"

I nodded in shame and lifted my hands up to cover my face as the tears pricked my eyes. When I raised them she noticed my wrists. She pushed my sleeves back to reveal the raw, bloody rings around them. She looked up into my eyes and read the pain, the fear and the sadness in them. Taking me by the hand once again, she led me upstairs and gently bathed my wrists. Afterward, I lay quietly on my bed. She reached over to stroke my face, then left me to rest. At the door she turned back.

"Anyone who would lock up a child should have been put away themselves. Forever."

As she quietly closed the door and left me, her words finally released my tears. I turned over and sunk my face into the pillow. I cried for the boy I had been and the man I had become.

I did not go out for a week after my visit to the police station. I swore to Christine that I would never do anything like that again, but I was afraid the presence would become too strong for me. Eventually I could take no more of my housebound status and ventured out. It would take time to overcome my embarrassment and regain my former level of comfort in walking our familiar streets.

*   *   *

The occasional tender moment aside, the psychological stress under which I lived caused more than the rift between Christine and me. Jean and Louise avoided me whenever possible although Jean was at least politely civil to me when we did meet. After the way I had treated him in the street that night in early July I did not blame him for his change of attitude. To both the Vaillancourts' credit, they continued to assist Christine when they could and to think of her as part of their family. I no longer could say the same about myself. I had unknowingly reverted back to my old manner of remaining distant and aloof, with a cold demeanor that discouraged all socialization. Poor Robert and Deliah avoided me like the plague, choosing to do their duties around the household at times when I was not around. Other people with whom I had dealt regularly tried hard not to show their reluctance to talk with me. I slid back into somewhat reclusive behavior and spoke to no one who did not speak to me first.

Even Father Etienne seemed hesitant to spend much time in conversation with me; he always seemed to be too busy. The presence had its claws sunk deeply into me, and I could not shake it loose. For the first time since I had come to New Orleans more than two years ago, people crossed the street to avoid me. The thing that lived inside me manifested itself in a hostility that radiated from me in all directions.

My true nature, the gentle, creative and loving nature which only Christine and a few others really knew, came through now only for her. After the events of the last night I had spent in our bed I tried to be as solicitous of her as possible. We maintained some semblance of a relationship, but all the growth in it had stopped, especially after the way I had treated her in our bed. I could not even bear to think of the physical closeness we had always enjoyed that I now dearly missed. We talked but said nothing. While I continued as church organist and playing chess with Paul, my heart was no longer in them.

Paul and I had enjoyed our special friendship for almost a year and a half. He was one of those few who knew the real Erik, the one who was now becoming deeply buried under my renewed hostility and confusion. Sadly, everything ended for us abruptly in

July of 1884 when I was stunned by the news that he had been found dead in his bathtub. It was said that he had succumbed to "congestion of the brain" brought on by his entering a cold bath after a heated walk. I wasn't so sure about the cause of his death, but I missed my friend terribly.

I took solace in my music and my wife. Christine accompanied me to Paul's services to share my grief. I had stood in that cemetery many times studying those very vaults, but they no longer held any fascination for me. She had met Paul on numerous occasions and always felt rather sorry about his inability to handle the success and acclaim that his marvelous talent tried to bring him.

His death plunged me deeper into increasingly frequent depressive moods. I cannot express in words the way I felt after Paul's death. One of the blocks in the foundation of my life had suddenly been knocked out from under me and I floundered in my confusion. Months earlier I had been confident that I could manage the two conflicting halves of my life. Now I felt torn between my two worlds, suspended between Christine and the evil presence that grew ever stronger within me—each of them fighting to win the prize of my very soul. Each day the presence devoured a little more of me, slowly but surely eating its way through my sanity. Christine knew nothing of the battle in which she was now engaged, but the presence was fully aware of what it was doing to me. Bit by bit, it was slowly and methodically taking me apart.

The hours that I had spent with Paul were gaping and empty and I filled some of them with more bourbon. I always stopped before I thought I would show the signs, but I was probably consuming a lot more than I realized. Christine knew, and even she began to avoid me.

I had reached a plateau of success in the local voodoo world. As in many pursuits throughout my lifetime, once I conquered it the novelty was lost for me. My enjoyment of my activities on North

Rampart dwindled as time went on. I continued to participate but it did not hold the fascination for me that it had for almost a year and a half. To be honest, I was also getting weary of the nightly activity because the lack of sleep was finally catching up with me. I was tired. The only thing that could retain my interest for long was my music.

The signs were staring me in the face but I refused to see them. The signs were there that I was entering a phase of my life that eerily paralleled that which had enveloped me in the years before I knew Christine; the years that I had spent hidden away and totally alone while haunting the Opera House.

Back then I had been living my life one day at a time, almost not knowing when day turned to night. I felt no emotion and had become almost totally indifferent to what went on around me. I had been deep in the clutches of depression then, and I was heading to that same place now. How long would it take for me to hit the bottom? What would happen when I got there? I still had enough presence of mind to know that my previous and current situations had one major difference. I had Christine with me now, and all I needed to do was go to her for help. It was a simple enough thing for me to do. Why couldn't I just go to Christine and ask for her help? I knew why. The presence would not allow it. I needed something stronger than the evil thing inside my head to stop me from falling further into the fires of hell that surely awaited me at the bottom.

18

★

I thought I could not sink much lower, but I proved myself wrong when on Thursday night of that week I could be found walking briskly toward one of the roughest sections in town. The street ran right along the Mississippi waterfront, which provided a convenient arrival and departure point for all sorts of illicit operations. As I walked further away from familiar territory, I heard the voice.

So, you are curious about what's down there, heh? Don't be nervous, you've lived in places like that all your life. It's where you really belong, you know. Those people are no match for you. You can handle them. You made sure of that, didn't you?

Yes, I made sure of it. Neatly tucked away in my inside coat pocket was my lasso. When I lifted it from its place in the drawer it felt oddly comforting, and I worked it in my hands to soften it to its former suppleness. At the appointed hour I turned the knob at the address I had been given and, with a quick glance over my shoulder, slipped inside.

I closed the door behind me and peered down a darkened hallway that ran beside a steep narrow staircase. The only light came from the end of the hallway to the left. I walked down the creaking hallway and stopped in the doorway. Seated at a table in the dimly lit room were two men who looked oddly familiar. The surroundings themselves were familiar—dimly lit rooms and dark shadows had always followed me through life. They ceased their low conversation and looked up expectantly at me. I recognized them as the two men who had been talking about me in the street on the day I had landed myself in the clink. My eyes narrowed to slits as I wondered what connection they had to this business. I was just about to ask who had summoned me there when a dark shape rose from a stuffed chair in the far corner. Just then I saw a tiny glow just below eye level. Francois. Suddenly I made the name connection. Francois was the Frank whose name I had overheard on that fateful day. Who in hell was he and what did he want with me?

"Welcome, Mr. Devereaux," he said. "I see you got my note." At my slight but careless indication of surprise he went on. "Oh yes, I know who you are. I know exactly who you are. In fact, I know more about you than you might think."

He stopped in the middle of the room and eyed me. He was mistaken, of course. There were too many things he didn't know about me that could be bad for his health. I judged him to be a low-class vermin who was fond of hearing his own voice. But, for whatever reason, I decided to hear him out.

"So you know who I am," I said. "Then tell me why I am here. I have other business, and do not appreciate being summoned by strangers without prior knowledge of the circumstances."

"Ah, yes, your 'other business'. We're all familiar with what that is, aren't we gentlemen?" One nodded quickly before dropping his eyes to the table again. The one I had almost strangled did not look up. Francois took a long drag on his cigar before he turned his back on me and returned to his chair. "Please, Mr. Devereaux, have a seat."

Warily I went to the only empty chair on the opposite side of the table from the two silent men and sat down.

"Let's talk about this other business of yours," he continued. "You have rather quickly wormed your way into a world that normally does not open itself to white men, and indeed you seem to have become a favored right hand man. Quite an unusual situation for an upper class gentleman living in the Rue Royal who rubs elbows with the elite of New Orleans to be involved in wouldn't you say? But then, you are not the average city gentleman are you, Mr. Devereaux?" He leaned forward in his chair. "One look at you confirms that fact."

"State your business. I am losing my patience," I demanded with an edge on my voice. I was growing uneasy.

"Yes, of course. I can see you are a man of action, and that is precisely why you are here." He crushed out his stub of a cigar in an overflowing ashtray and took his time lighting a new one. "I have a business proposition for you. You could call it a side business of what you are already doing. We have noticed that you possess some unusual...talents. We think those talents of yours could be of great use to us, and we are willing to cut you in on a nice chunk of the profits in return." He paused. "If, of course, you are interested."

If that was all I had come to hear, I had wasted my evening.

"Gentlemen," I said. "I have no interest in your proposition, whatever it might be, and even if I did I would not partner with the likes of you. You might think you know all there is to know about me, but I assure you that you do not have the slightest idea of with whom you are dealing, or of what 'talents' I might possess. I am no stranger to activities of an illicit nature and I have no intention of getting involved. Good night."

I got up to leave and had reached the door when his next words stopped me cold.

"You have a very pretty little wife at home, don't you Mr. Devereaux?" he asked in a malicious tone. Something froze in the pit of my stomach at his mention of Christine. He went on talking to my back.

"Yes, she's very young too, and for some unknown reason she appears very attached to you. But appearances can be very deceiving, can't they? You of all people should know that." He paused for maximum effect. "Does she know where you go so many nights, Mr. Devereaux? It would be a pity if she found out. Or maybe the good Father would be interested in what I have to say. He might like to know what you're up to when you're not sitting in his church trying to play your way into heaven. Either way, the little wife will hear it one way or the other."

Dread filled my heart as I thought about the consequences of his words. I did not doubt the sincerity of Francois' threat. A vision of Christine's horror-stricken face popped into my mind and I squeezed my eyes tightly shut at the thought of how she would react if he got to her with his information. I barely heard Francois' last words as I walked stiffly out the door.

"Do think about it, Mr. Devereaux. Saturday night, same time and place. I'll fill you in then."

Christ, what had I gotten myself into now? Threats were common to me in years past, but I never had to worry about consequences to anyone but myself. I had been prepared to turn Francois down no matter what he said, but the minute he brought Christine into it he had me over a barrel. Someone had been spying on my life with Christine and I felt violated. Real fear inched its way with icy fingers up my spine—fear like I'd never felt before. I could lose everything over this. Christine would be devastated to discover the extent of my lies and deception. Beyond that, the truth about where I had been at night and what I had been doing would drive her away for good. She would never understand. Hell and Goddamn, I didn't even understand it myself any more.

I walked homeward with heavy steps through the empty streets. I felt no relief when I arrived home. It was different from the other nights when I had returned home to leave my other world behind in the darkness. On this night I walked into my home and the darkness followed me. I went to my lonely room and paused to look out the window into the moonless night. I was cornered. As a cornered animal will turn and fight, I would do whatever I had to do to fight my way out. My hand went to my pocket to absently finger the soft coils waiting there.

I agonized over what to do. I had gotten myself into a fix that would require very careful handling to diffuse. I must be at my best both defensively and offensively. I realized then that I could possess no more formidable weapon than my own experience. I had tried to leave my former life far behind me, but the lessons of that life were firmly entrenched somewhere in the recesses of my mind. All I had to do was find them. I had to rediscover the Erik who had learned and used them well; the Erik who lived on in the presence that constantly haunted me. My path was clear. I would use the evil wisdom and cunning of the presence to my advantage. I must cease to fight it and let it take control of my mind. Only in this way could I deal with the problem at the level of expertise that was required, since I was no longer at the top of my game, as it were. This was the only way I knew to get myself back on top. It would be very difficult to keep my life together while under the control of the dark memories of my past. Until I had removed the threat hanging over our happiness, every waking moment I spent with Christine, Etienne, Jean and Louise or anyone else who knew me would be a precarious balancing act. I would become even more divided in my personality; maintaining some semblance of my true self at home while accepting the challenge of allowing myself to once again become what I had been fighting ever since leaving Paris.

The dangers were many. If I pushed my wife too far, I would lose her anyway. If I allowed the presence too much control, I may not be able to force it into the background again when this was over. If I failed in my efforts to get this threat out of our lives, we would both be lost forever. Above all else, if I could not protect my soul from my own ravaged mind, there was no point to any of this. Even after recognizing the dangers, I knew I had no choice. I had to protect us. Over the next two days I prepared myself.

Saturday night found me walking with briskly confident strides along the darkened streets. I was indeed Erik...the Erik of twenty years ago.

In the space of those two short days my metamorphosis was complete. I had willingly succumbed to the relentless pull of the evil that lurked inside me, and it had been so strong—so overwhelming—that I physically felt the precise moment when my mind lost its battle. I ceased to hear the voice of the presence speaking to me, for I had become one with it. While I continued to live physically in the present, my mind functioned as it had twenty years before.

I had taken a startling trip back in time. The images that had haunted my days and nights since the first nightmare became active memories once more. I felt alone and ostracized. My hostility and contempt for the human race came flooding back to me and it was all I could do to suppress it when needed. As I walked briskly toward my rendezvous, I pushed my present life into the darkest corners of my mind and let my hostility feed and strengthen me.

*　　　　　*　　　　　*

"Come in," said Francois with a sly smile of victory on his heavy face. He offered me a chair at the table where the other men sat silently. This time he sat himself down across the table from me. "Now, Mr. Dever..."

"No." I interrupted abruptly. "If I am to cooperate you will not use my real name at any time. Is that clear?"

"Yeah...sure." He was taken aback by my manner, which was considerably more hostile than at our previous meeting. "Have it any way you want. So who are you?"

I cast around in my mind for an innocuous name without taking my eyes from his. "Jake. Just Jake."

"Suit yourself." He shrugged and lit a cigar.

"Get on with it," I demanded impatiently.

"Okay, Jake," he said conspiratorially as he leaned his elbows on the table and blew his smoke over my head. "You know that Marie Laveau has got a pretty decent business over there on North Rampart. You must also know that she gets a pretty good dollar for her services. What you don't know is that a fair amount of her business is courtesy of this little group right here. If it wasn't for us, she'd be spending a lot more of her time fixing fancy ladies' hair than she does. For years she's been paying me to bring her a bit of business...you know, kind of spread the word that her services are available. Me and the boys here, we make out pretty well on what she pays us. Call it her advertising budget. Thing is, there's a part of this that she don't know herself."

"And what might that be?" I asked without much interest.

"You've been part of that racket for a while now yourself, haven't you ever noticed that white people with problems just keep on coming and coming? And that some of those people are pretty high up in this town? Well, yeah. It's because we send 'em there. But these rich people don't always have the problems they think they do. You're a smart one —you get my meaning?"

"You're setting them up. Child's play. What do you need me for?"

"Laveau is getting difficult. She's one powerful old lady, but lately she's been balking at what she's paying us and she's not getting the repeaters like she used to. There's a girl who's been learning from her, her name's Bess. She was there the night you got my note."

I remembered the girl. I had been impressed with her performance. I nodded.

"I want Bess in and Laveau out. I don't care how you do it."

"Why her?" I asked.

"Bess will cooperate," said Francois with a smirk. "She knows the score and will play by the rules."

"You're asking me to double-cross an old woman who has nothing but her local fame," I retorted with disdain. Marie had been good to me, and even in my present state of mind I could not forget that. Still, my primary concern now was for Christine and myself. I stood up and placed my hands wide on the table to lean over into Francois' flabby face.

"I will take care of it."

*   *   *

Around midnight a week later I soundlessly closed the door to my bedroom and stepped out into the hallway. I came face to face with a sleepy Christine who was carrying a glass of water and a candle. It was the first time she had actually run into me during any of my late-night comings or goings. An awkward silence prevailed as the flickering flame revealed that I was dressed to go out. At the look in her eyes, I hunched my shoulders and silently turned to go down the stairs and out into the night.

I became even more involved with the ceremonies of voodoo than before, if that were possible. My attendance was required on a nightly basis. By calling on my extensive experience in the art of deceit, I convinced Marie that Bess needed more experience if she were to one day take over the operation full time. Since Marie was no longer a young woman she went along with the idea readily enough. Unwittingly she asked me to do the very thing I needed to do; spend more time instructing Bess. I promised Marie that I would give her regular and informed reports of the gatherings, which meant that I could keep her off site indefinitely if need be. It was harder for me to work at ingratiating myself in Bess's eyes. I wanted nothing to do with her when it became apparent that she was an arrogant and untrustworthy young woman who would stop at nothing in her desire to gain Marie's position of respect in the voodoo world.

"Bess," I said after one night's performance, (I do not use that term loosely; those ceremonies were performances, no more or less.) "You did well tonight."

She glanced at me sideways, her dark eyes overly confident.

"I have been chosen for a reason," she stated pompously as she wiped ceremonial wine from her bare arms and legs with long, slow strokes and raising her skirt hem immodestly high while doing so. "You should know that. It is your job to assist *me* now." Her light clothing was plastered to her body with wine and sweat. She made no attempt to hide what was plainly showing through her blouse.

"It is Marie's wish that I instruct you," I said condescendingly.

The sentiment was lost on her. I turned to shake the heavy red cloak from around my shoulders. My shirt was also laden with sweat and sticking uncomfortably to me. I was plucking it away from my body when I glanced over to catch Bess watching me closely. She came to stand in front of me and slowly raised her hands. Her hands hovered for a moment in mid air, then lightly straightened my collar. Her eyes met mine and she smiled conspiratorially. She turned away and was gone. I breathed a small sigh of relief. The stakes were high enough in this game.

                    *   *   *

My relationship with my wife felt more strained with each passing week. I returned to life as a recluse, venturing out of the house as little as possible during daylight hours. I could not avoid my church duties without attracting more attention to my changing lifestyle, so I continued playing there while managing to avoid Etienne almost entirely by sneaking in and out like a common thief. Every move I made was carefully weighed and calculated. I saw nothing of the Vaillancourts, and I knew they wanted nothing to do with me. When they came to collect Christine for daily afternoon outings I watched them from behind drapes and doorways. No one else came to the house. I kept the drapes drawn, shutting out the light and along with it all the happiness of my adopted city. I sat in the parlor with my darkness and my hostility and a drink in my hand. My servants kept such low profiles that I had almost forgotten what they looked like. Christ knows what Christine thought of all this, since we were barely speaking to each other. There was no anger, we just were not connecting and our relationship was totally adrift. All my thoughts were concentrated on one task, and that was clearing Francois out of our lives.

On the few occasions when I made an effort to exhibit my real personality it was forced and unconvincing. I was coming from so far into the dark recesses of my mind that I was finding it more and more difficult to relate to anyone at all. I was uncommunicative and moody. My body finally rebelled against the increased nighttime activity and I began to sleep during the day, rising uncharacteristically late in the morning. Usually the sound of Christine's carriage pulling away woke me just before noon. We lived together yet apart, and neither of us had a choice in the matter. It felt like years since I had been welcome in Christine's bed.

One evening, just after dark, I was sitting in my courtyard looking up at the stars. My enjoyment of the soothing quality of the darkness had never left me, and I morbidly looked forward to the setting sun each day. Christine came out of the house and wandered past my shadowed bench without noticing me. I watched her walk past me and then return. I said nothing, but something caused her to peer into the darkness. I heard her sharp intake of breath as she finally saw me there.

"Erik," she stammered, "you startled me."

"I am sorry," I spoke softly as I held out my hand toward her, "I didn't mean to frighten you. Please, come sit with me."

Hesitantly she came and sat gingerly on the bench beside me. I sensed her discomfort. How far we had fallen from the life we knew so well! And all of it was my fault. Christine had become an innocent pawn in my dark game of life. If I had been more careful from the start we would not have been sitting there like two strangers in our own home. We sat silently for several minutes, but it was not the easy silence of two people who know each so well that they communicate without speech. Slowly I reached out and put my arm around my wife's thin shoulders. She tried to hide her slight recoil from my touch. I leaned toward her and brought my lips to her cheek to brush it with a light kiss.

"Christine," I murmured in her ear. "I miss…"

"Erik please, I'm very tired. I…I think I'll go to bed now," she said quickly and stood up and returned to the house, leaving me with my arm stretched out into space. The pale lamplight from the window revealed her furtive glances back toward me and proved what I suspected. My own wife was afraid of me. That knowledge plunged a knife through my heart.

*   *   *

"Jake," Francois waved me into the room with a particularly wet looking specimen of cigar in his stubby, stained fingers. "Laveau is still around. You said…"

"That I would take care of it," I interrupted in a low voice. We were alone, but I did not take the indicated chair and remained standing. I was tired of this man and his requests for reports on my activities. "These things take time."

"Bess tells me you report to Laveau on everything that goes on. Why do you do that when she will be gone soon? Bess doesn't like it."

"I don't give a damn what Bess likes or doesn't like," I countered. "She is an arrogant and foolish girl who will never achieve what Marie has in this town."

"She does business with me, and that's all I care about," Francois said with a note of annoyance. "It's time to be rid of Laveau—permanently." He tried to gauge my reaction to his words but there was none. "Do it."

"I will remove her when the time is right and not before."

Francois rose slowly and pointed the wet end of his cigar in my direction. "I'm telling you…"

My fuse had been burned to the bottom. I lunged at him, grabbing a handful of his coat with my left hand and setting my right forearm hard across his miserable fat throat. I slammed him back against the wall as beads of sweat began to pop out on his face. The few dingy portraits jumped on their hangers. The offensive cigar fell to the floor and glowed, threatening to ignite the ancient, shredded carpeting.

"You will tell me nothing!" I snarled into his face. "It was your decision to blackmail me into doing your dirty work, but it is my choice how and when I do it." I increased the pressure on his throat. His face turned more florid and his eyes began to roll around. The stench of his foul breath was overpowering. "I would advise you not to push me, or by the end of this you will wish you had done business with the devil himself." I then threw him into the overstuffed chair in the corner where he sat gasping and rubbing his neck.

I turned to go, but looked back over my shoulder. "Or perhaps you already have," I added, and walked out with a venomous chuckle low in my throat even as I saw tiny flames began to lick their way across the carpet. As I reached the street door I heard him scrabble across the floor to beat them out.

Francois was right about one thing. It was time to end this. He had finally tipped his hand and spelled out exactly what he wanted me to do. He wanted me to dispose of Marie Laveau in such a way that she would never be seen or heard from again. To my mind, there was only one way to guarantee that result.

I had my own plans to bring this disastrous situation to closure. Francois did not know how fortunate he was that one former capability had not returned to me when I invited the dark personality of my past to re-enter my life. Without certain irrevocable changes that I had undergone since leaving Paris, Francois would have been in no position to put out the fire eating away at his carpet that night.

*   *   *

Bess was working hard on preparations for her first important ceremony out at Lake Pontchartrain. Per usual I was to be a major attraction, but that week I spent most of my time instructing her on the correct handling of the snakes used extensively in the more public locations. I'd kept Marie tucked away at home for several weeks with the help of a little herb concoction that made her feel considerably but harmlessly under the weather. I had plans for her at the lake also. It would be a night no one present would easily forget.

A week before the event, I was assisting a reluctant Bess with the art of draping live snakes around her body without alarming them. One does not want to make these large reptiles uneasy, for they can tighten themselves around one in a powerful vise-like grip that can be quite painful if not worse. Care must be taken with them, but Bess was impatient and cared little for details.

"Do not squeeze them," I instructed firmly as I reached around her to remove the long, heavy body from her shoulders. "You must move slowly. Be gentle with them and respect them."

"Show me," she said.

I lifted the large boa constrictor carefully and draped it around my own neck. Then I arranged its 8-foot length completely around me. I enjoyed the feel of its weighty warmth coiled snugly around me and I stroked it gently. Contrary to what many people believe, snakes are not cold. They are warm and smooth, and quite underrated as creatures of amazing physical capabilities.

"Now, stroke it gently in one direction, like this." I took her hand and directed it to the thickest part of the body, which extended from my shoulder, across my chest and around under my arm. Her thin brown fingers slid over the smooth surface. She walked around me several times following the curve of the snake, then stopped behind me. I felt the pressure of her hands move from side to side. Her fingers brushed against me as she slid them along the snake's round body. Then her hands were not on the snake at all, but on me. She lifted them to my shoulders and began to knead them. It felt good. It had been much too long since I'd felt a woman's touch. She could not reach enough of my shoulders because of the snake around them so, without giving much thought to what I was doing, I reached up to remove it and walked over to set it gently in its crate. I straightened up and waited with my back to her. Sure enough, I soon felt her hands slide up my back to resume her massage of my shoulders.

"Like this?" she whispered from behind me.

"Yes." I was powerless to do anything but stand there. I had no intention of allowing the situation to go any further, but the girl's touch was so soothing that I did not readily stop her. I did not realize how tense I was until she began to dig her fingers into the muscles of my back and shoulders. She worked until I felt them loosen and relax. She eventually worked her way around in front of me. I did not protest when she unbuttoned my damp shirt and slid it from my shoulders, nor when her remarkable fingers worked around my collarbone and into the upper muscles of my chest and arms. I stood with my eyes closed, trying to mentally assist her in driving away the tension.

As my muscle tension relaxed, her touch changed from one of deep searching massage to that of a caress. Around and up and down, her hands were suddenly all over me. Still I kept my eyes closed, as if by not seeing what was happening I could consider it acceptable. I kept them closed even when I felt her lips linger on my upper arm, then flutter around my chest. If I had been living fully in the present I would never have allowed her to touch me at all, but most of my conscious mind was thinking only the thoughts of twenty years before. To have any woman show intimate interest in me back then was a novelty that I would have been a fool to refuse. Certainly this was one danger that I had never anticipated when I decided to bring back my own past for use as a weapon.

The Erik of long ago stood still, eyes closed, and allowed Bess to continue with her light kisses and increasingly intimate caresses. Her behavior was unexpected, because I had been sure of our mutual dislike for one another. Even so, I found my body responding to her advances. I opened my eyes when she slid her tongue across my chest.

I could no longer remain impassive. I raised my hands and pushed my fingers deep into her woolly hair. I cradled her head in my hands and lifted her face to me. At the moment that her large brown eyes locked into mine an alarm went off somewhere deep inside me. I pushed it away, not wanting it; not understanding it. I dropped one hand down to her blouse and began to slide it off over one brown shoulder. Two buttons held it closed, and as I undid the first of them another alarm sounded from deep in my muddled brain. Again, I tried to ignore what was becoming a persistent nagging from somewhere within me. I flicked the last button open. The sight of her nakedness reminded me of how lonely I was, and I felt the warm rush of desire begin to center itself within me. Now employing a highly erotic (and obviously well practiced) writhing motion of her shoulders, Bess worked the blouse back until it fell to the floor behind her. Her movements also had the desired effect on me, which she noted with a slyly sensual smile. Warnings continued to sound off in my head as she pressed herself against me. I moved my hands around the sleek smoothness of her back, tracing the outline of her shoulder blades under her silky dark skin and sliding a hand down the side of one fabric-covered thigh. She wore nothing beneath the thin skirt, and I fingered the single button at the back. She ran her hands slowly up the length of my arms and up toward the back of my head. Through a fog of conflict between increasing desire and reluctance, I suddenly knew exactly what the little bitch was after.

My hands shot upward immediately and my fingers locked around her wrists before she could grasp the thin cord of the mask. I pushed her away from me as I finally recognized the warnings in my head. My deep and abiding love for Christine was fighting its way through the layers of darkness under which I had temporarily hidden it. I looked at the devious, half-naked girl standing before me and felt nothing but contempt for her.

"Get dressed," I said shortly as I wrestled into my damp shirt from where it was hanging still tucked into my trousers. "Tonight's lesson is over."

Bess angrily snatched up her blouse from the floor and pulled it on, leaving it wide open.

"You bastard! If you think you can lead me on like that and then walk away, you are dead wrong," she hissed. "You and your secrets are no match for me. I will soon be the most powerful woman in New Orleans!"

I locked down the top of the snake crate and reached for my coat.

"Don't flatter yourself," I sneered and walked out.

I did not care about Bess at all; I did not even like her. But, damn it, I have to admit that on that particular night, I wanted her. We were two people using each other—nothing more. Even so, I came very close to doing something that I would regret for the rest of my days. I could have blamed it on my state of mind at the time, but no matter how much I tried to rationalize it, the result would have remained unchanged. Nevertheless, I have wondered what might have happened between us if Bess had not tried to take my mask. I will never know the answer to that question, but I will always believe that the love of my Christine speaking to me through my conscience would have stopped me before it was too late. I knew sacrifices must be made when I began this experiment in madness, but betraying my wife was never part of my plans. Regardless, I had to put the incident from my mind and concentrate on finishing the job at hand.

I canceled my remaining session with Bess. She knew enough that one more session wouldn't matter, and I refused to spend any more time on her. I used the time instead to finalize my detailed plans for the upcoming ceremony. Two days later I had good news for Francois. The event scheduled for Wednesday night at the lake would be the final step in my fulfillment of his wishes. He chortled happily as I left, and lit another cigar.

*   *   *

A few more drops would probably be wise, I thought, as I made my final preparations in the early morning hours of Wednesday. I added a few more for good measure and pushed the cork stopper securely into the neck of the vial. I held it up in front of the single candle on the table and noted the correct tint in the liquid. I slipped the vial into my pocket and walked over to unlock both of my doors. Locked bedroom doors would be hard to explain to my wife, even considering my recent behavior. I flipped open my pocket watch and slanted the face toward the candle. Two o'clock. By this time tomorrow night it would all be over.

*   *   *

As was usually the case, Christine had already left the house when I walked downstairs early the next afternoon. I was unusually hungry so I went to the kitchen and foraged some cooked meat and several slices of bread. I took my food with me into the parlor and stopped at the sideboard for a large glass of bourbon to wash it down. The one glass would have to do, for I needed to have my wits about me. I ate my meal slowly while staring at the silent piano. Christ, I hadn't played it since the day Francois first summoned me. I could not have sent my wife a more blatant signal of distress than to ignore my music. Come to think of it, the only time that music hasn't dominated my life was during the years that I was now reliving in my mind. Survival had been foremost in my mind then, and so it was again. I spent the remainder of the afternoon behind the closed door of my bedroom.

The sound of the front door closing announced Christine's return in the late afternoon, but I could no longer face her.

Dusk found me on Marie's doorstep. She looked weary and old as she let me into the tiny cottage. A single candle burned on the table, throwing long shadows in the gathering darkness.

"Marie, you must attend tonight," I continued as she repeatedly shook her head. She did not feel well and did not know why, but I did. "It is imperative that you be there."

"Why you make a sick old woman go out inna night?" she asked sadly. "You yo-sef been tellin' me to let da girl take over. Well, tonight she take over." She placed both her hands flat on the table before her and stared at them, rocking herself slightly.

"You must not give up." I was beginning to worry about her. She had to be at the lake. I reached across the table and took her tiny hands in mine. "Marie, there are forces at work against you. I need your cooperation. You must trust me. Everything will be all right if you will do exactly as I tell you. Do you understand, Marie? You must not question anything I ask of you tonight."

She looked up at me and searched my eyes. After a long moment she said, "Aw right. I'll go, but I go for you, not me. Marie is tired."

                    *   *   *

The throbbing beat of the drums was heard long before Marie and I approached the far end of the beach in a small rowboat. Bess had the ceremony in full swing when I grounded the boat and helped Marie from it. The sounds of chanting rose into the night air and accompanied the silhouettes of people dancing in the firelight. In the center of a ring of fire stood Bess, passionately writhing with a snake coiled around her neck. Apparently she had absorbed at least some of what I taught her. Marie and I walked up through the trees to the gathering place. Just before we emerged into the clearing, I turned to her.

"Marie," I said, parting my robes to take the tiny vial from my pocket. "Do you trust me completely?"

At her silent nod I handed her the open vial. "Drink this."

She took it and drank the contents without hesitation. I nodded to her again and we broke through the trees.

A cry rose up as Marie was spotted approaching the firelight. The sea of people parted to allow us entrance, and I led her to the center of the circle and bowed dramatically before her. She smiled as she drank in the appreciation of her people. Bess reluctantly stepped back to allow Marie and me to attend to our duties.

We were halfway through the festivities when Marie began to falter. The people noticed nothing and went on with their dancing, singing and drinking. Watching her carefully, I had just begun to move toward her when Marie shot me a look of alarm. She swayed precariously on her feet, then fell into the soft sand. I rushed to her side and held her gently as a sudden silence descended in the clearing. The faces began to close in on us until I held up my arm, motioning them back. Slowly I brought my ringed fingers to the pulse of Marie's neck, and after a moment I bowed my head over her in defeat. A soft collective gasp rose around me. I raised my hooded head.

"Marie Laveau is dead."

A man rushed from the crowd and knelt beside us. When he could find no pulse, he stood and solemnly announced, "It is true."

I carefully picked Marie up and stood facing the people. One of her arms dangled lifelessly and the sight caused the silence to stretch on. I caught the red glow of Francois' cigar at the very edge of the crowd. The look of triumph on his face was unmistakable, and it was mirrored on the face of Bess, who stood beside him. He nodded to me imperceptibly and melted away into the night. The evening was over. People started to disperse with the uneasy quiet that death always brings, sometimes stealing a look back at the lone red-robed figure standing in the firelight holding the dead woman whom they had come to see. I lifted her body ceremoniously toward the smoky night sky, then turned and walked slowly into the woods.

Once in the trees, my steps quickened and I hurried to the beach. I laid Marie's body in the bow of the boat on a blanket and rowed out onto the dark lake. I could waste no time. After shipping the oars as quietly as possible, I threw off my robe and knelt by the old woman while searching my other pocket for a second vial. Locating it, I tipped her head back and poured some liquid from the vial into her mouth and rhythmically worked her jaw so that it trickled down her throat. Working in that manner I managed to get most of the contents into her. It occurred to me that she must have done the same to me on the night I had been almost beaten to death. Satisfied that she had ingested as much of the liquid as possible, I dipped my handkerchief over the side and bathed her face with the cool water. I could do no more. I wrapped her in the blanket, then reached into the bottom of the boat for my own robe, which I tossed over the side. I removed the heavy rings from my fingers and tucked them inside a pocket in Marie's robe. She was still unconscious a half hour later when I rapped softly on the door of a small home on St. Ann Street, but she was breathing regularly when they took her from me.

The following evening Marie smiled at me weakly as I approached the bed. I patted her hand and told her that soon she would be back where she belonged. Even as I spoke, the New Orleans voodoo world mourned the deaths of its two most revered figures. It would always remember the great Marie Laveau, who had been stricken down during a public ceremony, and the well-known but still mysterious figure in red who had apparently mourned her so desperately that he had thrown himself into the lake. His empty robe had washed up on the beach the next morning. Neither his nor the old woman's body had been found.

*   *   *

"You have done well," Francois said to me begrudgingly. We stood on a dark section of pier on the night following the lakeside ceremony. The newspapers had been filled that day with accounts of the sudden death of the local voodoo priestess, apparently from heart failure, and the disappearance of her ghostly attendant. The reports implied that her absence from the scene for some weeks prior to her death had obviously been due to poor health.

"Now that Bess is in charge we'll all be happier," Francois continued contentedly. He cast me a sideways glance. "Bess told me about your little late-night rendezvous with her," he confided with a low chuckle. "She is looking forward to getting to know you better, if you know what I mean," he finished with a lascivious smile.

"Bess presumes too much, " I said flatly, "and she is a liar as well. I have no intention of working with her or anyone else. I have done what you asked. My involvement ended with Marie's death last night."

"I'm afraid I'll have to disagree with that," Francois said as he threw his cigar into the river and crossed his arms. "Bess needs help, Devereaux, and you're going to give it to her. The rich folks won't come if they don't get the usual show."

"I'll not say it again. I am finished," I said evenly. "I will expend no more effort for a petty thug who requires the help of a professional to get a simple job done. Christ, you even advertise your ineffectuality with delusions of grandeur," I added with a note of mockery. "I daresay you have a bit of an identity problem,

Frank." I eyed him contemptuously. "I have wasted enough of my time with you."

Francois stared at me, then turned on his heel and walked a few steps before he stopped and looked back at me. "We will see what your little wife thinks about that."

He turned his back on me a second time. Before he'd taken two steps I had the lasso around his neck and hauled him backward toward me. At the same time I swiftly grabbed one wrist and wrenched it painfully back and up behind him so far that his stubby fingers almost touched the back of his neck. I neatly wrapped a few loops of the lasso around the wrist, so that the more he struggled the tighter the noose became around his neck. With his free hand he clawed at the catgut where it was settling into his throat. His neck was so fat he could not get his fingers under it. I maintained my grip on the catgut connecting his neck and wrist and coldly addressed him from behind.

"If you ever come near me or my wife and friends again, I will find you," I hissed in his ear, "and when I get through with you, you will beg for death." I dropped my voice to a smooth and dangerously low conversational tone. "If you doubt my experience in these matters, do you wish to consult my references?" I asked with feigned innocence. "On the other hand," I continued thoughtfully, "that may be a bit difficult. You see, many of those who have observed my best work can no longer speak for themselves. Unfortunate, of course, but true."

A tiny smile crept across my lips. I was enjoying myself, and recognized an almost forgotten surge of malicious pleasure in this sort of business. I twisted the captive arm a bit for emphasis, and noted his gasp of pain with satisfaction. My next words came from low in my throat.

"I advise you not to test my skills. I guarantee that you would not be disappointed."

I released his wrist, flipped the noose off his neck and shoved him away from me. I calmly coiled the lasso and put it back in my pocket while he stood bent over trying to catch his breath.

"Remember this," I said to his hunched form as I nonchalantly rearranged my cloak around me, "the most dangerous enemy one can have is a man left with nothing to lose. And without my wife, I have nothing to lose."

I had turned and begun to walk back to the street when I heard a grunt behind me.

Francois had recovered both his breath and his stupidity. Enraged, he came barreling at me with his head down like a bull stuck full of spears. I quickly stepped to the side to avoid being hit by his heavy body without noticing how close I had been standing to the edge of the pier. He sailed past me into the open air and, with flailing arms, descended toward the muddy waters of the Mississippi. He landed with a huge splash and sunk like a stone without a sound or a struggle. The powerful current swept him away before I could have reached him, but I never considered going in after him. Along with him into the dark water went the threat that had been hanging over our lives. His lackeys would pose no threat to me without him. It was over. I watched the swirling current for a few minutes before I calmly walked away.

19

---★---

My eyes flickered open to the morning sun peeking through a gap in the drapes. It was unusually early for me to be up and about, yet an hour later I was sitting in my sunlit courtyard. For three days I had forced myself to awaken early and get out into the light. It was a necessary step in my efforts to break the stranglehold that the presence had over my mind, to get back to where I was before I began my descent into the darkness of my past. I had to crawl back out of the hole before I lost my wife, my home and, eventually, my very life.

Once again I paced back and forth across the flagstones of the courtyard. I listened for the voice, for I knew that, until I heard it speaking to me from inside my head, it was still in control. I resisted a steady urge to go back inside and draw the drapes; to hide myself in the dark. I sat down and let the sun beat down on my head, warming me and penetrating the darkness in my mind.

For three days I had forced my mind into thoughts of Christine, Jean and the other people and things I cared about. I saw Christine's face—the laughing, loving face that I missed so much and had not seen in months. I searched in my memory for the things that made me happy—tours of the city, dinner at favorite restaurants, my music, our friends, our wedding and our love. The other more sinister thoughts tried to intrude, and I pushed them back again and again.

I felt inexplicably restless and got up to repeatedly pace the area. I could not stay still for a moment. Memories began to crowd my mind in a mixed up jumble of the good and the bad. They suddenly started coming so fast that I could not sort them out. It felt like my mind was becoming unhinged, that I had no connection with it. An endless parade of faces and events flew past my mind's eye as if I was reliving my entire life in the space of a few minutes. Faster and faster they came and I was spinning out of control! I clutched my head in my hands and moaned when I fell to my knees on the flagstones. The roaring in my ears was deafening, and the house and yard spun around me. The colors blurred together and I could no longer see anything but spinning, spinning color! The roaring in my ears threatened to split my head apart!

"No more! Please! Nooooooo!" I screamed. The sound of my agony bounced off the stone walls of the courtyard. I clamped my hands tightly over my ears and pressed them together to squeeze out the confusion. The pressure inside my head built higher and higher until suddenly my mind exploded in a shower of confused light, sounds and pain! I bent at the waist and my head went down to strike the ground with a dull thud.

Again, I opened my eyes to the brilliance of the sun. I shifted my weight uncomfortably on the hard surface, until I became aware that I was lying on the ground in the middle of my courtyard. How in hell had I gotten there? When I sat up I noticed the ache in my head and the sweat drenching me. I put my hand to my forehead and felt a sizeable lump there. Then I remembered. I slowly picked myself up and walked unsteadily toward the house. Fortunately, Christine had taken to staying away from the house all day and had not witnessed this or any of my recent courtyard battles. I went to the sideboard and poured myself a drink. I felt drained and emotionless while I mechanically went through the motions of fixing myself a hot bath. I soaked myself, my drink handily beside me, until the water turned cool. I pulled on a pair of trousers and lay down on my bed in exhaustion. I was nearly asleep when I heard it.

"You goddamned, ignorant fool," it said. *"You couldn't handle it. You had your chance and you threw it away. Fool!"*

With a deep sigh, I rolled over and slept like a baby for almost 24 hours.

*   *   *

The presence had not left me—far from it. After that afternoon of my partial victory it resumed its onslaught on my nights and its haunting of my days. I resumed my normal activities of previous months, although it was hard to deal with the increased, yet understandable, avoidance of me by my wife and friends. Aside from that, I seemed to be no worse off than before. I no longer worried about clandestine entries into the church, so I encountered Etienne several times on my way in or out. He acted surprised to see me. While I still could not open myself up to him as I once did, I made the effort to be cordial.

During a fortnight of staying relatively housebound I tried to be as solicitous as possible of Christine. If she noticed that I was no longer leaving the house at night, she did not mention it. We had several evening meals together, and although the sparse conversation was strained, I was content just spending the time with her. One morning as she was about to go out the door to Jean's waiting carriage (they never even entered my house these days), I gave her a quick hug and a goodbye kiss on the cheek. She looked at me strangely and made an effort to smile. I watched her pull away, and then went to sit at the piano, where I spent the afternoon.

*   *   *

I had been to see Marie once since the voodoo world had been shocked by her "death". I had prepared her with the items she would need when she shocked the city again less than two weeks later with her equally remarkable reappearance.

Bess had been confidently overseeing the ceremony when Marie appeared out of nowhere in a sudden and dramatic flash of red smoke and firelight. The believers took it as a sign that Marie's power was limitless and Bess was made to stand aside. She had not been seen anywhere in town since that night. Neither had anyone seen the tall figure in red so indispensable to Marie for so long. He was still considered dead by drowning, presumably by his own hand.

Marie reached across the small table to pat my hand affectionately after I finished explaining the use of the devices I was giving her.

"Ah owe you," Marie said. "You is still ma special one. Don't evah forget dat."

"You do not owe me for anything," I replied. "But I regret that I can no longer work with you. You have taught me many things."

"I be awright," she remarked with a smile. "You be awright too. But you got to let it go now. It is time."

"I don't understand," I said. "Let *what* go?" I paused to think about her words. "And you keep calling me special...what do you mean?"

Marie smiled again and stood in front of me. "You will know. Everythin' will be clear soon. Just take Marie's word."

I stood up and placed a kiss on her wizened cheek. I knew I would not see her again.

*   *   *

I was gathering up my music after mass. I stuffed it into my satchel and turned around to find Etienne standing behind me. It had been a long time since we'd shared any conversation since I had successfully avoided him for weeks. My recent attitude undoubtedly was responsible for the look of hesitancy on his face. He meekly and politely asked me to come to his office, as there was something that he wanted to discuss with me.

"Erik," he began hesitantly after we were seated. "I wish to speak to you about your playing."

I never considered that my playing would necessitate an office conversation.

"What is the problem, Father?" I asked, not able to conceal the note of suspicion in my voice.

"Well, it may not be so much a problem as perhaps an...adjustment," he said uncomfortably. "Quite a few members of my parish have complained recently about the volume of your music." He hurried on. "Now that's not to say that the Lord's music should not be played with strength and with power, that's not it at all. But it seems that you are playing so loudly that you are hurting their ears."

Was that all? I could certainly back off the volume a bit. "I understand, Father. I shall play with lower volume in the future."

"There is one other thing which I feel I should mention," Etienne continued as he looked at me curiously. "I myself have noticed a certain, how shall I put it...a certain *violence*...in your music lately. Yes, that's it, violence. Frankly, it sounds as if you are angry with the Lord and I really can't have that during my masses. Do you understand what I'm saying?"

I stared at him as the cold crept around me and imprisoned me in its icy grip. I heard the presence quietly laughing at me. The sinister sound was so real to me that I half expected Etienne to hear it.

Etienne looked worried. "Erik, if there is anything you would like to talk to me about I would be happy to make myself available to you. I noticed at Mr. Morphy's services that you and your wife do not appear to be as close as you once were. I would hate to see anything happen…and neither do I want to have to look for someone else to play my organ. There is no one else who can make it sing the way you can."

I politely thanked him for his offer and promised to "adjust" my playing.

"So," I told the presence out loud as I came out into the street, "you want to take this away from me too, do you? It isn't going to happen!"

Christine was not home when I returned and I went straight for the bourbon. I tossed one full one back, swallowing the lot of it in one huge gulp. I took off the mask and dropped it carelessly on the table. The structure of my life was coming down around my ears.

"What in Christ's name do you want from me!" I shouted to the presence. The sound filled the empty spaces of the house as I sloppily refilled the glass. "You've already taken my sleep and my peace of mind, you're taking my wife and *now* you want my music!" I was becoming both very angry and more frightened. "I gave myself to you once! Didn't that satisfy you? When will it be enough?"

Down went number two. I looked down at the mask staring up at me from the table. That damned mask; the symbol of all that I had been denied in my life. I'm just like everyone else inside! I thought wildly. All I ever wanted is to be like everyone else! Why can't people understand that? *Why?* I picked the offending thing up and flung it across the room.

I began to pace the room like a caged animal, and soon my third and fourth glassfuls were gone. I looked at the empty glass in my hand and then whipped my arm back to throw it as hard as I could at the back window. The glass broke through the window-pane, leaving a hole in it, and I heard it shatter on the flagstones of the courtyard. Not satisfied, my eyes fell on the sideboard where the heavy cut crystal decanter still held a good amount of bour-bon. Grasping it by the neck, I raised it to my lips and drank deeply from it, pouring half the contents down my throat while slopping some of it over my chin and down my shirtfront. I stopped to look at it, licked the overflow from my lips and tipped it up a second time. The liquid burned its way down my throat as I gulped it like water. Then I violently heaved the decanter at the same window. The remainder of the window exploded on impact, sending shards of glasses everywhere. I ducked as they flew around me and landed with a tinkling sound on the carpet. I looked up to see my best bourbon running in ugly brown streams down the wall, spattering the drapes and collecting in puddles on the floor.

Suddenly it was all too much for me. The two sides of me were tearing me apart and I could take no more of it. I ran from the room and up the stairs to what had been our bedroom. I rushed to the music box that I had brought with me from Paris and given to Christine on our first Christmas. Whimpering like a lost child, I wound it up frantically, almost knocking it off the table as I lis-tened impatiently for the first notes of the intricate melody it played. I knew those notes by heart, for I had built this very box many years ago. When I heard them I hugged it to me and ran my shaking hands lovingly over the smooth rosewood case and the lit-tle window in the lid, which showed the movement of its delicate inner workings. The haunting notes finally soothed me and once again became the gentle friends they had been during the years of my solitude. I was there in that room with my arms wrapped tightly around the music box, reeking of whiskey and with tears drying on my face when Christine came home.

She was immediately alarmed when she saw the broken window in the parlor and quickly came upstairs looking for me. I sat huddled on the floor in a corner hugging the box. The music had wound down some time ago but I had not noticed to rewind it. I sat with my eyes closed, rocking the box and whispering, over and over, "You won't get it, you won't get any more." Christine hesitantly laid a hand on my arm and I jumped. I looked up into her face and began to cry. I was scared, so scared! I didn't want to go back to that other place of darkness and silence again! I'd just been there and I didn't want any part of it! I wanted to be here with Christine in the new life we had made together. I told her that, and she looked at me oddly.

"What do you mean 'go back', Erik? Please talk to me! Don't keep shutting me out!"

Sitting on that floor with my beloved wife imploring me to let her help me, I knew I couldn't go on like that any longer. I was being torn apart inside and I could not help myself. I had tried to push it away but it didn't work. No matter how hard I fought, it just kept sucking me down, deeper and deeper. The presence was too strong and powerful for me to fight alone any longer. I haltingly explained to her that there was something inside me that was determined to drag me back to the way I had been before I met her...back into the unspeakable life I had led before entrenching myself so firmly under the Opera House. I finally admitted that the constant nightmares I still suffered were all scenes from my own violent past and that I had not told her about them because I didn't want to frighten her.

"Christine, there are so many things I can never tell you about. The things I *have* told you only scratch the surface of the man I once was. You would hate me and I couldn't bear that. This thing ruins my sleep and haunts my days. It intrudes on everything. Etienne even told me today that it is in my music...my *music,*

Christine! It is taking everything I love from me! When that part of me takes control I am not responsible for what I do or say." I looked down at the floor. "I'm being punished for the sins of my past and I'm dragging you down with me. I don't deserve you, Christine...that's what this is all about. It will haunt me until I let you go or I die. I was wrong to have taken you from Paris." I began to rock the box again, cringing with the memory of one awful night. "The last night I came to your bed...Oh, Christine, it wasn't me that night...I never meant to hurt you that way...it wasn't me, it wasn't me..." I broke down in sobs.

Christine tried to take the box from me, but I would not let it go. I continued to rock it back and forth, sobbing and apologizing for what I had done to her. She persisted in trying to get it away from me, and finally I let her have it. She set it on the floor beside us and wound it up. With the background of delicate and soothing melody, she took my tear-streaked face in her hands and lifted it so that I had to look at her.

"We knew there would be bad times along with the good, Erik. You told me that yourself." Christine said gently. "You've been so different lately, like someone I've never met before. I haven't known...I've been so frightened of..." At that admission my tears began again. She wiped them away, her fingers tracing my ugly features with love and tenderness. "I want back the Erik whom I married, the Erik who is loving and gentle and a very good person. The person you've always been underneath all that you were forced to become. The Erik whom I love so dearly and whom I've missed terribly! Please, my darling, let me help you."

Then she took me in her arms. Christ, it had been so long! I clung to her tightly, feeling like I was home again at last. We sat there together, just holding each other, until long after dark.

20

---★---

We sat in the courtyard having our noon meal with our second anniversary only a week away. I had tried very hard over the last few weeks to make amends for the pain I had caused everyone. I mended my friendship with Jean and Louise. Together Christine and I explained to them about my nightmares. Or, rather, she did. I sat next to her holding her hand like a lifeline with my head bowed. I was ashamed to face my good friends after the way I had treated them. We told them a sanitized story about my having a past that I was not exactly proud of and that my nightmares were caused by painful memories. It was basically the truth, and without the actual details it didn't sound too bad. Christine made such good work of smoothing things over that I gathered my courage and tried to explain my drinking as the result of my increased tension and anxiety. They were obviously relieved that Christine and I were once again on better terms, and graciously forgave my behavior. Of course, I did not mention my activities on North Rampart Street. I caught Jean looking at me with a knowing expression, but either he actually feared my wrath or he wished to spare Christine the information. Whatever the case, he remained silent.

Since the nightmares continued without interruption, I opted to remain in the adjoining bedroom. I promised Christine that I would not "walk them off". It was an easy promise to make, considering that I would no longer be spending my nights hiding under crimson robes and scaring the hell out of the local colored community. No doubt she wanted to ask about the real reason for all those disappearances, but I suspect that deep down she may not have wanted to know the answer. Regardless, her questions would have gone unanswered. (I admit to those activities here only because they represent a crucial element of my journey. If not for their contributory effects on the man I have become, they would have remained hidden forever.)

Many times I could shake my dreams off myself and, when I couldn't, Christine always came running in to help me. At least there were nights when she could get a full night's sleep even when I couldn't. There had been many occasions during recent weeks when the presence threatened to reveal itself. My mind would try to slip back into that dark place I was trying once again to forget and, when that happened, I grew moody and distant. Armed with her new knowledge of my struggle to deal with my inner demons, Christine could now recognize the intrusion of the presence in my eyes, my voice, and my behavior. She was not afraid of it, for she knew the presence was only another part of me and it was a part she was determined to conquer. No matter what I was doing when the presence intruded upon me, she took my face firmly in her hands and forced me to look at her and told me firmly that I must stay with her, that she was there to help me drive it off. She helped me to force the darkness from my mind before it could take full hold of me. I was grateful for her help, for I truly feared that if the presence ever gained full control of my mind again, I would not recover it.

It was very difficult to curb my excessive drinking, but my willpower had always been strong when I chose to call upon it. I successfully dropped my consumption immediately to my earlier social level although the urge to imbibe more heavily remained strong for quite some time. It had been a habit born of my nighttime environment, so staying home at night helped me tremendously with overcoming it. I remained thinner than usual although my appetite had returned, but the lack of sleep and the stress and terror of my nightmares prevented me from gaining back the health I had enjoyed during the first year of our marriage. Christine made no secret of the fact that she was worried about me. It had been eighteen months since my heart attack and in that respect I felt good. Even so, neither of us could forget André Sorel's warning that I could have another one at any time and it could be as bad, or worse. If I had one any worse, I would not survive it.

Christine and I resumed our physical relationship, but not with the same frequency or abandon as before. She was too tired. Lately she had been retiring early and rising late. Several times I brought her breakfast upstairs to her bedroom and ate with her, but she never seemed to want much to eat.

Now, as we sat in our sunny courtyard, I looked at her a certain way and saw that she did not look well at all.

"Do you feel all right, my love?" I asked with concern. "You look a bit under the weather."

She looked up from her untouched plate. "Now that you mention it, Erik, I do feel a little tired. I'd like to go inside."

I pulled back her chair and she got to her feet. We were halfway to the door when she fainted. I carried her upstairs to her bed where I gently patted her face with a cold wet cloth until she opened her eyes. I told her to remain lying down and I went downstairs to call the doctor. I had not used the telephone much. I

usually preferred to do my business in person rather than listening
to the annoying crackle of a distant voice in my ear. However, I
was glad of its presence as I cranked it up and was connected
quickly with Dr. Sorel.

I was sitting with Christine when he arrived. After he shooed
me from the room I wandered downstairs and eyed the bottle of
bourbon that we still kept, but thought better of it. I went back
upstairs and nervously paced the hall until he opened the door.

"Mr. Devereaux," he said. "Your wife will be fine. I have examined her and everything appears to be in order." He turned back
to Christine. "Follow my instructions and everything will be fine.
Good day." He smiled at me and went down the hall, leaving me
standing there in confusion. I went back in to Christine.

"What was that all about?" I asked. "What is wrong?" When I
leaned over her, she put her arms up around my neck and whispered into my ear.

The baby was due in the early spring of 1885. I was ecstatic.
Having this to look forward to would surely take my mind off my
own problems. I was overjoyed until I began to think about the
news a little more. Later that night after I went to bed I counted
back the months and realized with horror that Christine had most
probably conceived on the very night that I had come home drunk
and crazed from Marie's and treated her so badly. That night's sex
had not been the result of my intense love for my wife. It had been
a purely carnal and animalistic act of lust. I had used her and hurt
her that night and love had nothing to do with it. Our baby would
be born from a violent beginning and that fact saddened me. It
also frightened me. One look at my own face in the mirror
reminded me all too well of what can happen in the womb. I
pushed my depressing thoughts aside with difficulty, and I never
mentioned them to Christine.

We celebrated our second anniversary in quiet and contented fashion by having Jean and Louise in to dinner. Christine seemed in perfect health so there was no reason for her to stay at home; we just preferred it. In the afternoons I usually took her driving or to the church with me, where I continued to play. I managed to align my playing with what Etienne wanted, although I still found myself occasionally fighting the urge to use a heavier hand. Instead, I poured my fears and frustrations into my own compositions. I had shelves full of them by now. Some of them were as gentle as a summer rain, and others pounded the listener with violence and anger. My compositions ran the gamut of emotions, reflecting a mirror image of what I felt at the time that I wrote them. In retrospect, I have come to realize that my music tells a story—the story of my life. Each composition represents a chapter. From the living hell of my younger years to the relative contentment of my life in New Orleans, these musical chapters chronicled my journey through life better than any diary ever could.

*   *   *

The humid heat of the city in summer gave way slowly to the cooler temperatures and pleasant nights of the fall and winter months. We both loved New Orleans but the climate was definitely a little heavy at times. After living for so many years amid the cool dampness of the cellars it had taken me some time to acclimate myself to the sub-tropical heat and humidity of Louisiana. I welcomed the winter months as a much-needed break from the relentlessly heavy heat of summertime. Christine and I took it rather slowly since we received the news of her condition. It was a wonderful anniversary present and we both looked forward to the birth in the spring. I had not returned to her bed permanently because of the nightmares but it may have been just as well; she looked very tired and had a difficult time during the warmer days. She spent many hours contentedly reading her novels in a chair tucked into the corner of our courtyard where the shade from the house and trees was heaviest.

It was late November and I was readying myself for bed. I had just come from Christine's room where we had been talking before I tucked her in like a child and kissed her goodnight. Now, back in my own room, I was sitting on the edge of the bed when I felt tightness in my chest. I tried to remember what I'd had for dinner but the fish could not be responsible. I lay down on the bed and tried to relax. I was not going to alarm Christine if I was suffering from indigestion. After a few minutes the tightness began to ease off. I breathed a sigh of relief, but I could not push the anxiety from my mind. I had not felt anything like that since the awful day when I'd collapsed on the floor of our home. Dear God, please...not again. Christine needs me more than ever and I need to be strong for her. I got into bed and fell asleep with my troubled thoughts.

I didn't sleep long. Within an hour I was dragged once more into the terrifying world of my dreams. This one began with screams, louder and more piercing than any I had ever heard in my life. They were the screams of a woman but I couldn't tell who it was. Suddenly faceless people surrounded me and they were all laughing and pointing at me. Their faces moved around me as if I was being spun around like a child's toy top. Faster and faster they went until I could make out nothing but blurred images. Abruptly my spinning was stopped as I backed up against a wall. Before me there appeared a pyre of flames and, as I watched, a woman's form appeared in the flames. Up and up she rose until I could see her whole body silhouetted against the searing brightness. She vanished into the flames only to be replaced by a large snake—a serpent—writhing and twisting in the heat. The serpent stretched its length out toward me, but there was nowhere I could go. I was backed against the wall. I turned to the wall and tried to claw my way up but it was too smooth. Over my shoulder I could see the serpent coming closer; then its tail wrapped itself around my ankle like a huge tentacle. Pulling me off my feet, it inexorably began to drag me toward the flames!

I was on the ground, scratching at the floor in a desperate attempt to find something to hold on to. The serpent dragged me closer and closer to the pyre and I began to scream when I felt the heat upon my body. I twisted around and sat up to kick and scratch at the serpent's tail, trying to loosen its ever tighter grip upon my ankle as it pulled me toward the flames. I couldn't get loose! The heat intensified and I began to scream as I felt my clothes incinerating and my skin start to shrivel...No! Help me!

Christine found me on the floor. Lying on my stomach, I had dragged the bedding off the bed with me in my frantic attempts to free myself from the serpent that clutched me in the dream. The sheet was wrapped tightly around one ankle. I could still feel the heat from the flames as they licked my body. I was still screaming.

"Erik!" Christine fell to her knees beside me. "Erik! Erik! Wake up!"

She grabbed one of my clutching hands and held it while she shouted at me. Finally her voice penetrated my consciousness and I stopped fighting. I opened my eyes to see only the floor in front of me. I was panting so hard I could hardly catch my breath. When Christine left me to get some water, I dropped my head to the wood floor in exhaustion. She was gone longer than I would have expected, and when she returned she held a small glass of bourbon.

She helped me to sit up. I was still breathing hard, and I swore I could still feel heat. It must have been emanating from my own body. I looked with surprise at the drink in her hand.

"It doesn't matter," she assured me. "You need it."

I took it and sipped it slowly. Soon my breathing calmed. I reached out one arm and she came into my embrace. I set the glass on the floor next to me and held her.

"I'm sorry I woke you again, love," I said after taking some more of the bourbon. "It was one of the worst I've had. I just couldn't get away…"

I shook my head and closed my eyes, sighing as I leaned back against the bed. The bourbon was helping. How did she always know exactly what I needed?

"Get away from what, Erik? Can you tell me about it?" She snuggled in next to me against the side of the bed.

"Snakes, fire, faces; I don't know what else. It's odd, but I can't seem to connect anything in tonight's dream with my past. These things seemed totally unrelated to me."

That wasn't entirely the truth; the snake was one of the most prominent symbols of the voodoo world. I had worked with many of them, and it brought back unpleasant memories of the night Bess had tried to outsmart me. It was the only connection I could think of but I certainly would not mention it.

I glanced at my wife sitting on the floor beside me. What would I do without her?

"Please, Christine, go back to bed. I am fine now and I've never had more than one in any given night. I touched her face. "You need the sleep more than I do now."

She made no move to leave. Our eyes locked and I moved my hand from her face to the lower area of her abdomen. I spread my fingers across its width as if willing the tiny life inside to be all right. Christine placed her hands on top of mine and leaned forward to kiss me. Our lips gently met and I thought how good it felt to be close to her again. It was a soft kiss between two people who need each other more than anything else in the world. My large misshapen lips now molded perfectly to her smaller delicate ones, and kissing my wife continued to be one of life's finer experiences. It still never failed to amaze me that she could so totally accept the horrific appearance of my face, especially that close up. I always thrilled to that aspect of human contact that I had so often dreamed about. One's face is the source of so much of the communication between one person and another. The face is the window upon which all emotion is displayed. One can easily judge moods of joy, anger, confusion, fear and love just by looking into a face. I'd always been envious of those around me who could express their thoughts with as little as a "look". To me, the idea of two people joining together at the lips represented the most intimate form of all human touch. A kiss can express how one is feeling more than any touch of the hand and it seemed much more intimate to me than the actual sex act. Such a tiny little gesture, a kiss, but so important! Our first kiss, on the day I proposed to Christine, proved to me that she truly did see past my ugliness to the man I was inside. As far as I was concerned it was the ultimate test of Christine's ability to accept me for who I really was.

We sat together on that hard floor in the middle of the night enjoying the intensely intimate moment. I could have spent the rest of the night sitting with Christine on the floor just kissing her. It appeared that she could do the very same thing, but she needed her sleep. I told her again how much I loved her and persuaded her to go back to bed. After she returned to her room I lay in the remade bed pondering the meaning of this latest dream. With the possible exception of the snake figure, I could find no relationship to it from anything else I knew. I finally fell asleep again and the remainder of the night passed without incident.

*   *   *

Several weeks later, I was sitting at the piano working. Christine's shriek from somewhere upstairs brought me running in a panic. She was sitting on her bed with her hands splayed over her stomach.

"Erik!" she cried as I ran into the room. "Here, quickly!"

Was something wrong? She grabbed my hand and planted it firmly over her lower abdomen. Then she pushed my hand down hard. I was about to protest that she might hurt the baby when I felt the tiny fluttering movement from deep within her.

"Is that...?" I stammered.

"Yes!" she cried, her eyes shining.

I will never forget the feeling that struck me to my very core when I felt the first movement of our child. I looked at her joyous face and the love I felt almost was too much for me. I took her in my arms and kissed her. Soon our light kiss intensified and I began to give in to my desire until I remembered.

"Christine, perhaps we shouldn't..." I began breathlessly. "It might hurt the baby."

"No, my darling, I asked Dr. Sorel," she replied. He said if we weren't too overly enthusiastic..." She smiled at me with the devil in her eye, "that it would be fine for several more months."

I was sitting next to her on the bed. When I kissed her again she lay back with a sigh, pulling me over and down with her. When her hands crept between us to begin unbuttoning my shirt, I lifted my head and caught the familiar darkening of her blue eyes. We spent the remainder of the afternoon in a tender and gentle love-making that was as passionate in its own way as anything we'd ever experienced. When we finally decided it was time to get up for some dinner, we felt the baby move again. It was the sweetest thing I'd ever known.

*   *   *

Jean and Louise were delighted at the prospect of a baby and we promised them that they would be the child's godparents. In early December we were returning home after dark from a dinner at Jean's house where we had enjoyed dinner and conversation until I suggested to Christine that it might be time to get her home. I treated her very gently these days, and was probably a royal nuisance to her when it came to what she ate and when she went to bed. She usually had the good grace to submit to most of my fussing without comment. I felt I owed it to her after all I had put her through.

We clattered over the cobblestones slowly with Christine's arm through mine. I began to hear sounds from somewhere in the neighborhood, but I could not identify them. Suddenly Christine asked me if I smelled smoke. When we rounded the corner at Royal and St. Ann I looked off in the direction of Chartres Street. I was dismayed to see an orange glow from further down Chartres. Whipping up my horse, I begged Christine's indulgence and covered the two blocks in seconds.

Rounding another corner revealed the reason for the smoky smell. Several doors down was a house on fire. The flames were beginning to lick through one of the second story windows. There were several people in the street but no one was doing anything. I pulled my horse up a safe distance away and looked over at Christine. Her hands were at her mouth and she was staring in horror at the burning building. When her wide eyes met mine I read her thoughts. Was there someone inside? I handed her the traces and jumped to the ground, then removed my cloak and threw it up to her. I took my handkerchief out of my pocket and quickly tucked it under my mare's bridle and over her eyes. There is nothing worse for a horse than their fear of fire, and I did not want her bolting with Christine in the carriage.

"Erik! Don't you go in there, do you hear me?" I heard her shout as I ran up the street.

I went straight up to the small group of men who stood across the street. They were standing in a close circle watching the flames grow in intensity. Why weren't they doing anything?

"What is going on here?" I demanded when I reached them. "Has the Fire Company been summoned?"

One man separated himself from the group. I don't think he could see me all that well in the dim flickers from the fire.

"Yeah, they've been called, and there's nothing we can do until they get here."

"Is anyone inside the house? Who lives here?"

"A woman and her daughter, I think. We don't know where they are; no one has seen them out here," he replied sheepishly.

"What do you mean you don't know!" I roared, grabbing the unfortunate man by his coat. Looking over at the others I shouted, "Did none of you check for anyone in there?"

Several of them looked at the ground. I looked from one to the other hoping to find some help but they were all miserable cowards, every last one of them. With a shake of contempt I pushed the man I held away from me. I looked back over my shoulder at the flames that now showed from several windows on the second floor. The first story looked untouched.

I ran across the street to the front door. The knob was cool. It was unlocked and I cautiously opened it. I heard Christine scream my name from down the block. I promised her silently that I would not leave her and then I stepped inside.

21

———————— ★ ————————

I heard nothing but the roar and crackle of the flames upstairs. The rooms downstairs were dark and flame free but the smoke was thick. I held my arm up over my nose and mouth. The light from the flames in the upstairs windows spilled out into the night and was reflected back from the windows across the street. I could barely make out the staircase to my right in the dense smoke. I slowly climbed it, feeling the heat increase with every step. Up in the hallway I saw a flickering glow from the right hand rooms. I had gone most of the way up the stairs when I froze. I had heard something. I stopped and waited while keeping my eye on the glow above me. There!

Adrenaline surged through me. Someone was on the second floor. At that instant something exploded in one of the rooms above. A ball of flame shot down the hallway toward me. I ducked down quickly on the stairs and it went over my head, but the carpets and furnishings in the hallway began to burn. I must find whoever it was quickly and get the hell out of there. Crouching at some spots and jumping over flames at others I ran quickly and carefully down the hallway. At the end were two rooms and both were afire. I shouted as loudly as I could, asking if anyone could hear me. I heard an answer from the room on the right.

The door was open. The flames had apparently jumped across the hall to it from the room opposite. That door was closed but the fire had eaten its way across the carpet under the door, setting the hall ablaze along with the room into which I now looked. I was soaked with sweat, but my mask, hat and clothes had so far protected me from the worst of the heat. Ironically, the mask was coming in handy. I peered around the corner into the room. Only part of the room was burning and in the far corner I thought I could see someone crouched there. I dropped to the floor and crawled around the bed to the corner. The woman was paralyzed with fear. She looked from me to the flames and back again. Before she could protest I grabbed her by the arm and dragged her toward the door. The flames were spreading across the floor and ignited the drapes and part of the bed. I had to move fast. When we reached the hall I stood up and pulled her to her feet. Holding her arm I started down the hall toward the stairs but she wrenched away from me and ran back toward the flames to stare at the other bedroom door. Through the thickening smoke I could see the flames licking out from under that door. She noticed them at the same time and began to scream. She screamed and screamed. I went back for her; I would have to take her out of there bodily. She continued screaming incoherently. She fought me as I tried to get her to the stairs and I made out one word—*daughter*.

Christ, there was someone in that room! I lifted the woman off the floor and hefted her up over my shoulder. She beat her fists on my back and screamed as I carried her down the stairs to the front door. I shoved her out into the street and took several deep breaths of relatively clean air. Maybe those cowards will do something for her now, I thought nastily. Without looking down the street in the direction of my parked carriage, I dove back into the smoky blackness.

The smoke was extremely thick. I could barely see where I was going and could only advance on my hands and knees. I crawled up the stairs to an almost totally involved second floor. I didn't know how I was going to get to that back room but I had to try. I shouted, hoping to hear an answer, but there was nothing. Maybe I was too late. *Please, don't let it be too late.* At the top of the stairs, I quickly charted my way through an obstacle course of fire. I pulled my hat down as far as it would go around my head, pulled my collar up and ran quickly through the flames to the door. The door was hot, but there was someone in there. Standing to the side, I used the pocket of my coat to slowly turn the knob. Damn! It was locked! I backed up a few feet and raised my foot to send it crashing against the bolt. The door sprung open with a bang.

A blast of heat hit me full in the chest and knocked me back across the hall to the opposite wall. My head hit the wall hard enough to make it spin. Shaking it off, I looked into the room before me. It was full of flames. Some of it was burning so intensely that the flames appeared blue. Everything was aflame; the bed, the draperies, the furniture and the carpet. In the middle of it, in the only area of floor not involved, crouched a young woman. She didn't move, but stared into the flames with a grotesque fascination. Ignoring the smoke, I moved through the door and around the corner. She caught sight of me and stood up, reaching out her arms to me in a silent plea for help. I was surprised that she could see me through the thick smoke. I moved along the wall to one side where the flames were less intense, hoping to reach her from there. At that moment something else in the room ignited in a ball of fire and the added heat forced me back against the wall. Flames sprang up all around her and she finally began to scream. I stared for several precious seconds at the deadly tendrils of flame that were beginning to dance their way closer to her. Her arms reached out to me...the heat...she kept screaming...*my dream!*

I began to cough in the heavy smoke. Neither of us had any more time. The heat was suffocating and my clothing was getting hotter. The level of combustion in the room was so high that my sweat soaked coat sleeves were smoking. I had to let some heat out of the room. I picked up a wooden chair that stood against the wall next to me and hurled it with all my strength at the closest window. A couple of panes were already broken from the heat but when the chair crashed through it the glass exploded. The flames leapt a little higher but the heat level was lowered by a few precious degrees. The mask was protecting most of my face but was getting so hot that I thought the leather would burn me. I could no longer feel my hands. The flames were now only inches away from the woman's skirts.

I had to move now! I lunged toward her with the flames licking at my legs. Christ, it was hot! I wrapped my arms around her and she fainted. I put her over my shoulder and tried to capture her voluminous skirts under my arm. I turned to stare in horror at the wall of flame that had sprung up between the door and us. Frantically I looked around me for an available window but there were none that I could reach. The heat was unbearable and I could no longer breath. I felt my chest constricting with the smoke I had inhaled. I knew if I didn't get out of there immediately they would find my charred remains in the morning with the blackened bones of my arms still wrapped around the woman I held. Coughing violently, I closed my eyes and plunged through the flames.

By some miraculous stroke of luck I managed to hit the doorway on my first attempt while banging only one shoulder painfully on the way through. I ran down the hall through the flames and smoke, only to find the carpeted stairway ablaze as well. Several of the steps were burned almost through and the flames beneath them blinked wickedly at me through the widening holes. I could see only one way down. Shifting the unconscious woman to hold her tightly in both arms, I hiked up one leg to sit upon the smooth banister. After a hasty glance behind me at the approaching flames I slid quickly down the narrow rail to the bottom. We landed heavily on the floor of the entryway just inside the front door with the woman's body sprawled on top of me. I looked up from the floor in relief to see several firemen at the open door. They lifted the woman from across my chest and carried her outside. Two of them helped me to my feet and out the door into the fresh air.

The smoke in my lungs and the heat finally overcame me. My knees buckled and the firemen literally dragged me away from the building and into the street. Safe at last, they allowed me to sink to my knees in the street coughing and gasping for air. I leaned over and rested my head on the wet cobblestones where the air seemed to be the cleanest. There were people everywhere by then, milling around in confusion. The Fire Company was finally getting some water on the flames and beginning to knock them down. Since I got the women out the ladder wagon had not been needed. The pumper was doing its best to keep up with the need for water. Its hissing blasts of steam could be heard over the sounds of men's shouts, spraying water and general clatter. I felt as if I had been in that burning hell for hours, but in fact it had only been several minutes. I began to gag and was spitting up a vile black mess when Christine reached me.

"Erik!" She flung her arms around me. "Oh, Erik! Thank God you're all right!"

She was crying hysterically and was all over me. When I looked up into her frightened face I noticed she was covered with soot. I finally sat up and looked at myself. My white shirt was streaked with gray and black shades of soot, as was every inch of myself that I could see. My coat was like dried paper and was coming apart. My hands were burned and blackened with soot. I suspected my lower legs were as well when I saw that the bottom edges of both trouser legs were burned away. All I wanted was to go home. I asked Christine to help me up. She pulled my arm across her shoulders, and although she could not have supported my weight if I fell, I appreciated her gesture. I was slowly limping to my carriage when I was stopped by one of the fireman.

"Please wait, sir!" he called. Catching up to us, he took one look at me and whistled. "My God, man, you need a doctor."

"I'll be all right, my doctor is on my way home," I answered hoarsely, anxious to be away from there.

"I should tell you, sir, that if you had not gone into that building those two women would have perished tonight. They owe you their lives and we owe you a debt of gratitude." He paused, then added, "I wish we had more men like you in this town. Thank you." He reached out to shake my hand, but when I lifted it he saw my burns and did not touch it. "Get to that doctor, please." Then, with a nod, he turned back to the business at hand.

I had almost reached the carriage when a commotion behind me caused me to turn around a second time. A small carriage pulled up and the woman whom I had brought out of the house first was helped down from it. She hobbled over and threw her arms around me, sobbing wildly.

"Oh sir," she wailed, "you saved our lives! How can I ever repay you?"

She clung to me until a man pulled her away.

"You and your daughter are alive; that is payment enough," I said with even less voice than I'd had a minute ago. My throat burned and I felt slightly sick to my stomach. The daughter, who, I learned, was only seventeen years old, had been taken to the hospital and the mother would be joining her. She was helped back into the carriage and driven off quickly. I looked back at the house. The fire was out, and people were beginning to drift away.

At Christine's insistence she drove me over to Dr. Sorel's house immediately. I could not drive so I had little choice in the matter. When he opened the door to see my blackened face he blanched and hurried me inside. I was very uncomfortable, to put it mildly. My eyes were almost shut from the smoke irritation and my head ached from hitting that wall so violently. I could not stop coughing. The burns on my hands and legs hurt like hell. I became violently ill when he began to dress the burns, but after seeing the blackness I had thrown up he considered it a good thing I'd done it. Dr. Sorel sent Christine to the kitchen for a glass of water for me. I knew he wanted to get her out of the room.

"You know, Erik, you took a huge chance in doing what you did tonight, and I don't mean from the fire," he said soberly as he eyed me stretched out on his examining table.

I knew what he meant. I had told him about the tightening in my chest the night I'd had the fire dream. He listened to my heart but when I tried to breathe for him it just set me off coughing again. He set down his instruments and leaned back against the counter, crossing his arms in front of him and regarding me with grave seriousness.

"I don't know if what you felt is related to your condition or to tension, but I don't like the sound of it. You have felt good for quite a while now but that doesn't mean the danger is over. It will never be over. An attack could strike at any time and the next one could leave you bedridden or it could kill you." He helped me off the table. "A word to the wise, Erik. Be careful. If you experience anything at all unusual, please let me know."

A few minutes later Christine was driving us home. She did not know of my conversation with Dr. Sorel, and she wouldn't, at least for now. Before we left the doctor's house we all enjoyed a good laugh over the fact that no one had seemed to notice my mask at all during the whole incident. I had to chuckle along with them when they told me that both my face and mask were so blackened with soot that no one could see where one ended and the other began. Indeed, when the artist's rendering of my heroic rescue appeared in the paper the next day, there was no mask to be seen on my normal looking face. The one aspect of my appearance that unequivocally identified me around town had not even been noticed. I was an unidentified savior who had appeared in the night to save two lives, and disappeared just as quickly. That drawing was the most handsome I'd ever looked.

In bed that night as Christine tucked the sheets around me I tried to explain in a croaking voice about the dream.

"It was the dream, Christine, do you understand what I'm saying? That one was not a memory, it was a premonition!" I struggled with my rapidly disappearing voice. "When the flames blew me back against the wall and I saw that girl standing there with her arms reaching out to me it was the same as what I'd seen in my mind!"

"I understand, Erik. Please stop talking and go to sleep." She touched my face with a loving caress and leaned over to kiss me goodnight. "I was terrified when I saw you go into that house, Erik," she said softly. "I didn't know if you would ever come out, and when I heard the explosions…I…" She began to cry. "I was so afraid…."

I lifted my thickly bandaged hands to pull her to me. "Christine, I had to do it. No one else was going to get those women out. I was their only chance."

I refused to think about the huge possibility that, had the slightest thing happened differently in that house, all three of us might just as easily have died that night.

I lay in bed thinking about the evening, and something occurred to me that I had not thought of before. Marie Laveau, in some odd wisdom of hers, had told me that I was special. I never knew what that meant. I had figured out from the start that her initial fascination with me had principally been for the purpose of my unique masked mysteriousness and the fear that my abilities could bring forth in people. I was a sideshow for her. Although I believed that her power over people had more to do with their fear of the unknown than her ability to produce actual magic, I had wondered about her words to me for a long time. Was what had happened tonight what she meant? Was it destiny that Christine and I left Jean's at that particular time and saw the fire? Was I meant to get there in time to save those women? I would never know, but something had drawn me to that spot tonight and it had driven me to risk my own life to save the lives of two others. I had seen it before it happened, so something had sent me there. *Take that*, I said to the presence, which had been quiet and thankfully dormant for months, probably gathering its strength for an all out attack on my healing mind. *I saved two lives tonight and there was nothing you could do to stop me*. I felt stronger inside than I had in months and I slept well that night.

The next morning found me in my carriage, with Robert at the traces, on our way to St. Louis Cathedral. I'd lost my voice completely overnight and was still coughing painfully. All I could do was whisper, but I wanted to speak to Etienne myself about my playing; it was too important an errand to leave to a messenger. I looked down at the white bandages covering my hands. Dr. Sorel said that my skin was badly damaged, but he did not know if the muscles and tendons had been affected. He was confident the skin would heal reasonably well, but my movement? He could not say.

Etienne was saddened when I told him that I could not play for an indefinite period, but he was also surprised to find out exactly who had gone into the burning house after those women. Apparently not many people had found out and I preferred to keep it that way. I kept my hands tucked under my arms in the carriage. My legs had been luckier. Although I would walk stiffly for a while, they would heal quickly.

It was a difficult meeting for me. I was extremely worried about the future of my playing and my music. I could not compose correctly without playing. The danger involved had not occurred to me when I entered the burning building. Rescue had been foremost in my mind. The excitement had worn off and now I was terrified. I could not contemplate life without my music, and the thought of never again being able to play the magnificent organ whose pipes soared above my head at this very moment was beyond my comprehension. Etienne assured me that as soon as I was ready to come back I was welcome, but he must hire someone else to play in the interim. It was hard for me to think of anyone else playing the manuals that I had come to think of as my own.

I would be going to Dr. Sorel's office every day for new dressings until my hands healed. I stopped off there on my way home for my first visit. When he unwound the bandages I could not believe that I was looking at my own hands. Angry red and swollen, they were barely recognizable. I could not bend my fingers at all and he reprimanded me when I tried. My heart caught in my throat as I looked at my once graceful hands and recognized the very real possibility that I might never play again.

"Erik, please don't get concerned too quickly. It will take a while for the swelling to go down," Andre said when he saw my concern. "Once the skin has healed I will give you some exercises that will get your fingers moving again." But just getting them moving isn't enough, I thought as I limped to my carriage.

Robert took me home. Christine met me at the door and I took her awkwardly in my arms, wincing from the pain in my bruised shoulder. Words were unnecessary. I felt the empathy in Christine's embrace.

*   *   *

That night I had another dream related to my past. Unlike my previous nightmares, this dream was slow and quiet, with none of the formerly frenetic pace and flying images. I was peacefully rowing my boat on the lake beneath the opera house. I thought the water looked a little darker than usual so I leaned over the side to look more closely at it. I could see my own reflection in it, which didn't make sense because the lighting down there had always been too dim to show me any reflections in the water. As I watched, my reflection became brighter and brighter, but there was a red tint to it. I reached down with both hands to swirl the water around, which dissolved the picture. I returned to my rowing and finally entered my underground house. (Seeing it so vividly in my dream was odd, because it had now been close to three years since I had left it. What did it look like now? I pushed the thought away.) When I lit the lamp in my parlor and removed my cloak I was horrified to notice that my hands and forearms were completely covered with blood! I ran quickly to the tub room and washed my hands. It was on my sleeves so I changed my clothes. I had to rinse the basin several times to get the blood out of it. Where in hell had that come from? I decided to go back out to the lake and take a look.

I walked back down the short passageway to the water's edge. I lifted my lantern and looked out over the expanse of water. It looked totally normal to me. I held the lantern down close to the water. It still looked the same as it always had. I shrugged and went back to the house. Setting the lantern down on the table, I reached to put it out. My hands were again covered in blood! *I had never touched the water on the second trip.* I grabbed the still burning lantern and raced back out to the lake a third time. This time when I held the lantern low, I could see that the water was a deep red color. The entire lake was filled not with water, but with blood! Suddenly I could smell it; fresh blood has a disgustingly distinct odor that is unmistakable once one is familiar with it. I ran back to the basin and scrubbed my hands raw. The basin and the wall were covered with red spatters from my feverish attempts to wash the blood from my hands. I scrubbed and scrubbed my hands, but I could not get the blood off them! Where did it come from...why wouldn't it come off? Why wouldn't it come off...I can't get it off. I can't get it...off!

I sat up in bed abruptly, breathing fast. My hands were throbbing. Holding it awkwardly between my bandaged hands, I took a drink from the water glass on the table beside me. I got out of bed and went to stand at the window. I fumbled with the latch and when I flung it wide open the cool winter air rushed into the room. It felt good upon my naked body. The night was calm, clear and peaceful. What was the presence trying to tell me? I do have blood on my hands. I do not deny it. Murderer, killer, assassin, executioner; call it what one will, I have been all of those things at one time or another, long before I found the love that had turned my life around. I could only guess that the symbol of the bloody hands was a haunting reminder that my past would always be with me. This dream was not the first in which I had seen that image, although it appeared in different ways. Usually it was in fleeting glimpses, but not this time. This dream had centered upon it.

22

---- ★ ----

Christine was entering her sixth month when Christmas of 1884 arrived. I saw the strain the baby was putting on her. She was very tired and began to eat less instead of the larger quantities that I expected. Still, she set aside time every day to assist me with my recuperation. It had been almost four weeks since the fire. I was told after two weeks that I could begin work on getting my fingers moving again. I was sickened by how stiff and ugly they were. They certainly would never look the same again. I could not bend them at all and it hurt to try. Along with my own efforts to bend them, Christine sat me down several times a day and massaged my hands. Using a fragrant oil, she worked her fingers between and around mine, moving them every way possible. I was fortified for these sessions with a glass or two of bourbon but it was still exceedingly painful. She slowly but relentlessly worked my fingers and gradually they began to loosen. Aside of the pain, it was a very special time for us. Often while she worked on my hands we would enjoy a long kiss over our task. It helped to take my mind off the pain.

Playing music was out of the question. I tried, but the effort only served to frustrate me. I was pushing myself too fast and I knew it, but I was impatient to get back to my work. I tried working on some of my scores, but my hand quickly became too fatigued to hold the pen. I had always abhorred incompetence in others, and now I transferred that impatience to myself. I could hardly bear to enter the parlor and see my piano sitting there silently. Everything was exactly as I had left it, yet now it only served to distress me. I knew that if I could never play again, I would never hear Christine sing again. All along I'd held out some hope that she would show some interest in returning to her music, but now that seemed quite impossible.

Christmas Eve was spent quietly at home. We would again be having dinner the next day with Jean and Louise but we reserved the evening for ourselves. After dinner we retired to Christine's room. She was getting larger and I was too afraid of hurting the baby to make love to her. She announced that if I would allow her to work on my hands one more time that night she would give me a Christmas present. I didn't know what she could possibly mean since she had not left the house for a while but I extended my hands to her in anticipation. She worked on them with her gentle but firm touch and I lay back on the pillows and closed my eyes.

I had drifted off to sleep, or so I thought. From the heavens I heard a beautiful sound, as if the angels themselves were singing. Beginning very gently, the heavenly notes soon grew stronger and louder until I was taken up and carried away on a cloud of wonderful music. Suddenly I was aware that Christine had stopped rubbing my hands, and was quietly holding them. I opened my eyes.

She was sitting up next to me in the bed. Her eyes were closed and she was singing—she was singing! It was Christine's lovely voice that I heard, and it was still as pure and perfect as it had been in Paris. I sat up to see tears dropping from beneath her dark lashes. A more beautiful sight I had never seen. It was an old French Christmas hymn, and I sat listening with rapture until she had finished.

"Christine," I whispered in amazement. "What...?"

"I thought it would make you happy, Erik," she said softly. "Merry Christmas, my darling."

"Nothing could have made me happier, my love," I said in an awed whisper. "You are the most beautiful woman in the world, with the voice of an angel. You were truly sent to me from the heavens." I lowered my eyes to my stiffened hands and added, "I only wish that I could play for you."

"My darling, you will play for me. We will keep working until you can. No matter how long it takes, I know in my heart that my Angel of Music will play for me once again."

"You have not called me that since we left Paris. Do you still think of me as your Angel, even after all the pain I have caused you?"

"Always," she said quietly.

I gathered her into my arms and brought her down with me to snuggle deep under the covers. My hand strayed down to the growing curve of her body and caressed her soft skin. I was just beginning to regain my sense of touch and her skin felt like silk. We spent the next few minutes enjoying each other as much as possible without taking undue chances until we were both too sleepy to continue. I fell asleep with my wife in my arms for the first time in six months.

*   *   *

The new year began and with it came our renewed hopes for the future. Christine and I had weathered an extremely rough time in our marriage. Those bad times, which had encompassed more than a year of our precious time together, were solely the result of my inability to deal with a past that continued to torment me.

I had always believed that I could do anything I wanted to do if I set my mind to it. I believed that I would never need anyone's help in anything; that the only person I could ever fully rely upon was myself. I was wrong. Christine had shown me that I could not handle everything by myself, that I was not the invincible and omnipotent man I thought I was. I was foolish to wait so long to ask for her help in fighting my demons. I was foolish to try to handle it myself when I had my wife to lean on for support. I'd not had much experience with trust and it was a very difficult concept for me to grasp.

Consider what I had put her through. Battling my inner demons, my drinking, my endless and unexplained absences, my rages and my generally unpredictable and volatile nature all the way back to my original deceptive manipulations of her and others, my kidnap of her and our disastrous wedding night. Through it all Christine had remained steadfastly at my side. Why? Why did this woman not leave me and run as fast as her legs would carry her to someone who could help get her away from me?

She stays because she loves me. Christine really and truly loves me. She loves me even with all my faults and my shortcomings, my unpredictability and my ugly face. I don't know how or why, but she does. And God knows I love her. I love her with every breath I take, with every part of my being, and with every beat of my heart. Almost three years had passed since I had taken her away from Paris and changed both of our lives forever.

Together we looked forward to the birth of our baby, but my happiness was tempered by my concern for Christine's seemingly fragile condition. André Sorel assured us that it was not unusual for a woman to have a hard time with carrying a baby. As Christine's pregnancy progressed he recommended that she get as much rest as possible. I spent hours at her side talking or singing to her. I sang to her all the time now that I could not play for her, and many times she sang along with me. It would have been a totally joyous experience were it not for my concern over her health.

We continued to work on improving my manual dexterity. I could move my fingers almost normally, but I had not recently tried playing the piano. My earlier failure was too fresh in my mind. Christine's relentless manipulation of my fingers had worked miracles and one day in mid-January, while she rested upstairs, I sat down at the piano. I laid my fingers on the keys and closed my eyes. I willed my fingers to move with every ounce of my concentration. Very slowly the keys began to speak as my fingers moved over them, gently pressing them in almost the correct sequence. I forced my mind to send its instructions to my unwilling hands, and in between the inevitable mistakes I slowly began to hear the sounds I wanted. I had managed to pick out a good part of one piece when I felt Christine's hands on my shoulders. Taking encouragement from her touch I continued, feeling her strength flow into my body and transfer itself to my stiff and recalcitrant fingers. She sank down onto the bench beside me and began to sing. I joined her in the soft song and our voices blended together with the music. When it was finished I lifted my trembling hands from the keys and turned to look at her. Her eyes said everything. She took my aching hands in hers and looked at me in triumph. I was just about to kiss her when her expression changed to one of surprise as she looked over my shoulder, causing me to turn around. In the doorway stood Robert and Deliah, and both of them were smiling at me. I returned their happy smiles before I turned back to Christine and kissed her anyway.

The musical gates reopened for me, and I resumed my habit of spending hours at the piano. By the end of January I returned to the organ at the cathedral, much to Etienne's delight. I could not play long before my hands ached with fatigue but with each passing day my endurance grew. One day not long after I returned to the organ I was getting ready to leave for home when a slight but ominous tightening in my chest sent me a silent warning. I tried to relax and sat on the bench without moving for several minutes until it passed. I made a mental note to inform André of it.

Christine entered the last month of her pregnancy and spent all her time at home, either reading in the courtyard or napping. I still slept in the other bedroom even though I'd had fewer nightmares since the fire. It was my turn to help Christine as she thrashed around in her bed trying to find a comfortable position. She lost sleep constantly and it showed. Many nights I sat in her bed holding her while she went to sleep, only to have her wake after I had returned to my own room. Her irritability increased with her size, and I could not blame her. She looked exceedingly uncomfortable.

I had never been able to explain the dream about the lake filled with blood and my bloody hands. Then I had one that was even more perplexing. This dream, like the lake one, was quiet but it was very brief. It was also unusual, because Christine was in it. In the dream, Christine stood looking at me silently with a look of sadness upon her face. I reached out to her but she stepped aside, revealing a small child standing behind her. The girl looked to be about four years old with fair skin, long dark hair and large blue eyes. Christine turned to look at the child and reached out to her. The child lifted her thin arms but was moving away. Anxiously she stretched out those tiny arms again to Christine, but they could not reach each other. Christine went down on her knees as if to beg but the child, now peacefully smiling at her, moved farther away. Just before she disappeared into the darkness, her gaze shifted to me. Her eyes stared steadily into mine and I was filled with the oddest feeling that I knew the little girl. Her gaze was intense as it bore deep into mine but the meaning behind its intensity escaped me. For a long time we looked into each other's eyes, and a connection of some sort was made between us. I opened my mouth to speak to her, but even as her tiny lips curved upward in a warm smile, her hand rose to me in farewell and she was gone.

I woke up slowly, and I could remember the entire dream. What on earth had it meant? I'd seen no bloody hands or anything remotely frightening. Only this beautiful child who had seemed to want to come to us, but could not. Still trying to place her, I went back to sleep with great difficulty.

*   *   *

I was at the piano on a sunny afternoon of the following week when I heard an unmistakable cry of pain. Taking the stairs two at a time, I found my wife leaning heavily on a small table in the upstairs hallway. Her face was white and her eyes were wide with pain and fear. She doubled over again in agony.

"Erik, help me!"

She moaned when I picked her up. I took her quickly into the bedroom and laid her on the bed. She was wearing only a thin dressing gown and when I eased my arm out from under her I saw the blood. Pain tore through her again and I stared numbly at the crimson stain that began to soak through her gown.

"Erik!"

The intensity of her cry broke me out of my stupor and I ran downstairs to the telephone, almost tearing it off the wall in my frantic haste to crank it up. Upon hearing Andre's promise to come right away, I hastened back upstairs to follow his instructions. She was breathing hard and her gaze found mine through a fog of pain. The plea for help I saw in them broke my heart. I lifted her gown and was horrified to see the blood pouring from between her legs. For someone who has seen as much blood as I have in my lifetime, I was surprised by my slightly squeamish reaction to seeing Christine's. I swallowed hard and tried to ignore it while I tore the upper sheet from the bed, pushed her knees up and held the wadded sheet as tightly as I could against the flow. Over and over I promised her that it would be all right, but I do not think she heard me. Oh, the blood! There was so much blood! Each time her body clenched in pain the blood pumped out of her with renewed vigor. I couldn't stop it! Hurry, André, please hurry!

"This isn't...something is wrong!" Christine gasped through clenched teeth.

She had not seen the blood, and I would not let her. I told her to lie back, that the doctor was on his way. She whimpered, and she was losing her strength fast. It seemed to be taking such a long time for him to get there. I didn't know how much longer she could hold on. My arms ached with the effort of trying to stanch the flow of blood. Christine fell silent; I looked up at her face and saw signs of her slipping away from me. I called her name but she did not respond. Her eyes were half closed and her face was stark white. The bed and I were both covered with her blood.

I was holding the sodden mass of sheeting against her and calling her name when André burst into the room. Taking no time for formalities or pleasantries he grabbed me by the shoulder and pulled me out of the way. He took one look at my wife and swore loudly.

"André, what's happened? It's not time for her to have the baby!"

"Erik, this baby is coming out right now whether it is time or not! Now, get me all the clean sheeting you can find along with some hot water!" I guess I did not move fast enough, for he shouted at me, "Get them!"

I returned quickly with the things he needed and was promptly barred from the room. I closed the door behind me and for the first time looked down at my hands. They were a solid red up to my elbows.

My hands were covered with blood.

Oh, dear God, no! Was it Christine's blood I saw on my hands in all those nightmares? With a sudden certainty I knew that this was exactly what I had seen in all those dreams. I was living it just as I had lived the dream of the fire. I had seen the future again, but this time I could do nothing to stop the awful sequence of events. I was powerless to help her. Only the doctor and God could help her now.

I fell to my knees in the hallway and prayed to the God I had denied for so long.

God in Heaven, please hear me! Don't take my Christine from me! I have changed, I swear to you I have changed! I am not the man I once was! You must not punish this innocent girl for my sins! Do what you will to me but spare her! I cannot go on without her, please! I need her, oh how I need her!

I looked with longing at the closed door beside me. With a heavy heart I got to my feet and started down the stairs, blinded by the tears streaming down my face.

It was a long time before André came downstairs to find me sitting in the parlor staring out the window. He appeared beside me and I got up to look expectantly at him. He looked exhausted.

"Erik, your wife should be all right. She lost a lot of blood and her recovery will be difficult, but I believe she will pull through. She is asleep, and will probably sleep for many hours. She is very weak…and very lucky."

"Thank God." I breathed a sigh of relief. "And the child?"

André put his hand on my shoulder. "I'm sorry."

Part of my world collapsed in ruins at my feet. Acute sadness cut me like a knife. I turned back to the window. I removed the mask and pressed my hands to my eyes but new tears did not come. I lowered my hands and turned again to André. It was the first time I had ever willingly faced anyone but Christine without the mask. I took a deep breath and asked him what happened. There had been a problem with the cord, he said, and the baby had suffocated sometime before Christine began hemorrhaging. I don't remember the medical terms he used, and they do not matter. Our baby was dead and my wife lay half dead upstairs, oblivious to all that had transpired. André assured me that it was no one's fault and there was nothing anyone could have done.

I did not believe him. How could I? It had surely been my fault, because this child, like myself, had been doomed from the beginning. I knew it as sure as the sun came up in the morning. I thought back to so many things that I had done wrong, including my early experimentation with many questionable narcotics and my drinking. And finally, on the night of conception, my behavior toward Christine had been despicable and inexcusable. This was my penance. André adamantly denied that anyone was responsible. When I demanded to see the child he did not have the heart to deny me.

I cradled the small bundle in my arms, hesitating for only a second before I gently pulled the blanket back from the little face. I fully expected to see my own hideousness reflected in a tinier version, but that was not what I saw. What I saw was an exquisitely beautiful baby girl. The instant I looked into her face I knew I had seen her before. I had seen her in my dream! The lovely child who had looked into my eyes so steadily while reaching for Christine was my own daughter. Through the eyes of premonition, she had appeared to me as the four-year-old daughter whom I would never know. My tears began to fall upon her blanket and André gently took her from me. I leaned over to place a kiss upon her tiny forehead, one kiss that must last her—and me—for eternity. Promising that he would begin making the arrangements, Andre left me alone with my grief.

I could not talk to Christine until the following day. She took the news very hard. She was so weak she could not sit up and our tears mingled together when I leaned over her to softly kiss her cheek. Soon, much too soon, her tears dried and she turned away from me. She did not speak for the remainder of the day.

I completed the arrangements for the interment of our child myself. Christine refused to discuss the subject at all. I named her Angelina Christine Devereaux. Two days later Etienne performed her early afternoon service with Jean, Louise, André and me in attendance. Robert and Deliah had tearfully paid their respects earlier, presenting themselves at my door with sadness and the hope that "Miz Devereaux" would recover soon. Christine was physically unable to attend, but I doubt she would have anyway. I did not like what I saw in her eyes during the brief moments when she had looked at me. Soon the brief and simple service was over. I was left alone to say goodbye to my daughter.

I sat before her vault for a long, long time. I could think only of how much I already missed her. Of how much I would miss spending time with her, teaching her to sing and to play the piano. Of taking her for walks in the park, teaching her to ride a horse, spoiling her shamelessly. Everything I had ever learned in my life I would have passed on to the little girl who would instead lie forever inside a cold stone box.

I could not be strong any longer. There was no one else around and I could not contain it. I removed the mask to cover my face with my hands. Suddenly I was consumed by the most intense grief I have ever known. I wept as I had never wept before, for anyone or anything. I wept for Christine and for our child. I wept for my parents, because I now understood how they felt when they first laid their hopeful eyes on my hideous face. Finally, I wept for myself and for all the years I had wasted with my self-pity and my hatred and my hostility. I wept until there were no more tears or emotions left in me.

I was left totally exhausted by my overwhelming grief, but when I finally looked up into the setting sun it was all gone. All my self-loathing and hatred were gone. The vengeance and the bitterness that I had carried with me for so long were gone. Surprised by a curious feeling of emptiness inside me, I listened intently for the evil voice inside my head and heard only silence. For the first time in my entire life I felt completely free. Almost at the same instant that I recognized the absence of the evil presence, the place near my soul where it had lived began to fill with the most wondrous feeling of acceptance; my own acceptance of myself as a flawed but worthy human being.

I looked with love upon Angelina's name engraved in the stone, and I traced the outlines of her name with my fingers. The gentle breeze dried the tears upon my face. Her death had not been my fault. I knew that now. It was meant to be for reasons beyond human comprehension, and nothing could have changed it. She was gone, but she had left me a very precious gift. She had come to me in my dream, and I would carry the image of her lovely face with me in my mind and my heart for all the days of my life. I knew the child she would have become had she lived, and in her eyes I recognized her immense love for me, her father. Hers was an unconditional love, and with her total love she understood and accepted me completely.

Marie had been right; I was special, because I had someone who loved me whom I loved in return. I was as special to Christine as anyone is to those who love them. Christine taught me to love, but until that moment in the cemetery I confess that I really did not know what I was doing. Yes, wise Marie, it was time to let it all go.

Suddenly everything was straight in my mind, and along with my new freedom and clarity of thought I finally realized the full potential of the love that I had inside me. Angelina had shown herself only to me, and in doing so, she had accomplished what I could not. She had purged and cleansed my soul of all the pain of my life. She had freed me from my inner darkness and walked with me into the light.

I looked back one more time at her name and calmly walked out of the cemetery. When I passed through the gates my past did not follow me. I had finally left it behind, in the loving and eternal care of my daughter.

23

———— ★ ————

Christine worried me.

More than two weeks after Angelina was laid to rest she still had not left her bed. André assured me that she should be able to get around a bit; it was her mental condition that had us both concerned. She ate little and spoke even less. She would not even look at me if she could avoid it. I waited upon her hand and foot with help from a Deliah whom I did not recognize. She came to my aid without hesitation and went out of her way to make Christine comfortable. She showed no fear of me as she went about her business in the house. She worked right around me and even asked me to move if I was in her way. Deliah was a very warm hearted and kind woman once her true personality came out and I was grateful for her help. It touched my heart to see the devotion both Deliah and Robert showed for Christine. After being served several particularly nice lunches that she prepared especially for me, I finally had to ask Deliah why she seemed to have changed her opinion of me overnight.

"Mista' Devereaux, any man who grieves for dat dead chile and dat po' woman upstairs like you does cain't be all bad."

I tried not to show my grief in front of my wife. She was having a hard enough time on her own. When I was away from her, loneliness overtook me. I had lost my daughter and the wife I knew and loved had disappeared inside a shell of indifference. Even after she began to move around the house Christine was unresponsive and uncommunicative. She spent most of her days in her room, and during those times I often saddled Onyx and rode to the cemetery to spend time with Angelina. I talked to her a lot. I hoped she would show me some sign of what I could do to help her mother.

Louise came often, sometimes staying with Christine for a good part of the day. When I passed her bedroom door I heard Louise gamely keeping up the conversation with only an occasional brief comment from Christine. It became a habit of mine to linger in the hallway for it was the only way I could hear Christine's voice. When I entered the room, her lovely face would turn away, her soft voice would cease and she shut me out thoroughly. After several weeks I began to play the piano again. I had not played at home since the child's passing. The music I wrote and played now was incredibly different from what I had done in the past. It lacked the anger of my previous work. I hoped the new music would break through the walls Christine had built up around herself to defend her mind and her heart from the pain she could not face. That must be it, of course, she was not ready to accept the death of our child. She will come around, everyone told me. I did not see any change.

No one knew the dangers of severe inner conflict better than I did. If only she would talk to me! Our situations were reversed. When I had been dealing with my own inner torment I refused to confide in her. I thought I could handle it myself. I had learned the hard way that I could not handle it, and neither could Christine. The thought that somehow she blamed me for our loss gnawed at me.

Two weeks later, André assured me that Christine was physically recovered and need not be confined to the house. Her recovery meant two things. While I was relieved to see her up and on her feet again, it also meant that she no longer required my constant care and attention. Since she would not acknowledge my presence, I had no contact with her at all. I felt helpless and totally useless.

She began to receive callers. Louise, Jean and many of Christine's society friends began a steady stream of visits. When there were people in the house I usually could be found working behind closed doors in the parlor or with my newspapers in a secluded corner of the courtyard. Some of the women were still made very uncomfortable by my presence. The endless stream of others in the house was confining, but I opened my home to the constant parade. If their silly giggling and petty gossip benefited her then I was all in favor of it. They gathered in her room or in the courtyard and chattered away. She made an occasional comment, but for the most part they talked to her and around her as if she were an important part of the conversation while she remained silent.

As the weeks passed, however, Christine's friends were heard to grumble about the fact that she did not appreciate them. Louise had quite a time convincing them that Christine enjoyed their visits. They continued to come but were not enthused about it. My concern grew and I had several long conversations with both Etienne and Jean about Christine's lack of progress. I had watched and waited for many weeks and saw no appreciable change. We came to the mutual conclusion that something more must be done.

I decided to take action. I would begin taking Christine out, whether she wanted it or not. I could no longer allow her to languish at home. On a bright sunny morning toward the end of May I marched myself up to her room. She was sitting up in bed, reading, after eating her usual light breakfast. I sat myself optimistically on the edge of her bed. She continued to read without looking up. I watched her turn a page. From her relaxed manner I knew that she was not making a conscious effort to ignore me. I simply was not there to her. Her eyes moved back and forth over the printed words.

"Christine, I am taking you driving today," I announced pleasantly. "If you would please get dressed we can have a nice ride in the sunshine and be back by noon."

If she heard me speak she gave no sign. I grew impatient when she turned yet another page in that damned book while I sat not two feet from her.

"My love, you need to get out of this house. André says you don't have to stay home any longer. Please get dressed for me."

Nothing—no acknowledgment, no movement, no recognition. I left her and stalked out to Deliah's house. Trying to get my impatience under control, I forced myself to knock softly upon her door. When she answered I asked her calmly to go and prepare my wife for an outing. A smile split her dark face when I told her my intentions, and she hurried away to get Christine ready while Robert went to ready the horse and carriage. I went to wait in the parlor. When I heard sounds from the foyer I hastened in. There stood Christine, fully dressed and ready for me, with Deliah still fussing over her skirts. I gave Deliah a grateful nod and took Christine's arm.

It was like leading a doll. She walked along beside me but there was no emotion in her face and no life in her step. I picked her up to set her on the high seat and the feather lightness of her tiny body shocked me. I acknowledged the look of hope on Robert's face, then climbed up beside her and we were off.

That first day we spent more than two hours driving slowly around the Quarter—two hours during which not one word passed Christine's lips. I kept up a steady conversation, but it was infuriating to speak to someone who would not respond. Each time I looked over at her she was staring straight ahead. At least I was doing something for her, and just being with her made me feel better.

I took her driving every day from then on. We covered most of New Orleans, rediscovering both its old and new sections. I loved taking her through the quietly elegant Garden District, with its grand mansions and lush gardens. We drove along the waterfront, where the ships emptied their cargo and the busy sounds of shouting men and machinery filled the air. We went out to Lake Pontchartrain, where the familiar site of the voodoo ceremonies looked vastly different in the bright sunshine. One day, after several weeks during which I had seen little improvement, I stopped the carriage under the giant oaks beside the lake. I slipped a feedbag over my mare's nose and went to fetch Christine down. I led her by the hand down to the shore of the lake. The warm wind blew softly through the leaves in the towering oaks above our heads. The worst heat of the day had not yet arrived, and it was pleasantly warm by the water. Birds sang and a light breeze made ripples on the blue water in intricate patterns that fluttered and redesigned themselves with each fresh puff of air. I deposited Christine on a large rock and sat down beside her.

The silence stretched between us. The only sounds were the wind, the birds and the gentle lapping of the water below us. I moved closer to her and gently put my arm around her shoulders. We sat like that for a long time. We were totally alone. There were no visitors, no doctors and no concerned friends. I looked over at the impassive face of this woman whom I loved so dearly and my heart cried for her. My grief and loneliness took over, and as I sat there looking at her my composure gradually slipped away from me. I slid off the rock and knelt before her, taking both her hands in mine.

"Christine? Christine, my love, please talk to me." There was no response. She looked over my head at the water beyond, but I don't think she saw even that. Seeing her like this was killing me.

"Christine, my love!" I cried, my voice breaking. The sound of it echoed over the water. "I promise you that I will find a way to bring you back to me! Can you hear me, my darling?" I was pleading with her, and tears came to my eyes as I desperately searched her face for some sign of life. "Christine, I can't make it without you, I need you...I will bring you back, but I can't do it alone! I...I need your help. Please help me, Christine! I need you!"

I was crying then, and I dropped the mask carelessly to the ground. I'd never begged anyone for anything in my life, but I'd never wanted anything as badly as I wanted my wife back. I buried my face in her lap while silent sobs shook my body. My hands twisted themselves into the folds of her dress. My fear for my wife and our future poured out of me into her frail lap.

Minutes later, I felt something lightly touch my shoulder. I raised my tearstained face to find Christine's hand resting there. When I straightened up it fell away, but I lifted my eyes to her face in time to see one large tear begin its slow descent down her cheek. Her face was still without all expression and her eyes still stared ahead, but there was no mistaking the meaning of that lone tear. My beloved Christine was in there somewhere, and she wanted to come back to me. She was trying to come back to me! I reached up tenderly to wipe her single tear away. I stood up to take her hand and lead her back to the carriage. Ignoring her vacant expression, I gently put my arms around her and pulled her close. She did not object and I held her for several precious moments before I lifted her into the carriage.

I drove slowly through the streets toward home with renewed hope. The seclusion of the lake had been wonderful, and suddenly it occurred to me that I might have found the answer. I would take

Christine away. I would take her away to where she had no bad memories, where there would be just her and me. Christine had lifted me from the depths of my despair and saved my life more than once. Now I would do the same for her. She would see a new Erik—an Erik she had only glimpsed before. Freed at last from the mental chains that had bound me, I would be romantic, attentive and charming. Unfettered by the demons of my past, my true nature could at last emerge completely and without constraint. I would shower her with love and affection and drive her desolation away, releasing the woman inside who was trapped behind a wall of grief and loss. I could bring Christine back from this place where she had gone after the death of our child.

I had to.

24

---★---

Isn't it amazing, the twists and turns that one's life can take? Researching a location to which I would take Christine felt familiar, to say the least. When I approached Jean early the next morning to ask for his help with my plans, he was thoroughly in favor of them. Obviously, he could not draw the parallels that I did to this task. No one had ever known about what transpired between Christine and me back in Paris. Indeed, not a soul knew what had brought us to New Orleans or of our circumstances when we arrived. When I had done this same thing before, it was to serve my own purposes; I took Christine away from everything she knew just because I desired it. It was fortunate for both of us that things had worked out, because my selfish action could just as easily have destroyed her. This time my intentions were solely for her benefit. If getting her away was what she needed, then so be it.

I immediately warmed to Jean's suggestion of a plantation homestead upriver. He knew of one that might be available, and he promised to contact the owners post haste to investigate the possibility of a lease. Located on the east bank of the Mississippi, the home was large, opulent and very secluded. Having been closed up recently due to a family death, it had no staff. I would take our own servants. They both loved Christine and would do anything for her, and Deliah had finally discovered that I would not bite.

For five days I waited impatiently for word from Jean on the house. Finally he appeared at my door with a written lease in his hand, ready for my signature. I could not get him into my house fast enough. I signed the lease and noted that I could take possession immediately. Thanking Jean profusely, I hurried to give my servants the word.

The months following my decision to temporarily move Christine out of the city are difficult for me to write about. Waiting patiently for my wife to return from wherever it was that she had gone was one of the hardest things I've ever done.

I am unable to list the study of mental disorders among my accomplishments. I had no idea why Christine had so completely closed down. It seemed out of character for her. This was a woman who had, ever since our flight from Paris, dealt with my significant problems with a strong heart and a clear head. The loss of the baby had been a severe blow to us both. Apparently the effect the child's death had on Christine was totally opposite from the effect it had on me. While it had torn my heart out to lose the child, I had nonetheless emerged from the experience as a better person.

From the moment I told her that the child was gone, Christine had drawn inside herself where I could not reach her. The tears that shone in her eyes at the news dried almost before I got all the words out. Ever since that day in March when Christine turned her drawn, white face away from me, I had not seen even the tiniest sign that she understood what had happened to her. Why didn't she grieve? I began to understand the frustration she must have felt when I had been so secretive and hostile just a short time ago. I had communicated nothing to her during those long months and kept her firmly on the outside of my torment.

No one else dared to mention the child in Christine's presence. Her society friends sidestepped the issue as delicately as they would a puddle in the street, and Louise was too concerned about hurting her further to say anything. I could not even get her attention, much less have a serious conversation with her. Christine had lived in a world of her own for too long and it was time for me to put things back on track. It helped that I had the support of our dear friends. That support was a new concept for me, and it was very encouraging.

*   *   *

Christine and I traveled upriver by boat. There were only a few to choose from. It was no longer like the stories I'd heard about the grand tradition of river boating on the Mississippi; the war had effectively put an end to that glamorous world. Some thirty years earlier the river pilots were a revered species, and the profession carried much prestige in the towns and cities located along the more than fifteen hundred miles of riverbank. The arrival of rail service helped to kill whatever aspects of river shipping that the war had not. Instead of the dozens of gaily painted and filigreed boats that years ago could be seen proudly lining the levees of New Orleans, one now might notice a paltry five or six of them, mostly in sad condition. However, it remained the only way for us to travel to the location I had chosen aside of a tedious and hot route over land.

I led Christine aboard after saying goodbye to our friends. We would arrive at our destination in the morning, and we spent the afternoon sitting on deck watching the riverbanks slide by us in a slow and easy manner, much like the entire pace of life in the South. There were many houses along the river, and in between them were sprinkled the last of the huge sugar plantations which had been so active before the war. The home to which we were headed had also been a sugar plantation, but production had ceased years ago. So many of these splendid homes had been lost to the Union forces' burning and pillaging, and it seemed a shame that so few were left.

Christine had shown no opposition to anything we had done since leaving home. She did not speak, but she did as she was asked and allowed me to tuck her hand under my arm when we walked. As we sat in the shade after a light mid-day meal, she leaned her head back against her chair and closed her eyes. Her hand dangled out over the edge of the chair arm and I gently took it in mine, bringing it tenderly to my lips. She turned her head slightly to glance at me, then closed her eyes once again.

There were few passengers on board. We could have gone part of the way by rail, which would have been faster, but that was precisely what I did not want. We had time. There was no hurry. After the events of the past year, it seemed a luxury to just sit and enjoy the peaceful setting. The only thing missing was my wife's smile and the twinkle in her eyes when she directed her gaze at me. The lack of passengers suited me nicely, but not for the reasons one might think. I had gone past my innate fear of being seen in public. I had gradually become accustomed to being stared at over the course of our years in New Orleans, but my epiphany in the cemetery had finally banished the last of my concerns for a part of my life over which I had no control. I no longer worried about others' reactions to my appearance. No, Christine needed the quiet and the solitude; she did not need scores of people around her. There were few enough people on board that we could keep to ourselves for most of the journey.

After another simple meal in the dining area we retired to our stateroom. There was no choice of accommodations. We would have to make do with two small but clean bunks, a mirror, a small closet, and a washbowl and pitcher. It was a far cry from the manner in which we were accustomed to living, but it would suffice for one night.

I gently closed the door behind us and turned around. My wife stood in the middle of the tiny cabin looking at me with her big, impassive blue eyes. Since I had sent Deliah on ahead with Robert to transport our baggage and horses via road, it would be up to me to do everything for Christine aboard the boat. Would she allow me to prepare her for bed? I carefully began to remove her clothing. Seeing her lovely body again brought back waves of desire that I had not felt for months. I suppressed the trembling in my own body before it could get the better of me. Her eyes showed no emotion, but they followed my every move. As I dropped the nightgown over her head her eyes rose to mine. I could read nothing in them, but they remained locked on mine for several seconds before she dropped them to the floor. I motioned toward her bunk and she obediently crawled into it. I tucked the blankets around her as I would a child and leaned down over her, with one hand on either side of her shoulders. She looked up at me sleepily and closed her eyes as I kissed her gently on the forehead. Later that night, as I lay curled into my own inadequately sized bunk, I was awakened by something I could not readily identify. I listened intently, and finally identified the sound as Christine quietly crying into her pillow. It broke my heart.

*　　　　　　*　　　　　　*

Occupying a spit of land along the river some twenty miles above New Orleans, the manor house was elegantly and symmetrically designed with white Doric columns enclosing three sides of it and which supported wide shaded galleries. It sported dormer windows that projected from the hip roof on all sides. Atop the two and a half story home was a glass-enclosed belvedere. If the house were not splendid enough, the approach certainly was. The long drive was lined by a magnificent stand of mature oaks that reached their massive branches across to each other to form a cavernous and cool leafy hallway to the home's front entrance.

Robert met us at the river landing behind the house. Behind the main house was a very unusual six-sided garconniere in which they would live. We entered the cool front entrance of the main house to face an intriguing circular stairway. I immediately thought I should have to study it, as it was masterfully crafted and rose seemingly unsupported to the attic. The decor of the rooms was elegantly understated, and I was overjoyed when I entered the parlor to find an enormous grand piano next to the black marble fireplace. The draperies were "puddled" on the floor, and looked as if their length had been misjudged. They were not, as this was a style of decor which signified affluence. It's a tradition I never understood or liked, and would never have in my own home. Otherwise, the entire home was tastefully and impressively decorated. Upstairs I found a massive poster bed in the room I chose for Christine and I to use. I would never sleep apart from her again.

Our first night at the house was a repeat of the previous night upon the river. I slowly undressed Christine for bed, but this time I could not stop myself from gently touching her, my hand lingering here and there upon a shoulder or hip, as I removed one article of clothing after another. It was a slow process owing to the many layers that made up ladies' wear, and a frustrating one for me. I longed to have her thin arms reach out to encircle my waist or neck. I yearned to feel her breath against my face as it felt just before she kissed me. And how I needed to feel her soft lips against mine! Once again she looked up at me when I put on her nightgown. Our eyes met and I reached out without thinking to take her in my arms. She did not embrace me, but her body melted into mine effortlessly and I felt her chest rise and fall in a deep sigh. I picked her up and laid her in the big bed and covered her. Christine silently watched me while I undressed and got in beside her. How good it felt to share a bed with my wife again! It had been so long; first my habits had forced her to deny me the privilege, then came her long and difficult pregnancy during which I stayed away for her sake, and most recently due to her withdrawal since the loss of the child. Christ, it had been almost a year since I had awakened next to her—an entire year out of the less than three years we had been married. What a damnable waste.

I moved over to kiss her goodnight, once again on the forehead. Her eyes met mine and I ventured to place a light kiss on her cheek as well. I settled down next to her and went contentedly to sleep.

The next few weeks were spent in much the same manner as our time in the city. I took Christine driving in the early mornings before the heat of the day descended, bringing the high temperatures and humidity that ultimately forced us indoors. Needless to say, our drives were quiet and peaceful. I could keep up a running one-sided conversation for only so long before I, too, fell silent and we rattled along the rutted paths without speaking. The sounds of the birds in the trees and the rustle of branches and leaves were the only sound to be heard above the crunching of the ironclad wheels and the rhythmic clip-clop of my mare's hooves. One mustn't misunderstand; those hours were among the most peaceful that Christine and I had ever spent together. For the first time since I had known her, time slowed virtually to a stop. Our life together had been so tumultuous and unpredictable from the very beginning that it was a refreshing change to do absolutely nothing. Frustrated as I was with Christine's continued silence, I found myself feeling reasonably contented. We were experiencing the mythically unhurried pace of life in the Deep South and we were doing it together.

*   *   *

Sunlight streamed through the huge windows of our bedroom. I turned my head to find Christine sleeping peacefully beside me. Her dark curls were spread across the pillow and her face was flushed with sleep and the added pink of renewed health. The sheet had fallen away and I watched her chest rise and fall with each breath. I propped myself up on one elbow and quietly watched her; noting the way her dark lashes lay against her cheeks and the slight twitching of her lips as she slept. The warmth of love flooded through me followed quickly by a more intense desire for her than I had felt in a long time. I reached over to lay my hand along her cheek, and ever so slowly leaned toward her. My gentle kiss was not enough to wake her, but it certainly awakened me. Fire raced through me when my lips met hers. I drew back and got out of the bed as quickly as possible without disturbing her. I could not lie next to her a minute longer and expect to maintain my composure.

Christine could now attend to her own needs so I was already downstairs when she arrived for breakfast. I was surprised to see her come right toward me when she entered the room and even more surprised when she stopped in front of me. She looked up into my eyes and I thought I saw a tiny flicker of life in her deep blue ones. I smiled at her and she came into my arms, melting into my body as if she had never left. She still did not speak, but I knew then that my Christine was on her way back to me.

*   *   *

"I think we had better head home, my love," I said, as I looked upward. We'd begun our drive under blue skies but the clouds had rolled in quickly. We were miles away from home and I feared the storm would catch us out. "Hold on," I told her and whipped up my mare. From the look of the sky, the afternoon storm promised to be a serious business. Christine stole a look at me and then firmly grasped the seat as we took off for home.

We were several miles from the house when the skies opened with a torrential downpour and a tremendous crash of thunder. I've experienced rain all over the world, but nowhere had it seemed more spectacular or more drenching than in Louisiana. Our light open carriage provided no protection and we were both soaked in seconds. I kept going, as there was no shelter to be had anywhere. Lightning flashed all around us. I pushed my poor horse even faster over rough tracks that quickly became a quagmire of greasy mud. The delicate wheels of the carriage cut deeply into the softening road, causing the carriage to slew wildly from side to side. I had to trust that Christine was holding on tightly, because I could not take my eyes off the road as we careened down it. My arms and back ached with the exertion of keeping the nervous horse under control.

Just as we came abreast of an enormous oak that stood at the edge of the road, the tree exploded with a lightning hit. My horse reared in terror and came down sideways, overturning the carriage and throwing both Christine and me from it. It happened in mere seconds; I was thrown high into the air, my eyes were filled with fire and sparks, I heard the splintering of the carriage and the screaming terror of my horse. There was no time to think about anything else before I hit the ground.

*   *   *

"Erik! Erik!"

I thought I heard my name, but I could not be sure. I didn't even know where I was, but the lower half of my body felt strangely heavy. Awareness slowly returned to my dazed mind and I felt pelting rain hitting my face and heard it splashing into the puddles beside me.

"Erik, please! Oh dear God, please!"

Hands clutched at me. Suddenly I realized that it was Christine who was calling my name and I opened my eyes. The rain went into them and blurred my vision, but not before I saw her face swimming above me.

"Oh, thank God!" she cried when she saw my eyes open. She took my face in her hands and leaned down to look into my eyes. My mask was gone and her hands felt cold against my face. My vision cleared and I saw her frantic expression turn to one of relief. I reached up with both arms to enclose her in them, grateful that she was all right.

As I released her, realization suddenly dawned on me. I tried to get up but I couldn't. I looked down at my legs and saw the large section of tree limb lying diagonally across my upper thighs. I pushed at it but it would not budge. It was long and heavy and it was cutting off the circulation in my legs. My elation at hearing my wife's voice again would have to wait. She pushed my shoulders back down onto the ground and shouted above the wind and the rain.

"Erik, we have to move the tree!"

"You cannot move it by yourself!" I looked around and saw my unfortunate mare standing a short distance down the road, still hitched to the wreckage of the carriage and, apparently, unhurt. "Take the horse and go for help!" I shouted.

"No! I won't leave you here alone!" Her voice was high pitched with tension but sounded amazingly strong. Perhaps it was because I hadn't heard it in such a long time. I looked into her face and saw the determination there. I knew my precious Christine was back and I also knew what she was thinking. Without warning she struggled to her feet, her wet skirts wrapping around her legs, almost tripping her. Shaking them out, she ignored my objections and ran through the mud to the horse. I could barely see her through the rain, but it didn't take her long to unhitch what was left of the carriage, leaving most of the harness hanging down over the mare's back. Positioning her beside me, Christine fumbled with the stiff, wet leather straps and tried to get them around the bulk of the limb without hurting me. I sat up as far as I could and took them from her. Speech was useless over the roar of the rain and wind, but as I took the leather from her my hand closed over hers. She stopped and stared at me with the most intense look of concern and love in her eyes that it almost took my breath away.

Tearing my eyes away from her, I tied the harness leather around the heavy limb as best I could. Christine moved to the bridle and began to urge the mare forward. When the limb began to move I felt the pain. I groaned as the weight shifted, but slowly and surely it was lifted from me. I prayed that the leather would hold, for if it snapped the harness would not be the only thing broken. After what seemed an eternity during which I held my breath, I was able to roll free.

I sat up and conducted a quick appraisal of the damage to my legs. Fortunately they were not broken, only badly bruised. I looked up to see Christine standing at the horse's head a few feet away. Her dress hung limply on her and her beautiful hair was full of mud and tangles. Rainwater sluiced down her face and she blinked to purge it from her eyes. One shoe was gone and she was standing in muddy water. She was a bedraggled mess and she was the most beautiful sight I had ever seen.

"Well don't just stand there, woman, help me up!" I announced with authority. Without a word she took my arm and helped me to my feet, then she bent to retrieve my muddy mask from a puddle. She tried to wipe most of the mud from it with her equally muddy skirt, then handed it to me. I looked down at her face and laid my hand alongside her cheek. She tilted her head against my palm and my arms went around her. Then I lifted her onto the horse and painfully climbed up behind her. She lay back against me and we began a slow walk home.

Deliah immediately took charge of Christine upon our arrival. Both she and Robert had been worried when the storm hit and were relieved to see us home although Deliah clucked incessantly like a mother hen over our wet and filthy condition. She spirited my wife off so fast she had no time to notice that things had changed between us. I let her go without comment. Christine needed a warm bath and dry clothes more than she needed me at the moment.

It was some time later when I shuffled to our room wearing the dry clothes that Deliah had brought me and feeling infinitely better. I softly closed the bedroom door behind me. The click of the latch sounded very loud in the silence around us. Christine stood with her back to me in the middle of the room. My painfully bruised legs were forgotten as I moved slowly toward her.

She turned around. When her eyes met mine I saw my beloved Christine in them. No longer were they the eyes of someone out of touch and distant from the world, they were alive and warm. I smiled at her and she came into my arms. Her small form melted itself into the contours of my body as if we were two halves of the same person.

"Oh Christine, I've missed you so very much," I said tenderly as I ran my hands over her small back.

"I missed you too, Erik," she said quietly. "Are you all right? I thought you had been killed out there today, and I...I couldn't bear the thought...I was so frightened! I sat up and saw you just lying there..." she whispered with tears in her eyes.

"You can't lose me that easily," I said. "I have worked too hard and waited too long to have you back to go anywhere now."

"Erik, I'm sorry I..."

"No. You must not apologize for anything. The trials of these last months have not been your fault, or anyone else's."

"But I..." she began again. I placed my finger across her lips.

"My love, you are here with me now and that's all that matters. That is all I want; that is all I have *ever* wanted. Only you, Christine, only you."

I reached up to smooth her freshly washed hair back from her face. I lifted her chin and tilted her head back to look into her eyes. I slowly lowered my lips to hers. Gentle at first, the kiss soon caught fire and I pulled her to me tightly. She felt so good in my arms! Her arms snaked around me and she began to kiss me back ardently. My hands roamed her body and every part of me ached with a desire that had been unreleased for too damned long. Breathing heavily against her lips, I started on the many tiny buttons at the back of her gown. The fools who designed ladies' clothing must never have been married. Spreading the back open, I pulled my hands forward over Christine's shoulders, bringing the gown with them. As I drew it forward I bent to kiss her soft neck and shoulders as they were revealed to me. My lips traveled around to the base of her throat and her head went back. My lips felt the warm pulse beating there and it drove me half-mad for her. I moved lower, and suddenly Christine stiffened. She clutched her arms to herself, clutching the top of her gown and preventing me from going any further. I looked up in confusion to see the anxiety on her face.

"I can't..." she stammered with tears shining in her eyes. "I just...I'm sorry!" With that she turned and ran into the dressing room and closed the door behind her. I stood dumbfounded and alone in the middle of the room.

Christine's rudely abrupt departure angered me. I had waited too long to get her back, and being rejected hurt me deeply. But as my heart finally slowed, I could not erase the fear on her face from my mind. Could Christine be afraid to make love to me? Why? We'd always been so good together.

I went to sit on the edge of the bed. I never expected this. I thought that once she came back to me that everything would go back to the way it was in the days when we had been so happy. The days while we waited for the birth of the...

I leaned forward with a sigh to lower my head into my hands, my elbows resting on my knees. That was it, of course. I was stupid not to have realized the impact that losing the child would have on my wife. She had awakened today as if out of a dream— a dream that she had entered on the day of our loss. There had been no chance for her to grieve, and no chance for her to face the reality of a suddenly childless future. My mourning had been done with long ago, but for Christine it was just beginning.

*   *   *

I lowered my book to see Christine standing in the doorway of the parlor. It was late, and the only light came from my small table lamp. The grandfather clock in the foyer slowly ticked away the minutes. Its soothing sounds were lost in the rustling of Christine's skirts as she slowly walked toward my chair. The sight of her reminded me of the first night we had spent in our own home after our wedding; the night she helped me overcome my fear of loving her. But tonight was different. She looked like she had been crying.

It had been many hours since she had left me standing alone in the bedroom. I laid the book aside and held out my hand to her. She sank down onto my lap and rested her head against my shoulder. I wrapped my arms around her as if I could protect her from what she was feeling, although I knew that nothing could shield her from the pain she held in her heart. I did not speak. She would talk when she was ready. We sat there together for a long time, saying nothing, until I followed her up the stairs to bed.

I was awakened in the night by the sound of Christine's weeping. I briefly wondered if I should leave her alone but the sounds tore at me. When I leaned over her she turned and buried her face in my chest. I had never in my life heard a woman weep so wretchedly as did my poor wife on that night. All I could do was hold her as she poured her grief out for what seemed like hours. She finally drifted into an exhausted sleep, leaving me to lie awake for the remainder of the night.

Several days passed before Christine mentioned the child again, during which I waited patiently for her to come to it in her own time. We were out driving when she pensively asked me if I had seen the baby. The question shook me, and it was all I could do not to pull the horse up abruptly to stare at Christine in surprise. Somehow I managed to pull the mare to a slow stop and turn to my wife calmly. At my gentle affirmation, the look in her eyes told me that she was finally ready to learn about what had happened. We walked hand in hand through the trees to find a spot by the river. We sat on the grass in the shade of a huge oak tree where I proceeded to tell her about that fateful day, while emphasizing what the doctor had said about it being an accident of nature and that it would be unusual for it to happen again. She listened intently while her eyes glistened with tears. Once in a while she lifted a hand to brush them away. When I was finished, she reached up to wipe my own tears from my face.

"Angelina," she said softly. "What a lovely name, Erik, and so fitting. I shall always miss her. But I still have my Angel...I still have you."

25

————— ★ —————

"Madame Devereaux, you'd best find your finest silks and satins, for I'm taking you to dinner at the best restaurant in town this night!"

I burst into the bedroom just as Christine was awakening from an early afternoon nap. She sat up and rubbed her eyes. With her chemise twisted tightly around her she looked like a child being made to rise early on a Sunday morning. I went over to the bed and grabbed her hand, pulling it to my lips with a flourish and bowing low, causing Christine to giggle at my exaggerated formality, which was exactly my intent. Some life must be brought back into the House of Devereaux, and for the first time in my life I was just the one to accomplish it. "I shall expect you to be ready to leave promptly at six o'clock this evening, Madame, for that is when your carriage departs." Before she could say a word, I swept out of the room. As I walked down the hall I smiled to myself at the look of barely hidden delight I saw on her face as I left the room.

At a few minutes to six I presented myself in the foyer, dressed to the hilt in a formal black tail suit and cloak. I tugged impatiently at the snugness of my waistcoat while I waited for my wife. Christine had not seen me dressed like this for a long time, and I have to admit I was a bit uncomfortable in it after years of cooler and more casual attire. However, drastic situations call for drastic measures, and I would not allow a little discomfort to deter me. Christine had been in her room all afternoon fussing, I hoped, over her dress for her "evening out". She had several to choose from, thanks to my foresighted hope that everything would eventually be well with her. All recently purchased by me, I hoped she would like them. As the clock in the hall struck the hour of six, she suddenly appeared at the top of the stairs.

My heart thudded in my chest and my breath caught in my throat with a sharp hiss. Christine was lovelier tonight than I remembered. It had also been a long time since I had seen her so formally dressed, but how could I have forgotten how devastatingly beautiful she was? Even in her currently too-thin state she was breathtaking. Her red satin gown trailed down the steps behind her as she descended them slowly, the dress falling down each step in turn like red liquid. Her bare shoulders were creamy in the dim light and her dark hair was piled atop her head in a cascade of curls. Rubies flashed at her ears and throat. I took her outstretched hand as she reached me, and I once again bowed low over it and pressed it to my lips.

"Mrs. Devereaux, you look ravishing tonight." I said in a choked whisper, which was all I could manage.

"And you, Mr. Devereaux, are exceedingly handsome," she replied with a shy smile.

"Now, my dear lady, let's not overdo," I said with a smile. "Come, our carriage awaits."

"Where are we going?" she asked as I helped her into our carriage. "There is nothing around here for miles."

"You shall have to wait and see then, won't you my love?" I said with a sly look. I took up the traces and promptly drove down the length of the oak-lined road and out the gates, where I made a large turn. Not looking at Christine, I drove back through

the gates, up the oak lined road and pulled up with great ceremony in front of our own house. Leaving the horse for Robert to
take care of, I helped Christine out of the carriage while trying
hard to suppress my laughter.

"Erik Devereaux, what in the world are you doing?" she asked
in confusion as a smile played around her lips. Wordlessly I
presented her with my arm and escorted her back into the house.
The dining room doors had been closed all day to hide the
preparations on which Deliah, Robert and I had worked so hard.
I threw them open to reveal a table laid with an exquisitely
intimate dinner for two, complete with candles recently lit by our
loyal servants before their hasty retreat to their own rooms.
Christine's hands flew to her mouth as she stared at the room.
When she looked back at me I smiled. "Welcome back, my love."

I sat back in my chair and watched Christine daintily finish the
last of her meal. I longed for the day when I would see her wade
into a meal like she used to. Laying down my napkin, I walked
over to the sideboard where I had placed a small music box. I
found it in one of the bedrooms, and although it didn't have the
sound of Christine's own box, it would do. Winding it up, I
offered her my hand. The dance was slow and gentle. Just having
her in my arms again felt like heaven and as we moved around the
large candlelit room I could not take my eyes from hers.

"Do you remember the first night we danced together on the
ship, my love?" I asked quietly. "You taught me so much more
than how to dance that night."

"I do, my darling. I was just beginning to discover who you really
are. Little did I know I was beginning to fall in love with you."

"And it was on board that ship that I finally realized that I
already loved you with all my heart. While on that ship you taught
me how to live, how to laugh and how to love. I will never forget

those nights. They are precious to me and I did not even know then what our future held."

"I was blind, Erik. Blind to what was right in front of me. However could I have failed to see how much I cared for you? I wasted so much time..."

"No," I whispered, putting my finger to her lips. "Our time is now—here." I kissed her.

We continued to move slowly around the room as the music wound itself down, but I was unaware of when it did stop. When I lifted my head to see the smoldering in Christine's darkened eyes the little music box was silent and the candles had burned low and almost out. I looked into her eyes until I was sure of what I saw in them. I swept her into my arms and started for the stairs; doctor's orders be damned. By the time we reached the bedroom she had my shirt and waistcoat undone. I hastily kicked the door closed behind us and set her down, devouring her mouth with mine while she pushed my coat, waistcoat and shirt from my shoulders in one motion. My lips tasted every inch of her face, neck and shoulders before moving farther and farther down as I clutched her to me, not wanting to let her go ever again. The red satin gown fell at her feet, leaving her gorgeously naked and shaking with desire. I pulled the pins from her hair and buried my face in it, drinking in her smell and her softness. She worked at the waistband of my trousers, and they fell away as her hands slid down along my hips. Anxiously I picked her up again and lowered us both onto the bed.

"Christine, don't ever leave me again!" I shouted breathlessly as the huge wave hit me and took me over the edge.

We lay wound around each other in the darkness afterward, contented to lie in each other's arms forever. We were home. I swore aloud that nothing would ever keep us apart again. Christine was silent.

"What are you thinking about, my love?" I eventually asked as I absently stroked from her hip to her breast and back again.

"I was thinking about the time I spent with you under the Opera. I was frightened of you, but there was something about you...I couldn't stay away. I didn't understand it then, but I wanted you to touch me...touch me in ways I'd never thought about before...touch me the way you touch me now." Her voice was barely more than a whisper in the darkness. "I wanted to feel your graceful hands upon my body and it terrified me. I was as frightened of my own feelings as I was of you. Raoul never made me feel like you could, no one else could. The way I felt about you was like nothing I'd ever known."

"Christine, if you had realized how much I wanted to touch you all those nights you truly would have been frightened, my love, so frightened that you would have never come near me again. It didn't begin that way. I only wanted you to spend time with me. I was so lonely, Christine...so desperately lonely! You were so close, yet you seemed so far away. I did not understand that there could actually be people who would see past my ugliness. You were a beautiful dream, a dream that I would never reach..."

"But my darling, you did reach me. And when I finally realized I belonged with you, I came to love you so, so much! Even during our worst times together I've still loved you more than I ever thought could be possible. But, you see, when I lost the baby I thought that was gone forever. I thought I'd never be able to love you again the same way...that somehow the way I loved you was to blame for what happened. Our love is so intense, so consuming and so passionate that I thought somehow it had to be wrong, that I was being punished for loving you so hard. I just couldn't face you, my darling. I can remember you telling me about the baby, then...then nothing.

"Christine," I began.

"No, please let me finish," she said. "I proved to myself tonight that I can still love. And I owe my love and my life to you. You stayed by me and didn't give up. You were so patient and kind and you let me work it through on my own."

"Christine, I would do anything for you. You must know that by now."

"Yes, Erik, I do. You've told me that from the beginning. But there is something different. You are different. There's a new calmness in you that I have never seen before. When I look into your eyes it's like…it's like I can see all of you now, that there are no secrets. The part of you that I could never reach isn't there anymore. If I didn't know better I'd say you'd made your peace with someone."

"I have, my love, I have." My wife's silence meant that she was waiting for an explanation. I smiled to myself in the warm darkness and settled her more comfortably against me. "I have finally made peace with myself, Christine, and I am going to tell you a wonderful story."

I began to tell her an unbelievable tale of a little girl whom neither of us had ever met, but who would live in my heart and in the window of my mind forever. A little girl who helped me to finally understand the world around me and how to accept my unique place in it.

When we settled down to sleep that night I pulled the blankets up close around us and tucked Christine's body more closely against me. She fell asleep immediately, and I leaned over to place a kiss upon her lips. They were slightly parted and her breath moved gently in and out through them. My lips lingered on hers and as I felt her life's breath flowing in and out against my own mouth, I marveled once again that this beautiful, vibrant young woman had chosen me to be at her side for the rest of our lives. As sleep overtook me I was filled with a feeling of complete contentment.

26

———————— ★ ————————

I felt the tension in my chest at the same time the sounds of the birds calling in the trees outside the window interrupted my sleep. I lay perfectly still and tried to breathe deeply. Stealing a glance over at Christine's sleeping form, I prayed that it would go away quickly. I did not want to wake her with this kind of news. Patiently I waited, and after several minutes the constriction finally began to ease. I breathed a sigh of relief and, taking care not to disturb Christine, I got out of bed, grabbed a robe and went into the dressing room. I looked into the mirror while I splashed water on my face. Funny how mirrors didn't hold the horror for me they once did. Ah, well. My problem with mirrors was just another annoyance that I had put behind me.

I was leaning on the washstand looking into the mirror when it happened again. With disbelieving eyes I watched my own face turn gray and then white. The pain was more intense this time when it wrapped itself around me like a vise and threatened to force all the breath from me. Pride and masculinity be damned, I tried to alert Christine.

"Chris…" I gasped out. After taking another couple of labored breaths, I finally got it out. "Christine!" I heard her sleepy "What?" as I began to feel faint. "Come…here!"

I tried to stay on my feet by clutching the stand, but I was losing the battle when she appeared in the doorway.

"Oh dear God, Erik, no!"

She caught me and helped me sink to the floor. I leaned against the wall while Christine wiped my face with a cool wet cloth. The sweat poured off me even as I shivered with cold. I thought I was gone, that it was all over. I looked into my wife's face with regret and sadness before I closed my eyes in pain. Suddenly the chains encircling my chest broke, and life-giving air flooded into my lungs. The pain had gone as abruptly as it had come. I looked up again into Christine's worried face and sighed with relief.

"You can't have any more of these, do you hear me?" Tears of worry stood in her eyes as she knelt beside me. I reached out to her and she put her arms around me. Soon I felt strong enough to get up and we went back into the bedroom.

"You remember what André said to us after my heart attack, Christine, that I could have another one at any time. We must be prepared. We must..."

"No, no! I can't think about that now." She clutched nervously at me, pulling my robe closer around me, stroking my face and straightening my hair. "We just got our life back, and things are finally going right for us! I don't want you to have any more of these!"

I finally got Christine calmed down enough to talk some sense into her, and she agreed that we should talk to André. For quite some time I had been fighting the knowledge that this might happen again. I had hoped it would not be so soon.

                    *   *   *

We had been back in the city for a little more than three months, and they had been some of the most enjoyable and fulfilling months of our marriage. The first thing I had done upon our return home held great symbolic importance for me, although Christine could never have understood exactly how important an act it was. I led my wife by the hand out into the sunlit courtyard and stopped in the middle of it. She looked around and asked me what we were doing.

"It's all over, my love," I said as I looked deeply into her eyes, "the darkness, the pain, the fear and all the ugliness of the past. It's all gone forever."

She looked at me uncomprehendingly. I reached into my pocket and slowly withdrew my catgut lasso. Without a word, I uncoiled it and held it up between us so that it hung down straight from my fingers toward the ground. Christine knew what it was, of course, but she didn't know just how recently it had seen action. While she silently watched, I struck a match and held it to the bottom end of the thin line. The tip blackened, and then a tiny flame began to eat its way upward toward my fingers. I looked past the climbing flame to the love and contentment glowing in my wife's eyes, which mirrored an identical expression in my own. When the flame approached the top I dropped the tiny end to the ground, where it shriveled into nothing. I met Christine's eyes again, took her hand and led her back toward the house. We were barely inside the doorway before the mask was off and my arms were around her. Then, hand in hand, we went upstairs. My past would never hurt us again.

The dark times of our marriage fell away to the recesses of memory. We were deliriously happy. The hot weather finally gave way to the comfortable cooler temperatures of winter in New Orleans and, with only a few weeks to go before Christmas, we cheerfully anticipated another holiday with our friends. This Christmas would be different from the last two, for there were finally no secrets, no intruding past and no darkness in our lives. After a visit to the cemetery soon after we returned, Christine had finally put our loss behind her as I had done. My account of what had happened to me on the day of Angelina's burial had served to release Christine from her sorrow as well. For the first time since we'd met, we were totally free to love each other the way our love was meant to be.

After spending two extra weeks in the country, we had returned home to the open arms of Louise and Jean. They were relieved to see Christine well again, and I caught a very satisfied look on Jean's face several times when I noticed him watching me. Of course, they had seen the difference in me before I had taken Christine to the country but now, with my wife almost back to normal, the change in me was complete and unmistakable. I was contented, relaxed and truly happy for the first time since the day I was born. When I looked at myself in the mirror I saw what everyone else saw. My clear, dark brown eyes were warm and sparkling and peaceful. I was ready to meet life head on, so as I sat on the edge of the bed that morning with my wife fussing worriedly over me, I was understandably upset by what had been the most severe recurrence of pain since my heart attack.

Upon examination by André, he once again hung the sword of doom over me, as it were. As usual I tried to make light of the situation, but the faces of both Christine and André dampened my mood considerably. These damnable episodes were the only form of ill health I had ever suffered, and I did not take well to the news that I must curtail my activities further. No strenuous activity whatsoever, proclaimed an adamant André while I intently examined the carpeting at my feet. I should continue walking but I could drive or ride only short distances. I got him to agree to my driving as far as the church, where, to Etienne's delight, I had resumed my playing almost immediately upon our return to New Orleans. But I was damned if I was going to have Robert drive me around everywhere like an invalid. At my first opportunity, I cornered poor André and, drawing myself up to my full and considerable height and looking as fierce as I could these days, I told him frankly that I would not give up making love to my wife. If I must give that up, I declared, he'd best shoot me through the heart right then and have done with it. I think he got the message.

Christmas of 1885 and the new year were ushered in under a note of caution at our house. I tried hard to behave myself, because I didn't want to leave Christine any more than she wanted me to leave her. I obediently took walks every day and, once again, I became a familiar sight around the streets of the Quarter. Perhaps sensing the cloud hanging over our heads, Christine began taking some walks with me. We spent many hours talking as we strolled arm in arm through the familiar streets of this city which now felt like it had always been our home.

On Christmas morning my wife presented me with a beautiful ebony walking stick. The large and heavy ornament of gold at its top was fashioned into the shape of a horse's head, and bore a striking resemblance to my black gelding Onyx. It fit my large hand perfectly, and pleased me immensely. I had no further use for material gifts, but this one was functional and handsome. It also underlined Christine's concern that I might have need for it one of these days. I knew without a thought that I would carry it with me always.

My gift for Christine had been trouble even before the day she opened it. The little terrier pup had already chewed one of my shoes and shredded several of Deliah's good dishtowels during our attempts to hide him for several days; moving him between houses so Christine would not see him. I daresay keeping the dog a secret was one of the most challenging attempts at subterfuge I'd made in years. The more indelicate messes he made do not bear mentioning, aside from the fact that he enjoyed making himself a nuisance in any way he could. The delight on Christine's face when he bounded out of the box to lick her face was worth all his trouble, and, morbid as it sounds, the thought occurred to me that she would most likely have this little dog at her side longer than she would have me.

So, our family now numbered three after all. The pup was summarily christened "Pierre" and Christine often took him with us for our walks and even in the carriage. I also became quite fond of him, as I have always had an affinity for animals. I suppose that was normal, because for many years I had half considered myself to be of that level of life form. Animals of all sorts and I have always gotten along admirably and Pierre was no exception. I did not, however, take kindly to waking in the morning to find Pierre snugly sleeping in the bed between us. He eventually learned to retire after I had gone to sleep, so the little demon usually won those battles. Too often, I turned over to put an arm around Christine only to realize that Pierre was the recipient of my affection. The day I awoke to find myself nose to nose with him has not easily been forgotten, but even that was made more palatable by the sight of Christine lying on the other side of him trying in vain to contain her laughter. Pierre knew how to get around me though, and he licked my face before I could throw him off the bed, thus reducing me to laughter as well. Although the dog did spend considerable time lying in wait at the bedroom door while Christine and I tended to important business, I could not bring myself to shut him out all night.

As winter turned to spring and the Mardi Gras season approached, I had several other warnings that my health was once more a very real threat to our happiness. I began to fear my own mortality, which was certainly a departure from my thoughts on the subject through most of my life. My greatest fear was for Christine. She was very happy in New Orleans, but I was not comfortable with the thought of her being left alone in the event of my death. I had promised to take care of her always upon our flight from Paris so long ago, and I felt that I would be going back on my word. That was foolishness of course, because not even the Opera Ghost can live forever and I am, after all, considerably older than my wife.

We did not go to Mardi Gras that spring. We observed the festivities from the gallery of our home, but did not venture into the madness in the streets or to the ball. Everyone agreed that it might be too much for me, and I had to go along with them. For the past several weeks I had been losing weight and my appetite was not what it should be. André could find nothing specifically wrong, but he was worried all the same. I had always prided myself on my strength and physical prowess and, aside from my face, my appearance had always been exceptional and impressive. I was only fifty-two years old, but my physical condition now resembled that of a much older man. In light of the changes that were going on and unbeknownst to Christine, I sat down to have serious conversations with Robert and Deliah and with Jean and Louise. Each couple expressed their concern and promised to look after Christine in their own way should anything happen to me. That knowledge helped me, but did little to alleviate the growing concern I harbored for my wife's future.

Spring turned once again to summer and my deteriorating condition seemed to reach a plateau and level off. I was considerably underweight and did not feel particularly strong, but neither did I feel ready to keel over. I hate to admit it now, but the weight loss made me look exactly like I did when I lived in the cellars of the Opera Populaire. All the heartiness and strength I gained from our life together above the ground had disappeared, leaving the unbelievably thin, gray-skinned walking skeleton who had first observed a young singer through a mirror. Back then I had been thin but strong and firm, and now even that was gone. André believed I suffered from circulation problems and indeed, despite the warmth of our climate, my hands and feet were often cold.

One evening Christine caught me changing for bed in the dressing room. I could not admit to her that I felt embarrassed over my weakening body. I thought that if she were to see me that way she would not want me. I said nothing but she guessed it anyway, and came to me with empathy in her eyes. She led me back into the bedroom like a child and undressed me. She lovingly stroked my sunken chest, protruding ribs and hollow stomach. Her hands framed my loosening gray cheeks and moved on up into my rapidly graying hair. She pulled my head down to hers and met my lips with firm persuasion. Deeper and deeper that kiss went, until her tongue finally ignited the fire deep inside me that I never could resist. The further I fell into that unbelievable kiss the less I thought of my current state of affairs. I raised my cold hands to loosen Christine's clothing and consign it to the floor. My arms wound around her and still that kiss went on until I couldn't hold back any longer. Feeling stronger than I had in weeks, I eased her back onto the bed and joined her, starting with another helping of that huge wet kiss. Thankfully, there was one part of me that still functioned normally. I never felt more a part of her than I did on that night. We both leapt off the cliff at the same time, crying out with an intensity of feeling that was overwhelming. I collapsed on her, completely out of breath.

"Erik, are you all right? Maybe we shouldn't have done that, maybe it was too…"

"Please, my love…just give me a minute…to…catch my… breath," I panted.

She tried to get up but I held her down beneath me. "But darling, you don't sound very good, we can't do…" Her concern was beginning to dampen my mood. When she opened her mouth to speak again I covered it with mine and gave her my own version of the type of kiss she'd just initiated on me. I was exhausted, but there was considerable time spent that night exploring other equally impressive pleasures.

*   *   *

August brought a heat wave to the city that was ultimately not only my undoing, but that of many others as well. Some died from the excessive heat and humidity and it sapped the strength from me until I could do no more than sit inside the house during the heat of the day. But even as the physical strength slowly left my body my creative juices seemed to flow more freely. A relative prisoner of my home for much of the day, I turned once again to the piano as my salvation, and the piles of music on my shelves grew with each passing week. I wrote feverishly, as if I was running out of time.

When the heat finally broke I regained some of my ability to get about but I was weak and breathless. In early autumn I made several more attempts to play Etienne's wonderful organ before I reluctantly informed him that I must resign as his organist. It broke my heart to give it up and, sensing my sorrow, he adamantly told me that I should come whenever I felt up to it. I sat on the bench and ran my hands over the keys and the soft, smooth wood, lovingly tracing the contours of that magnificent instrument with my fingers and committing it forever to my memory. I knew I would not be back. With tears shining in my eyes I shook Etienne's hand and, placing my walking stick deliberately with each step, I walked slowly out through the great doors of St. Louis Cathedral.

27

———————— ★ ————————

Four years! I could not believe Christine and I had been man and wife for four years. I sat looking at her from across the table at Antoine's on the evening of September 27, 1886. We traveled in style that night, having ridden over in our well-appointed and elegant new brougham. She was also wearing the emerald and diamond drop earrings and necklace that I had given her and her face was as radiant as her jewels in the candlelight. I had lived an entire lifetime in those four years. I reached across the table to take her hand and her fingers intertwined with mine. I would cherish the way Christine looked that night for the rest of my life, and that image would mingle with all the other pictures of her that always crowded my mind. My wife...my love...my life.

Throughout the autumn months the ominous warnings of my body continued. Not only did I experience frequent chest pain; I also began to lose feeling in my right arm. Some days I could barely lift it, and when it wasn't numb it hurt like hell. Something was seriously wrong with me. I took to holding the arm against my body while hooking my thumb in the top of my trouser waistband. That, along with the way I now stooped over my stick, gave me a decidedly unwanted elderly appearance. I played the piano less and less, choosing instead to reread many of the classics I had discovered in my lonely youth. By playing with one hand, I managed to finish several more pieces before I gave up on the piano completely. It had become increasingly difficult for me to compose in that manner. I kept up a brave front for Christine's sake, but when she began to see me at the piano less often she knew how ill I was. Frankly, I didn't feel well at all. As if she were trying to fill the musical void in my life, Christine began to sing again. I sang with her when I could, and her beautiful voice and my books became the center of my life. I saw André often, of course, and had many visits from the Vaillancourts and Etienne, who always brought me armloads of new books. I took great delight in their frustration, for I read the books faster than they could bring them. They grilled me on content, hoping to prove that I was not really reading all those thick volumes, but they were able to prove only that my superior intellect remained intact.

Robert took me driving several times a week. It became such an effort to get up into the carriage that I was reluctant to try but, as usual these days, my wife got her way and I was taken out for short rides. Eventually Christine began to go out on her own every afternoon, and initially I encouraged her. I loved her company, but didn't want her to waste her days sitting with an old semi-invalid when she should be out and about seeing her friends or shopping. She insisted that she cared for none of these things, but she did agree to go out. Christ, she was only twenty-six years old and much too vital to be stuck at home with my decrepit self.

Nighttime remained our special time. Our lovemaking was a shadow of what it once was but we continued in whatever ways we could. Even as weakened as I was, I would never lose the passion that consumed me whenever my wife lay down next to me and kissed me or stroked my body as I fell asleep. I never failed to feel the thrill in the way Christine's body felt beneath my hands. Often we snuggled beneath the covers and just talked. Christine never said much about her outings, and it began to bother me. Like anyone who is frequently confined to his or her home for whatever reason, I became ravenous for news from the world outside. It annoyed me that she could spend an entire afternoon away from home and return with nothing to tell. Hell, I had more to tell her from my short jaunts around the block than she did from a four-hour absence.

As autumn turned to winter I felt increasingly frustrated with my situation. I became short-tempered and irritable. My body was betraying me, and there was nothing I could do about it. This would be a very difficult state of affairs for anyone who has been in command for most of their life, so imagine what it was like for me. As I became weaker I had to rely more on Christine for the simplest things. She or Robert had to help me get dressed some days, for Christ's sake! If that weren't bad enough, the stairs became enough of a problem for me that they actually tried to convince me to move into the downstairs room to sleep. I adamantly refused, saying that I would not sleep apart from my wife for another night as long as I lived. When Christine said that she intended to move with me, I finally relented after remembering the last several times I had tried the stairs. I was saddened at the thought of giving up the lovely room where we had enjoyed each other so much, but if it bothered Christine she did not show it. She only said quietly that we would make new memories in the new room. I retorted with a bitterly sarcastic comment that drove her from the room. I sat on our new bed and watched her walk out. Tears of frustration pricked at my eyes. I was only fifty-two! Why was this happening to me? I'd planned to grow old with Christine, not leave her during what should have been prime years in my life. Jean was several years older than I was, but he was healthy! It just wasn't fair. Why did God give me so much so late only to take it away so soon? I did not understand. I looked down at my almost useless right arm. The tears began and I could not stop them. I was sobbing aloud when Christine ran back into the room.

"Christine, I'm so sorry," I sobbed, "I've become such a burden on you and I never expected that, never wanted that."

She put her arms around me. "You could never be a burden on me, I love you. I'll take care of you."

"That's just it, Christine," I sniffed, "it is I who promised to take care of you. I am letting you down."

"Now you listen to me, Erik Devereaux! When we were married I said 'in sickness and in health' and I meant it! I'll hear no more of this talk from you. Lord knows you've spent your share of time taking care of me."

That night, our first night in our new room, Christine did her best to make me feel loved and wanted. We both knew that it changed nothing.

*   *   *

Day after day, Christine went out. If I thought I was frustrated before, it was nothing compared to the increasing impatience I felt with myself. I was trapped inside the prison of my body. My mind fought to free itself through my books and the music that continued to swirl around in my head, but the walls of my failing body bound me like no chains ever could. Pain became a constant companion. By the time 1887 became a reality I was never free of pain, and the supply of morphine I had kept for years steadily dwindled until I swallowed my pride and asked Andre for more. I struggled on without the drug during the day, but at night it had become impossible for me to sleep through the pain. Indeed, I was amazed that I had lived long enough to see yet another new year. I became even thinner, if that was possible, and my hair was almost entirely gray. I was shocked by how fast I had gone from a relatively healthy man to what I had become. Why, less than two years ago I had been preparing to become a father! I thought often about Angelina and about how I would have handled her childish energy in my present condition. She would have been a bouncing child of almost two by now, with a father who could do almost nothing but talk or read to her. There were days when I thought that what had happened was for the better, then I would scold myself for those same thoughts. After all, if the child had lived Christine would not be left alone. These thoughts were typical of what ran through my mind during that time, a constant parade of confused thinking and emotions that took me from one extreme to the other, from depression to something close to happiness. The one overriding joy in my life continued to be my precious wife. She never mentioned the possibility of another child, but as time went on and it became apparent that there would be none, I secretly despaired that once I was gone there would be nothing left of me but what lived on in Christine's memory. That is not a hell of a lot to show for fifty-odd years on this earth.

*   *   *

"Erik, we are going out tonight."

Christine's statement took me by surprise. I hadn't even left the house for drives since the damp and cold of winter had set in. I didn't know what she was thinking, and my confusion was revealed in my abrupt tone of voice.

"What do you mean, 'going out'? How in hell am I supposed to go out? Or haven't you noticed that I can't even get up from this chair today without help?" My sarcasm was biting, and although I hadn't meant to be hurtful, I saw her turn away quickly to hide her expression. I immediately felt sorry for the remark, and my voice softened. "Please, my love, forgive me. I don't mean to sound ungrateful, but surely you must know that I didn't expect you to suggest such a thing."

"It doesn't matter, Erik," she said as she turned around again, her face fully composed. She continued to bustle around the bedroom, dragging things out of the wardrobe and flicking lint from my best formal dress suit. "We are going out tonight and that's all there is to it."

"What can be so important that I have to be dragged out on a winter's night, may I ask?"

"There is an event being presented tonight at the Opera, and we shall attend. And we must look our best, as there will be many important people there tonight." She glanced over at me to notice the uncertainty on my face and suddenly stopped her preparations to kneel beside my chair. "Oh, Erik, please. You haven't been out for weeks and I thought the music would cheer you. Besides," she continued, "I can't go to an event like this unescorted, can I? And you, dear Erik, are my one and only escort."

"All right, my dear," I sighed. "I can never resist your charms and you know it. You know just how to get arou..." I was silenced in mid-sentence by her delighted kiss.

*   *   *

I stood in the foyer leaning heavily on my cane. Yes, damn it, a cane. It was no longer a walking stick to me. When it became a necessity for every step it became a cane, and all the depressing connotations of the word applied. My frail body swam in what used to be an elegantly fitted suit. Christine swept in wearing an absolutely stunning gown that I had never seen before. A deep sapphire satin, it was shot through with gold threads and gleamed in the lamplight with every move she made. Her manner reminded me of the way she had been just prior to leaving Paris, when her stage presence and confidence had been at their peak. There was something different and exciting about her tonight, but I couldn't quite put my finger on it. When she saw me decked out in my formal suit, cloak and hat she pretended that she hadn't helped me put them all on. Her approval shone in her eyes and she brushed my cheek with a light kiss.

"How wonderful you look tonight, my darling," she said with admiration. "I'm so happy that you agreed to come with me."

"My dear Christine, you didn't leave me much choice in the matter." I smiled at her and drew myself up to my full height for the first time in months.

As a formally dressed Robert helped me up into the carriage, I began to feel excited in spite of myself. I put my arm around Christine and settled back into the soft leather seat. The thought of an evening of music was lifting my spirits even though I knew how tired I would be afterward. I had seen nothing of any special event in the newspapers, so I briefly wondered what the fuss was about. We covered the short distance to the Opera House in relative silence.

The scene outside the Opera was bedlam. Carriages were everywhere and people were congregating at the entrance doors waiting to get in. I worried about walking through that crush of people, but Robert drove our carriage around to the side entrance, which was deserted. Christine said nothing, but led me to the side door as if she had planned to use that entrance. It appeared to me that they had made special arrangements to get me there. Once inside, Christine paused to search for available seating. When she spied two seats in the first row center, her exclamation was so natural that I had to smile to myself. Of course. She had arranged for the best seats for us and did not want me to know of all her special little plans. Well, I could go along with this if it made her happy. Leaning on my cane and a little more heavily on Christine's arm than I intended, we made our way to our seats without delay. I needed to sit down. I felt tired already, but the excitement of being in a theater again encouraged me to push my fatigue aside.

A full orchestra was warming up on stage. I was curious to know what this event was all about. Finally they appeared ready to begin. Christine took my hand to hold it in her lap as the silence of anticipation descended upon the sold-out house.

Twelve bars of music had been played when the hair on the back of my neck stood on end and I felt the warm rush of shock spread through my body. Motionless, I stared with widening eyes at the conductor's back as he went through the gyrations of leading the enormous orchestra through a complicated and intensely soulful piece of music. I knew that music well.

It was mine.

I couldn't breathe. Everything around me disappeared until the music was all that was left—the music and the pressure of Christine's hand upon mine. I dared not look at her. I didn't understand what was happening...how did they...?

Piece after piece they played, and soon I realized that many of my compositions had been interwoven and joined together in such a way that they appeared to be parts of a whole...a whole that I had envisioned in my mind but never had the chance to assemble. As each movement was presented I could remember exactly when I had written each section. To my immense satisfaction the music, as played by a full orchestra, conveyed exactly the emotions that I had intended.

I finally looked over at Christine. She smiled knowingly and squeezed my hand. Suddenly I knew where she had been going all those afternoons for so many months. She had been secretly removing my music from our home and working with someone to mold it into the beautiful symphony we were now hearing. How could I have been so blind? I had become impatient with her for her absences and her refusal to talk about them. She had been doing it all for me.

The music soared into the very rafters of the Opera House, filling every part of it. After the initial shock wore off I was able to relax and enjoy the fruits of my many years of labor, something which I had never thought possible. And it was good! Oh, damn, it was good! All those years I doggedly wrote and wrote and wrote, never expecting anyone else to hear it. I closed my eyes and let it wash over me, reveling in the knowledge that my efforts had not been in vain. I was completely lost in it when the music crashed to an explosive ending.

The applause was deafening. I had never heard such an ovation in all my years of observing productions in Paris or anywhere else. I sat there listening to it in stunned, wide-eyed silence, hardly daring to believe that my work could be so well received. The conductor turned around, sweating profusely, to acknowledge the admiration. The look on his face was triumphant, but it could never match the feeling of fulfillment that was growing inside of me. He motioned for the house to quiet down as he prepared to speak.

"Ladies and Gentlemen! Welcome to this very special night of musical entertainment. Tonight we have the distinct pleasure of enjoying a truly magnificent work written, over a period of many years, by an unusually gifted and talented composer who lives right here in New Orleans. Tonight marks the premier of his work in public and from the reaction of this audience I would say that this is only the beginning. This gentleman has risen above tremendous personal adversity to carve an impressive niche for himself in the music world. Would you all please join me in honoring our composer, Mr. Erik Devereaux!"

Applause thundered through the theater behind me. My eyes moistened as the entire orchestra rose to applaud me along with the conductor and the rest of the house. I was so overwhelmed that I didn't notice Christine rising and pulling on my arm. She pulled me to my feet and then, from somewhere deep inside myself, I found the courage to turn and face an audience for the first time in my life.

I stood tall and straight as I looked into the thousands of faces around me. The house lights were up and I could see them all, even in the balconies, standing and applauding. I acknowledged them with a wave of my hand. After what seemed like an eternity I turned back to Christine and we sat down. I was shaking with emotion and fatigue and could not have remained standing for another minute.

I cannot convey in words how I felt as the orchestra launched into the second half of the program. More of my music, arranged so perfectly that I could not have done a better job of it myself. I knew I had Christine to thank for that, for she knew most of my music almost as well as I did. As they reached the end of the last movement I could only thank the Lord above that I had lived long enough to see this night. Perhaps this was what He had been waiting for.

The evening's emotion had worn me out. I began to think about getting home but a hush then fell over the house and once again the conductor turned to address the audience.

"Thank you, Ladies and Gentlemen. It may interest the audience to know that Mr. Devereaux was brought here tonight under false pretense. He had no prior knowledge that his work would be performed anywhere at all, let alone here tonight. We hope we have sufficiently surprised him."

He glanced at me with a smile and I nodded in response.

"You may also be unaware that Mr. Devereaux is married to the former Christine Daae, an accomplished singer in her own right, and a former star of the Paris Opera. Mrs. Devereaux?"

I turned to Christine in surprise as she left her seat and was escorted up the stairs at the side of the stage. I didn't know what she was up to, but I couldn't take much more excitement. She took her place center stage and turned into the lights. I was instantly transported back to the first time I ever saw her, singing so hesitantly while almost cowering upon the stage of the Opera Populaire. That frightened girl was a far cry from the self-possessed and talented young woman who became so much in demand in the months following her debut. It was a period of success that was cut terribly short by the desperately selfish behavior of an old man who could see nothing but his own obsession. My breath caught in my throat as I looked at her standing there and saw once again the bright star she had been in Paris.

"Thank you, Mr. Michaels," Christine began as she faced a spotlight for the first time in almost five years. "And thank you, everyone, for your generous reception of my husband's work. We truly appreciate it."

She paused and looked directly at me.

"Erik, this is a very special night for you, and I wanted to add something of my own. You have made my life complete. Over the years and through all our ups and downs I have loved you more than I ever thought possible. You are the sun, the moon, and the stars to me and I don't know what my life would have been like without you. With my appreciation and my love, this is for you, dear Erik."

The orchestra took up their instruments and softly began to play. Tears flowed unchecked down my cheeks when Christine began to sing, soaking the inside of the mask and running down onto my suit. It didn't matter. Nothing mattered but my beautiful Christine up there on that stage. It was a sight I thought I would never see again. She sang a composition I had written for her. We had sung it together for the first time the day I returned to the piano following the fire rescue. Her voice was powerful yet pure and sweet, and from the sound of it I knew she had been practicing hard for this performance. Too soon she finished the song and took her curtsies. Amid renewed and deafening applause, I rose from my seat with the strength of my love supporting me and slowly walked to the front of the stage. Christine came forward to meet me and knelt at the edge. I reached up to her as she leaned down to embrace me.

"Congratulations, my darling," she said into my ear.

I was speechless.

The rest of the evening is a blur. I remember what seemed like thousands of faces coming forward to shake my hand on my way out of the Opera House. Somewhere from the depths of the crowd Jean and Louise appeared with tears in their eyes. With Jean on one side of me and Christine on the other, I somehow managed to walk with dignity through the theater while murmuring my appreciation to the faces closest to me. I remember the incessant chattering of people around me; accolades coming from all directions in such a muddle that I could not sort them out. By the time Robert met us at the side door with the carriage, I was barely able to stand up. Christine and Jean were doing their best to support me without being obvious about it, which I appreciated since we were still surrounded by people. At last we were safely seated inside the safety of the carriage and on our way down Royal. I reached for Christine and I didn't let her go until we arrived at our front door.

That night is second only to one other event in my entire life. That would be the day I married my Christine. In bed later I tried to tell her how I felt about what she had done. I wanted to tell her how much the recognition of my years of work meant to me—that my name would not die with me. Already there had been talk of publishers and performances. But, more importantly, the knowledge that my music would live on completed the one circle in my life that until that night had no closure. There was so much I wanted to tell her, but the words would not come. Emotion and exhaustion got the better of me, and it would have to wait until morning. We went to sleep wrapped in each other's arms and with the vision of my wife singing on that stage burned into my heart.

28

---- ★ ----

My journey is almost at an end. All that remains is the final chapter which, unless I actually do become a ghostly entity through some oddly ironic circumstances, I shall be unable to write. I sit by my window enjoying the spring breeze, a view of my lovely flowered courtyard, and the sounds that surround me. These are the sights and sounds of life, and I have learned how precious they are. For the past several months I have been busying myself with writing this chronicle of my acceptance of life and my place in it—an acceptance that took me a lifetime to accomplish.

I have been two very different men during the course of my lifetime. The first, obviously, was the misunderstood and abused boy who grew into the misunderstood man who abused others in turn. That was the man whom the people of Paris knew as the Phantom of the Opera, or Opera Ghost, and whom many people had legitimate reason to fear and hate. That man began to die the day a beautiful young woman chose to spend her life with him. The changes in me began on that long ago voyage across the sea. They were complete by the day of my daughter's burial, when the horror of my past life was finally laid to rest. As the butterfly leaves its cocoon or the snake sheds its skin, I crawled out of the rotting carcass of my former life and left it behind forever.

The man I became is the one who sits here in this chair on a sunny day in New Orleans, but in retrospect I realize that I have not become a different man at all. I am convinced that through Christine's love and acceptance I have simply emerged as the man I was always meant to be—the man I was born to be. My true personality had been beaten down and hidden under a constant barrage of hatred, derision and abuse. I defended myself in the only manner I knew; deeply burying my sensitivity, creativity and warmth beneath as many layers of stone as I could manage, both figuratively and, in the case of the Opera House, literally. A man of stone cannot be hurt.

My stone walls of defense began to crack the day I peered around a marble column and saw a beautiful dark-haired girl standing below me on the stage. Somehow, in that instant, I knew my ugly world would never be the same.

Christine brought me happiness and filled my life with wonder, love and the only real joy I have ever known. I hope she knows what was in my heart all along. It is what I could not understand for a very long time…that I loved her from the first moment I saw her. I believe now that it was God's plan for me to take up residence at the Opera Populaire—to endure all those years of desolation—and thereby meet the beautiful woman who would at last bring happiness and peace to my tortured and undeserving soul and save me from eternal damnation. I was like the moon, destined to float in the dark for eternity. Christine, like the sun, burst in on my darkness to drive it away forever. She lit a light inside me and the heat from that light will warm me for the remainder of my days. I regret that I did not recognize my feelings as those of love from the beginning, but how could I? Love was a completely foreign emotion to me. No one had ever shown me love before, so I didn't recognize it until almost too late. Oh, the time that I wasted! Then again, perhaps our troubles were a necessary part of our journey, a journey upon which we embarked together, to help us both discover the true meaning of love. But, most importantly, it has been my own personal journey—a journey of the mask.

As my heart grows weaker and my body wastes away, I think with regret of the years that Christine and I will never see together...years that should have been ours for the taking. I will never understand why I am to leave this life so soon after finding it, but I must believe that God has some other plan for me. Through the love of my wife, His hand has finally touched me and I feel its warmth upon my shoulder. It is there not to do battle with the relentless approach of death, but to comfort me in leaving Christine behind, for that is what I fear above all else. I try to talk to her about beginning again with someone else, but she will not speak of it. It is my wish that she does so—I do not want her to be alone. She made it possible for me to see life as it should be seen. I will love her for eternity.

I grow tired. My hand is weak, but before I lay down my pen forever I must write, one last time, the four most important words I have ever spoken.

Christine, I love you.

Epilogue

———————— ★ ————————

Christine Daae Devereaux—June 1887

Erik passed away on 2 April 1887. He was only fifty-three years old. He took a large piece of my heart with him. The last eighteen months were very hard on him, and it hurt me to see my strong and virile husband reduced so quickly to the invalid he became in the end. What hurt even more was watching him struggle with the frustration of it all.

Several weeks after his death I was finally able to go through some of his things. I knew he had been doing a lot of writing in his last months but, in deference to his privacy and his pride I did not ask him about it. If he'd wanted to tell me he would have. When I came across the thick sheaf of papers in the drawer it took me several weeks to summon the strength to look at it.

I sat down to read what Erik had written. The writing was very difficult to read, and became increasingly hard to decipher toward the end, illustrating how hard it had been for him to write all that he did. When I finished, tears were blurring his words. I never realized the depth of the pain with which he lived in both the mental and physical senses. He had told me something of his past life—the indifference of his parents, his painful growth to adulthood and the constant rejection and scorn that became the backdrop of his life—but he never mentioned the agony of his relentless pursuit of my love.

Reading his words made me remember little things that should have alerted me to the torture that I put him through. I blinked back tears as I read his view of my own confused feelings. I didn't know then that I could love him. If I had, things would have been so different, but it is too late for retrospection now. I wasted precious time resenting Erik for his manipulations of my life but, in the end, I loved him all the more for it. I don't know what my life would have been like if Erik had not taken it upon himself to bring me to America. Yes, I probably would have eventually married Raoul, but I know I could never have let go of what I shared with Erik. I belonged with him and to him. His misguided action ultimately gave me the best anyone could ask for. I will always love New Orleans because it reminds me of the years Erik and I spent together in a world of our own making. I have no desire to live anywhere else.

The day before his death, Erik suffered another massive heart attack. God only knows why it didn't kill him on the spot. I guess Erik was as stubborn with death as he was with everything else. We were taking tea in the parlor when his sudden intake of breath startled me. He clutched at his chest and whimpered in pain. Before I could react, he had tumbled from his chair and lay gasping in agony on the floor. I called for help and quickly returned to his side. He did not speak, but what I saw in Erik's eyes when he looked up at me will stay with me for the rest of my days. Fear, pain, regret and a plea for help were all reflected in those beautiful brown eyes. My heart bled for him as I held him and tried to comfort him until help arrived.

André sadly informed me later that Erik would not recover...there was too much damage to his heart. I somehow knew the truth the minute I saw Erik fall and, to be honest, I felt he could take no more of the way he'd been living. Since he had sworn we would never sleep apart again, I insisted that he be put in our bed. If it would harm him further to have me there alongside him it didn't matter; it was where he wanted to be.

As Erik lay dying, I sat with him for hours. He said little and drifted in and out of consciousness. That night I crawled into bed beside him and wrapped myself around him as closely as possible. I lay with my head on his chest and listened to the weak and irregular beat of that great heart...the heart that had remained strong despite all that Erik had been through in his life. When I woke in the morning I found his arm around me. How and when he had put it there I didn't know, but I savored the comforting weight of it around me for what I knew would be the last time. It was a long while before I moved out from under that arm and laid it gently upon the bed. Throughout that day I held his hand, dreading the moment when I would have to let him go...a moment which finally came in the late afternoon. He opened his eyes and they were clear and free of pain for the first time in months. He looked up at me.

"My love, my Christine. I will always love you," he whispered.

"And I love you, Erik, forever and with all my heart," I softly replied, and bent toward him.

My lips melted into his, each of us tasting for the last time the love that made us so strong together. Erik put all he had left to give into that gentle and bittersweet kiss. His lips moved softly upon mine and he conveyed through them more than words could ever say. When his hand crept slowly across the coverlet to weakly grasp mine tears ran down my face to mingle with his over that last beautiful kiss. I finally raised my head to look deeply into his incredible brown eyes one last time before he closed them forever. He sighed and slipped into sleep. A few minutes later he left me. It is fitting that, after dreaming of it his whole life, a loving kiss was the last thing he knew.

I put my arms around him and held him while the warmth slowly left his body and my tears dried on his face. I listened once more for the beating of his wonderful heart, but it was still. I rose and went to the dresser. Reverently, I lifted his most finely crafted mask from the top drawer. I kissed my husband's face once more, placed the mask on his face and went to tell our friends.

*   *   *

When I realized how hard Erik had worked to write down the story of our life together, I felt compelled to clarify some of what he had written.

Erik was and will always remain the love of my life. I have in turn feared him, hated him, thrilled to his sensual touch, shared his pain and his passion and finally loved him beyond all else. Though all too brief, our passionate life together was a constant series of ups and downs that carried us from the lowest depths to the highest heights of what life can offer.

One might ask how I could be with a man who looked like Erik and who had done the things he had done. The answer is simple. I loved him. The man. Not his face. Not his voice. Not his body. I loved the person inside.

He did frighten me at first. I was terrified of him, but the stories I'd heard and the things I'd seen in Paris did not seem to fit with the man I was beginning to know. Of course I'd heard all the frightened talk in the theater about a ghost phantom that terrorized and murdered people but I could never connect any of that with my Angel. He was very careful to keep the truth about himself hidden from me. I did not see his darker side until much later, but by then it was too late. I was hopelessly in love with him.

Erik meant many things to me over the course of our relationship. He was, in turn, my angel, friend, father, protector, husband and lover. As he moved from one role in my life to another, he never let the former roles go, and eventually he became a combination of all of these things. That is a lot to ask from most men, but not from Erik.

I knew from the beginning that Erik was different. No matter what he chose to do, he never gave less than one hundred percent. He threw himself into everything he did with equal abandon. He was a relentless perfectionist and was extremely demanding of himself and of those around him. Sometimes I fear that I may not have lived up to his impossibly high standards. He would adamantly deny that fact if he was here, but I believe it is true. Erik had an incredibly quick mind and he absorbed information like a sponge.

Those are some of the traits that made him the man he was, but what first drew me to him? His angelic singing voice, of course, but his voice provided only a hint of what he was all about. Frankly put, Erik was the most erotically exciting man I will ever know. From the moment I first saw him, I was totally lost in the sensual aura that surrounded him. Of course, the first time he led me down all those stairs to his home under the Opera I still believed he was an angel. That was a perception that he had worked very hard for months to create in my mind, and he was undoubtedly frightened to death to reveal himself to me in human form. When I tore the mask from his face, I stripped him of the only defense he had against a world that had shown him nothing but hatred. As the mask was removed, so were my illusions of angels. That knowledge threw me into a state of confusion in which I would remain for months, for the thought of dealing with Erik as a man was far more frightening to me than thinking of him as an angel.

To confuse matters further, Raoul was courting me at the time. My relationship with him was safe and predictable. The only issue that marred our supposed happiness was that his titled family would not have approved of our marriage. We were two innocents involved in our first love and thinking only of a rosy future together. I loved the feel of Raoul's arms around me...they made me feel protected and safe.

Erik did not make me feel safe or protected. His very presence touched the raw ends of every nerve within me and laid me open to feelings and emotions I never knew existed. Even when we came to know each other better those feelings of detachment and awe lingered for a long time. Part of the power Erik had over me was in that amazing voice. Whether charged with anger or caressing a word of love, I could not hear enough of it. I could not think straight when he was near me. I don't remember the first time he actually touched me. I was too entranced by his magnetism to remember any reaction at all, but I felt the heat of his hand upon me long before he ever touched me. He frightened me, but I found myself waiting for him to touch me, wanting it, dreaming of it, and wondering if his touch could possibly surpass what his voice did to me. He did not really touch me for a long time; the only contact we had was when he politely offered me his fingers to escort me over the stairs. Speaking of his hands, I have never seen hands like Erik's on any other man. They were elegant, expressive and graceful. Even after the fire his hands, although scarred, remained graceful. Indeed, every movement Erik made was smooth, graceful and sensual. He did not walk across a room—he glided. His sense of the romantic was infallible. He always appeared so controlled and in command that I never guessed how difficult those times were for him until I read his words. No, with Erik I did not feel safe. I felt alive.

I was devastated when I saw the newspaper and thought of him dying alone. I could not make Raoul understand why I had to go back. I didn't understand it myself, but I felt that I owed Erik at least that much, even considering the events of the last night we saw him. Sometimes I wish I had left with Erik when he first asked me and saved us all a lot of pain. That last night of insanity was terrible for Raoul and me, but also for Erik. Witnessing a man's desperation and subsequent mental collapse is not easy, regardless of the situation.

I was very angry with Erik when I realized, on that ship, what he had done to me. I was terribly hurt that he would tell me a lie of such magnitude, and that he would use my friendship to that extent. I was also once again frightened of him, although he seemed once again in command of his mind, for I'd seen how volatile he could be. The situation was simply overwhelming. I wanted to go home where my life used to be uncomplicated and simple. My singing career had just taken off and it was just what my father would have wanted for me. I had a devoted suitor in Raoul who made me feel needed and loved. I thought I had everything. I did not want to be confined on a ship in the middle of the ocean with a mysterious masked man who thrilled me and terrified me at the same time. I was determined to go back to Paris.

I began to see more of the man behind the manipulator on the night I agreed to go to the music room with him. I was weary of being angry and tired of doing nothing. It surprised me that Erik would even suggest such a thing. The least I could do was to go with him. When he almost fainted I began to understand what he was going through for me. He was always loath to show vulnerability of any kind and reading what he wrote of that evening makes me appreciate all the more the monumental effort he made to please me.

In spite of my anger and my disappointment in him, my feelings for Erik grew with each passing day of our voyage. The glimpses I was getting of what might be hidden inside him made it increasingly difficult for me to stay angry with him. I am afraid I was quite dreadful to him in the beginning but that did not deter him. He had a stubborn streak in him that was quite aggravating at times, but in this case his stubbornness eventually enabled me to see the truth of my own feelings. By the time we docked in Virginia I had sorted them out only enough to know that I could not just return to Paris and leave Erik behind to fend for himself. He needed me, and I was beginning to realize that perhaps I needed him as well.

So how could I love that face? I was hopelessly under the spell of Erik's incredible voice long before I saw him, and later on I was totally mesmerized by his overwhelming presence. Honestly, I don't know how I did it either, for his face really was truly awful. But when I looked into his deep brown eyes and saw the sadness and the loneliness there, his face disappeared from my sight. Those eyes were windows through the hideous wall of his face, and they were the deepest, most expressive eyes I have ever seen. They had to be expressive; they were all he had. The afternoon in Virginia when Erik collapsed probably did more for his case with me than anything else. While I bathed his naked face as he lay unconscious on the floor, I studied him without embarrassment. It was something he would never have allowed me to do had I asked outright, and it gave me the opportunity I needed to accustom myself to his appearance and put it behind me. His trusting gesture in allowing me to touch him afterward satisfied any remaining curiosity I felt over it. The lurch I felt in my stomach when I saw him fall also proved to me how much I cared about him.

I began to think of Erik in new ways before we arrived in New Orleans. The thoughts I was having about him made me feel wicked. His unexpected show of passion in the dark street was certainly not that of either a friend or teacher and made me even more confused. We were in a strange country where I was forced to rely completely on this strange, mysterious man who was suddenly revealing emotions that I couldn't deal with. I did not *understand* what I felt for him but I could not walk away from the pull of it. His description of that night is surprisingly accurate and I am amazed that he read the situation so well.

When I was with Erik I forgot everything else. After we were married he could finally let loose all the passion he'd been holding inside and, at times, I was nearly suffocated by the intensity of it. Erik had an enormous amount of love in him that he was desperate to share with someone. It took him many years to acknowledge that fact to himself. We discovered the art of love together, and I blossomed from a naïve child into a passionate woman under his sensual touch. I will never know that kind of love again as long as I live. He told me what it would be like between us and he was right. His written (and surprisingly candid) descriptions of the passion that we shared can't hope to capture the true extent of what we felt for each other. Intense, powerful and overwhelming, Erik's love was like a tidal wave that washed over me, pulling me under and obliterating everything but him.

All Erik ever wanted was to love and be loved for himself, and to live life "like everyone else". We did not live our lives like everyone else. That could never happen, although I believe we did a good job of trying. Erik's appearance would always hamper us so we remained on the outskirts of society to enjoy our few friends, our simple pleasures, and each other. Admittedly, there were many bad times along with the good, as Erik so eloquently confessed. He took a very deep and probing look at himself, then revealed his innermost thoughts and admitted his mistakes in a startlingly frank manner.

I never knew of his involvement with voodoo. He was correct in thinking it would upset me. Perhaps I was blind, but one must remember that my husband was a master at keeping secrets. He'd done it all his life and he could lie with the best of them. He gave nothing away when he lied; he could look one square in the eye and lie to one's face without a qualm. To this day I have no idea if

Erik actually told the captain of that ship that I was mad or if he just wanted me to believe he did. When he was in full possession of his faculties he could make anyone believe anything he wished. It wasn't until his heavy drinking began to dull his senses that I could see through some of his lies. I knew he was repeatedly leaving the house at night, I knew he was drinking too much and I knew almost everything to come from his mouth in those days was a lie, but he would not let me help him. The alcohol contributed to his downfall, but it provided me with the only tangible evidence I had that something was seriously upsetting him. All through that lengthy period during which he fought alone with his past I watched him slide hopelessly into a world of misery where I could not reach him. As he withdrew further and further away from me, I despaired that I would ever see my loving Erik again. It cut me deeply to see the hurt in his eyes when I banished him from my bed, but I had no choice. I could not lie next to him another night only to have him crawl quietly and secretively away to do God knows what. I never believed that he was seeing someone else, and I hurt him yet again when I suggested such an absurd notion. That was the only time that I remember ever making a remark that reflected on his appearance. He appeared to deflate a bit before he recovered himself to come back at me with his equally absurd retort. In those few awkward seconds before he spoke I knew I'd hit him hard in the spot that would hurt him the most. I wanted to take it back, but I couldn't. Those few lines of intentionally hurtful conversation in the bedroom that day were the lowest moments of our life together. I didn't know what to think of what was going on, but the truth was beyond my wildest dreams. I will never forget the wild look in his eyes on that one awful night when he returned from the darkness acting like someone I didn't know. I had never before seen that kind of ugliness in Erik; and indeed never expected to. I don't know who came to my bed that night so drunk and demanding, but it certainly was not my husband. Frightened as I was by his unexpectedly brutal behavior, I was even more disturbed by what might have caused it. I was losing him, but to what?

He became more terrifying than he had been in Paris as whatever drove him reared its ugly head and pulled him down. As Erik's attitude gradually became more hostile I began to understand why people had always been so afraid of him. The glimpses I had of his former personality alarmed me when I finally realized just how angry he really had been. It still frightens me to think of the chances that he took to protect us against that awful man from the docks. Erik had been fighting his own past with everything he had, yet he was willing to risk it all by allowing himself to slip back into that dark place he was so desperately trying to forget. As for his encounters with that young woman, I don't know what to make of that. All I can do is believe, as Erik did, that the strength of our love would have prevented his making an understandable, but painful, mistake.

It was during those weeks, obviously, that Erik became the most terrifying. I saw some very frightening changes for the worse in him almost overnight, which is, in fact, what did happen by his own admission. It was then that I began to seriously consider going to someone for help. I recognized that I was living with a secretive, unpredictable and possibly dangerous stranger who bore no resemblance whatsoever to the man I had married. I am thankful now that I told no one of my fears, because I believe that would only have made matters worse. Erik's mental condition was too precarious to confront him over a situation that was, in reality, out of his control.

If only he had let me help him sooner! The memories and the pain that he carried with him were eating him alive and I could only stand by helplessly and watch them devour him. Only when he hit bottom did he reach out to me. Thank God he finally did. It was only after he explained to me about the thing that he had living inside him that I understood the two faces of Erik that I had seen for so long. It was then that I could forgive him for all of it and give him the help that he so greatly needed.

How sad for Erik that it took the death of our baby girl to finally free him from his agony! I never saw him happier than when I told him that we would have a child. I was not able to help him with the awful task of burying her, but once again his indomitable inner strength prevailed and he did it. Then he came to me and brought me back through the sheer force of his love. Erik was a totally different man after we returned from the plantation house. He had become the man whom I knew he really was underneath the shell of his past.

He had changed a lot since our departure from Paris. He was happy, warm and loving with me but there was always an edge to him that he could never completely hide. I told him many times that I could see it in his eyes. Even during the best times of our life together that edge remained; it was deeply buried but it was there. Perhaps it was better that I was not with him that day in the cemetery. He needed that time alone with our daughter to work things through by himself. The circumstances that brought him to that dismal place were finally enough to allow him to let it all go. His grief for our lost child, his concern for me, and his just being so tired of fighting it all, made him realize that his past didn't matter anymore. The man who was there for me when I woke out of my own grief was the man I always knew Erik could be. When I looked into his beautiful eyes on that night when we danced and renewed our love I saw only kindness, warmth, honesty, and the fire of our love. It is a shame that he was taken from me when we were entering the most satisfying time of our marriage, but he died happy and contented and I thank God for that.

My dear Erik. I loved him so very much and I shall miss him every day of my life. But I am not alone, for he will be with me forever in my mind, in my heart, and in my soul.

There will always be a place in my heart that no one else will ever touch. That place belongs to Erik alone. That place ached with emptiness and loss as I drew the sheet carefully around Erik's body. Good-bye, my love.

*   *   *

I buried him in St. Louis #3, next to the child he had wanted so desperately. The small group of mourners consisted of Jean, Louise, André, Father Etienne, Robert, Deliah and myself. Erik would have enjoyed it. A few words were said. I leaned forward to place a single white rose atop the marble plaque that bore his name. The chain I wore around my neck upon which Erik's wedding ring was suspended swung out from my breast. I looked down at the other, tinier gold ring on my finger. I never knew until I read his story that he had bought the ring for me before we left Paris. I never knew what that simple band of gold meant to Erik or why he wore it. It was the symbol of our future together; a future that lived only in his hopes and dreams until the day I told him I would marry him. My hand closed around Erik's ring lovingly and I brought it to my lips in a gesture of fond farewell.

*   *   *

Two months after Erik's death, a firm knock sounded on my door. I was still receiving an occasional condolence, so after shooing little Pierre from the room, I opened the door without hesitation. I looked up and into the handsome face of Raoul de Chagny.

I finally found my voice and invited him inside. Raoul was very nervous, and kept looking around the room. He said he was traveling in the South on business and he had, by pure chance, caught Erik's obituary in the newspapers. (Owing to the impressive debut of his music, Erik had been honored as a celebrity in many newspapers, both local and otherwise. The presentation of his music was the last thing I had been able to do for Erik of any importance and it meant everything to me that he had been so happy at the end. That last night at the Opera fulfilled his one remaining dream.)

Raoul had never known Erik's last name, of course (and, according to my husband, apparently neither did I), but I had also been mentioned in the notice and it was my name that caught his eye. Up until the day he appeared on my doorstep Raoul had no idea of where I had been since early 1882. He told me he should have forbidden my return to the Opera, and that no matter what the authorities thought, he had always believed "that monster" had done something terrible to me. I bristled at his use of the word "monster" and he saw my reaction plainly. He then talked of his search for me and of the life he had led since then. He had finally married three years after I left Paris. He didn't elaborate, but she was most likely a titled innocent of an approved family. As I listened to him talk, I thought of how different my life would have been had I married him. I watched the man sitting across the room from me and I sadly realized that he meant nothing to me. Anything I had felt for him back in Paris must have been the remnant of youthful infatuation and childish adoration. I was a woman now; a woman who had been loved by the most passionate man ever to walk the earth.

I felt no desire to explain anything about my life with Erik. Raoul would never have understood. I offered very little information, and after some sidestepping of the issue he finally had to satisfy his curiosity. He bluntly asked me how I could stay with someone like Erik. Why hadn't I tried to contact him?

"He tried to kill me one night, you know," he continued with a trace of arrogance.

"You mean on the night you shot him?" I countered with growing impatience. His eyebrows went up at that. "Oh yes, I know everything. I did not know you were capable of something like that, Raoul."

"It was in self defense," insisted Raoul. "He would have killed me…"

"Oh yes, he could have, very easily and at any time. But he chose not to. You ask how I could live with Erik? My dear Raoul, I loved my husband very much. For your information, he realized his mistake and offered me a return to Paris. It was my decision to make my life with him. He made me very happy, and for me there will never be another man to equal him. Now, if you will excuse me, I must summon my carriage. I have an appointment to go over more of Erik's scores for publication. It's been very nice seeing you again, Raoul."

I closed the door gently behind him and smiled to myself. I had made the right decision back in Virginia. Call it destiny or fate, Erik and I had been meant for each other. How I missed him! I turned to see Erik's gold and ebony walking stick leaning against the piano, where it would remain as long as I lived in our house. With a smile on my face and my husband's presence filling my heart, I went to gather my reticule and a new pile of Erik's scores. I must not be late for my appointment; Erik wouldn't like that at all.

About the Author(s)

———————— ★ ————————

Nancy Hill Pettengill lives in New Hampshire with her husband, her three children and her horse. She works full-time as an Administrative Assistant at a local college. When not on horseback, she also enjoys singing, musical theater, water and snow sports, history and reading.

0-595-12484-4